# Losing My Siren Luna

## Book One of the Hidden Cove Series

C. Hazlewood

ISBN:9798388003300

Cover design by: Zhandre Dex G. (MC Damon)

Library of Congress Control Number: 2018675309

Printed in the United States of America

This book is dedicated to all my loyal readers (my Hazlenuts) who have been with me through this amazing book-writing journey.

# ONE

***Elelira***

Tonight is the night. Just five more minutes, and my husband, now ex-husband, of the past 2 years will learn the truth.

It's too late to change the past. It's too late to go back and fix all the wrongs I have had to endure in this forced marriage of the past 2 years.

He claimed he was searching for his mate, searching for the one he was fated to, while unknowingly married to her. Neglect, adultery, verbal and mental abuse are just a few of the things I've been forced to endure, but that all ends tonight.

The treaty agreement is breached. It has been two years of our marriage, and just like he and my uncle agreed, if no child was produced in two years, he would be free to divorce me and choose another. I never revealed to my uncle that the man he forced me to marry had never touched me. In the two years living in the coastal, castle-like packhouse, my husband has brought many women into his bedchambers, but none of them were ever me.

I knew. I knew the moment I stepped foot in the packhouse he was my mate.

I knew at our wedding as my uncle, the Lycan ruler of the western realm, walked me down the aisle, when I laid eyes on Lachlan for the first time, I knew. I knew he was destined for me, but I was confused by the disgust on his face as he glared back down at me.

He didn't feel it. Of course he didn't. He was a Lycan, and I was only half. I was a hybrid, unknown to my uncle at the time, who thought my mother was impregnated by one of the countless men he used to force on her.

No, my father was not a Lycan, or even a shifter of the land. He was of the fairy realm, and the fae, all races of the fae, do not come into their magic until their 20th birthday, at the precise moment of their birth.

Without my magic, he couldn't detect me, but I detected him. He was fully adult by Lycan standards, so I knew the moment I caught his scent and my Lycan's eyes saw his through the veil of our concealed magic. I knew, and my heart shattered millions of times in the last two years, every time he rejected me. Every time he took a new woman to bed, which was often, I felt it. I felt the pains in my chest and the tearing of the Lycan beast resting inside me until even she came to detest the man we were forced to marry.

He only married me to appease my uncle, and form an alliance between our packs. My uncle offered me in place of his own daughter, because I was disposable; an orphan left in his care, and he was saving his daughter for someone other than the Lycan ruler of the south, who rumor said was cruel and heartless.

The rumors were true. Though he was strong, and a sight to behold, I had not once experienced kindness from my husband. In the past few months especially, his cruelty knew no bounds.

He neglected me for the first year of our marriage, not granting me an audience to speak with him and reveal what we were to beg him to stop. Stop taking women, and crushing my soul each and every time. After the first year, when I became numb to the pain, and could bear it and grit my teeth through it, he began to show his face to me periodically, only to insult and belittle me. Calling me skinny, or ugly. He would insult the straw color of my hair or the way my skin stayed fair, even though I spent endless hours outside in the sun, walking alongside the beach as I dreamed of my freedom.

Just months ago, he started to watch me intently. If I spoke to anyone, he would storm my room later in the evening when I was all alone, berating me, calling me names and insulting me for being a whore. It was no secret that my mother's sole purpose for my uncle was to reward his loyal men, and help when negotiating treaties and agreements for the pack. She was the sister of the Alpha, but treated like a pack whore.

He accused me of being like my mother, even if all I did was ask a worker to bring firewood to my room. I was forced to do everything for myself from that point on, and that included carrying firewood up the four flights of stairs to my drafty, heatless room the last few months.

At least he never touched me. I became grateful for the lack of intimacy, viewing him as nothing more than dirt I wish to one day trample upon. I quietly took the torment and the belittling, never letting it break me. He took my hope of fated love, since Lycans, unlike werewolves, do not get a second chance mate. He took my hope of that, but that was all he had from me. My innocence and my pride remained intact for this satisfying moment.

I checked the clock, and saw I had two minutes until the moment of my birth.

This morning, my *husband* paid me a final visit in my chambers. A visit I would be eternally grateful for.

He brought me the annulment papers. Having gone two years without an heir, it was finally time. The only words he uttered as he set the papers on the writing table in my meager bedchamber were, "Bring them tonight, signed, then leave my lands at once."

With this I will be free.

After the clock strikes 7:02, I will be free to reject him, and I can finally live my life in peace.

I crossed the marbled floor of the ballroom, where many of the pack are gathered before the run that commences every full moon. My bare feet made no sound as I padded towards my now ex-husband, who is speaking in whispers to his Beta, Nilo. Lachlan's back is facing me, but Nilo saw my approach. He eyed my scantily dressed frame in confusion, then nodded to Lachlan to turn to face me.

Lachlan's eyes went wide momentarily as he took in my appearance. I'm in nothing but a silk slip, wearing just the necklace my mother had given to me from my true father before she passed away. I did not want to take anything of Lachlan's or my uncle's with me when I left, and even this slip would be left behind as I went.

I won't need it. I won't be needing clothes ever again if I can help it.

After the look of surprise subsides, agitation replaced it on Lachlan's features.

"What the hell are you wearing, Lira?" he hissed.

I raised my chin in an act of defiance, the only one I have ever shown. I am done here. He can not hurt me anymore.

"Here," I handed him the papers, then checked the clock on the wall again. I can feel a surge beneath my skin, as if my blood is rushing backwards and my heart is pulsing in a melodic rhythm. "It is signed. We are no longer married, though I can't say the last two years were really a marriage at all. "Twenty more seconds. I can feel the magic buzzing inside me, awakening for the first time.

Lachlan's eyes ran down my body, then back up to my face, a confused look upon his face. "You don't look ready to leave. I thought I made myself clear, Elelira. You are to-"

"One last thing before I go," I smirked, looking back up at the clock, ignoring the growl that escaped him at my interruption.

It's time.

The moment my magic was upon me, I felt as if my entire body was engulfed in light, my hair lifting and twirling with the rush that came from my inner mana breaking open inside me. It's flowing through my limbs, to the tips of my bare toes, my fingers, even seeping into every lock of my hair.

I am fae, and with my magic unlocked, I know he can feel it. He can feel the bond, but it's too late. I won't have him.

His eyes went wide, his mouth went to the ground as he sank to his knees.

As I got my bearings once again, I quickly scanned the room, and saw others in a pose much similar to Lachlan's, scared of the light and the magical aura that emanated from me. Even Nilo leaned against the wall in surprise, shock evident on his face.

"You, Elelira, you...you are…." Lachlan stumbled over his words, coming to terms with what had just occurred. I can see the understanding and recognition in his eyes. He feels it, the mate bond, but it's too late.

"I *was* your mate, the mate you claimed to be looking for all along, but were too arrogant to notice. I tried telling you countless times, but you dismissed me, abused me, forced me to endure as you brought countless women to your bed." I took a step back, bracing myself physically for my next words. "I, Elelira Meline Lambert, reject you, Lachlan Stiles, as my mate, and as my Alpha."

"No," he gasped right before he buckled over from the pain of me severing my end of the bond.

All he needed to do is sever his connection with me, and we can both be free. Free from each other, and free from the burden of the ugly fate we were forced to share. He was the worst of my past, but I can be free to be happy in my future.

"Alpha!" Nilo drops to the ground beside him, helping to support his body as he bore the pain of the rejection. We did not bear each other's marks, but he was finally feeling the two years of the suppressed bond. All the weight of the neglect and pain of his betrayals is resting on his shoulders, and that is a heavy burden to bear.

I know. I endured it for years.

My Lycan inside me whimpered, but the pain isn't nearly as bad as his. My Lycan and I have faced rejection for years. This is his first time. He will live, but I hope the pain lasts just a bit longer so he has an idea of just a fraction of the pain I have had to endure.

"*I do not wish to watch him suffer, Ela. Let's just go. I am done with him, and ready to face our future.*" 'All alone', Valerina leaves unsaid. We will be alone after this as we search for our true father, a true family where we can finally belong. He will not get a second chance, and we won't either.

Good.

I do not let the flickers of lingering pain show, keeping my head high as I glare down on my suffering ex-husband and ex-mate. "Good-bye, Lachlan."

I turned, and walked towards the doors that led to the walkway and the ocean shore. That will be our escape.

Pack members moved aside as I strode past. I did not bear a glance at any of them. I am but the pitiful woman their Alpha was forced to wed. I never received a kind word or help from any of them in the last two years. I am as done with this pack as I am their Alpha.

As I reached the door, I turned to face the room, staring blankly at Lachlan who was straining to get up off the floor. Nilo tried to help, but Lachlan pushed him away. He was staring after me with an unidentifiable emotion, one I had never seen from him before. I think it was regret.

"I, Elelira Meline Lambert, reject Hidden Cove Pack, as a member," I took a deep breath, closing my eyes as I murmured the last words, tearing myself completely from my mate and his pack forever, "and as its Luna."

Lachlan, who had just stumbled to his feet, collapsed again to the ground, screaming out in excruciating pain, along with every adult member of the pack.

He deserved this, but they don't. They don't deserve to pay for his misdeeds, but that is his burden to bear. He made his bed, and with countless other women. I need to be strong and stick to my resolution, no matter how much it hurts. Their pain will lessen in seconds, while mine lasted years.

With my eyes closed, I take the straps of the gown on my shoulders, pushing them to the side and down my arms until the whole gown falls, pooling around my feet.

I'm naked, and free, finally ready to leave.

As my eyes opened, Lachlan was staring across the room at me, trying to force himself to his feet again as tears ran down his face, a longing in his eyes that was never there before.

It's too late, Lachlan. You are now nothing to me, and that is how it will forever be. You will stay as a bad memory that I will try my hardest to forget.

With no emotion, just the coldness I felt for him resting on my face, I turned my back one last time, walking towards the open waters and freedom that lie beyond the pack's shores.

When my feet hit the water, the magic beneath my skin's surface surges forth again, making my skin take on a translucent glow. The deeper I got into the water, the more the magic pushed forth, until my limbs quivered and the siren inside of me breaks free, transforming my body, granting me a glorious, metallic and rainbow-scaled tail and fins. Gills emerged on my neck, on the soft spot below my ears.

My first breath of the salty ocean water sends tingles down my spine, like a jolt of adrenaline as I dove down, feeling truly free for the first time in my life.

My necklace felt as though it is pulsing against my throat, a steady drumming, but comforting in a way. The feeling of the jade and emerald stones gives me a sense of home. The ocean felt like my home with it. It is like this was my true fate all along.

The water was exhilarating, rushing past me as I dove deep, twisted my ductile new body and pushed back up to the surface.

As I broke past the surface of the water, I look back to shore in the distance, at the beautiful castle I once thought was my future. Now, it is nothing but part of the nightmare of my past.

Good riddance.

Before I dove back down, movement on the shore caught my eyes.

Lachlan. He is wading into the shallows, calling me that damn nickname he has taken to calling me the last several months. Lira.

What right does he think he has to call me a nickname? Any name at all? He should just be thankful he is free from me now, because heaven knows I am. I am free of him, and no matter what name he calls me, I will never come back.

Losing My Siren Luna

# TWO

***Lachlan***

"Any sign?" I asked Nilo as he walked up to where I'd been standing at the docks for hours now.

When my guilt and my sorrow become too overwhelming, this is where I find myself, in this very spot, staring out at the sea.

She was gloriously beautiful, from her glowing hair to her broad, translucent fins, glimmering in the setting sunlight. That last sight of her before she dove beneath the water's surface has been haunting my dreams for months now.

"No, Alpha. The ocean is too great. We will never find her, I'm afraid. I am sorry, but I don't think there is any hope."

No. There will never be hope of her return after the pain I put her through. I can see that now.

"I told you," Killian, my Lycan snarls in my mind, "I warned you, begging you to be kind. You ruined everything. She was what we were looking for, but you turned her against us forever. She will never return. And….I don't blame her. I just hope she finds the happiness she deserves. The happiness that she never found in us, her true mate."

"Are you saying you could tolerate feeling the continuous pain of betrayal if she were to find happiness in another? Because I couldn't. I can't." She was ours. Two years we had her in our grasp, but never noticed the bond.

I did not and will not accept the rejection. If she chooses another, I will know, and it will haunt me, pain me like I did to her for the longest time.

It will be no more than I deserve, but I will never give in.

How was I to know she was a hybrid? A fae? Her uncle claimed she was a pure Lycan, fathered by one of his strongest warriors while also bearing her mother's alpha genes. How was I to know she was fathered by fae and not a lycan like he claimed?

I dismissed her after our forced wedding, knowing that if our contract marriage resulted in a child, I would be forced to fully mate her and reject my fated mate. I didn't want to risk it, though she tempted me.

Her beauty was otherworldly. Her clear, flawless skin, her slim waist, her womanly curves and the rosy hue of her cheeks and pillowy lips. I wanted her, but hated myself for it.

I didn't want to betray my fated mate by being stuck with another, so I constantly rejected her, thinking she was a temptation sent from hell to torment me and break my resolve.

Unknowingly, I betrayed my mate right in front of her, weekly, and sometimes daily when I couldn't get the image of her beautiful face out of my mind.

I did not want to permanently bind myself to Wayne's niece. The alliance was necessary when we were coming out of war with the northern clans, but I didn't want to be stuck with that bastard in an alliance forever. He was just as likely to stab me in the back as the vampires and demons of the north.

For all the reasons I had to avoid Lira and bide my time to annul the marriage, it never changed how much of a temptation she was for me. I should have given into the urge instead of fighting it. I should have…..

"GAHHH!" I screamed, clutching my chest and sinking to my knees.

No…. NO!

She can't be. Please….. no, my Lira.

"Alpha!" Nilo drips down beside me. "Is it..?"

The tightening in my neck as I strain myself to nod sends a stabbing pain down my spine. My heart feels as if it is being ripped in two. Killian is snarling and howling inside me, right at the surface, on the cusp of breaking free.

Is this the pain she endured? How? How did she endure it?

Every day of the first several months of our marriage, she would beg my men for an audience with me. Is this why? Was she trying to warn me, to beg me to stop?

The pain inside me intensifies at the realization.

Lira. My Lira. What have I done?

"She is betraying you," Nilo states, worry etched on his scarred features.

No. I betrayed her. She rejected me. After months, she is just moving on, which is something I can never do.

I hope he enjoys his time with her, because I will get her back, if that's the last thing I do.

~

***Elelira***

Pain. Intense, like no other, radiates through my torn and broken body.

Two weeks. I have survived two weeks in hell, and I pray this is finally the end.

Returning to the western coast to search for some sign or clue as to who my father could be was a mistake. A huge mistake.

I came to land once, but once was all it took to be thrust into a hell worse than any other.

Now, here I lay, in a bed of my own blood, locked in a cell just waiting to die. I am praying for death, and I feel its crushing weight closing in on me.

Finally.

There is no other escape. My fate is now the same as my mother's. How much pain must I endure in my short life? Not even 21 and I have faced every torture this life could hold.

I'm done fighting. I choose death. That is the only freedom I will ever know.

"Holy shit, she is still alive," a man snickers from outside the cell door.

"I thought she wouldn't survive after last night," another says.

"That was way cruel. Too much for my taste."

"Should we help her? She is a fine thing. They left her for dead. If we help her heal, maybe we can keep her for ourselves?"

"The alpha would have our heads if he were to find out."

"How would he know?"

"Your mate would know," one snickers.

"It would be nothing new to her. She would ignore it and keep her mouth shut like she always does."

"Ahh, you trained her well."

"It's all in the back of the hand and the flick of the wrist."

The men cackle and snort while laughing with each other.

"I'm sorry, Ela. They inhibited me. I can not shift to change us; to save us. I'm sorry."

" I'm sorry too, Val. I'm done. I can take no more."

She whimpers, knowing what's to come, but accepting it, knowing it's our only way out.

My uncle must have discovered the truth, because he knew how to inhibit not only my Lycan, but my magic as well.

With the last of my strength, I can do just this, emptying what is left inside me for my final escape; the last of my life.

"Goodbye, Valerina. I am sorry you were cursed with such a pitiable counterpart."

"Don't say that, El. Don't take-"

Her words are cut off as I pull on the last remaining shred of magic inside me, calling them forward, then coating my heart with the force.

One thought is all it takes to end it. End it all.

~~~~

"Elelira!"

I groan as I turn in bed.

"*Elelira!*" Val's voice filled my head.

A bed? How did I come to be in a bed? Did those men take me? Was I unsuccessful? There is no way….

My eyes shot open and I sat up, alarmed and unsteady, gazing around at the familiar room around me.

No….

Why am I here? In this bedroom? The chambers I kept for two years. 2 painful years in the south.

Hidden Cove Pack.

Why am I here? Did Lachlan find me somehow? Why? Why would he?

*"El, I don't think-"* Val starts to say, but knocking at the door cuts her off.

"Elelira. It is time to wake up. The omegas arrived to help you prepare for the wedding."

"Wedding?" I echoed. What wedding? Whose?

Niomi, a familiar face, the elderly woman who once helped me in my adjustment to the south, opened the door and I gasped.

It really was her.

She died. After one year of life here in the south, the only person who
~~~~

ever showed me an ounce of kindness died of an incurable disease. How can she be here now?

"Niomi? Mimi?" I stumbled to my feet as I murmured the nickname I once called her, gawking in disbelief. I hastily stumbled towards her, practically falling into her arms as I wrapped my arms around her in a warm embrace.

She is taken back for a moment, but just a moment. Her hands quickly started patting my back, hesitantly at first, then with more purpose as I began to sob in her arms.

"What is this? We just met yesterday but I am glad to see you have accepted this old woman already."

"Yesterday?"

It had been almost three years since we first met, two since her death and I last saw her.

Her death.

She was dead. She can't be here.

She nods and smiles at me kindly, making my heart pang. "Elelira, dear. Your uncle and future husband are waiting. We must begin the preparations if we want to make the ceremony on time. It's your wedding day!"

"My wedding?" I asked hesitantly.

I release my hold on her, but continue to stare in disbelief, trying to hold back my tears as I begin to contemplate in disbelief and horror of what happened.

"Yes, dear. Your wedding to Alpha Lachlan Stiles. You have yet to meet, and you wouldn't want to be late."

I don't know how, and I don't know why, but I'm back in time. I traveled back to right before the wedding to Lachlan.

I don't know what I did wrong. I thought I was ending it all. I thought I was finally going to find freedom and peace in death. I guess even that is too much to ask for. Here I am, back at the beginning of my hellish marriage.

"You look so beautiful, Elelira, dear," Mimi coos as the omega doing my hair finishes pinning the last tendril in place.

"Ela. You can call me Ela," I told her with a warm smile as I stared back at her reflection in the mirror. Her soft, wrinkled cheeks glow a soft pink as she smiles back, an all-too-familiar motherly smile.

I loved Niomi, my Mimi, because she always smiled at me this way, filling that motherly void. When I needed support through the first year of my marriage, before I had completely closed myself off to my husband for good, she was there, holding the pieces of me together, then showing me that motherly smile, telling me how proud she was of me for enduring the pain.

She thought the pain was from a fated mate I left behind, without rejecting, in my uncle's pack. I never told her it was Lachlan. I wanted to, but I was scared. I was scared of what others would do if they found out I was part Fae. I was past the age where pure Lycans are able to find their mate, but because my lycan was cloaked in my repressed magic, no one would believe me if I told them I was the Alpha's fated mate. Not without me revealing why I could detect him, but he couldn't detect me.

This pack has a long history of wars with other races. That is why Lachlan holds the brutal reputation that he bears. The reason Lachlan entered this alliance with my uncle in the first place was to prevent a coming war with the northern covens and clans over land as they sought a passageway to the southern sea. Lachlan needed the alliance to give him time to rebuild and strengthen his army.

Uncle wanted to keep Lachlan on a leash, hoping that my marriage to him would result in an heir to the pack. When I was captured by my uncle's forces, that was what he revealed to me. I had failed, so I was rendered useless, like my mother, and given to his men. He did not want the threat of my magic and my true father's revenge on his pack, so I was to be done away with when the men had enough of me.

The hell and horror I faced during those weeks made the betrayal pains seem like tickles and mild heartburn.

It has turned my heart into stone, and I truly never want a man to touch me ever again.

There was some *good*, if you can call it that, that came from my uncle confronting me one last time. He knew who my true father was, and I now have a small clue about how to find him.

~~~~

*"Well, look who came back. I had my port guards and warriors on alert for the chance of your return, but I didn't think you were this idiotic to actually come on shore. Not when your ex-husband is on the hunt for you." My uncle smiled menacingly, crouching down in front of me, where I was being held in place, kneeling on the floor*
~~~~

*between two guards.*

*I just wanted to sneak on shore for a moment. Just a moment to visit the public record office, to see what fae or siren representatives may have visited in the months before my birth. I had been searching the seas for months, and was no closer to finding the entrance of the siren liars.*

*I knew that they visited land with the fairy courts when they sent out their delegation parties every seven years, but I had no idea how to find them.*

*Coming to land was my last resort, and what led to my tragic capture.*

*"When that monstrous asshole sent word demanding atonement for lying about your birth father, I knew. I knew that the reason your Lycan side was weaker, and why, after your twentieth birthday, you were able to escape by sea. It was that he was truly the one who fathered you. He always showed your mother favor above the other whores." Uncle cackled in his sick, gravely voice. "You have greatly angered your husband. Or should I say, ex-husband. You are more worthless than your mother," he scoffed. "You had one job. Open your legs and give him a son. How am I going to control that pup and his ports now? My own daughter has just found her mate. Looks like I will have to take this to war. There is no other choice now. And you," he chuckles menacingly, "You failed to open your legs properly for him, but I'll let you atone for that until your death now."*

*Valerina growled menacingly through me, and Uncle looked up at one of his guards, nodding with a sick smile. The guard produced a vial from his pocket while the other bent over me, holding my head in place, pulling my jaw down with so much force I felt it dislocate with excruciating pain as the other poured the contents of the vial down my throat.*

*I sputtered, but without the use of my jaw, I couldn't fully close my mouth. Valerina couldn't heal me enough in time before the medicine kicked in.*

*My magic was already being suppressed by the black diamond and pearl cuffs on my wrists, and now my lycan was being restrained inside me.*

*"I think we broke her jaw," one of the men mused like it wasn't that big of a deal.*

*Uncle just snorts. "A broken jaw might be useful for the only purpose she can serve now. After you men are finished with her, make sure she is taken care of. I already have Lachlan, that bastard, demanding her return. He probably wished to eliminate her himself after the embarrassment he faced. But, if her father were to suspect I'd been using and mistreating his own blood, he would retaliate, and that would not bode well for us. She is to be disposed of when she can no longer serve the men. Understood?"*

*"Yes, alpha," the men recite together with devious smirks, eying my scantily clad body in a sick way that makes my stomach roll.*

~~~~

"Elelira? Ela!" Mimi calls out to me, snapping me out of the memory.

"Yes?" I met her eyes in the mirror as a look of concern masked her face.

"Are you alright, child? Is something not to your liking? We can change the accessories if you-"

"No, no. It's fine," I smiled at her.

I take in my appearance; my youthful face, no longer containing the heavy bags under my no longer dull eyes from all the nights of fretful sleep. My glowing skin, unmarred by the harsh elements that I had to battle daily the last year of my marriage to supply my own firewood, food, doing my own laundry in the stream a mile inland so as not to disturb the maids. Lachlan made it clear I was not his true Luna and could not order his staff as I pleased. I hated that trek to wash my laundry. Without proper shoes to travel across the rocky landscape, my feet would be blistered and bleeding as I came back every time.

Mimi would take care of all that for me when she was alive, being able to order the maids and staff as she pleased. I did not have that ability. After she died, I was truly on my own.

"Do you have to do this again, Ela?" Val asked me. "Can we not just run away?"

"If we leave now, where will we go? Without our fins and our gills, we would be stuck on land and could easily be captured and returned to Lachlan, or worse, my uncle. Also, we need to reject him, Val. If we don't, we could be living our entire lives with the pains of betrayal. We know he won't touch us, and no one else will during our time here. We could face worse out there."

"There has to be a way to attain your fins and gills before your magic comes in. If not, how do siren children survive?"

"They are born from siren mothers and so are born in their siren forms. We had a Lycan mother. We can't access that form until our seal is broken."

Val whimpers, not wanting to face the endless rejection of her mate again. It hardened my heart, but hers is still longing for the one she was fated for. She never met Lachlan's beast. She doesn't hold the same closure I was able to attain in the rejection.

This will be the first night the pain begins. Our wedding night was his
~~~~

first act of betrayal.

I waited for him, hoping he would come, only to be struck by the greatest pain I had ever felt up to that point while he entertained himself with another woman that night.

This night will not be any different.

No, there will be a difference. I have known greater pain than he could ever give me. I have been subjected to far worse than betrayal.

I will not wait for him. I will not long for him. I will not let a single tear fall from my eyes as my chest burns and throbs for hours on end.

My heart is already closed off, and there is no hope for me in this marriage, fated mate or not. I will just endure once again, biding my time until I can finally be granted my freedom.

# THREE

***Lachlan***

It's the day. I've been fighting and longing for this day for so long, and today has finally come. The day I see her again. My restart, the reset I've fought for. I've killed for it.

I couldn't believe it had worked. He told me he could do it, but I had my doubts. The incessant demands and the rules he set made me believe that he was full of it. I expected him to bring her back, then keep her for himself.

When I awoke in my own bed, feeling unchanged, I thought that he had deceived me, but then the omegas started pouring in to ready me for my wedding day.

Seeing my appearance, the younger face, without the worry lines and wrinkles, and with no beard laced with gray from the months of constant stress and regret, I knew it had worked. He had fulfilled his end of the deal, and now I must fulfill mine.

Two years.

I have Two years to make her fall in love with me, which shouldn't be hard considering she is my fated mate.

I remember the look on her face on our wedding day the first time it happened. I remember the awe and the longing.

She knew.

She knew the moment our eyes met that I was hers; I was too stupid to realize it. She could have been mine on that night, but I fought my urge to go to her and take her, and spent the night in the brothels, fucking through a series of women with the image of her beautiful face haunting me the entire time.

I should have known she was a siren. Everything about her called to my soul, but I spent the whole two years of our marriage fighting it. Now I know why, and I will not make the same mistake.

"You better not. If you hurt her in any way ever again, I will end us. I would rather kill us than let her ever feel that pain again."

The betrayal pains we felt changed my beast. The realization and physical reminder of the pain she always felt from us made him go mad for some time. It took feeling her death for him to give me back control.

Worse than the pain of betrayal, the pain of her death, and the final tether holding our souls together was too much for him. It broke him, and I know he would go to any lengths to prevent her from hurting ever again.

We both went through great lengths to bring her back.

Now that we have got our second chance, I will not ruin it. She will be showered with my love and admiration from the moment our eyes meet in the ballroom.

I will let myself be enchanted by her beauty, and tonight, I will fulfill the bond.

One of the rules that was set was that I can not reveal that I was the one who brought her back. I can't say how I know that we are fated mates or let her know the lengths I had to go through to bring her back from the dead. That will not matter, though. She wanted me on our wedding day. I was the one that ruined the special moment we should have shared.

I won't make that mistake again.

"Alpha?" Nilo opened my bedroom door. The omegas making last-minute adjustments to my clothes started working faster to finish. Last time, I did not care how I appeared at the wedding. I just wanted to get it done. This time, I wanted to take her breath away. I want her to be so enamored with me that fulfilling my end of the deal that I struck with her father would only take a day. A single night. Our wedding night is all I will need.

"It's time, Alpha. Everyone is in place and the officiant has just arrived. I received word that Elelira is ready herself as well."

"Good, good," I smiled at my Beta before turning to check my appearance one more time.

Everything was in place. My outfit accentuates my physique, and my face is radiant with the joy I'm feeling, knowing I am about to come face to face with my mate once again. I am being given the chance to do everything right.

"Let's go," I told my Beta, waving off the omegas and righting my collar around my neck.

Before, on my wedding day, I wore black to match the mood and my emotions. This time, I had them change my undershirt and my accents to gold, to match the color of her hair, and the rings we will exchange are adorned with green emeralds to match the color of her luminous eyes.

When I told the staff to fetch me a jeweler to purchase the new rings the first moment after waking up, they thought I was mad. I had already had plain gold rings, thin and fragile like our original marriage prepared.

That wouldn't do.

This was to be forever, and the rings needed to reflect the eternal love I would shower her with from this day forward.

It was expensive, but she is worth it. She will be worth all the treasures in the world, and I plan on giving her it all.

My fingers traced over the box with the rings in my pocket, a smile playing on my lips.

"Are you sure about this, Alpha? I do not trust Wayne, and this seems too forced for a marriage alliance. Are you sure you want to go through with this?" Nilo asked as we walked together towards the ballroom.

"I've never been so sure of anything in my life," I grinned.

He eyed me speculatively. "You sure changed your tune. You were dreading this just yesterday. You told Yasmin not to worry and that you would be back to see her tonight."

I cringed internally. I forgot about the brothel girls.

"Forget about them again. Forget about all of them. You will not be hurting her," Killian growled at me.

"You have nothing to worry about. I will never lay a finger on another woman again."

"I know you won't. I won't let you," he snarled.

Like I would ever ruin this chance. It hurts to even think about the day she rejected me, and all the pain and heartache that came after.

I took my place proudly at the front of the hall, Nilo at my side, and we turned to face the doors my bride and mate would soon emerge from.

It is only minutes, but the wait is excruciating. My longing for her is almost too much to bear as the moment of our first meeting drew closer and closer.

I breathed deeply, readying my heart for that admiring and awestruck look that will come over her face when she enters through those doors. I plan on pouring every bit of my love into the gaze I return back to her. This is the moment I will remember as the moment our love began.

When the doors finally started to open, my heart began to beat out of my chest and I forget how to breathe. This is it. This is the beginning of our….

Wait.....

Everyone turned to stare, whispering among themselves, no doubt as amazed at her beauty as I was the first time my eyes met hers.

This time, though, her eyes are trained on the ground, her face blank and uncaring. When she does look up, her eyes don't go to mine. They are staring straight ahead, cold and distant.

The hold she has on her uncle seemed forced. His smile was cruel and calculated, as it usually was, but hers is much different from what I expected. When I remembered this moment the first time it happened, I had always longed for a redo; to go back and accept her from this moment, to change the course of everything.

There was no emotion to connect with this time. She looked as if she was marching to her death, dreading the marriage and everything about it.

She doesn't want this. I can see it on her face. She doesn't want this marriage to the point she won't even look at me.

"*WHAT DID YOU DO?!*" Killian roared in my head.

"NOTHING!" I exclaimed, "I haven't even seen her yet. The last I saw her was the day she rejected me, but that hasn't happened yet."

Killian was silent for a moment, and so was I as we raced through what could have changed this time around. This should be a fresh start. This should be exactly like it was in the….

"Wait. Would she still have her memories from before like us?" Killian asked.

Could she?

She was directly in front of me now, and her uncle is ready to pass her off, but she still won't meet my gaze.

My heart shatters, its shards stabbing straight through to my soul, Killian howling in pain, not knowing what to do.

We got our redo, just like he promised us, but the task of making our mate fall in love with us will be impossible if she remembers the mistakes of our past; of our future. To make matters worse, we can't reveal anything to her.

When her eyes finally did lift, meeting mine only momentarily, I felt it. Her hatred and her rejection, like ice being thrown over the fire that was burning inside me.

~

***Elelira***

As Mimi and my escort walked me to the room where my uncle had waited for me, I retreated into my shell of numbness, going on autopilot until this whole ordeal is over.

I suspected numbness will be a constant for me again, since the pains of my *husband's* betrayal will begin tonight.

Val whimpered at the memory. She was locked inside my mind, enduring it with me, her heart shattering over and over along with mine. It was his human side having the affair. His lycan had no part, which was the hardest for Val. She could never extinguish that hope for her mate because she could never know if Lachlan's lycan was in agreement with that action.

This marriage right now was entirely to his human side, so she was trying her best to retreat into the darkest corner of my mind and wait in sorrow until it was over.

When we entered the room, and my eyes landed on my uncle and his men, I tried to maintain my numbness and not outwardly show my disgust and discomfort.

Some of the very men that had tortured and ravaged my body in my last days were standing around the room, their sickening stares making Val snarl in my mind.

"About time," Uncle growled. "Bad enough I had to wait to use you for this till the day you turned 18. Let's get this over with. I have a *meeting* in town right after this."

"Meeting my ass. He and his filth should do the world a favor and fall off a cliff on their way out," Val sneered before retreating back to her dark corner.

I agree, but this world has proven to be unfair over and over again. We would never be that lucky.

I somehow managed to rest my hand on my uncle's elbow, hiding my disgust and scorn. Just five minutes. I can be near the monster for five minutes, and it will hopefully be the last five minutes I ever see him again in this life.

I will kill myself again before ever going back to the West.

He will only correspond with me through letters after this day, and send messengers to me when he wanted to communicate something that more than a few lines on a page. Five minutes. Just five minutes and he will disappear from my life.

I went into a trance, focusing on the floor as I let the numbness take over. I did not wish to see Lachlan and the resentment on his face as he looked upon me for the first time. I did not want to show my hurt and pain from his rejection. I will remain numb and try my hardest to not meet his eyes once during this entire ceremony.

The first year of our marriage he won't seek me out once. Not once. I can hold onto my numb facade, then steer clear of him for at least a year. It won't hurt me. It won't break me. I have already been broken beyond the limits. I will merely exist until the day my magic returns and I can seek freedom in the sea once again.

At the thought of the sea, I looked up, staring out the massive plane window in front of me, my eyes taking in the majesty of the stormy waters.

The waves crashing into the shore seemed to be beckoning for my return. I wished to return. I wish for the escape.

Two years. Just two years, and I will never leave the sea again.

My dread of the next two years was probably showing on my face, and I had to work hard to mask it once again. When I finally felt like I had control of myself, letting the rhythmic waves in the background soothe my dread, it was time. It's time for my uncle to pass me off to my dreaded fate.

I allowed my eyes to trail over Lachlan only for a second, not lingering on any part of him for any amount of time. He was nothing to me. Nothing. I just need to remain numb until this ceremony was over, then I could retreat back to my room and avoid him as much as possible.

"Dearly beloved. We are all gathered here today for the joining of Alpha Lachlan Stiles, the ruler of the South, to Lady Elelira Lambert of the West. As a result, joining two kingdoms in an alliance through holy matrimony ...."

The officiant droned on, and I kept my eyes unfocused, staring off at the area behind Lachlan, keeping myself numb and uncaring.

None of this matters. This marriage was nothing to him, and it would remain nothing to me. I am no longer the naive girl I was the first time we went through these motions. I know what he thinks of me, and I will not delude myself into thinking there is a hope to change his mind.

I don't want him to change his mind. I want him to remain uncaring, because that is how I feel. I want him to keep his disgust of me, because I am more disgusted with him. I want to stay away from him as much as he desires to avoid me, and once this ceremony is over, I will resolve myself to do just that.

Once this is over, I will change out of this embellished gown with its diving neckline and clinging fabric into something much more comfortable. I will take a bottle of wine from the reception that I know my *husband* will barely attend, then retreat to the shore and walk along the stormy sea.

The clouds in the distance might be depressing for others, but I know the calming and soothing effects a good storm has deep under the water's surface. The beauty of the rolling waves above and the comforting swaying of the currents. It's like a baby being rocked in its mother's arms. I loved storms from under the water, and I plan on treasuring the storms above the surface just as much now that I know their true value and beauty.

"Do you, Lachlan Stiles, take Elelira Lambert as your lawfully wedded wife, and the Luna of the Southern pack?"

"I do," he resounded, squeezing my hands that were numbly resting in his. The determination and passion in his voice broke my daze, and I met his eyes for the first time in this life.

After sliding a ring on my finger, his eyes trailed up to mine. He was not looking at me with disgust or disdain. No. The emotions radiating in his eyes startled me, because there was no malice or anger. They were not the eyes I was familiar with when I remembered them from before.

He almost looks….grieved. Hurt and scared, but determined.

Determined for this to be over?

"Elelira Lambert, do you take Lachlan Stiles as your lawfully wedded husband, and as your Alpha, choosing to lead his people beside him, for the good of the pack?"

I blinked out of my trance, looking away from Lachlan and towards the elder officiating the ceremony. His kind eyes and warm smile stung as I considered rejecting this marriage. The numbness was shaken off at the shock of Lachlan's appearance, much different than before, and the fear of the unexpected weighed heavy on my chest.

Valerina stirs in my mind, her fear matching mine.

Can we do this again? Can we survive the impending future?

We have to. There is no choice. If I say no, what is to become of us? My uncle will take me back with him, and I will face the same ending as I did before, only this time, I will die with the regret of never feeling the water flow over my fins. I'll never experience the storms in the ocean and the freedom swimming in the vast ocean brings me.

I can't reject it.

Val whimpered as I started to breathe heavily, trying to find the numbness in me once again. We can do this. We have to.

"Lira," Lachlan's voice whispers the familiar and hated nickname he gave me from before.

I hated it when he called me that. I hated the way it resounded in my heart as the name left in a sneer from his lips.

He was not sneering now. I can't detect a hint of malice or hatred from him. Just concern and fear.

Fear of what? Me? What reason would he have to fear me?

I stared down at the ground, closing my eyes as I focused inward, Val helping to pull the numbness back over me. After several seconds, that felt like hours, I reopened my eyes, keeping them unfocused as I stared past the man in front of me, who was still tightly gripping my hands, blankly staring at the wall just past him.

"I do," I murmured, my voice sounding dead and cold, even to me.

# FOUR

***Lachlan***

"She knows," Killian whimpered. "She remembers everything. She hates us."

*"She can't. She can't hate us entirely. We're her mate,"* I told him, but that didn't stop the fear from rising up inside me.

She can't hate me. I can't lose her again. If she rejects me again, I would rather die than try living without her. I know what life without her is like. I know what living with the pulsating pain of regret constantly residing in my chest is like.

I can't live without her. I won't.

Her hesitation at our vows made knots form in my stomach, and acid rose in my throat. The bitterness of reality matches its taste. When her father had placed all the rules on me, rules I made a blood promise not to break, I never thought he would bring her back with her memories intact as well.

This should have been easy. We could have lived blissfully in love for years until the mate bond fully revealed itself, then I could have marked and mated her with no stipulations.

Now… I'm going to have to fight. Fight even harder to change her opinion of me, and I'll have to do so without being able to tell her why I'm so different this time around. I can't reveal why I wanted her when last time I treated her so poorly.

It's our wedding, and I could see the fear in her eyes now that they had finally met mine. She is fearing for tonight, I'm sure. It's the first time I betrayed the bond. Even though I didn't feel it, she did, and she probably laid in agony all night because of me.

It will be different this time. I will never take another, but I can't tell her why. I can't reveal that I know we are mates. I can't tell her that I remember the life we had before as well. Her father created a contract in my blood, and it is unbreakable. Even my desire to tell her everything right now is causing me agony.

"Lira," I whispered her name like a prayer, and to my surprise she met my gaze, her emerald eyes shining with unshed tears.

It broke my heart to see her fear of me. I did this. I brought this on myself.

She moved her gaze to the ground, then took a few deep breaths, closing her eyes as she collected herself.

People around the room began to whisper, her uncle glaring at her with a sneer on his lips. He was the reason I was untrusting of my attraction to her. He was the reason I rejected this marriage in every way except on paper while I was still in it. He's conniving and manipulative. I could see the hidden motive behind his actions, but I didn't have a choice before. I couldn't refuse this marriage, for my pack would have suffered without the alliance. In our weakened state, the North would have come for us, attacking us in our own land, devastating our home while we recovered from the war that just came to an end.

I needed the two years to rebuild our forces, and now it looks like I will have the added and even greater burden of rebuilding the bond between my mate and me.

When Lira looked up again, her eyes were once again a vacant stare, looking past me as her passive, cold face returned.

"I do," she stated, her voice soft and monotone.

The ring bearer handed her the ring to place on me, and she went through the motions without even looking at the rings. The rings just hours ago I agonized over, picturing her surprised face when she gazed upon their beauty. Now, she doesn't take notice of them at all.

Killian whimpered and cried, feeling her disinterest and coldness towards us.

"I present to you all, your Alpha and Luna, Lachlan and Elelira Stiles!" the elder recited with a joyous look that neither Lira nor I felt.

I sent word to him before we began to change one part of the ceremony from our previous life, and now my fear is caught in my throat with the realization that Lira will not like it. She will hate it. She may reject it on the spot.

"Alpha Lachlan, you may now kiss your bride!"

She startled hearing that, looking at him, then jerking her head back at me in horror.

My heart pulsed painfully in my chest at that look. When I pictured this moment, I imagined her lovestruck face staring back at me with anticipation and want. That is the opposite of what she is expressing now.

The color drained from her cheeks. She wanted to run. I could feel it. Killian could feel it, and he was crying while snarling at me in my head.

I hoped for a sweet, romantic first kiss, but the reality of the moment was nothing but fear from both of us and for different reasons.

If it wasn't for my hands holding firmly to hers, I felt like she would make a run for it right now, and because that is my greatest fear, I couldn't seem to let her go. We were now standing before half the pack awkwardly. We couldn't back down. I couldn't back down from this.

"Lira," I whispered, making her panicked eyes meet mine. "Just….please," I pleaded with her, begging her to not reject me, or to fear this.

I pulled her hand, taking a step closer to her, but she took a step back. In my panic, I wrapped an arm around her waist, pulling her toward me, and she went stiff as a board, not responding at all to my lips as they meet hers.

I swore I can feel the sparks, even without the bond, and Killian stops whimpering and purrs slightly. Her lips were as soft as I imagined. For years I imagined what they would feel like. This is beyond my expectations.

My elation was short-lived as I pull away from her, and am met with her hate-filled glower.

She looked away, towards the congregation. The music was bellowing a joyous wedding march, but this moment feels any but. Her hand was stiff as I led her back down the aisle to the waiting room at the end. The pack and attendees are cheering for us, waving ribbons and banners, but her face remained passive and cold.

As the doors close behind us, I tried to explain myself.

"Lira, I'm sorry. I-"

SLAP!

"You will not ever touch me again. Don't even show yourself to me after tonight. I don't know what that was, but I'm as uninterested in this union as you are."

I pressed my hand against my throbbing cheek, but the pain didn't compare to the pain in my heart. "Lira, I'm not-"

"I know," she whispered in a dangerously low voice. "I know what you think of me and this marriage. I know you're not invested in this, and neither am I. Let's just bide our time, and annul the moment the terms on the alliance contract are up. I will stay out of your way. You can live your life as before and I will live like the dead, being sure to never cross your path."

No…..No, no, no.

I reached for her, taking a step in her direction, but then the doors behind me reopened and people began to pour out to offer us their congratulations.

She sent me one last death glare, then turned towards her handmaid, Niomi, who came out ahead of the crowd. Niomi was looking between the two of us with concern. Many of the guests were looking at us with concern or confusion, but still offered their commendations. We must have put on quite a show there at the end. Niomi accepted all the praise aimed at Lira, then begged their pardon so she could assist Lira in changing her dress.

Together they walked off down the corridor to change her from her gorgeous wedding gown to the simpler dress for the reception, leaving me to receive all the congratulations on my own. A task I felt unworthy of and sick while doing.

"Alpha Lachlan," Alpha Wayne, her uncle, greeted me with a handshake. "I look forward to hearing good news soon. My men and I have a long journey ahead, and will have to miss your reception. Tell my niece I look forward to hearing from her in the near future."

This. This right here is why I was so suspicious of Lira. I know now that Wayne was just trying to use her as a pawn, and she really wasn't in a conspiracy with him. I nodded, not trusting my voice to not show my malice and hatred for the man.

He grunted, then he and his men walk toward the front of the manor to set out on their journey, which I knew from before was not to their home, but to the brothels and bars in town. It was quite embarrassing running into him and all his men there last time. Luckily, he thought I had enough of my wedding night with my wife, and had come to town to celebrate more rounds without her. He was that sick of a man who thought nothing of having multiple partners in one night, and that it was normal to cheat on your wife.

Tonight, we will not come upon that awkward situation. I will be loyal and faithful, even if she remembers and hates me.

~

***Elelira***

The reception went much the same as the first time. Many of the pack members came to congratulate us as we sat at the head table, but we didn't speak to each other again.

I was polite, even pasting on a smile at times, but inside I felt numb. I knew what tonight would hold for me, and I thought I was ready, but then he went and kissed me.

What was that? That didn't happen the first time. It stirred up Val, and it took me so long to get control of her again.

She felt it. Fully. The bond, the sparks. It was….exhilarating. It made me feel alive for a few moments….then reality hit me. As I was walking down the aisle hand-in-hand with Lachlan, the reality of what was to come if I succumbed to my bond felt like it was choking me. Momentary elation would mean nothing by tonight.

Out of anger for my Lycan, fearing what the ugly strands of hope he just fed her would do to her tonight, I slapped him. I slapped Lachlan, and spewed my venomous words all over him, not fearing at all what his reaction would be.

I won't tolerate it. I won't tolerate him hurting Val like that.

After changing into a lighter, simpler dress for the reception, I went back down with Mimi and was led over to my seat by Nilo, who told me my *husband* would be joining me shortly with a snicker.

When Lachlan did show up, he sat quietly beside me, and I continued to sip wine and accept greetings numbly from his pack. We didn't speak or acknowledge each other again.

There was one difference in the reception. The first dance. I had been dreading it, but when Nilo gave a short speech, snickering as he wished us a happy two-year alliance, he didn't end his speech by welcoming us to our first dance like he did before.

No. This time, by the end of the speech, his eyes glazed momentarily and he started to sweat. He looked nervous as he stared at Lachlan, then finished the speech with "To the bride and groom," as a toast. That was it.

I wouldn't have to let Val suffer from his torturous and tempting touch again, so I was grateful.

Lachlan chugged his champagne, then pushed himself from his seat, leaving with the mumbled excuse of needing to speak with his Beta.

I was happy to see him go. With him gone, it was acceptable for me to step out as well, and there was only one place I wanted to be.

Grabbing an open but nearly full wine bottle from the beverage cart, I slipped out of the hall while everyone was distracted with their meals that were starting to be served. The bride and groom were served first, while Nilo was speaking, so no one would notice my absence for a while.

I took the familiar path around the stone walls of the castle, past the main docks, leading to the private dock only for Lachlan's use. His boat was docked to the side, which is why I liked coming here. It hid me from view as I sat on the dock's end, letting my feet hang off the edge, skimming the water's surface.

Feeling the water between my toes brought back the longing to feel the water all around me. I love the ocean, and the freedom it brings. I've never known anything but sorrow and confinement on land. I want to be free in the sea again.

I'm staring down at the water under my feet, marveling at the foaming waves as they crashed against the structure beneath me when suddenly, I felt like I was being watched. I sigh deeply, thinking it's going to be Mimi or one of the guards asking me to return to the party. I looked up, took a big swig of wine, then froze, bringing the bottle back down as I'm startled.

Out in the distance is a figure, very human-like, floating above the water. I can't see his face, or anything other than a manly profile thanks to the angle and reflection of the sun, but I knew somehow that he is watching me.

I slowly stood, trying to get a better view so I could see his face when the figure dove below the surface, and a magnificent tail caught the sunset in its scales as it flicked against the surface.

A siren. In all my life, I've never seen another. Not even when the representatives come to shore every several years to discuss diplomacy with the packs. I was always told to stay out of sight, in my room, even by my mother.

Seeing one now brought tears to my eyes. I want to be in the sea. I wanted to dive in, swimming out to where I saw him go under, searching for him and pleading for him to take me. Take me back to your lair, to your kingdom.

*"Can we call out to him? Is there a way to signal him to come here?"* Val asked, as eager as I was to find a way to escape into the sea. She was just recovering from what being near her mate did to her. The agony of knowing you are so close to a mate that doesn't want you and can't feel you, it kills her, but she knows he is hopeless. A lost cause. He will start hurting us by tonight, and there is nothing we can do to stop it. Not without making ourselves vulnerable, which I will not do.

"I don't think he wanted us to see him. He dove under right when we noticed him."

"What if he is just swimming to us? He could be coming this way now."

"No. This distance is nothing in the water. He would already be here."

I'm tip toeing on the edge of the dock, considering diving in when I heard that damned nickname again. Val whimpers in my head, not ready for another encounter with him. Maybe I should dive in. I can make it pretty far by swimming even without my fins. I can make it to the other side of the castle, then sneak away to my room, hiding for the rest of the night.

"LIRA!" he yelled, and I knew he caught sight of me. I groaned, throwing the sea one last longing glance before turning to face my insufferable *husband* once again.

"Retreat, Val. Just tune him out and wait for this moment to pass. It will always pass with him. Close yourself off and I'll let you know when he's gone."

She whimpered, but was quick to listen, hiding herself deep in my mind, closing herself off to all my senses so she wouldn't have to feel her mate being near.

# FIVE

*Earlier.....*

***Lachlan***

"What the hell was with that speech?" I growled at my Beta. "Two years?! Did you have to put a time limit on us in front of everyone?!"

Nilo stared at me in confusion, trying to loosen my grip on the collar of his shirt. "Alpha, I showed you my speech beforehand. Just yesterday you said it was okay. You even said to make sure the pack knows that this is only temporary. That you will find your true Luna once this bullshit with Alpha Wayne is over."

Shit. I did say that. I remember now. I even held a special meeting between my most trusted subordinates and ranked Lycans, telling them to keep their eyes on Elelira, to be wary of her and that she was not to be trusted. I truly thought Wayne was using her to trap me in some way.

I released Nilo's collar, pushing away from him, cursing under my breath while I paced, running my hand through my hair.

"Alpha?" Nilo watched me carefully. He probably thought I'd gone crazy. Maybe I have. I just know I couldn't let things continue the way they were. I will never earn her trust if history repeats itself.

"She's my Luna, Nilo. She's my…." my throat burned, the blood promise preventing me from saying it; saying she's my mate. I can't reveal that myself until the day of her 20th birthday.

Her birthday…..

Shit. That's today. Today is her 18th birthday. That's why her uncle chose this day to begin with. I had forgotten.

"She's your what?" Nilo disrupted my distressing thoughts of forgetting something as important as her birthday. "Are you saying she's your mate?"

I swallowed, anticipating pain, but luckily, when I nodded my head in answer, I didn't feel anything indicating I was breaking the terms of the contract. I couldn't tell him, but he could guess. Good. That's good to know. It should be the same for Lira then. I can get her to guess that I know we are mates....if I can ever get that close to her to have those kinds of conversations.

"Holy cow. She's your mate? Is that why you were so nervous during the ceremony? I thought you both were acting weird. You must have been uncomfortable because of the bond and not being able to just mate her in front of all those people. How are you holding yourself back from taking her now?"

Killian growled at the crassness of his question. We don't yet feel the bond. That's how we were able to hold ourselves back, but I couldn't say that to him now. My throat burned with the mere thought of telling him.

When I first felt the bond right before she rejected me, it was like gravity was pulling me towards her, but I soon went crashing back to earth as the rejection left her perfect lips. The pain in my heart was so great, and Killian was tearing me apart on the inside, blaming me for his loss of her.

His growling turns into whimpers at the memory.

"Hell, I thought she was glaring at you. I guess she was just overcome by the bond too and was trying to hold herself back. It looked like she hated you. Imagine being used as a pawn by your own family but the marriage turned out to be with your mate. She must feel so relieved."

I flinched at his words. "She hates me," I mumbled.

"Hates you?" Nilo questioned. "Why would she hate you? Because of the rumors about you? Well….I guess you do spend a lot of time at the brothels. It's widely known that you're the cold-hearted warmonger who likes to keep his bed warm with women. This is going to break several ladies' hearts. They were expecting you back tonight on your own word that this was just a marriage on paper."

"Shit, will you stop," I groaned. He doesn't know when to shut up. "I'm never stepping into a brothel again. There will never be any other woman but Lira again. Understand? So don't say anything to anyone to suggest otherwise."

He held his hands up defensively. "Hey, I get it. You should tell this to Cherum and Meldec as well as the rest of the commanders. You told them all not to regard Wayne's niece as Luna, since she would be gone after two years. You even told the servants in the packhouse to address her only as

Lady Elelira and not Luna. You told them not to regard her with favor since she was only here temporarily."

He's right. I remember once saying all those awful things. I needed to fix this situation now.

"Tell the staff she is their Luna, and to treat her as such. Now. I will not tolerate any disrespect towards her. None. I want her to feel welcomed and treated like a princess." That's what she was. She just doesn't know it. I will never treat her as anything less.

"What about her room? You had her placed in the tower furthest from your room. Do you want me to tell the staff to move her?"

I was hoping we would share my room from this day forward, but with the way things turned out, that isn't possible. I couldn't even dance with her, knowing how uncomfortable that would make her feel.

The first reception we had, Nilo teased me after his speech by calling us to share our first dance. I stopped him before he could do the same this time. After that slap, I don't want to be on the receiving end of her anger again. I won't touch her again until she is ready for it. She doesn't trust me now, and I won't earn her trust by going against her wishes.

The room I had her put in was the least desired room in the castle. Less so than even the servant's quarters. It is drafty, making it humid and hot in the summer and freezing in the winter. Even the fireplace does little to fully warm the room.

"Change her room. Move her down to my hall, as close to me as possible. Have Niomi start tonight."

"You got it, Alpha. Anything else?"

I looked towards the reception hall and the people there celebrating our wedding. Killian was urging me to return and check on our mate, worried about how she is being treated in our absence. With the way I spoke to my men in the past about Elelira, I don't think any of them would be looking out for her, or making sure she was treated well. I can't even remember how she was treated at our reception the first time around.

I had sat with her out of obligation, but spent all my time ignoring her until Nilo's speech and that blasted dance. Once that was over, I excused myself, then retreated to my bedroom to rest before my night in town. I didn't check on her once, though I do remember dreaming about her during that nap, which frustrated me to no end.

What did she do after I had left, I wonder? I avoided her like the plague, and didn't have a proper conversation with her once. Besides Niomi, who was the most disposable omega in the castle, which was why I originally assigned her to Lira, I don't think she was close to anyone else.

Niomi had passed away before Elelira rejected me. I asked the other omegas about her and how she passed her time, but no one knew. They didn't even know who was helping to manage her room or look after her.

A stableboy recalled seeing Elelira wandering into the forest, up the stream about once a week. Was she meeting someone then? A friend? I never found out.

She was completely alone in the pack, it seemed, which is why she had no qualms about rejecting the pack and her position as Luna. The anguish the pack felt as she severed her ties to everyone was my fault. I treated her like an enemy, so they did too. Many of the staff and warriors grieved for a long time about their treatment of their true Luna. Their regret and guilt deepened mine.

I won't have my pack members have those same regrets.

"It's her birthday," I told my Beta.

His eyes grew big. "You're right! I had forgotten that was the arrangement made by Wayne. He had to wait until today so she would no longer be a minor." He then made a face at me. "You cradle robbing scamp. She's -"

"It's not that much of an age difference. Seven years is a common age gap," I growled.

"If you say so," he shrugs, still looking disgusted.

I've been Alpha since I was 18, thanks to my father and then mother dying in the war. I then spent the next 7 years in constant battle and war with the North. I may look much older than her, but her radiant beauty would be hard for anyone to match. I look a lot less used and worn out than I did before coming back. The time I spent searching for Elelira and then meeting all her father's terms to bring her back weathered my appearance greatly.

"So, what do you want to do about her birthday? Do you want me to send out for a gift? I can tell the staff to embellish her new room with flowers and have gifts delivered by the time you both retire to your rooms."

"Do it," I ordered, not knowing what else to do for her.

"You could start with wishing her a happy birthday," Killian muttered, "And apologizing for the kiss. If she is comparing the current you to you of before, give her a reason not to. Start with not abandoning her at our wedding reception."

He's right.

With a final run-through of the plans for moving her room, Nilo walked off to carry out the tasks, and I hurried back to the reception hall.

When I got there, I didn't see her at our table, and with a quick glance around the room, I could see she was no longer there.

"Alpha! You're back! I thought you had retired for the evening to get your rest before we head out tonight!" Cherum came up from behind me, slapping me on the back in the cheerful way he used to.

I haven't seen him like this in so long. He's my Delta, and he's supposed to be Luna's aide and protector. Because of my order to not treat Elelira as Luna, he neglected his duties, snubbing her completely. He may have been the only one who came close to feeling as bad as I did when everything came to light.

"I won't be going out tonight, or any night from this night forth," I told him in a terse tone, "Have you seen my wife?"

"Your wife?" he questioned me, "I figured you sent her away. I saw her leaving not long after you left the hall with Nilo."

My eyes grew big and worry hit me. "She left?"

He nodded, pointing towards the door that takes you to the back passage to the docks.

I sprinted out of the hall to find her, praying she wasn't trying to escape to the sea again. That image has haunted me for so long. I can't lose her already. Not like before.

I ran towards the docks, frantically, then saw in the distance the silhouette of a siren utterly still in the sea, staring at something at my personal dock. I gasp, realizing who it was, and what he must be staring at. He must have heard my gasp, because he quickly looked my way before smirking and diving under the water's surface. His hearing is as excellent as always, I see.

I ran the distance from the castle walls to the dock, maneuvering around the stone trail so I didn't fall off the cliff in my haste. It still takes me far longer than I would like, and I'm in full panic mode by the time I get near the dock.

"LIRA!" I yelled as loud as I could, my throat and lungs burning with the force. "LIRA!" I screamed again, finding her at the end of the dock, dangerously close to the edge while staring down at the water.

Don't do it, Lira. Don't leave me again.

"Lira," I panted out as she turned gracefully to face me, her golden hair streaming behind her like dancing sunlight in the sea winds.

Her sunny hair was such a contrast to her icy expression. She looks exasperated, like I had disturbed her greatly with my presence.

"Yes?" she muttered coldly, making Killian whimper.

"Wha-what are you doing out here?" I asked like an idiot. "Why aren't you at the reception?"

She furrowed her brows, "Why would I need to be there when you aren't?"

I cringed, knowing she was referring to our first reception when I left early, leaving her on her own without any regard for her.

"I'm sorry. I just had to speak with my Beta for a moment. I was coming right back."

"How was I to know that?" she snapped.

I tried not to cower in her fierce gaze. It was so much the same as the way she looked at me when she rejected me. My stomach was now in knots, and I couldn't think of any other way to carry on with a conversation with her. Should I try groveling at her feet, begging for her love and acceptance? Will she find mercy for me? Pity? I will accept anything but rejection. I won't survive another rejection from her.

She sighed deeply, realizing I had nothing left to say. Good going, idiot. You yelled at her, and now you can't find your voice to apologize or say something that may help you to win her favor.

She took one last lingering and longing look at the sea, then walked past me, back towards the reception.

I watched her go, frozen in place by her cold demeanor until she could no longer be seen.

"Good going. You should never have left her in the first place," Killian snarled.

"You were the one that told Nilo to meet us out in the hall while he was giving his speech," I reminded him.

He *humphs* and retreats to grieve in the back of my mind, distraught at our mate's scorn.

"You didn't think I would make it that easy for you, did you?" a deep, musical voice questioned me. I turned to see the man I saw in the water staring up at me from the space between the dock and my boat. Lira's father.

His long hair is fanning about him in the water, the same golden color as Lira's. The embedded crown around his head, signifying his status as king, shone in the waning sun. His broad body was massive, even in the water in this form. He was the reason I got a second chance, but he's also the reason Lira remembers everything.

"King Brennus," I gritted my teeth, knowing an outward display of my anger towards him would do me no good. "You never said she would keep her memories as well."

"Why would I do you that favor? It was your mistreatment that led her to run away in the first place. I told you that I would give you a second chance. Nothing more. In all honesty, I hope for your failure. She deserves better, and if it were not for her locked magic, I would take her back with me now. I wish to," his voice dropped slightly, then he looked towards the castle as if he really wished to come on shore and retrieve her.

"She could have told me about the bond before. Told someone," I murmured in defense. She never gave any indication that she was a hybrid to anyone, or that she was my mate.

"If she were to tell your people that she was your mate after your treatment of her, they would have called her crazy. And how do your pack members view the other races? I know it is the consequence of endless wars for your territory, and your dealings with the dark fae of the north, but your kind does not view the fae races or demonic races favorably. If she said she was half siren, your own commanders might have killed her thinking she was truly a trap sent by her filthy uncle."

I know by the way he always refers to Wayne that his hate for the Alpha of the West far outweighs his hate for me.

He's right. We don't treat fae very kindly. Sirens were derived from fairies and mermaids mating over centuries, and have magic we never trusted. Our pack has suffered so much because of the dark fae races of the north that my people could have possibly hurt Lira out of fear.

"She tried to tell you," Killian told me, coming forth again, "She tried requesting an audience with you multiple times, and you always turned her down. It wasn't until she stopped trying to seek you out that you even bothered showing her your face, and by then she was probably set on rejecting us, so why would she try after that?"

He's right. She may not have trusted my people with her secret, but she did try to reach out to me. I was the one that prevented her from telling me anything.

"I don't want to hurt her again," I whispered. "I will do anything to gain her trust."

King Brennus must have taken pity on me, because his cold eyes softened. "Because of our agreement, and for your help in bringing her back to this point, you have 2 years. 2 years to gain back her trust and maybe even her love. I think I was more than generous to give you that. I have countless other means to keep her safe and secure until her 20th birthday. I am allowing you another chance. One you do not deserve."

He lifted one of his hands from the water, a stunning necklace with glimmering jewels embedded in an intricate pendant, the pattern reminding me of a crashing wave in his palm. "This is my gift for my daughter on her birthday. Be sure she gets it."

I leaned down, taking the necklace gingerly from his palm, enamored by the way the last of the sunlight dances on the cut stones.

I was so fixated on the necklace that I didn't notice the smirk that came over King Brennus's face as he reached up and pulled me into the water. My wedding attire is ruined, and I was now a sopping mess.

I sputtered as I pulled myself back onto the dock, still gripping the necklace in my hand. King Brennus was laughing like a hyena, bellowing loudly and making me growl.

"That's my gift to you , my new *son-in-law*, on your wedding day."

"Trying to drown me?!" I sputtered.

"No," he chuckled one last time before his face turns serious, "*Not* drowning you, though you deserve it."

That's the last he said before diving back into the sea. I will have to be on my guard. That man will be watching us closely over the next 2 years. I'm sure. If I step out of line once, he would waste no time in taking his daughter away from me.

# SIX

***Elelira***

Walking back to the reception hall, I tried to let the numbness overtake me again, taking a final swig of the wine before leaving the bottle on the pathway' I did not want to draw any more negative attention to myself by coming in with it nearly empty.

There were already many differences during this second time marrying Lachlan. Not just the kiss, which was unexpected and confusing enough, but Lachlan coming to look for me after.

Once he left the reception before, he never came back. I was on my own the rest of the evening until Mimi led me back to my room for the night.

What reason would he have to come search for me? I thought he and his subordinates would be readying themselves for their night out about now.

"Luna," someone said, disturbing my thoughts. I looked around and saw Nilo and Cherum, Lachlan's Beta and Delta watching me as I reentered the hall. I didn't know which one addressed me, or why they would be calling me Luna, so I just stared at them in confusion.

"Pardon my late introduction," Nilo says, smiling kindly, "I am the Beta here, Nilo Gossling. This is our Delta and your personal protection and aide from this day forth, Cherum Rosewood."

"Luna," Cherum bowed his head respectfully. "I look forward to serving you from-"

"That's alright," I rushed to interject before he made a vow or anything of that sort to protect and serve me. In this strange second chance, I still did not wish to cause qualms or be the reason anyone broke a vow. "Like the Beta said during his speech, I have but two years here. That is such a short time that I will be in the care of this pack. After the contract is fulfilled, I have no desire to burden you any longer. If you will excuse me,"

I bowed to both of them before hurrying off towards my seat.

I didn't miss the way Nilo flinched when I mentioned his speech. I wonder why he cared, or why they would bother talking to me? They didn't the first time. Cherum would always sneer or growl at me, not wanting anything to do with me before, and Nilo, though not as hostile, would be the one to turn me away every time I sought Lachlan out.

I didn't want to bear ill-will towards either of them, but those memories remain, so my bitterness does as well. I only want to live like the dead, the same as before, surviving until my 20th birthday.

I sat alone in my seat for quite a long time, watching the others around the room mingle and enjoy the celebration. People are dancing, and the wine is flowing at every table. Even my own. Alcohol doesn't affect us the same as humans, but many in the room are starting to act drunkenly. I have a much higher tolerance, since I am a hybrid, I suppose. I used to try to use alcohol to numb the pain of Lachlan's affairs, but it never fully worked.

Now, I am just enjoying the wine, which seemed to be my only companion again in this marriage.

Lachlan, though he claimed he was coming right back, still hasn't shown up. I was about to wave Mimi over so I could retire for the night when he finally came back in, dressed entirely differently than before. He always favored black, but he wore more gold during our ceremony, and now he is in a white linen shirt with his signature black pants. You could see the contrast of his tan skin with the white shirt, making him more attractive and less severe-looking.

I'm sure the women at the establishment he frequents will go nuts over his appearance tonight. Good for them. Someone should feel happy on the day of our wedding. It isn't either of us.

He sat in the chair beside mine, and I didn't even bother acknowledging his return.

"I'm sorry for my delay. I, uh, had a mishap on the dock and fell into the water. I had to go dry off and change."

I could smell the saltwater on him, and his hair was still damp. I suppose he is telling the truth, but that is of little consequence to me. "I understand," I muttered, so as not to be rude and disrespect him in front of his people.

"Lira," he said the name softly. I wish he would stop calling me that.

"Elelira," I muttered.

"What?"

"Elelira is my name. Not Lira. No one but-" I stopped myself before I say *you call me that.* "No one calls me Lira."

"I wish to," he whispered in a deep, husky voice, making Val whimper with desire. I turned my head to look at him. His body is leaning towards mine and his eyes are begging me for something. For what, I do not know. "You will always be my Lira."

With the tender way he said it, I almost believed him.

The silence stretches between us, and Val was stirring inside me, curious, and maybe a little hopeful about the intentions behind his words.

"Uh, here," he murmured after a while, looking down awkwardly. He hands me a beautiful pendant necklace. The cool-toned jewels and pattern somehow remind me of the ocean, and my hand reaches for it without a conscious effort to do so, like I'm being drawn to it in some way.

"What is this for?" I asked softly. The metal in which the jewels are embedded is cool to the touch, and tingles ran up my fingers. I would mistake the tingles for the mate bond if I wasn't familiar with the sensation from before. Magic. The necklace is embedded with fae magic, much like the siren magic I possessed after my 20th birthday. Siren magic is fae magic, since sirens are one of the many races of fae-kind. "Where did you..."

"It was a gift. Not from me," he let me know quickly, "It was given to me by, uh, someone who wished to pass along the present to you."

"Who?" I can't help but ask.

*"It has magic like ours in it,"* Val mused in my head, fascinated by the feeling we get from holding the pendant. It almost felt like it was redirecting its magic to flow into us. *"Who gave that to him? Does he know that it has magic in it?"*

"Werewolves and Lycans cannot sense magic like hybrids and other races can. I doubt he is aware."

"Someone who wishes for you to have a happy life here," he smiled nervously.

I couldn't help but to snort in a very unladylike fashion. I doubt I'll have anything close to a happy life here.

"Lira, I just want to say, I do hope you can find a way to live happily here with me and, well, happy bi-"

"Alpha!" a group of young women interrupted whatever he was about to say. They are all dressed alluringly, with low necklines and bodices to push their breasts almost to their chins. They came to his side of the table, a few of them ignoring my presence, and the others sneering in my direction before turning overly sweet smiles towards Lachlan.

Lachlan looked panicked, in an uncomfortable frenzy like he wasn't sure what to do. One of the women, a beautiful brunette with thick lashes and voluptuous curves, pushes up against his chair, sending me a mocking grin before bending over to rest her arm around his shoulder, her chest imposing on his face.

I scoffed, and Val whimpered inside my head. We knew better. I almost considered holding out hope for this second life and this marriage to my mate. Almost. I'm glad I didn't now, because he clearly hasn't changed.

"Alpha. We wanted to offer our condolences after listening to all your mourning *all night long* last night. We look forward to seeing you again later this evening."

He started to growl, pushing her away from him, but I quickly rose to my feet, maintaining control of my outward emotions. The only display of my annoyance is my painfully tight grip on the pendent in my hands. "I think I will retire for the evening. Have a wonderful night, ladies. Alpha," I bowed my head, and started walking out of the hall. I do not wish to cause Val any more pain than she is currently feeling, and my walls are fully erect around my heart and my emotions once again.

"Lira!" Lachlan called to me, but I ignored him, done with his fake niceties for a lifetime.

~

***Lachlan***

"Alpha?" Leona pawed at my chest while pulling my arm. I shook her off and stepped away, intending on chasing after my wife. She was gone, though. She didn't even turn back when I called her.

"Why?" I growled furiously as I slowly turned towards the women. "Why would you think that was okay? To disrespect your Luna like that on our wedding day, why would you-?"

"Lanny," Leona pathetically whined out the nickname many of the girls call me, cutting off my question. "Don't be like that. You looked like you were struggling, so we came to help. You told us she wasn't going to be anything more than an annoying guest," she popper her hip out to the side, "You said she would never be our Luna, Lanny. I don't know why you are being so mean."

I pinched the bridge of my nose, focusing on containing my Lycan, who was trying to break free and tear this woman apart for insulting our mate. How am I going to get close to Lira now? How am I going to overcome this misunderstanding?

"Alpha?" Yasmin, the girl I used to frequent more than the others because she was the least clingy. "I'm sorry if we offended you. We can leave," she murmured, pulling Leona back meekly. "We will see you later," she bows politely, many of the other girls following her lead.

"You won't," I told them coldly. "I won't be coming back again. I'm a married man, and I won't betray my wife."

Leona scoffed, "Lanny, you can't be serious. You said-"

"I SAID," I yelled above her, using enough of my aura, letting Killian push to the surface to make my point, "I will not betray my *wife* and *your Luna,"* I glared at her menacingly until she submitted, bowing her head in compliance, but still bearing an arrogant grimace on her lips. Most of the guests had stopped to observe the confrontation and my bout of anger. Good. There will be many to witness me sending these women away. "Do you understand?"

"Yes, Alpha," she murmured before joining the rest of the girls as they flinted off to the open bar. I sent a quick mind link to Nilo to get them out of here. I saw him across the hall, and he nodded before moving towards the group to carry out my order.

How did they get into the packhouse? Most of the women are human, though Leona isn't. She is a half-breed, whose parents died in the war.

She probably led the rest of the girls here, now that I think about it. The packhouse is open to all Lycan and werewolf kinds in my pack, so she would always be allowed access.

I'll deal with that later. I'll talk to the guards and warriors about preventing Leona from running around as she wishes, causing problems for my mate and wife.

"If that bitch pulls a stunt like that again, you had better deal with it. It's your fault she thinks she can come and go as she pleases."

"*I know, damn it."* I was a real prick before. I got so overwhelmed with my desire for Lira before that I would invite women into the packhouse and into my bed all the time. Leona and Yasmin would often visit me in the packhouse before Lira came whenever I called for them. It got to be where

Leona would seek me out after a while. I never discouraged her, which I should have.

I forgot about that. After Lira rejected me and ran away, I didn't see Leona, Yasmin, or any of the other brothel women again. I didn't touch another woman. Killian wouldn't have let me if I wanted to, which I didn't.

"Damn right, I wouldn't have. We had the perfect woman given to us, and you spent two years pushing her away. You hurt our mate enough. I wouldn't let you do it again."

"You're like a broken record sometimes," I growled.

I was walking as fast as I can towards the room I had Lira originally set up in. It's on the farthest side of the castle, far from the rest of the rooms, and I had to climb two flights of stairs to make it there. I need to apologize and explain to her that what just happened will never happen again. I just need to see her and make sure she is alright. That she is still here, and hasn't run away again.

Just as I got near her room, I came to a stop and backtracked around the stairwell, spotting Lira in the hallway outside of her bedroom talking to Cherum, my Delta.

"Luna, please. I am only here to serve you."

She sighed loudly. "I told you, it wasn't necessary. This is only temporary. I will be gone in two years."

Cherum shifted uncomfortably on his feet, but Lira didn't back down. My heart dropped to hear her say she was still planning on leaving me after 2 years.

"I'm sorry, Luna, but I still wish to serve you. At least let me help you move your belongings to your new room."

"New room?" she asked.

I snuck a glance around the stairwell and saw that she was tilting her face in an adorable way. She looked graceful and lovely, even in this awkward situation. Killian was purring at the sight of her. I wished I could just run my knuckles down her supple cheeks and their rosy glow.

Cherum nodded enthusiastically. "Alpha ordered for you to be moved to be near him. Probably so you both could start sharing a room soon. If you are up here, how can you-"

She held her delicate hand up, stopping his words, a look of agitation crossing her face.

"I have no plans to ever share a room or anything else with your Alpha,

Delta Rosewood. I would rather stay up here. Now, I'm tired. It has been an exhausting day. I hope you men enjoy your night in town. It seems your Alpha you claim wants me closer to him is getting started with his *evening activities* downstairs in our reception hall."

"Evening activities?" he asked in confusion.

"Yes. The women of the night, I believe," she shrugged as if she expected it. As if it was normal for a husband to invite prostitutes to his wedding reception. She thinks so little of me. " Now, if you will excuse me," she bowed her head, then turned to enter the room, softly closing the door behind her.

*"You twit,"* Killian snarled at me.

*"I know,"* I groaned, leaning back against the stone wall and sliding down it, my hope of recovering the evening and apologizing all but gone.

She thought I called those women here. I know she does. Why wouldn't she? I'm fucking up this chance just as much as I fucked up my first.

"Alpha?" Cherum said in surprise as he rounded the stone steps. "Luna said….I thought you were with the night ladies. What are you doing here?"

I growled at his question, scowling up at him from where I was slumped on the floor. "I will never touch those women again."

He scratched the back of his neck, messing up his already messy red locks, before pulling on his full, bushy beard. "So Nilo wasn't lying? She is your mate?" Cherum asked, nodding in the direction of Lira's door.

"She's mine," Killian growled through me, baring my teeth possessively.

He held his hands up in defense. "I get it, Alpha. Jeez. I was just wondering, since it seems like she wants nothing to do with you or this pack. She doesn't even want to change rooms. Don't know why. You put her in the shittiest part of the castle. It's still summer and I'm freezing my nuts off up here. If she really wants to stay up here, I'll have someone come patch the holes in the walls and make repairs to the tower tomorrow. Don't need my Luna freezing come winter."

"She's not staying up here," I growled, "She's coming down to my floor. Whatever I have to do, I want her closer to me."

"But she said-"

"I DON'T CARE WHAT SHE SAID!" I yelled. "She's mine, and I won't be able to sleep at night with her this far from me."

"Shit. Okay, Alpha. I got it. I'll get her maids to move her since she won't allow me to help. Who is her handmaiden anyway?"

I grimaced slightly, knowing he wouldn't like my answer. "Niomi."

"The old lady?! Why? Why would you assign to her someone of such low rank? She was a kitchen maid, right?"

"Laundry, I think." I'm not sure what Niomi was doing before. She was too old to do anything significant, which was why I originally assigned her to Lira. "Get her a new handmaiden. Someone who can be her friend and who has more authority in the pack."

"You got it, Alpha," he said, reaching down to help pull me up to my feet.

# SEVEN

***Elelira***

When I went upstairs of my isolated tower, mentally exhausted and ready to retire for the evening, the Delta of the pack was waiting outside, looking about ready to enter the room for whatever reason.

"Why is he here? He didn't acknowledge us before. Why is he continually trying to get involved with us this time?" Val asked me.

"I'm not sure. Much has changed this time. It's a lost cause if he is trying to fulfill his task as my Delta. Lachlan obviously hasn't changed."

Val whimpered, thinking about the women that had surrounded Lachlan back in the reception hall. They all seemed more than familiar with him. I guess it comes with their line of work. Intimate and personal knowledge of my husband is not something I will ever obtain. After watching the women paw all over him, I'm now grateful I won't. I'm not here to intrude on their territory. It makes me sick to think about being with him after all of them have had him.

I left the reception early in my last life. Did he invite those women to our wedding the first time too? Was that where he disappeared to after his Beta had given that awful speech?

Looking in my hand, I was still holding the necklace he gave me. I probably should have given it back, but the magic in it was calling to me, urging me to keep it. I gripped it tighter as I approached the pack's Delta.

After telling him I have no plans on moving rooms, or having any closer relationship with his Alpha, I went inside my room, alone at last, and began stripping out of this reception dress.

I had just managed to unbutton the last button on the back, letting the dress fall to the floor, when I heard Lachlan yelling outside in the stairway with the Delta.

Still wearing my slip, I pulled a dressing robe from my bed and wrapped it around my body before slightly cracking the door to find out what was happening.

I just wanted a moment of peace away from him, but it seems Lachlan was set on making this life hell for me as well.

"I DON'T CARE WHAT SHE SAID! She's mine, and I won't be able to sleep at night with her this far from me."

Who was he talking about? Was he referring to me?

Val perked at the idea as we continued to listen in, but by the end of their conversation, both of us were growling in anger.

"He can't replace her. She is our only friend and support here. Does he want us to be completely alone?" Val asked.

"Why wouldn't he? That's all he wanted before. He will probably replace her with someone who treats us poorly from the start. Our time with Mimi was the only time we didn't feel helpless, and now he is taking that away from us."

*"Stop him,"* Val growled, no longer pining for her mate, but furious with him now instead.

"How? He is the Alpha?"

"And that Delta thinks you are his Luna. The Beta seemed to as well this time. Tell them no, and order them to keep her with you."

I grimaced, imagining how that might go. I paced my room as I thought things through, anxiety building in me. I don't want to lose Mimi. *"A Luna in name isn't the same as a mated Luna. I don't have the authority to command or order anyone in this pack."*

She growled in my head, irritated because she knew I am right. "Bargain with him then. If he wants you to change rooms or....be closer with him, then agree to do it as long as you can keep Mimi with you. She will die in a year. We can't let her die on her own."

Mimi, because she was an elderly, lower omega, didn't have much support. Maybe that is why we grew so close. I don't want her taken from me to die on her own. I want to love her and cherish her until her time comes, so she can leave this world knowing she is valued and adored, and not just an insignificant maid like she often thought she was.

"Let's go find Lachlan," I murmured out loud. Val snorted in my head in agreement.

If he wants me closer to him so he can keep a better eye on me, then fine. If he wants to…partake in his rights as my husband, then so be it, though I doubt that is what he truly wants. He never hinted that he wanted to before. I will endure whatever to keep Mimi with me.

I slipped back on my uncomfortable shoes given to me for my wedding day. My feet were aching from wearing them while climbing the stone steps, but I'm not sure where any other shoes are packed away at the moment. I would rather have gone barefoot, but the stone floors are too cold to walk on without causing my legs and feet to cramp.

I probably appeared indecent, roaming the castle in my slip and a flimsy overcoat, but I couldn't get dressed by myself in my reception dress again. Not on my own with all the buttons on the back, and I didn't want to waste time finding another dress.

When I got to the busier main part of the packhouse, I received curious glances from those still lingering from the wedding, but I held my head up high, not showing anything but confidence. Their opinions do not matter. I'm sure after Lachlan's little display with all his girlfriends, I couldn't be any more shamed than I already have been.

Reentering the reception hall, I found Cherum speaking with a group of young maids, probably searching for Mimi's replacement. I ignored the pointed stares from the remaining guest and strode over to him, not displaying anything but fierce resolve.

"Delta Rosewood," I spoke, causing him to turn and face me. The maids are surprised by my attire. You could see it in their expressions, but their expressions were nothing in comparison to the Delta's. His mouth dropped and his eyes went wide.

"Luna," he murmured, looking quickly around the room, then shrugging out of his jacket, offering to place it over my shoulders. I stepped away, not allowing him to do so.

"Where is Niomi?" I commanded, keeping my head up high.

"Um," he glanced around the room again. "She was reassigned back to the kitchens, or was it laundry?" he pulled his beard anxiously. "I was just about to send one of these women up to help you to-"

"I want Niomi," I told him. "I do not wish for another maid or handmaiden. I will not accept anyone but her."

He scratched the back of his neck nervously. "The Alpha said to assign someone more appropriate to you, Luna. I'm sorry, but-"

"If Niomi is taken from me, I will raise hell, Delta Rosewood. I can accept many things about this forced marriage and the hell that it will be, but I will not let you take Niomi from me. Where is your Alpha?"

He made a face, displeased with my wording, I'm sure. Referring to this situation as hell is a truthful statement, so I will not apologize for it.

"He is in his room, I believe," Cherum muttered after several awkward seconds of us staring at one another.

"I will address the issue with your Alpha myself. Dismiss these women back to their tasks. I'm sure they have much to do after this *reception*." I turned, not waiting for his reply. He is not the problem. His Alpha is. I am set to endure more hell in this pack. I won't let him take Mimi from me as well.

My robe billowed around me as I walked quickly towards the wing where his room was located. This part of the castle is well insulated and warm. I'm almost tempted to take off my heels as they are killing my feet, but I don't want to stop my momentum to do so. I will just have to put them back on when I go back upstairs anyway.

As I neared his room, I heard giggling outside of it. Of course, he isn't here alone. In my panic about Niomi being taken from me, I almost forgot what he would be off doing tonight.

The woman from before, the one who was pressing her chest into Lachlan's face, was standing outside his open door as he leaned against it. She ran her finger down his chest, and though I couldn't see his face, I do notice he doesn't push her away. He didn't know I was watching, not that he would care if he did. He never cared before.

"Alpha, you are so domineering. I love it when you get angry. It makes the night so much more passionate," she slurs. Is she drunk?

"Retreat, Val," I told her, hearing her whimper and feeling her pain, "I will be out of here as soon as I can. Retreat and don't look. You don't need to feel the pain."

I felt her withdrawal to the back of my mind, her heart crushed all over again. I think she was still holding out hope after hearing him claim us in the hall. That was all over now.

"Leona, I told you already that-"

"Alpha," I addressed him, drawing both their attention to me.

His head snapped around so fast, it is almost comical when combined with the panicked look that came over him. He quickly pushed the woman away, making her scoff with a grimace and hate-filled eyes that she turned towards me.

"Lira," he whispered my name, almost beggingly. He then looked at the woman and back at me. "This isn't what it looks like. I was just telling her to leave."

I held my head up high, not believing him in the least. He doesn't know I've lived through this already. "I just need a word, then you can return to your guest, Alpha Lachlan. It won't take long."

He growled, startling me for a moment, then his eyes softened with panic like he had just realized he scared me. "I'm sorry. I wasn't growling at you," he sputtered, then turned to glare at the woman, "GO! Don't come back here again. I will tell the guards you are not allowed past the gates if you try."

"But, Alpha," the woman puffed up her face in offense while pouting. "I always spend the nights with you." Her chest rose and fell like she was about to cry. Her hips are round, accented by her clothing, and she clutches her chest, making it spill out of her bodice even more. Is this why he never showed interest in me? Because he likes well-endowed women like this to keep his bed warm at night?

Lachlan growled again, more fiercely than before, and she jumped at the sound, hurrying away down the hall, right past me. She sent me the nastiest look as she walked by, but I just smiled apologetically. She can have him. I'm not here to take her client, lover, or whoever he is to her away.

"That was unnecessary, Alpha. I just need to discuss the matter of my maid, then you can go back to her."

"Lira," he said that awful nickname in that same pleading tone again. "It wasn't like that. Really. I was just sending her away. I won't touch another woman ever again now that we are married."

"What a beautiful lie," I smiled weakly. His face fell, but I maintained my indifferent air. "It is of no concern to me, Alpha. If you wish to take all those women to your bed every night, that is your business, not mine. What is my business is the matter of my maid, Niomi. Delta Rosewood told me she was reassigned. I do not want that. I will not accept anyone other than her."

He ran a hand down his stressed face, but I remained unmoving, not faltering, though I can feel his agitation. "I'm sorry I interrupted, Alpha," I murmured, "I won't accept Niomi being taken from me though."

"You didn't interrupt anything. Lira. Please, stop thinking the worst of me."

I scoffed, breaking my indifferent stance to roll my eyes. Who is he trying to fool?

"I'm serious. I was turning her away, but then you showed up. I didn't call for her or ask her to come. I didn't ask any of those women to come tonight."

"My maid," I brought the topic back to that, not wanting to hear more lies. He doesn't know this is my second time enduring this torturous night. I know exactly why those women were here. He wasn't going to take the only person who gave me any comfort while I endured it all.

He sighed deeply, knowing I didn't believe a word he says. "Niomi is old and frail. She never should have been assigned to you in the first place. We have many warriors' daughters who would be better suited for the task of your handmaiden."

"I only want Niomi," I told him stubbornly. "I will do anything to keep her, but if you take her from me, I won't forgive you."

I didn't expect that threat to do much, knowing he could care less about my forgiveness, but he actually seemed to fear my hatred after the words left my mouth. His expression darkened, like a weight was just placed on his shoulders.

"Will you do anything to keep her?" he asked after several awkward moments of silence and an intense stare-off between us.

A knot formed in my stomach, unsure of myself now that I offered. I'm doing this for Mimi, though. I don't want her to spend her last year of life in hard labor, feeling unappreciated until the day of her death.

I nodded solemnly. "As long as I can keep her with me."

"Would you move into my room with me?" he asked, biting his lip.

I couldn't stop myself from making an appalled face. "The room you have shared with countless other women?" I couldn't help but to comment. His hopeful expression fell once again.

"I will change rooms. Just sharing a room with you would be enough for me," he quickly explained.

I tilted my face, pondering his offer. His eyes softened as I thought about his terms. The strenuous mate bond made tingles build inside me under his stare.

"I do not wish to sleep in a bed many women have shared. Could I just allow for you to, um, visit me in my own quarters whenever you desire, um, *that?*"

His chest vibrated with a frustrated growl. "I told you, there will be no other women. Ever. But if that makes you feel more comfortable, so be it. I just ask for your room to be moved down here, so you can be closer to me."

I grimaced, not liking the idea, but seeing no way around it. "Fine. As long as you can assure me, Niomi will remain with me."

"Whatever you wish for, my wife," he grinned.

~

***Lachlan***

I thought all would be lost and it would be the final straw to break the camel's back when Lira walked up on Leona, coming on to me in her drunken state. There were so many mishaps tonight, I was sure any second her father would reappear to take her away from me, and I would lose my fated mate all over again.

This turned in my favor, thank the goddess. I got her to agree to move closer to me, and even though she was reluctant, she was open to sharing a bed with me, as long as it was a bed other women were never in.

Easy enough. I plan on never taking another woman again, so there will be no problem.

I don't know how I ever managed to get hard for women other than Lira before. She looked like an avenging angel in her white silk slip and loosely hanging overcoat. Her milky skin looked so soft and supple, and her sweet fragrance and beautiful face made my heart race. Her shoes were sinfully perfect with her sultry attire. If I wasn't so upset about the situation Leona put me in, I could have admired Lira fully.

"Nilo. Where are you? I need you to do something for me."

"What's that, Alpha? I'm briefing our commanders and warriors about the situation with our new Luna and your mate now."

"That's perfect," I grinned, "Bring a few with you and get this bed out of my room. Burn it. Have them make a bonfire tonight. I want it reduced to ashes by tomorrow."

*"You want us to burn your bed?"* He questioned me like I was crazy. Maybe I am crazy. Crazy for Lira. I would burn this entire wing down if she wanted me to. I'd burn down the entire castle and build her a new one if it would make her happy.

"Burn it. I didn't stutter. Then, I want construction to start on a new wing by next week at the latest. I want to build a family wing, with a grand bedroom for me and Lira to share."

"Uh, okay. Are you sure, though? Everyone that witnessed her confrontation with Cherum in the grand hall overheard her call this marriage to you hell. She said something about enduring it for only two years. The construction alone will take at least a year. Probably longer if we have a nasty winter."

We won't have a bad winter. Not this one, at least. Our second winter after marriage was a horrible one. I want this wing completed before then. She's not leaving me. Not after two years. Not ever. I just have two years to make her think this marriage is heaven instead of hell.

"*Just do it,*" I barked at him.

"Yes, Alpha," he sighed.

Lira went back to her old room to instruct the maids and Cherum on what to pack and take down to her new room. Nilo had the room next to mine cleaned during our reception and even managed to send for the jeweler so I could pick out more presents for her birthday. I still haven't wished her a happy birthday, and to suggest it being 'happy' might be too much of a stretch now, but I still wish to give her a gift. After all I put her through tonight, it's the least I could do.

That's what I was coming back to my room to do when Leona drunkenly started knocking on my door.

Now that Leona was no more of a worry, and Lira was busy moving rooms, I quickly picked out a pair of stunning emerald earrings that match her new wedding ring, along with a few other trinkets, and I'm anxiously awaiting her return.

# EIGHT

***Elelira***

This whole ordeal with changing rooms was utterly ridiculous, but at least I get to keep Mimi with me. She was in tears when she came up to my room soon after Lachlan sent me away to start packing. "I thought I had done something to offend you, my Luna. Thank you for believing in me," she sniffled. "I will serve you well, my Luna. These old bones are still strong."

"Just being here for me is enough," I smiled warmly at her, "and call me Ela. We're friends, remember. Formalities don't matter between friends." After that, she quickly dried her tears and got to work on organizing my room.

I don't plan on being Luna of this pack anyway. I'm not going to tell her that, not with so many ears listening and when she is feeling like she is honored by serving me, but this position isn't final until Lachlan either marks me or the mate bond is formed. Lachlan won't mark me, and I plan on rejecting him and leaving the moment my magic comes and the bond is formed again.

Mimi is taking her role as my handmaiden more seriously now, ordering the other maids as they pack the rest of my room and prepare to move me down to a room closer to Lachlan.

I hope he wasn't serious about sharing a bed with me. I'll do it for the sake of keeping Mimi, but I'm not excited about what that will do to my Lycan. Val will be affected by the bond so much more when the betrayal pains start again.

"I'll be fine. You will have to endure just as much as me. It's worth it to keep her with us," Val told me.

"If he wants to….to mate, you'll be able to feel his Lycan. It will hurt more when we break the bond." I said to her meekly inside my head.

I can feel her anxiousness at the thought, but her resolve doesn't change. Mimi was the only good thing we had here. Neither of us will abandon her.

"We will endure," she murmured, "We always do."

Yes. It seems we do.

With that, the discussion ends. Hopefully, he has retired to his bedchambers with his *guest* from earlier and has forgotten about me. It will be harder to avoid him if we are residing in the same wing, but we will endure, just like Val said. I can always come back up here to hide, and hide on the docks, away from the bustle of the castle. I know how to keep a low profile. My time here before taught me that. Living like the dead will be easy as long as Lachlan doesn't try getting into my bed, which I still doubt is likely this time around.

Everything was so different, though, so I have no idea what's going to happen.

I was sitting on my bed, folding my dresses from the wedding and reception to appear busy when the Delta clears his throat, causing me to look up.

"Luna," Cherum sounded nervous as he entered the room as it was being packed, "Your new room is ready."

I sighed heavily, "I understand. We will follow you once we are done here."

The dresses were folded as neatly as could be, and Mimi told me to leave the rest to the maids, so I stood awkwardly by the door as they finished. I was told I could head down first, but I'm not that eager to leave this room.

"Um, Luna?" Cherum muttered, watching me carefully.

"Yes?" I looked at him from the corner of my eye, contemplating correcting his addressing me as Luna again, but I think that's a battle for another day. There are only so many times I want to correct a man in a day. I know a lost cause when I see one. My first life in this marriage taught me that.

"Are you sure you wouldn't be more comfortable wearing my coat?" His eyes roamed down my body, looking unnerved. I'm still in the silk slip and thin overcoat.

"Does my body offend you, Delta Rosewood? You would think, with the frequency the ranked members of this pack visit the women of the soddy establishments in town, that you wouldn't be offended by this appearance. I have far less to show compared to them."

He groaned uncomfortably. "Luna, that was a misunderstanding. The Alpha has stated numerous times to us that you are his wife and he won't-"

"I've heard that plenty today, Delta Rosewood," I cut him off, "I do not wish to hear it again. Whether he takes others to his bed is none of my concern. Not when this is all temp-"

He coughed, cutting me off, and his eyes moved repeatedly to the maids, indicating they were listening. When I looked around, I noticed they are moving much slower, their heads all angled towards us to catch the conversation. Even Mimi was wiping the same spot on the table over and over again while pretending to work.

I rolled my eyes. "Like it is a secret. I'm sure he has already told all of you that I am not the Luna of this pack, that my uncle is using me to trap him, and that he's divorcing me after two years when the alliance contract terms are void."

"That's not exactly the case," he frowned.

"So he didn't say any of those things? He didn't put me up here to begin with to keep me away from him; so I stayed out of sight?"

He cringed with each word. "That was….I mean, I'm sure Alpha didn't mean that."

"I'm sure," I muttered, "I'm sure he didn't mean to be caught with one of those women at the door of his bedchamber by me earlier as well. I may be young, but I am far from naive, Delta Rosewood. You do not need to put on airs around me. I know who I married, I know what is expected of me, and I know not to expect anything from him. All that will bring me is heartache, and I've suffered enough of that."

He hung his head solemnly, looking defeated. "I'm sorry, Luna. I will think before I speak from now on," he frowned, "I just thought you might be cold. It is awfully cold up here. I'm sorry if I offended you."

Now it's my turn to feel awkwardly regretful. I thought he was indicating I was indecent, not commenting on my attire out of concern for my comfort.

I shifted back and forth on my feet uncomfortably. My feet were numb from the cold, which was helping with numbing the pain from the heels I was still wearing. I do have goosebumps on my chest and legs. Even my arms felt prickly in the sleeves of my overcoat from goosebumps. I was so used to the coldness of being up here that I didn't notice it before now.

"I am a bit cold," I murmured, offering a sorrowful smile.

He smiled, shrugging out of his jacket and placing it over my shoulders gingerly, like he was worried its weight might be too much for me. He's slightly awkward in his actions, but it was still sweet he cares enough to offer.

"I'm sorry, Delta Rosewood. It has been a....a trying day. I should not have snapped at you when you were not the one at fault."

He scratches the back of his neck. "It's okay, Luna. I would be upset in your shoes too."

We smiled awkwardly at each other, then stood in silence while the maids finished packing my room.

I did feel much warmer in his coat. It still had his body heat saturated in it, soaking into my chilled skin. I'm warming up quickly. The problem with that is now my feet are less numb and are starting to ache more. I don't know how much longer I can stand in these heels.

As the maids finished packing for me, we started the trek down to the Alpha's wing. The Delta insisted on having me grip his arm as I walked down the stone steps, and when my ankle rolled, causing me to almost fall forward, he quickly stopped my fall, lifting me into his arms like I weighed nothing.

"I'm sorry, Luna, but I can't let you continue to walk in those shoes. Your feet are turning purple and I wouldn't forgive myself if you hurt yourself."

He held me close, ordering one of the maids to rid me of the shoes before continuing down the stairs with me in his arms.

"Ela," I told him after a few stunned seconds once I got my reasoning back.

"Sorry?" He looked at me in confusion.

"Call me Ela, Delta Rosewood. I do not care for the formality of Luna, but you can call me Ela."

He smiled softly. "Okay, *Ela,* but only if you call me Cherum. Delta Rosewood sounds like you're talking to my dad."

I laughed gently at that. "Deal. Thank you, Cherum, for your help."

"Anytime, Ela."

~

***Lachlan***

I was pacing outside the room that would soon be Lira's. Nilo just came with a few men and took my bed and mattress from my room to be burned.

I don't need it. I plan on spending my nights with Lira in her room now that she has agreed to it. Her only requirement was not sharing a bed I shared with other women. There is now no bed that fits those disqualifications, so I'm in the clear. I'm giddy with excitement at the prospect of holding her in my arms at last.

That shit show with the women set me back momentarily, but I'll win her over. She won't be able to fight the bond if I'm touching and holding her. She might mentally fight it at first, but her body will crave my touch.

"Don't be an asshole and force her to do anything she doesn't want to do. Manipulating her with the bond she feels but we don't isn't right," Killian growled at me.

"I'm not manipulating her. I just want a damn opening."

"You don't deserve an opening," he growled, "I hope she punches you in the nuts for letting that nasty woman with all the fat touch you."

*"You'd feel it too,"* I snapped at my Lycan.

"The pain would be worth it. Don't let floppy boobs touch you."

"I didn't let her touch anything. She did it on her own. Did you want me to rip her hand off for it?"

"Better than letting our mate assume we asked for it," he snarled.

I know. Fuck, do I know, but I can't kill a member of my pack for doing what she thought she was allowed to do.

It won't happen again, though.

"I'll send Nilo to deal with those women to leave me alone tomorrow," I told my Lycan, trying to ease his nagging.

He scoffed, "Sending someone else would be better. He'll be too focused on getting his dick wet."

Killian was right. I should send Meldec, my Gamma. He goes with us often to drink, but doesn't touch the women. He has three sisters and a widowed mother. His father died in the war. He thinks the brothel is exploiting women with no other choice but to earn money with their bodies. He may be right, but in my first life, I didn't see it that way. Now I wonder if Lira found herself in similar circumstances after rejecting and leaving me. I felt the betrayal pains for some time before I felt her death. I never discovered where she was or what happened to her, but her uncle mentioned her being a whore before I killed him and took his dead body to her father. He could have just been throwing insults at random while facing death, but I never got the chance to find out.

I heard voices echoing down the hall, and perked up expectantly. Even Killian had his ears up and tail wagging with excitement.

She's here. She's finally here where she belongs, with me.

I saw their shadows on the wall before I saw them. The shadow in the front is obviously Cherum, but it's larger than it should be and oddly shaped. When he finally becomes visible, I see why.

A growl left me before I could stop it, seeing my Delta carrying my mate, her legs and feet seductive and bare, and his jacket wrapped tightly around her, though it didn't go past her waist. He had her slip bunched in one hand to prevent her ass from hanging out, but that just meant his hand was dangerously close to it instead.

What's worse, they were smiling at one another, laughing lightly like they were sharing an intimate joke. Jealousy pings my heart and made my chest swell. I've never seen her smile like that. Not since the day of her arrival for our wedding, the first time we married at the beginning of our ceremony, before I had crushed her hopes of acceptance and happiness.

All I got after that was sorrow and hatred.

"What the hell is this?" I snapped, drawing all their attention to me. Killian is saying something, probably telling me to calm down, but I can't hear him over the white noise of my rage in my head.

"Alpha?" Cherum slowed his walk, looking at me questioningly.

I nodded to his hand holding onto the skirt of her slip, pressed tightly against her thigh. Another fierce growl echoed down the halls from me, making all the maids jump in surprise.

He must've caught on to my mood and what triggered it, because he quickly set her on her feet, his hands lingering on her until she got her footing. I stepped out to help her instead, but she took a step back, backing into Cherum's chest so he had to hold her shoulders to keep her steady.

She avoided my touch, but seemed perfectly fine with his touch. That realization hurts.

"Ela almost fell going down the stairs," Cherum explained, "Her feet were hurting due to her shoes, so I helped her to prevent her from hurting herself more."

He's the Delta, whose sole purpose is to serve and protect our Luna.

This shouldn't surprise or anger me. His father would have done the same for my mother, but I couldn't stop the rampage of my jealousy raging inside me.

Not until I saw the look on Lira's face.

My flaring nostrils slowly calmed as the air froze around me. She's not impressed with my dominant display. Why would she be?

"Is there a problem, Alpha?" She asked coldly.

I sent a fierce look at Cherum before I could stop myself, then instantly regretted it when her expression grew even colder.

"Why didn't you call for me if Lira was having trouble walking? I could have come to assist her. I don't know how I feel about my Delta carrying my wife when she is dressed so provocatively."

"My name is not Lira," she snapped, "It's Elelira, and you can address me directly since I am right here. There is no need to talk to Cherum as if I am not present. I assumed you would be retired for the evening with your guest from earlier, who was dressed far more provocative than me. Why would we disturb you for something so menial when *my Delta* so kindly offered to help? It is very unbecoming of an Alpha to put down his own member and ranked warrior for just doing his job."

Panic filled me, knowing I messed up once again. Killian was snarling and cursing at me for my endless transgressions to our mate today when we were supposed to be winning her favor.

"I'm sorry," I hung my head, "I just don't like the idea of another man touching you."

She snorted. The sound would make me chuckle at the cuteness of it if I wasn't so worried about pissing her off more. "That's supremely hypocritical of you, don't you think?"

# NINE

We stood in an awkwardly, staring at one another. Her face remaining cold and displeased, and I was sure I looked like a total prick about to drop to her feet and grovel for her forgiveness. Cherum and Niomi started directing the maids to enter Lira's new room with her belongings. Niomi followed the last of the maids in, calling out agitated directions about where to put everything. She stopped momentarily at the door while looking back at Lira for any indication that she might need to stay with her. Lira nodded towards her, giving her a reassuring smile. Niomi sighed, then continued to direct the maids, moving about the room as they busied themselves with the task.

Cherum remained behind Lira, a protective hand still on her shoulder. Was he trying to protect her from me? I'm her mate and his Alpha.

A brief glance at his face and I could see disapproval resting there aimed towards me.

"Lira, I'm sorry. I reacted before thinking."

"Again, it's Elelira, and I'm not the one you should be apologizing to."

She wanted me to apologize to him?! I wanted to groan, but I knew better. Picking a fight with Cherum wouldn't do me any good right now, especially when it seems they are growing closer to one another. Close enough for him to be calling her by a nickname instead of calling her Luna like he should. I get scolded every time my nickname for her slips out. He can touch her and call her nicknames, and I'm not allowed to do either of those.

I fought to keep the glare out of my eyes as I turned them to look at him. "I'm sorry, Cherum, for misunderstanding the situation."

He pulled on his beard, twirling the tip in his fingers like he's contemplating my apology. "The growling really hurt my feelings too,

Alpha."

Oh, I'm going to run his ass into the ground during training in the morning.

Lira tilted her chin up expectantly, waiting for me to continue apologizing, I'm sure.

I sighed heavily, running a hand down my face, wishing I could wipe off the shame of this moment. Me, an Alpha, apologizing to my Delta for fucking growling. Growling!

"Serves your headstrong ass right," Killian growled in my head. "You don't deserve time with her anyway. Give me control and I'll do what you are too stupid to accomplish."

*"What's that?"* I snarled at him.

"Gain her trust and not act like such an intolerable brat. You are going to make her hate us more. She might hate you, but I did nothing wrong. If you keep messing up, I'll take over. Apologize to the damn Delta."

Even my own Lycan is shaming me. Goddess, I don't want to do this, but I'll do it for her. I can't make her any more mad at me.

"I'm sorry I growled at you and hurt your feelings." I told him begrudgingly out loud. "*You are going to pay for this later. I hope you know that,"* I growled at him in the mind link.

He tried to hold back the grin on his face at hearing my threat. "I accept your apology, Alpha," he says out loud, then adds in the link, "*And I think you will be paying more for this than I will. Seriously, Alpha. The lass dislikes you enough as it is."*

I growled again through the link, not liking the reminder of her disfavor. "*Keep your hands away from her butt and my jealousy might not flare up,"* I snapped. He snorted, not amused by my jealousy in the least.

Lira is looking between us, her eyes narrowing the more she studied our faces. She knows we're mind linking.

I tried to offer her a reassuring smile, but it didn't soften her disgruntled demeanor. Yeah, she hates me.

"*I told you,"* Killian grumbled.

"*Shut up,"* I snapped back.

Lira sighed wearily, then turned to look up at my Delta. I almost growled out loud again seeing the small smile she offered him. "Cherum, thank you for your help. I think I'll head inside to assist Mimi and the maids."

"Alright, Ela. I'll be here early tomorrow to show you around your new home," he said, gripping her shoulder reassuringly before letting her go.

She sent me one last nasty look before entering her new room, closing the door behind her.

"No wonder," Cherum mused, running his fingers through his beard while staring at her door.

"No wonder what?" I grumbled, glaring openly at the traitor now that Lira couldn't see.

He jerked his head to the side, indicating I should follow him as he starts walking down the hall. "*She can probably still hear us,*" He mind links me.

Shit, he's right. I sighed heavily and started to walk with him back down the hall towards the main foyer. When we are a good distance away, he answered my question.

"No wonder the Luna hates you," he stated, shaking his head disapprovingly, then looking around the halls to be sure no one was listening. "So, it's true you had a whore here with you earlier and she caught you?"

I groaned. "I didn't have a whore here intentionally. Leona showed up at my door drunk and wanting in. I was telling her to leave, but that was the moment Lira came. It was just a misunderstanding."

He nodded, continuing to pull on his beard. "She is your mate, correct? Ela, I mean."

I glowered at his nickname for her. "I told you she was. Why else would I go out of my way for that horrible man's niece? She's mine."

"I just want to be sure, because she is fighting the bond awfully hard. If I observed her actions alone, I wouldn't think you two were mates at all."

I ran both my hands down my face, feeling like I had aged twenty 20 years in one day. "We got off on the wrong foot," I mumbled.

We got off on the wrong foot, and kept stumbling down a rocky cliff into an endless pit of painful mistakes and regrets for two years until she rejected me. Then, we both came back to this day with those previous mistakes lingering over us. Add to that the countless misunderstandings and bad occurrences of today and I'm feeling as helpless as ever.

"I'll fix this," I stated confidently, more confidently than I truly felt right now.

"You better," Cherum said, "because all you are doing is proving all the rumors about you to be true today. If I lose my Luna because you can't get yourself under control, it is you who will have to answer to me. Quit mistreating my Luna, or I won't blame her if she rejects you. Hell, I might encourage it."

I couldn't even argue with him. It was his sole purpose to protect his Luna, even from me.

"I'm still running your ass into the ground in the morning," I muttered.

He chuckled at my threat. "That's fine. Just make sure you're just showing your asshole self to only us. Don't let her see that side of you. Not until she accepts you, at least."

When I growled at his insult, he held his hands up in surrender, "No offense, Alpha. I just don't want her to hate you more than she already does."

"Too bad she already knows that side of you, better than anyone else," Killian muttered in my head.

I threw my head back, staring at the ceiling, feeling helpless once again.

~

***Elelira***

Finally, I was in comfortable clothing; a thick flannel nightgown and my cushioned slippers I inherited from my mother. They were worn out from overuse throughout the years, but that just added to the comfort by making them buttery soft and familiar. The clothes combined with the necklace that had the familiar fae magic emanating from it are wrapping me in a cocoon of comfort.

"Are you sure this is okay for you, Luna?" Mimi grimaced at the faded pattern on my nightgown. "I'm sure I can find you much better sleeping attire for the night. It's your wedding night after all."

This is the third time she has asked, but the first time since the other maids have left. I can be more honest with her now.

I waved a hand, dismissing her line of thought about my wedding night. "I'm pretty sure your Alpha plans on spending our wedding night with any of those other women he invited to our wedding rather than me." I'm not concerned over making our wedding night something to remember. I remember our first one all too clearly. The endless pain of his betrayal kept me up all night.

It has been quite some time since I left him outside the room and he still hasn't entered my new bedroom. I think I'm safe for the night. I'm looking forward to my night alone before the pain starts.

Mimi made a disappointed face, understanding crossing her features. "I'm sorry, Luna. I just thought the rumors might be false, especially after he told all the staff that you were his Luna and to treat you accordingly."

"He did?" I made a face, not believing he would do such a thing.

She nodded adamantly, "He was quite firm about it. Beta Nilo has been running around making the necessary arrangements for you to be treated as such."

Hmm. That would explain Cherum's changed behavior. I'm still not sure why Lachlan would do such a thing. He couldn't feel the mate bond. He won't for two more years.

The grand clock against the wall indicated it was 9:02 at night. I'm eighteen years and two hours of age exactly. One year, eleven months, thirty days, and twenty two hours to go.

This room was much more comfortable than my last one, with a very large bed, adorned with carved flowers on the posts. The bedding is pure white and looks as fluffy as a cloud. It has an attached office and sitting room, as well as an ensuite bathroom, all things I did without in my first life. The bathtub even has a heater built into the flooring, and the fireplace has a fire raging in it now. It was almost too warm, something I never felt in the other room.

My favorite part of my new room was the large bay window overlooking the sea. A comfortable and cozy looking winged-back chair and drawing table were nestled in the space, and I couldn't wait to curl up with a blanket in the chair, watching the waves crash to shore.

The maids had finished with unpacking my meager belongings some time ago, all of which are hand-me-downs from my cousin or inherited from my mother. I never touched the belongings of my cousin in my first life. I do not plan on doing so in this life either. My uncle, not wanting to send me away empty handed and embarrassing himself, ordered for the oldest and least appealing clothing of his daughter's to be taken and given to me, which he quickly replaced with newer items.

I really do not have a relationship with my cousin, always being told that me being friends with her was beneath her, but I saw her plenty as she was flitting about the pack house in the West. She is much shorter than I am, and more curvy because she is actually fed real meals. Her clothes wouldn't have fit me in my first life, and I doubt that has changed, though much else has this time going about this marriage.

Lachlan, for one, has changed greatly. He was still the self-absorbed mutt, chasing any tail he could and behaving like an uncivilized mongrel, but in this life, he seemed to be trying to add my tail to the many he is chasing.

I'm his wife now. If he wants that from me in this life, I can't very well tell him no. I know he can't feel the bond, so I wonder what has changed his perspective this time around.

Earlier with the Delta, it was almost as if he was jealous. Of what, I do not know. If he is truly ordering his men and staff to treat me as their Luna, Cherum was only doing his job. It is very hypocritical of him to condemn Cherum for only doing his job when Lachlan has had women pawing all over him all day.

"Maybe he does feel the bond," Val suggested, "It would explain why he is showing interest in us now."

"Mmh, he would have claimed me the moment he saw me at our wedding. He's an Alpha. His Lycan would have demanded it."

"Then what do you think is causing all his abnormal behavior?" Val argued.

"Maybe we are in some alternate reality. One where he has to bed ALL the women, not just all the women who aren't me."

Val clicked her tongue disapprovingly. "He didn't bed all women. Mimi wasn't very fond of him in our first life. Called him a scoundrel all the time."

I chortled at the memory, "She wouldn't touch him with a ten-foot pole."

"She might have beaten him with one, though," Val snorted.

I giggled out loud at the thought.

"Everything alright, Luna?" Mimi asked me, looking at me strangely while organizing wedding presents on the table for me to open later.

"Everything is fine, Mimi, except you are still calling me Luna," I mocked disapproval, making her sigh with a smile.

"Ela. I'm sorry. That will take some getting used to. I'm not used to dropping formalities with those who are superior to me."

I snorted, "Mimi, I was very much your equal if we are speaking about ranks, up until the moment I said 'I do'. It makes *me* uncomfortable when someone uses polite speech towards me."

She cocked her head to the side, looking confused. “I thought you were the Alpha of the West’s niece. Does that not make you ranked?”

I grimaced, thinking of my uncle. “My mother was his older sister, the rightful Alpha of the pack in most places. She-wolves were not allowed to inherit positions in my previous pack, though." At least, that is what I was told. "My uncle treated her horribly so she wouldn’t forget her place, and in turn, I was treated as less than an omega.”

“Oh my,” Mimi pressed her hand to her chest, “I had no idea. You must not regard ranked members well then. No wonder you were so reluctant to marry our Alpha, even if you are mates.”

I looked at her questioningly. “Mates? He said we were mates?” Val perked up, hope building inside her.

# TEN

"Well, not directly, no. He had Beta Nilo tell all the staff you are his true Luna and to treat you as such."

"Hmm," I pondered the possibility of him feeling the mate bond like Val suggested. It seems more plausible now.

I twirled the ring around my finger; the wedding ring Lachlan had given me earlier today. Even the ring with this marriage was different. My first was dull and thin. It was a cheaply made ring to match our cheap marriage.

This ring is elaborate and beautiful. It may be the most beautiful accessory I have ever had in my possession. Well, besides the necklace, but Lachlan said that the necklace was given to me by someone else. The individual just asked for Lachlan to be the one to give it to me for some odd reason. I wish I knew who it was from, or wish Lachlan had finished explaining to me why he was the one to give it to me before all those women interrupted him. I would love to know who had access to siren or fae magic.

There was just so much difference in this life. Maybe he does feel the mate bond….

"I told you," Val muttered, "It wouldn't hurt to ask him."

"What if he doesn't, though? We would be left to explain to him why we asked if he doesn't feel it, and then we might be forced to tell him we are a hybrid, and could be condemned by his entire pack. Forget freedom. He might put us in the dungeons."

Val is was still wanting me to ask, willing to risk it. I'm not, though. He may be different in this life, but not in the ways that matter. He is still a womanizer and will only hurt us if we give him the chance.

"Okay, Luna-....I mean, Ela. If there is nothing else you need assistance with, I think I'll leave you to relax for the night."

I smiled sweetly at my favorite person in this castle. "Okay. Thank you for all your help today. I hope you have a good rest of your evening."

"You as well, Ela," she smiled, moving towards the door as I grabbed a soft blanket out of a basket in the corner by the bed and headed to finally sit in the winged-back chair. I wanted to let the waves lull and calm my soul.

Her startled gasp as she opened the door caught my attention. I looked up from staring out the window to see her face-to-face with Lachlan.

"I'm sorry, Alpha. I was unaware you were there," she managed to choke out after recovering from her surprise.

"It's fine, Niomi," he smiled stiffly, looking up and meeting my eyes. His smile turned hesitant before looking back down at her. He stepped to the side, giving her room to leave, and she hurried along, unnerved by the brief altercation, I'm sure.

"I didn't expect to see you again tonight," I said softly, turning to look back out towards the sea. The waves crashing into the shore seemed to be calling me, beckoning me to join them in their dance in the moonlight.

"I told you I wished to share your bed, Elelira," his deep voice husked, finally calling me by my name. If I didn't already know better, know the type of man he was, the way he spoke to me just now would have made me swoon. The bond I felt swelled with elation.

I do know better, though. This has nothing to do with the bond. He likely just wants my body before going off and having relations with those other women. Curiosity probably got the better of him.

"Fine," I muttered, standing to my feet.

I set the blanket on the chair, and made my way over to stand before him, unbuttoning the front of my nightdress in the process. "If this is what you want, let us be done with it. It would be rude to keep the others waiting for you all night."

"Lira," he said, reverting back to that damned nickname while stepping forward, resting his hands over mine, stopping my movements. "Stop. I just want to sleep tonight. I'm not here for....for *that.* Not until you learn to trust me."

Val was purring, practically doing somersaults in my head, but I was not convinced.

I scoffed. "You really just want to sleep in the same bed as me? Nothing more?"

He nodded his head. "Like I said, not until you trust me, Lira. I want your trust before anything else."

"You may be waiting a long time," I murmured, looking down and re-buttoning the front of my nightdress.

His fingers tilted my chin up to stare at him. The touch of his hand made fireworks erupt on my skin. "I'll wait as long as it takes."

Despite myself, my face leaned into his touch. Stupid mate bond. He obviously does not feel it like I do, or he would be much more unnerved. As it was, a small, triumphant smile graced his lips.

"I do wish for something of you tonight, though," he told me.

I move my chin out of his hold so I could think properly. I knew he wanted something.

"What is it?" I asked in an untrusting tone.

"I wish for you to accept these," he smirks, then whistles loudly.

A string of maids floated in, each with arms full of gifts. They all smiled kindly, setting the presents on the floor, on the furniture, and around the table. Some have bouquets of flowers, dozens and dozens of fragrant roses filling the room with their romantic aroma. There are packages in all shapes and sizes, some as small as my palm, others the size of furniture.

When the last maid made her way through, she handed a velvet box to Lachlan, then murmured a soft greeting to me before bowing and leaving the room, closing the door behind her.

My eyes must have been as wide as saucers. What is all this? "Are these more wedding presents?" I asked. I don't remember having anymore than what Mimi was organizing on the table the first time we wed. Did he keep the best gifts for himself last time?

"No, my wife. These are not wedding presents, but birthday gifts for you."

My mouth dropped. "From who?" I asked, touching the pendant on my neck, the magic in it helping to settle me in this confusing moment.

"Me," he shrugged, a cautious smile on his handsome face. "Happy birthday, Lira."

"You bought me gifts for my birthday?!" I asked in amazement. No one has ever given me gifts besides my mother. No one even celebrated my birthday before. It was just another day until the final birthday from my other life when I turned twenty and had access to my magic for the first time.

Lachlan nodded, a broad smile on his face as he cautiously rested his hand on my cheek. "I plan on showering you with more and more gifts every year on your birthday, and for every milestone and holiday we share together. You're my wife, Lira. You deserve no less."

I am was absolutely stunned. He *never* would have done this in my first life. The only thing he had ever given me was scorn and hatred.

"Maybe this isn't the same timeline, Ela," Val told me, "It can't be."

She was almost in tears of relief, that hope of being accepted by our mate blossoming inside her once again.

*"He would have told us if he felt the mate bond, though. Remember how you were the first time we laid eyes on him? If my uncle had not been holding on to us as we walked down the aisle, you would have made me run to him."* His indifference and cold demeanor were what prevented me from saying anything to him when I finally could speak to him at the reception, away from my uncle. His attitude was like ice water dousing me and waking us from the spell the mate bond cast over us.

"You are being pretty cold to him in this life. Maybe he is just too scared to say anything, just like you were."

"Well, I'm not going to be the first to say it now, either. If he feels the mate bond, he will tell me."

Val groaned, but doesn't argue further. She knows the dangers as well as I do what revealing our hybrid blood could bring.

Lachlan was staring down at me, hesitation all over his face. "Um, do you want to open your presents?" he asked cautiously.

My eyes left his to trail around the room. "There are so many," I whispered.

"Well, start with this," he extended the velvet box towards me.

My fingers twitched as I hesitated to decide what to do. Slowly, I reached out and took it from him, then lifted the lid cautiously, curiosity getting the better of me.

Inside, the most gorgeous pair of emerald earrings lay, as well as an intricate bracelet. I twisted my hand in the air to look at my wedding ring and noticed that the earrings and bracelet matched my ring perfectly.

"This is too much," I murmured, running my fingers over the delicate jewels.

"Nothing could ever be too much for you," he smiled, seeming pleased by my reaction.

"Alpha, I can't accept these," I looked at him warily, "Where would I even wear them?"

"Please don't call me Alpha, Lira. You are my wife," he said, making me furrow my brows. He wouldn't let me call him anything but Alpha before. "How about assisting me on visiting the village tomorrow?" he asked. "I overheard Cherum saying he would show you around the castle. Let me show you around the town. We can make it our first official date."

"I would be assisting you with a date?" I asked, confused by his wording.

"You would be assisting me with visiting the village and our people, so everyone can see the face of their new Luna. Then we can go on a date."

I quirked my brow, not sure how to respond. After a few nervous seconds, I muttered. "I've never been on a date before, and these seem far too fancy to wear on a simple date."

"There will be nothing simple about it," he smirked, "Trust me."

I don't. I don't trust him at all. I know he can see that on my face because his smile faltered.

He ran his hand repeatedly through his hair as he seems to think. "You accompanying me would free Niomi to move her room from the bunkhouse to one in the castle so she can be closer to you.," he then said, "If you are here, she will need to be trailing you all day, catering to your needs. If I take you out, it will free up her time. I could have Nilo assign a few warriors to help her move as well."

Mimi does have a bad room in the bunkhouse.... Well, if it was for Mimi, I guess I could go with him.

"I still don't think wearing this jewelry is appropriate, though," I said softly, running my fingers over them again. They were exceptionally beautiful, but not practical for a trip to town or the orphanage. "Your pack has suffered greatly from war. We could sell these and provide for widows or the children orphaned from losing their parents on the battlefield."

A radiant smile graced his face, and a breathless chuckle left him, making my heart flutter momentarily. "You are going to be such a loving Luna, Lira," he ran his knuckles down my cheek, making Val purr and my muscles contract in a weird way from the bond. Tingles traveled down my neck, making me shiver. I know he didn't miss the reaction. His eyes dance like he is elated by my reaction to him.

"I provide for the widows, Lira. They receive their spouse's retirement wages and we have housing specifically for them that is guarded and watched over by our top war-retired warriors. As for the orphans," he pursed his lips, thinking for a few seconds, "Would you like to see them tomorrow? We have facilities throughout the territory, but the one in the village we can visit. The children would enjoy meeting you."

I cocked my head to the side, more to get away from his touch so I could think again. Val was now a panting mess in my head and I was feeling foggy and confused. Not just by his kindness, but by the way his kindness made me feel.

I never knew he took care of the widows and orphans like that. Is this different too from my previous life, or was I just ignorant of the happenings of his pack before? I had never tried to get to know his territory or ventured into the village before. I really didn't leave the castle at all except to do my laundry up the river in the deeper part of the wilderness.

I really do want to see the village in this life if I can.

"We can go," I whispered hesitantly, "But I still wouldn't feel comfortable wearing these." I closed the lid on the velvet box and handed it back to Lachlan.

He pursed his lips, nodding and staring down at the box. If I didn't already know him, I would think the action was quite attractive, making his facial muscles tighten and contort his rugged face.

I know not to go down that road again, though. Not just yet anyway. I'm not convinced yet that the Lachlan in front of me is different from the one I experienced before.

"I'll have to find an occasion for you to wear them, then," he smirked, looking at me with hooded eyes and a crooked smile.

He set the box on the table with the many other gifts, then stretched his arms dramatically, making me want to chuckle. Even the yawn he produced seems forced. "Well, I'm tired. How about you? Do you want to open up the rest of these tomorrow while I am away at training?"

I am tired. Exhausted, really. I was getting ready to mentally and physically endure the pains of betrayal before he showed up with all these gifts, but it seems as though I will not have to worry about that. At least tonight.

I bit my lip and nodded, looking from him to the bed, wondering what his plans were exactly.

He held his hand out to me, a soft, reassuring smile on his face that stretched wide when I took his hand.

He led me over to the bed, encouraging me to sit with a wave. He then knelt down at my feet and pulled my slippers from my feet.

"Thank you," I murmured.

"You are welcome, my wife," he smiled, lifting one of my feet and kissing the top of it, making me gasp. The sparks from his touch traveled up my leg, and combined with his heated, mesmerizing stare, I was left not knowing what to do.

"*He feels the bond! He has to!*" Val practically screamed in my head.

"He said wife. Not mate, but wife," I tell her, "He would have called us mate if he felt the bond."

"But he is different," she argued, "He seems to care for us now."

"We will see," I told her, "We have two years. That is enough time to tell if he is different or if this is just some momentary fluke. We have until our twentieth birthday. That is plenty of time to see if he really does care for us."

"But that's so long," she whined.

"No. It's really not that long at all."

# ELEVEN

***Lachlan***

After slipping off her worn-out and beat up slippers, I couldn't stop myself from tasting her skin.

Her feet were adorable and smooth, and my lips were on them before I could stop myself. To my surprise, she didn't stop me either.

No, she seemed for a moment overcome by the bond and unable to do anything but react to my touch. Thank the goddess, something has finally turned in my favor. I thought she might kick me in the face or slap me again for kissing her.

Her reaction had Killian mewling for more. He was the one who told me not to push her, but now that the fire was lit inside us, seeing her body vibrate with want and hearing her sweet little gasp, that was all he could focus on.

"Not yet, you animal. She doesn't trust us yet. Calm down," I told him.

"She can trust us after," he growled, "Let's put a babe inside her womb, then that solves all our problems."

"No. It may get her to stay with us, but that's not how we are going to gain her heart and her love. When it's done, we definitely will lose any chance of getting her trust."

Killian grumbled, still salivating at the sight of our mate, but the mention of gaining her love and trust seemed to snap him out of his aroused state and helped to remind him what our end goal was.

Her father did not say we needed to get her pregnant or force her to choose us within the two-year time limit until her 20th birthday. He said we needed to gain her trust and make her love us again. Manipulating her with the bond and getting her pregnant would not be meeting those terms. I didn't want to manipulate her like that. I crave her heart more than her body.

I do crave her body, though. I am going to have to try hard to keep myself under control tonight.

"Just let me hold her," Killian whimpered, "I won't do more. Just let me have control for a bit and let me hold her. I'll calm down after that."

I looked up at Lira's beautiful face from where I was still kneeling in front of her. Her eyes are gleaming, like she was talking to her Lycan as well. Maybe her Lycan was as hungry for me as mine is for her.

"Lira," I said softly, breaking her from her trance. Her eyes focused on mine and my heart thumped wildly in my chest. Her green eyes shone so much more brilliantly than the ones in jewels I just gave her. "Would it be okay if my Lycan took control and held you for a little while?"

"Your lycan?" she cocked her head to the side, the movement so graceful and lovely that I almost backtracked on everything I just told my lycan and pounced on her, ripping that awful and ragged nightdress off her.

I nodded slowly, swallowing down my desires. "Killian wants to meet you. He won't do more than hold you while we sleep. I promise."

She looked deep in thought for a moment, her eyes gleaming over again, as she talked to her own Lycan, I'm sure. After the longest minute of my life, she asked, "Why does your lycan want to meet me?"

My throat swelled and burned with the desire to tell her that I'm her mate. I couldn't form the words, though, no matter how hard I tried. The blood-oath with her father wouldn't allow it.

"Because you are my wife," I managed to choke the words past my lips.

I might be mistaken, but her face seemed disappointed somehow, her expression dropping ever so slightly. It was hard to tell, though. She has seemed disappointed with me since the moment I saw her again this morning.

"Oh," she whispered, her eyes looking down at her hands knotting in her lap.

Was that not the answer she was looking for? Does she want me to tell her some other reason? Could I use practicality to convince her, like I had to when I was trying to convince her to go to town with me? Using Niomi was an excuse I invented on the sly, but I'm sure I could come up with an excuse like that again now.

I couldn't tell her that Killian wanted her because she's our mate, and she might trust me even less if I say it's because she is my love, my life, my everything. That might seem too forward and like a line to get her in bed for other reasons than to sleep, especially after the day of misunderstandings we just had.

She doesn't trust me. I haven't given her a reason to yet, and now that I am finally making headway, I don't want to falter backward now.

"I need her," Killian told me, "Can't you just tell her that?"

I need her too. I've needed her for so long. It's the raw truth of the matter, but I still don't think it's okay to tell her that yet.

"Lira?" was all I managed to whisper to draw her attention back to me. I cursed at myself internally for using the nickname again. She hates it, but I've been thinking and calling her that for years. It's going to be a hard habit to break.

She didn't correct me or look at me coldly this time when hearing my nickname for her. Her emerald eyes met mine again, making my heart thump violently and my nerves buzz with anticipation.

"Okay," she whispered, her voice sounding as unsure as I felt. "Killian is your Lycan's name?"

I smiled with relief. "Yes. His name is Killian," I assured her, then Killian growled at me to find out what her Lycan's name was. "Your Lycan, what is her name?"

Her eyes gleamed and I knew her Lycan had pushed to the front of her mind, listening to the entire conversation. "Valerina, but I call her Val," she said.

"*Valerina,*" Killian purred in my head, "*Beautiful.*"

I smiled in agreement. Valerina and Elelira. Our mates.

Her eyes were still gleaming, so I slowly reached up, resting my hand on the side of her face. My thumb stroked her soft cheek and to my surprise, Lira leaned into my touch, making my heart race. "It's nice to meet you, Val," I told her, holding her gaze as I stared not just into Lira's beautiful eyes, but Valerina's too.

Elelira offered me the first genuine, heart-melting smile in this life, something between a sob and a laugh leaving her. "She says it's nice to finally meet you too."

Finally.

That one word weighs heavy on me, knowing that my ignorance and arrogance is what prevented us from meeting sooner.

*"Give me control,"* Killian snapped, breaking me from my momentary grief. *"She said yes. Give me my mate,"* he growled.

I sighed deeply, annoyed I have to share the attention I'm finally getting from Lira with my beast.

"He wants out now. I'm giving him my body, and I'm not sure how he's going to act. If he does something you don't like, just tell me and I'll rein him back in."

She looked nervous, but nodded.

"Don't scare her," I told Killian, "Or you won't be seeing her again for a very long time," I warned him.

He huffed, "I'm not you, jackass. I would never hurt her."

I growled at him in warning, but still allowed for him to push forward as I retreated into the back of my mind, just in time to witness him jumping off the floor and enveloping Lira in my arms.

~

***Elelira***

I was nervous about meeting Lachlan's Lycan, hoping the decision wasn't going to hurt Val in the long run, but the moment Killian took over Lachlan's body I had the wind knocked out of me as I was pounced on, falling backward onto the mattress. My entire body was overcome by the pull of the mate bond, my skin erupting into mind-numbing sparks. I couldn't think about those worries any longer. I couldn't think about anything. I was all sensation and euphoria like I never felt before.

The bond inside us, that had once called out to Lachlan, but deadened with my deprivation over time, was jolted back to life. My whole body felt like it was singing from his touch.

Does he feel this too?

"Mmmh," the Lycan controlling Lachlan's body purred, making his chest vibrate against mine.

Goosebumps rose up on my skin, and Val, the pushover, purred back.

I couldn't blame her. It was too hard to fight the bond when he was touching me.

"Hi," I managed to mutter out in an airy voice.

"Hi, Elelira," Killian purred. I like how he calls me by the name I asked when his human counterpart wouldn't do the same.

"It's nice to meet you," I said, then giggled as his nose tickled the hair on the back of my neck. His weight was heavy, but felt almost comforting with the sparks from the bond. I didn't feel as apprehensive knowing this is Killian and not Lachlan right now. It's like a giant pet was lying on top of me and not a man.

Well, his hard body does feel like a man's body, but I don't feel any ill-intent or anything sexual from him. All I really feel from the spell the mate bond is casting over me is adoration. Killian obviously likes me.

"My mm-mmm-mm…." he struggled in a rough voice to form words. I pushed my neck into the mattress to lean away from him and saw his adam's apple bobbing up and down with much strain.

"My….mine," he growled after much effort.

"Yours?" I asked breathlessly, my cheeks flushed as I tried to overcome the bond enough to think and speak.

"My wife," he growled again, his nose skimming my neck, "You are mine."

*Wife*, not mate. Once again, my hope that he might feel the bond died. He couldn't feel the bond. It's just not possible until I'm 20.

"*He still called us his. He still wants us,*" Val said with relieved elevation. Even if it was as his wife and not his mate, Killian seemed to want us, which was all that matters to her.

She never got to meet his Lycan before this moment, and I could feel her tears of satisfaction from just being *wanted* in some way. It hurt her immensely, feeling like our bond was being rejected and abused every single day in our first life. I got to see Lachlan's treatment towards me, but she never got to experience Killian or see how he felt about her.

She had longed for this since the moment we very first laid eyes on Lachlan in our first life. She was finally seeing how Killian felt towards us, and even without the bond, he was accepting us. Accepting her.

"Can I come forward? Can I talk to him?" Val asks.

I think apprehensively, not sure if that would be a good idea. "You can't blurt out that he is our mate, Val. If you do, this could all end. It is different this time. Lachlan is different this time, I'll admit that, but what this pack has gone through with its wars has not changed. They will still be wary of other races and hybrids like us."

"But he wants us. He might not care," she pouts, impatient for her mate.

"Do you want to take that chance?"

She thought for a few seconds, then sighed, "No. I won't say mates. I just want to feel the bond myself, Ela."

This might be a different Lachlan from our first life, but I still didn't trust that he will not betray us, especially if he learns what we are.

"Killian," I murmured, trying to get his attention again. His nose is buried in my hair and his arms are wrapped tightly around me, holding me firmly against him.

"Hmm?" he hummed, his voice much deeper and raspier than Lachlan's. "What is it, my wife?"

His touch with the way he just called me his wife made a chill travel up my spine and butterflies fluttered in my chest. I don't know how I'm going to get any sleep if he plans on holding me all night.

"Do you want to meet Val? She is asking to come forward too."

He jerked his head back to stare down at me, a carnal smile spreading on his face. "She wants to meet me?" His expressions may look more wild, but the way he asked the question, full of surprise and excitement, reminds me of a child confirming he is about to receive a present.

"Yes," I chuckled, " if you don't mind."

"I don't!" he quickly responded, "I want to meet Valerina too."

Killian was cute in his earnestness. I already found him to be much more tolerable than his human counterpart.

"Okay, Val. Just stay in control of the bond. Please," I begged her before giving her control of my body.

I slowly receded into the back of my mind, letting Val come forward, but keeping a minor hold over our control in case I needed to take over quickly. I know how powerful the bond is. I just experienced it myself, and even with my guard up I was overcome by the power of it while under his touch.

Val still longs for our mate, unlike me. She might not be able to control herself.

"Killian," she whimpered in her velvety voice as she pushed past me, wrapping my arms around Lachlan's body.

She was melting against him, purring wildly as she rubbed her face against his cheek. To my surprise, Killian copied her, like they are both trying to mix their scents, marking with territories like a cat would.

"Valerina," Killian husked, turning our bodies so mine is practically on top of his, then gripping my face, now Val's face, between his hands, "I'm so happy to finally meet you."

Val whimpered, nodding between his large, war-roughed hands, "I'm happy to finally meet you too."

Killian stared up at her lips; my lips, and I can almost see the thought process going on in his head. It's the same as Val's as she studied our mate's annoyingly handsome face.

Her head dipped, encouraged by his hands, as he tilted his face up to meet hers.

*"Oh, no you don't,"* I growled, pulling back control, forcing myself forward and Val back to the back of my mind.

It's my lips that meet him now that I'm in control. I couldn't stop the act. I was a moment too late. My entire face felt like it was tingling and my heart was beating wildly in my chest, but I know better than to give into this sensation.

It took me by surprise the first time he pounced on me, but now I have my head about me, and can fight the bond and the power it has over me.

Pulling away, I stared down at his panting face. He looked as surprised as I felt. It takes me but a minute to realize it is no longer Killian, but Lachlan in control, and I was lying across his body, feeling vulnerable from the state our Lycans left us in.

# TWELVE

I felt disoriented for a few seconds, time standing still as reality set in.

I told him not to kiss me again earlier today, then our Lycans went ahead and did the act for us, leaving us in a very awkward position.

"I'm sorry," he panted, his hands still resting on the sides of my face. "I was yelling at him to stop, but he just ignored me."

I pressed my lips together, still feeling his warmth and moisture on them. I couldn't really blame him when Val initiated it as much as Killian did.

"That's okay," I mumbled, pushing my body away from his and kneeling at the end of the bed, "Val is to blame as well."

He looked disoriented and a little lost as he stared at me, still lying on his back on the bed. I felt self-conscious, wondering what he was thinking.

That was the first willing kiss I had ever had. The thought was wracking my brain. It may have been Val, but my body was still a willing participant. The thought was humbling, and made my stomach feel like a bottomless pit.

Every other touch I felt before this was forced on me, and the first time my body participated in an act of intimacy, I'm confused because I truly didn't mind kissing Killian, but I don't know how I feel kissing Lachlan, who I see as a man and not the adoring child or pet his Lycan was.

"Lira, I'm sorry," Lachlan said, probably seeing the disturbed look on my face. He sat up, looking concerned as he watched me. "I should have gotten control and stopped him sooner. It happened so fast, though, and Valerina seemed to want it, so-"

"It's okay," I smiled weakly at him, "I'm just…surprised," I mumbled out, trying to shake the disturbing images from my head.

He continued to watch me, not moving like he was scared he would frighten me away.

"I'm sorry, Ela," Val whispered, "I didn't mean to. I didn't want to bring up those memories. I was just so excited to finally meet him. I won't do it again."

I cringed at the mention of those memories. I don't know why the kiss triggered those images to reappear when the kiss from our wedding earlier didn't. Maybe because I was so guarded and overcome by my hatred earlier today.

Now, I was starting to relax around Lachlan, despite trying to maintain my indifference. Not being as guarded, let those disturbing feelings and memories, that really only just happened yesterday for me, come to the forefront of my mind.

"I don't want to feel like this, Val. I don't want to feel weak and helpless. Not in front of him," I managed to mutter out to her inside my head after some time.

She whimpered, not liking the memories either. She was a prisoner inside my mind when my uncle's men abused us endlessly. It was horrifying, and the fact that a consensual kiss with Lachlan, our mate, is what triggered those disturbing thoughts from returning was like a wake up call to her as well.

"I won't take control again. I can wait, Ela, however long it takes for you to trust him. Just please, don't blame him for my mistake. Don't blame Killian."

Her pleading for her mate took the edge off of my anxiety. I didn't want to hurt her, more than anything else, I didn't want to cause her pain or guilt.

"It's not your fault," I told Lachlan again. He looks on the verge of a panic attack himself. I tried to offer him a reassuring smile. I don't think it had the desired effect, though, because he looked more worried now, "I'm sorry. I must just be overly tired from the day. I can't seem to think straight."

Lachlan watched my face, his concerned eyes traveling over every feature, making me feel more self-conscious. I was thinking ill of him for having so many partners and being a loyal customer to the women of the night, when I am no better. I may be a virgin in this rebirth, but just yesterday to me, I was going through worse things than I'm sure he had ever done.

I felt filthy all of a sudden, like I was dirty and broken once again. I hate this. I hate remembering what awaits me if I go down the same, lonely path I went through in the past. All this stemmed just from a kiss.

If he wants to do more, I don't know how I can make it through.

Right then, the necklace that lay hidden under my nightgown around my neck started to pulse, and the comforting magic embraced me, helping to calm my racing thoughts.

"Let's go to sleep," Lachlan said after a while, moving off the bed and pulling the sheets and thick blanket down from the top of the bed, indicating that I should get under them.

I nodded, grateful he was not asking for more. He told me he wouldn't, but after being pounced on by Killian, and then that kiss, I didn't know what else to expect.

Val whimpered as Lachlan moved away from the bed after gently tucking the sheets and blanket around me. He's careful not to touch us, which I am grateful for, but Val was worried he was going to go visit those other women now.

To my surprise, and Val's relief, he moved to the other side of the bed, sitting on its edge and taking his boots off methodically.

He looked deep in thought, staring down at the task, then breathing deeply before turning back to face me, where I was lying flat on my back under the covers.

"Good night, Lira," he whispered, his voice thick with some kind of emotion.

He stayed fully clothed, which surprised me. He's still in the clothes he was wearing at our reception and they could not be comfortable.

He rolled over so his back was facing me as he pulled the covers to his waist. His back seemed tense, his neck muscles rigged and tight.

Did I make him mad with my reaction to him? I didn't manage my behavior or emotions very well. He always hated it when I showed any kind of emotion in my first life.

Pain, anger, annoyance, fear; they were all met with his anger.

My indifference over time was the only thing that would keep him from getting upset at me. If I went completely numb, not showing any emotions whatsoever, he would give me a look similar to the one he was giving me just now.

"Good night, Alpha," I whispered so softly, I'm not sure he heard.

It was automatic. If I didn't respond when he spoke to me in my past life, that angered him more than anything.

I was suddenly so mad at myself. Furious.

One kiss. That's all it took for me to revert back to the weak and vulnerable Elelira from before. I can't be weak. I can't be vulnerable. I can't let my walls come down. I need to protect Val, but to not hurt her, I can't hurt him. I'm lost in what to do and furious that I'm so helpless. I am doomed to always be weak and helpless.

The necklace once again started to almost vibrate against my chest, warmth and this sweet soothing feeling filled me.

I'm not helpless. I went through hell, but it made me stronger.

I have to survive. I desire nothing more than to protect Valerina and access our freedom so we can escape back to the sea…..

But now Val wants Killian more than anything.

I just don't know if I can bring myself to want Lachlan, or any man in that way ever again.

~

***Lachlan***

Shit, shit, shit.

"You tell me not to mess this up, then you go and scare her again like that!" I screamed at my Lycan in my head, facing the wall so Lira couldn't see the anger on my face and think I was mad at her. "We had her! Her walls were finally coming down! Did you not learn anything after the kiss earlier? We agreed not to do that shit until she trusts us!"

*"I know,"* he cried weakly, terrified seeing the look on Lira's face after she moved away from us, hurrying to kneel at the end of the bed in a meek stance.

We've seen that look plenty of times. We lived in war and battle all of our adult lives. That appearance is all too common for those who survive something truly horrifying. That was the look of terror that grips a person when nightmares that are all too real resurface, driving a person to the brink of madness and fear retakes them.

We did that. We made whatever nightmares plague her mind resurface, all from our touch.

I thought the mate bond would be enough to override my past mistakes, but I don't know now. I don't want to see her hurt like that ever again.

Letting her go might be better than letting her live a life filled with reminders of the horrors she once faced.

"We never hurt her," Killian murmured brokenly, "I never hurt her at all, but you only hurt her emotionally. That was not trauma from emotional pain. That was physical. It was triggered by physical touch, Lachlan."

He's right.

Emotional trauma is different from physical trauma. The way she was rubbing her arms, shaking slightly like she was freezing cold, despite the heat from the fire which was making the room almost stifling. That was how victims of torture or abuse react when triggered by some physical stimulus.

If I had yelled at her or started calling her names and she reacted like that, I would think the trauma was from me, but somehow I don't think it is.

Then, she apologized to me.

I hate myself that she went to a place where she felt she needed to say sorry to me.

"Valerina wanted me," Killian whimpered, "She wanted me, just as much as I wanted her."

"That may be the case, but Lira isn't there yet. She didn't want that. She told us never to kiss her again."

"No, she told you that, asshole," Killian growled. "That was me and Valerina until you ruined it. I bet Elelira wouldn't have even reacted like that if it was me and not you she was staring down at when she opened her eyes. Don't blame me because you messed up in the past. Even if you didn't physically hurt her, you still hurt her, and you are the reason she doesn't trust you. You don't get to blame me for that."

I bit down on my lips so hard I broke through the skin, drawing blood. He's right. He's one hundred percent right, and it makes me want to scream.

I know I told Cherum I was punishing him at training in the morning for touching my mate, but I might let him rough me up instead. I deserve it, and it's his job to protect his Luna. It's my job as well, but I don't know how to protect her from myself, or the memories that plague her.

"Good night, Alpha," Elelira breathed out. My heart can't take it, the brokenness in her.

She has been a beacon of strength and grace all day. This is the first time I've seen her acting so weak and frail.

Things were going so well too.

I rolled over to face her, longing to see her glimmering emerald eyes and the vibrant glow in her cheeks. She had already rolled away from me, though, and I was met with her slim silhouette and golden hair illuminated in the fire's light.

She's not sleeping yet. Her breathing isn't even enough for that.

"I'm sorry, Lira," I whispered. "I don't want you to be scared of me. I'm sorry I didn't stop my Lycan sooner."

The sweetest sigh escaped her, and she slowly rolled back on her back and turned her head to face me.

Her face was no longer filled with fear. It's back to the controlled expression she has had all day, far from the smiling face she showed Killian just moments ago.

Her walls were back up. She was back on her guard.

Shit.

"I told you, it's not your fault. Val wanted to do it too. I am not interested in those things, though. I….," she bit her bottom lip, her face looking momentarily vulnerable before the mask of control returned. She stares up at the ceiling and continued, "I don't think I ever will be. I know I agreed to it if you wanted those things for the sake of keeping Mimi, but-"

"Lira," I reached out and grabbed her hand, and to my amazement, she let me, "I don't want those things, not without your trust."

She turned those brilliant emerald eyes to look at me, stunning me momentarily.

I want to spend the rest of my life looking into those eyes, and I hope she lets me. I hope I never again cause her to feel like she wasn't safe with me or protected by my side. I want to keep her radiant and strong, not make her weak and broken.

"Okay," she whispers. "I'll believe you, for now."

For now.

Those words sting like I can't even describe. Even Killian was wincing inside me.

With that, Lira pulled her hand from mine, rolling back to her side, away from me.

"*We have a lot of work to do,*" Killian whispered. I can feel his anxiety and mournful tone, like we were losing our mate once again. "*I don't want to hurt her, but I don't want to lose her."*

"*I'm not giving up yet,"* I told him, watching Lira's body curl around a pillow as she tucked herself in to sleep.

Even her back is beautiful. Even if I never get to touch her more than just holding her hand, I'll be happy with just the image of her back every night as I close my eyes and let the night take me. I want the image of her back to be the last thing that is imprinted on my mind before going to sleep.

"Tomorrow is a new day. We will have to make it a good one from the start," I reminded my Lycan, "We have to show her she can trust us. We will make our first date with our mate a memorable one and show her how much she means to us."

# THIRTEEN

***Elelira***

It's hot. Too hot.

My body was a tingling sensation of warmth and comfort, soothing sparks enveloping me.

Something was weighing me down, preventing me from moving freely. I tried to roll over, as Val stirred awake in my mind, then it hit me. I'm being held by Lachlan.

I was so warm because I'm no longer in the drafty tower room, and I'm in the arms of my mate. A mate that doesn't know he's my mate, who hurt me beyond measure in my first life, and I was on the brink of a fit of terror from his touch just last night.

I'm not on the brink of terror now, though. I'm just hot.

And I need to empty my bladder.

I pushed firmly against Lachlan's arm, trying to get it off my body. His grip just became tighter, squeezing my torso and making the urge to pee ever stronger.

"Alpha!" I hissed, trying to wake him, tapping my hand on the side of his face.

"Mmh," he groaned, resting his chin above my head.

"Just wet the bed," Val yawned, "Maybe he won't try to sleep with us again."

"Tempting," I growled.

"LACHLAN!" I yelled, shoving him roughly against his chest.

"No, I'm Killian," he grumbled gruffly. His rough voice lets me know it's not Lachlan but Killian in control. "That idiot was worried he would scare you again, so he had me come forward."

"Whoever you are, I need to get up, please," I groaned, squeezing my thighs together.

"No," he groans, "I'm comfortable."

"Well, I'm not," I pushed against him again, "I need to use the restroom, you big puppy."

"Fine," he yawned, letting me go enough so I could wiggle free.

He grabbed my pillow after I got up, cuddling it to his chest as he went back to sleep, purring with his nose pressed to the fabric. I rushed to the bathroom, the sparks from our mate bond fading with each step away from him I took.

I wondered how and why I ended up in Killian's arms last night without noticing. I'm also wondering why I was okay with it?

Killian has a soothing presence about him, even in Lachlan's body. I have so many memories of Lachlan being horrible to me, but I never met Killian before yesterday.

*"He's wonderful,"* Val hummed in my mind.

"We barely know him," I rolled my eyes.

"But he's still wonderful," she sighed, "You even like him."

"I don't hate him," I admitted, "He's cute. Much cuter and less annoying than his human."

His aura even changed from Lachlan's. The mate bond becomes stronger but more comforting when he is near me. I know he won't hurt me, somehow. I don't feel that same way in Lachlan's presence. With Lachlan, I feel like I need to be ready for his anger at any moment.

It's funny how they share the same face, the same body, but are completely different to me.

When I was done with my business, and after washing my face and cleaning my teeth, I found a thick robe hanging near the large tub and decided to put it on before returning to the bedroom. My mother's nightgown had been washed thin, and though it is comfortable, it is quite cold now. The restroom's heating must not be on yet. It does appear to be early morning, far earlier than we should be awake for.

Coming out of the ensuite, I could tell right away that Lachlan took back control from his Lycan. His eyes were more hooded and his face full of worry lines and a deep scowl. Killian looked less reserved in his body. Lachlan looked like he was already upset about something.

"Um, good morning, Alpha," I murmured, going to the side of the bed to retrieve my slippers as his hooded eyes followed me.

He stared at me while I slipped them on my feet, then murmured a low "Good morning," in return.

I stood awkwardly beside the bed, while Lachlan was sitting on the edge, sliding his feet into his boots without lacing them up. He ran his hands through his hair then down his face, looking exhausted.

"It's still too early, Alpha. Why don't you go back to sleep? I think I would like to walk to the kitchen for some tea anyway," I said, shuffling nervously on my feet.

"Are you not tired?" He watched me warily.

I shook my head. I don't think I could go back to sleep now even if I was still tired. I felt like I was dreaming of something unpleasant, and then after waking up in his arms, I suspect that is why.

Or maybe not….

I felt surprisingly comfortable in Killian's arms. It was more the feelings behind whatever dreams I was having that were making me not want to close my eyes again.

Lachlan yawned again, standing up to stretch. "Why don't you lay back down and just rest before Niomi comes for you. I need to get to training, but I can have a kitchen omega bring you your tea."

With his eyes watching my every movement, I resisted the urge to squirm in discomfort. I felt like he was evaluating me, or judging me in some way. He was not as easy to be with as his Lycan, that is for sure.

"Okay," I end up conceding, getting back in the blankets on the bed after knowing he wouldn't be staying in it with me.

"Regular tea?" he asked. I nodded. "Sugar or milk with it?"

I shook my head, "Just black."

Sugar and milk were never things wasted on me before. Uncle made me eat with the omegas and staff, who were rarely allotted such luxuries, and after coming here, it was much the same. After Mimi died, even black tea was a rare thing for me here. When she was alive, I didn't like her having to fight and argue to acquire things for me that weren't necessary or allotted to the castle's staff, so I quickly learned to live without them.

He nodded, "Anything to snack on before breakfast?"

I shook my head softly again, not wanting to put him out. I barely ate the food yesterday at our reception, but, again, hunger is nothing new to me. I can wait to join Mimi with the staff for breakfast.

He made a face, his eyes scowling more than normal as he stared at me, but after a few awkward moments of scrutiny, he let out a heavy sigh and started to leave.

"I should be back to join you for breakfast. If I am unable, I will send Cherum to accompany you to the main dining hall. Or would you rather eat here?"

I furrowed my brows, "I'm allowed to eat in the dining hall?" Before, I was told to stay out of it. He didn't want to give the impression that we were in a true marriage or I was anyone's Luna.

"Yes, Lira. You are allowed to be anywhere you wish, as long as it is in this castle. If you wish to travel outside of it, I just ask you to let myself or Cherum accompany you. You are my Luna. Your authority and control surpasses all others. Even myself."

I scoffed at that last part. I couldn't help myself. No one's authority surpasses his.

He sighed again, looking momentarily upset by my reaction.

"I'm not spouting empty words, Lira. You are my wife. You are my mmmmh-," he took a deep breath, his face looking strained for a split second, "my Luna."

Wow, was saying those words so hard for him. Does it cause him pain even in this life to try and say I am his Luna?

My negative thoughts towards my husband and mate were interrupted as he approached me, resting his rough hand on the side of my face, his thumb rubbing soothingly on my cheek.

"Rest. It was a long night for you. I will have someone come shortly to bring your tea."

A long night? What did he mean by that?

"Maybe he is talking about how you panicked when we kissed yesterday? It was a stressful situation," Val suggested guiltily.

That must be it.

The sparks tingling on my skin from his touch help me to relax, my bond being comforted, despite my personal feelings towards the one I am bonded to. I rested back on my pillows, trying to reassure Lachlan that I would try to rest after he left.

~

***Lachlan***

I fell asleep watching Lira, mesmerized by everything about her. When my eyes eventually got too tired to stay open any longer, and sleep was heavy on me, that was when Lira started to scream in her sleep.

It was horrifying. Watching her go from peaceful tranquility, her angelic features relaxed and lovely, to seeing her wear a mask of pure terror, her screaming and cries jolting my heart were almost too much for even me. I don't know how she stayed asleep through it all.

I tried to wake her, worried she would break her jaw from clenching it so hard, or she would hurt herself by scratching at her skin too deeply. She wouldn't wake, no matter how loudly I called to her or how much I shook her, trying to be careful not to touch her directly.

The last thing I wanted was to touch her and make her even more terrified of me, but when Killian suggested doing just that, I had no other option.

He came forward, as I didn't trust myself not to scare her if she woke. When he pulled her against us, wrapping our arms around her slim frame, trapping her thrashing legs between ours, she started to settle down, and within minutes was back in a deep, restful sleep.

Every time we stopped touching her skin directly, she would start to get restless again, whimpering and crying in her sleep. It shattered my heart, seeing her so broken in her most vulnerable state.

I couldn't stop wondering if I was the one that did that to her.

Killian still suspects her condition is from another trauma, but he couldn't argue that my betrayal might have had something to do with her restless sleep. She would have felt it and had to endure every night I was with another woman, keeping that pain all to herself.

We felt it. We felt what betrayal could do to a person's sanity. I wanted to end myself so many times, feeling it endlessly for long periods of time, in the time before she died, and I felt our bond severed for good.

The betrayal pain could never compare to the pain of feeling her soul permanently detach and forever leave mine, but it was still unimaginable.

"She thought last night would be the first night we betrayed her. She kept telling me to go to my guest. Maybe she was reliving that night from our first life all over again," I told Killian.

"No, that sounded like she was reliving being physically harmed. She wasn't holding her chest where the betrayal burns the worst. She was tearing at her skin, like she was trying to fight someone off."

The thought of her fighting anyone off makes me sick and homicidal.

"Do you think it was her uncle?" I growled.

"He kept assuring us she was pure, though. Then she swam off after she rejected us. When would he have hurt her like that?" Killian said, thinking about the possibility and probability that her uncle could have been the one to hurt her.

The weight of what kind of attack she must have endured sits heavy on my chest.

She panicked at a kiss, and then the way her body moved around as she was having her nightmare…..

"Do you think she….."

"Was raped?" Killian finished my thought, "I think it is a strong possibility."

A growl, so fierce and deep, vibrated my entire body and echoed down the empty halls. Who would dare harm her? Who would harm my wife, the embodiment of grace and innocence, like that? Did it happen when I was neglecting her? Did it happen right under my nose, when I was so obsessed with avoiding her to resist giving into temptation? Did someone else take advantage of my mistreatment of my wife and abuse her here? If not, when else could it have happened?

"It could still be something else. Some other trauma. We do not know how she died yet. She could be reliving her death. It just happened yesterday, or the day before yesterday for her."

He's right. A traumatic death could have the same effect.

"*I wish we could just ask her,*" I groaned. But the contract with her father prevented us from revealing our knowledge of anything from our first life. I can't ask her for specifics like that.

I wonder if her father knows?....

My thoughts about this matter and how to approach it will have to be put on hold for now. The training grounds are just ahead, and with the sun just beginning to light the sky, the elite warriors and all my commanders will be here soon to begin drills.

I passed an omega who works in the kitchen as she left the warrior's barracks, clearly after spending the night with one of my men. I stopped her to order tea and a light snack to be brought to Lira in her chambers. I know she said she wasn't hungry, but I also noticed how little she ate at our reception yesterday. I spent most of the night holding her slim frame in my arms.

She needs to eat.

I want her to be healthy and happy. Happiness may take me a little bit to figure out, but I can start on getting her healthy now. I need to direct Niomi into ensuring Lira eats plentiful and filling meals, and snacks frequently in between when she can.

The embarrassed omega nods, hurrying off to the kitchen to carry out the task.

"Morning, Alpha," Nilo called as I entered the armory.

I strode towards the kettle hanging near the fire, needing coffee if I'm to stay awake this morning. I really didn't get any real sleep last night.

"Yeah," I muttered, pouring myself a cup and slurping down some of the gritty texture. Nilo made this. He makes shit coffee.

"So," he grinned like an idiot, "How was your night last night?"

I growled at him, baring my teeth as Killian pushed momentarily forward, pissed at his cheerful attitude, just like me.

"That good?" he snorted, "Cherum is going to have your ass, then, Alpha. He said if you mistreated his Luna again he would have you eating dirt for breakfast. He told us about the shit with Leona too. No wonder she was such a bitch last night. Cherum nearly banned her from the castle and stormed out of the bar after she wouldn't stop going on about Elelira not being Luna. She said the Luna was nothing more than a prissy western bitch who was more of a whore than her."

Killian pushed forward, growling deeply loud enough that the coffee shakes, spilling over my cup. "SHE SAID WHAT!?"

Nilo had his hands up defensively, shaking his head, "I told you! Cherum almost exiled her then and there. He put fear into her, that's for sure. I don't think she will say that stuff again, Alpha."

"She better fucking not," I snapped.

Nilo sighed, "You shouldn't have let her continue to visit you freely here at the packhouse, Alpha. After saying that Elelira would never be Luna, and you would be divorcing her the moment you could, all the girls were under the impression that treating her cruelly is what you wanted."

Killian snarled, but guilt filled me. I was horrible to Lira in our first life, that is for sure. Even before she got here, I was horrible to her just because she was Wayne's niece. I said horrible things.

Maybe that's why someone thought they could take advantage of her before…..

"I want the whole territory to know how I feel about my wife by the end of the day," I told my Beta. "I want there to be no question that, despite what I said before, she is now the most important person in the world to me, and to this entire pack. She is Luna, and without her, this pack would weaken. An Alpha needs their true Luna. A pack needs their true Luna."

"I got it, I got it," Nilo said, "I'll get a team together and we will set out today. Don't worry."

"Good," I snapped, slugging back the gritty coffee.

Nilo shifted on his feet, making it obvious that he had something he wanted to say, but he was nervous about whatever it was.

"Speak. Quit shifting around like you are trying not to piss yourself," I barked at him, making him jump slightly.

"I was just thinking ... .Why don't you plan a festival for her or something, so the people can see you treating her like the Luna. After the fuss you made about her not being your Luna, I think you need to show them that she is. It would reassure the pack that you really have found your mate and that she will strengthen you and our pack."

"Hmm," I scratched my stubble-covered chin, thinking about his suggestion. I'm taking her to town today to visit the orphanage and hopefully show her a more likable image of me. She's seen nothing but the bad in me, and I'm sure she has heard countless rumors about my thirst for blood and women. I want to prove that I'm no longer that man. I thirst for nothing but her and her happiness. Maybe a festival in her honor would help show her how important she is to me.

"Morning, Alpha. Beta," Cherum and Meldec walked in, walking straight for the nasty coffee.

Meldec lifted the pot lid then grimaced, scowling towards Nilo. He hates Nilo's coffee too. Cherum couldn't care less, filling a cup with the sludge water and taking a big gulp, smacking his lips together afterward like it hit the spot.

"Men. Tell the warriors training is canceled for today, in honor of my wedding," I announced.

"Really?" Cherum grinned, "Did you get on my Luna's good side last night? I guess we all knew you had no issues in the bedroom-"

I growled to cut off his crude words.

"You. Get presentable and make sure my wife gets a good breakfast. I want her to clear her plate. Tell Niomi to be sure she does that every meal from now on too."

He nodded, pulling in his beard, "Aye, the lass is a bit on the light side. She could put on a few pounds."

I growled again. "You touch my wife again, I will be feeding *you* dirt for breakfast, lunch and dinner for the foreseeable future."

He huffed, "I know, you overprotective mutt." I lifted my brows, tilting my head at his insult. "I mean, yes, Alpha," he added, then busied himself with drinking his coffee.

"What are you going to do, Alpha?" Nilo asked.

"*We* are going to plan out this festival to honor my wife. We need to get the basics planned out before you leave so you can spread the word."

# FOURTEEN

It was late morning by the time Nilo and I finished planning the dates for the festival and the major details. I am going to have him and the secretaries plan the minor details when he returns, but he has done enough to write up a decree, declaring an annual holiday and festival in honor of my mate.

"I hope she likes it," Killian said nervously, "She didn't have much love for this pack in the past."

He was thinking of the day she rejected us and then rejected the pack and her role as Luna, showing no sorrow or remorse.

"We didn't give her much reason to."

"You're right," he sighed, "I just don't want her to panic about having all the focus be on her."

"We will help her adjust," I told him.

"You mean I will help her. She still doesn't like you. She called me a puppy," he boasted.

"*Fuck you,*" I snarled.

"Don't be jealous," he replied.

I grumbled under my breath, really jealous about Lira being okay with Killian and not with me.

I went back to my old room to bathe and get dressed, still wearing my clothes from the day before. We strip to our underwear while training, so I didn't see the need to change when I left this morning, but I don't want Lira to see me all gross and disheveled now.

My room seems massive without a bed. A sudden thought as I looked around the space made me grin, knowing that Lira would love it.

I mind link Meldec, who dismissed the commanders and elite warriors from training, and was now at work, organizing the warriors' schedules and routes for the week, since they will have the added focus of keeping their Luna safe, especially while we are out today.

"Hey, Mel. Can you organize some of the lower warriors to get a new bed in my old room and help the maids to clear my belongings and move them to Lira's room?"

*"I can, but I thought the Luna didn't want you to share her room?"* He asked, not maliciously like Cherum would or teasingly like Nilo. He was just genuinely curious.

"How do you know that?" I asked.

"Cherum told us. He was pretty upset with you last night."

Fucking Cherum. I'm glad he is taking his role so seriously, but he feels like another obstacle for me now.

"Things changed," I muttered.

I don't want Lira to ever spend a night alone with her night terrors. I would rather Killian be there to hold her and keep her relaxed through the bond she feels every night, and if I tell her who is to be getting my room, I know she will agree.

"After my belongings are moved out, help Niomi move hers in. I want Lira's handmaiden to have my old room."

"Really?" Meldec asked in disbelief, "Your room is the nicest room in the castle. Wouldn't it be better to move Luna in with you and give the old maid her room?"

I sighed, "Lira does not wish to share a space with me that I have shared with someone else."

"Oh," he murmurs, "Okay, Alpha. I'll get it done today. I have a team ready to start bringing in materials for the new wing you requested too. An architect is being called in tomorrow to start the blueprints."

*"Perfect,"* I grinned, even though he couldn't see me, *"Thank you, Mel."*

*"You're welcome, Alpha,"* he said before I cut the link.

I grabbed my most used belongings, as much as I could carry, and started across the hall to Lira's room. I knocked, but she must already be at breakfast. The room was empty, except for the many present boxes opened around the room.

Good. Someone got her to open all her gifts. There were so many things she needed among them, like new sleepwear and slippers. The ones she wore last night were atrocious. I should throw them out for her now that she has better ones.

I deposited my belongings in the closet and the bathroom, and saw her nightdress and old slippers from last night on the settee in the bathroom near the tub. I lifted both, carrying them out with the intention of throwing them away, when I ran into Niomi and another much younger maid, almost making both of them fall with startled surprise.

"Alpha," Niomi pressed her hand to her chest, "I didn't expect to see you here. We can come back after you-"

She stopped talking, seeing the slippers and nightdress in my hands.

"Alpha, may I ask what you are planning to do with those? I can take those if you intend to take them to be laundered."

"I intend to throw these in the trash. She has much better to wear now, and I only want my wife in the best."

Niomi was old, so she probably doesn't realize how unfashionable and ratty these scraps of cloth are.

"I understand your intentions, Alpha, but if you do that, Ela will be most distressed. Those both belonged to her late mother, and she treasures them greatly," she told me, holding her hands out like she wanted to take them from my hands to keep them safe.

With her warning, I quickly handed them over, scared of Lira's anger more than anything else. "I had no idea," I stammered.

"I didn't either," Niomi smiled gently, while cradling the outfit to her chest, "I suggested the same to her last night and she told me. It was an honest mistake, Alpha. Ela will understand."

Ela. Everyone she is growing close to, she is having them call her Ela.

"Ela," I tested the name in a whisper.

"Isn't it a lovely nickname," Niomi sighed, "She also got that from her late mother. She told me just this morning when I accidentally called her Luna again. She now calls me 'Mimi'," she gushed, "She is a kind and loving woman, Alpha. I am so happy to be serving her. Thank you for giving me the opportunity."

I cringed inwardly. Just yesterday, I was trying to replace Niomi. I'm glad I didn't and Lira stopped me. Niomi cares deeply for her already.

"If you want to thank me, have your belongings ready to move this afternoon," I told her, making her face turn into a mask of confusion. "I am having you moved to my old bedroom so you can be at my wife's beck and call."

The maid behind her gasped in surprise, and Niomi's mouth was hanging wide open. I smiled smugly, feeling quite accomplished and knowing I had just earned some points with my mate.

"Thank you for your service to my wife. I hope you continue to be a great help to her and serve her well."

"Yes, Alpha. Oh, thank you," she smiled gleefully, doing a little happy dance with the other maid. Niomi looked half her age with how happy she is, which makes me happy in turn. For her and for Lira.

I left them to their celebrations, feeling quite proud of myself.

"All you did was give her a room. Everyone else is doing the work," Killian says, bursting my bubble.

"Can't you offer me any praise? You know as well as I that moving Niomi to my old room was an excellent move in getting Lira's favor."

"Quit calling her Lira if you really want to get her favor," he muttered, making me growl.

The dining hall is filled with pack members eating breakfast, many of which were calling out greetings to me as I entered. I didn't pay any mind to anyone other than my wife sitting at the center table, surrounded by Cherum and other warriors, laughing freely with them.

She was wearing one of the dresses I had bought for her. A velvet green one with simple but expensive pure gold buttons and accents. Her hair was braided loosely down her back, exposing her beautiful, slim neck and pale skin.

My momentary fascination was interrupted when I finally noticed who was sitting across from her.

Yasmin, the prostitute I used to spend the most time with in my first life.

She was sitting across from Lira, leaning in as they whispered something to one another, then both burst into a fit of giggles while looking at Cherum, making his cheeks blush.

What the hell is she doing here?

~

***Elelira***

I had the most marvelous morning that I could ever remember having before in my life. Shortly after Lachlan left, a maid scurried into my bedroom with a teapot, some pastries and fruit to snack on until breakfast. I didn't expect Lachlan to follow through. I thought he just wanted me to stay in my room.

I sipped hot tea by the large bay window in that chair that had been calling to me since I first stepped into the room. The fire was brought back to life by the same maid that brought my tea, warming the room while I watched the sun rise up in the sky over the sea and send the ocean into a glittering array of vibrant colors.

I was a little disarmed having woken up in Lachlan's.... well, really Killian's arms, but the rest of my morning was relaxing and comfortable.

Cherum and Mimi came once the sun was awake, and encouraged me to open all the birthday presents given to me by Lachlan, as well as our wedding presents. There were so many gorgeous items of clothes, accessories, shoes, purses, books, stationary, trinkets and even expensive-looking candies that I was overwhelmed.

I had never received so many extravagant gifts. I've never received any extravagant gifts. I'm amazed that he took the time to prepare all this for me.

"See. He's different. Everything is different," Val kept saying to me.

It was different. I couldn't help but to hope now that my life won't be so miserable here for the next two years.

Mimi and a few other maids helped me to dress in one of my new dresses. I asked for something simple, and Mimi truly tried to find the plainest one, which was no easy feat. All the dresses were extravagantly designed. She did find a simple green dress that would have to do.

Cherum stayed in my room waiting for me as the maids helped to bathe me and get me ready for the day in the ensuite.

I never had this before. I would bathe once a week with Mimi in the bathhouse that's for the staff, and no one besides Mimi would help to get me ready in the mornings, except the morning of my wedding when my uncle insisted on dolling me up.

My hair was brushed until it shined, then braided down my back. They tried to do more with it, but I asked them not to. If Lachlan and I were to be playing with children in the orphanage today, I don't want to worry about ruining whatever elaborate hairstyle they painstakingly came up with.

Once ready for the day, Cherum and Mimi accompanied me to the dining hall.

Nervousness ate away at me. I had never been allowed in there before. I didn't know what to expect. As we drew closer, the sounds and voices of the many pack members who were eating there were carried out into the stone hallways, and I deeply dreaded going in.

This was never my pack in my first life. All these people hated me, if they ever noticed me at all.

I was the unwanted bride forced upon their Alpha, trying to ruin his chances at finding his fated mate and for them to have their true Luna, as far as they were concerned.

Mimi urged me along, and when I tried to use the excuse of already being full from the snacks I was given this morning before their arrival, Cherum rather rudely told me that I shouldn't be missing any meals. Mimi reiterated this, telling me that she could see my ribs when helping me to dress, so I reluctantly gave in and went into the dining hall.

I was expecting scoffs and scorn, but was welcomed with quite the opposite.

Everyone wanted to greet me, it seemed, and they were all very warm and friendly. Every table I passed resounded with "Good morning, Luna"s or "Luna, hello".

Mimi sat me down at the center table, excusing herself, even when I tried to get her to stay. She insisted on going back to tidy my room with the maid that was assigned to be her assistant, Gemma.

Cherum ended up calling a kitchen server over, directing him to prepare a spread to be delivered to my room for Mimi and Gemma to eat while they worked. He told me that he planned on taking me around the castle grounds after breakfast anyway, and they would have plenty of time to eat and work at a leisurely pace before my return.

Cherum scared me in my first life. He, being the Delta and protector of the Luna, thought of me as an imposter, I believe. He never spoke to me, but he would glare at me when I was present. Now, he is going above and beyond to make me at ease, with his warm smile and gentle gestures.

Warriors that serve under Cherum came to sit with us soon after our meals were served. They are known as the Luna's guard. I had never met them before, as I was not allowed to act like even a member of the pack, let alone the Luna.

I was nervous when they first sat with us, feeling that cold panic creeping up my back and making me feel like I was choking, but my necklace started to pulse beneath my dress, sending out soothing waves throughout my body that helped to tamper down the distressing feeling rising in me.

After a few minutes, I saw I had nothing to fear from any of these men.

They all seemed eager and excited to meet me, making me feel guilty, as I still wasn't sure I wanted to stay, even though Val wanted to. She liked Killian greatly, and wholeheartedly believed that this was a different timeline we were taken back to. Like it was an alternate universe where we were accepted into our new pack, Lachlan wasn't a total monster, even without feeling the mate bond, and we could finally be at peace, at least until our 20th birthday.

I'm still not convinced. There are many differences, but there are also many similarities. Lachlan is still obviously a womanizer. He invited prostitutes to our wedding reception. He even had one with him outside his bedchamber after the reception until I showed up.

It was going to take more than presents and one night's sleep to convince me that he was a different man.

"Luna, try this," one of the men, Percy, handed me a large mug filled with a milky coffee.

"Don't give her that. The Alpha will have a fit if he sees her drinking alcohol this early in the morning," Maurice nudged his shoulder.

"The lass is just an adult as of yesterday," Cherum chuckled, brushing crumbs from the toast out of his beard. "I doubt she has tasted alcohol stronger than wine before."

"So I shouldn't drink it? Is it that strong?" I asked him, taking the mug and sniffing its contents. I smelt the faint sharpness of alcohol, but not stronger than a glass of wine.

Cherum shrugged, "You are a big girl now, Lass. I would never tell my Luna she couldn't enjoy a bit of liquor infused cream in her coffee if she wished for it."

I don't get drunk. I tried in the past to help numb the betrayal pains, but was never able to. I doubt this will do the trick now, and if I'm to spend the day with Lachlan, maybe being a little loose thanks to a bit of alcohol will help, so I don't have another panicked episode like last night might be needed.

I was about to try it, pressing the mug to my lips, when I heard a lovely voice behind me.

"Good morning, Delta. Good morning, Luna," a pretty girl with blonde hair and a sweet expression is smiling warmly at us as she slowly walks by. She seemed familiar somehow, but I can't place her.

She stopped, bowing her head respectfully to us, and that's when I realized that she is one of the women from last night. One of the girls from the brothel that Lachlan invited to our reception.

Now that I'm paying attention, I can tell by her scent that she is a werewolf. Val growls in my head, not liking her invading on our pleasant morning, but I don't think we should condemn her just yet for our *husband's* misdeeds.

"Good morning," I smiled back, trying to be as friendly as possible.

Her cheeks reddened, making her faint freckles stand out, and even Val's guard dropped at her shy expression. Her eyes were kind, unlike that other woman's from last night. I don't see any malice or ill-intent in her expression or body language.

She wasn't even dressed as a bar-maiden right now. She was in a simple tunic that covered even her throat and a heavy skirt, leaving no impression of her profession.

"Yasmin, I thought we made it clear that you all would not be permitted in the castle any longer?"

Her expression dropped, her eyes going wide as she looked embarrassingly from the Delta, to his warriors, and then momentarily resting on me before turning her eyes to the floor.

"I'm sorry, Delta. I was told to leave the, uh, brothel this morning and didn't know I couldn't come here. I thought that order was for Leona only. I'll leave."

"Wait," I reached out and stopped her before she could turn to the door.

On closer inspection, with her head bowed more and her shirt hanging a bit lower on her throat, I could see bruising that looked much like hand prints. I pulled her toward me, wanting to see if my suspicions were right, and pulled her sleeves up, noticing bruising around her wrists as well.

She gasped slightly, pulling her hand free from mine with a worried expression.

The men who were all sitting awkwardly, waiting for her to leave, stood from their chairs to see what I was looking at, one of them even growling when his eyes landed on the bruises. Cherum looked worried, holding his hand out for hers, which she hesitantly gave him after a few nervous seconds debating what to do.

He pushed her sleeve up again, and then sighed heavily at the bruises.

They were a nasty purple, with claw marks and silvery veins spotting them.

She was restrained by wolfsbane not long ago. That's why the bruising isn't being healed by her wolf.

"What happened, lass? Who did this?" Cherum asked, pulling her sleeve back down.

She shook her head, "It doesn't matter. They left town early this morning."

My heart contracted for her. I saw the panic in her face, and knew she feared telling the truth, and would rather leave now than do so. I know her pain all too well.

"Sit with us, Yasmin," I told her, cutting off whatever question Cherum was about to ask.

A man will never be able to understand that kind of pain, and I know his constant questioning may hurt her more than help her, especially if she can not get justice for what was done to her.

"And do not go back to that place again. I will need more handmaidens, correct?" I looked at Cherum, raising my eyebrows, challenging him to tell me otherwise.

"Uh, that would be up to Alpha," he said nervously, rubbing the back of his head.

I don't care what kind of bribe or promise I have to make with Lachlan this time, I won't subject this woman to more pain by sending her back to a place where she is being abused.

"Then I will deal with my husband later," I said with full confidence, even though I didn't necessarily feel it when it came to Lachlan.

Cherum laughed dryly, shaking his head with a big smile on his face. Maurice and Percy part, and Percy patted the seat beside him on the bench.

"Come sit, Yasmin, and we will get you some breakfast and some of my special coffee."

# FIFTEEN

"These are pretty good," I told Percy after taking a big drink from my second mug of his special coffee.

"I know," he smirked, "The cream is homemade. Only the warriors blessed to be in your service ever get to have it, Luna. Well," he smiled softly at Yasmin, "I guess your new hand-maiden can have it now too."

It warmed my heart how welcoming the warriors were to Yasmin. I could see in them at first that they wanted to find the culprit who hurt her and deal with them. I feel much the same, but it was going to hurt her more to demand answers here in the dining hall after Cherum almost threw her out.

She had no reason to trust them, or to even trust me, a stranger, enough for her to share that information or relive the horrors she must have been through.

I thought that with her profession, that the men here would assume that it was her fault that something like that happened to her. That was always the case with my uncle's pack. It was always the woman's fault, never the man's.

I used to hear all kinds of misogynistic reasoning in my Uncle's pack that it was the woman's fault if she was raped or abused. It would be the woman's fault if she dressed provocatively, or talked to a man in a manner he found to be flirtatious, even if she was just being kind. It would be the woman's fault if she was out alone at night or if she even talked to a man. If she was a bar-maid or a prostitute, it would be her *job* to endure that kind of treatment.

I once saw a merchant woman pleading for justice outside my uncle's packhouse because men came into her shop when she was alone and assaulted her. My uncle just said that it was her fault for keeping the shop open when she didn't have a mate to protect her. It didn't matter if the man or men who did the act were monsters. Men were never the ones at fault for their own monstrous deeds.

Here, in Lachlan's territory, I'm glad to see that isn't the case.

Cherum had a medic come and discretely drop off some medicine to Yasmin for the poison in her system from her wounds, then the men made sure she felt comfortable being here, making small talk about trivial matters and teasing one another until she became more relaxed.

Once she had one of Percy's coffees in her, she was laughing and joining in on the conversations.

"Why does only the Luna's guard have access to the coffee?" Yasmin asked curiously.

Kent, another of the guards, pushes Cherum's shoulder with a broad grin. "Tell her why, Commander."

Cherum narrowed his eyes at Kent while the other men chuckled. "You keep giving me lip, I won't be sharing my skills with the lot of you any longer."

"You make it?" I asked in amazement. "You make the cream?"

"Aye," she smiled proudly, "It was my mother's recipe. I even milk the cows and churn the butter to make the cream myself, just the way she taught me. Blending it with the liquor was my idea, though. She blended hers with maple syrup or lavender tea."

"The commander is an excellent baker too," Maurice smirked.

"How very domestic of you," I giggled at Cherum, making his face turn as red as his hair with embarrassment.

"He will make a great husband ... .or wife to his mate one day," Yasmin leaned across the table and whispered to me, making me laugh even harder, holding onto Cherum's shoulder so I don't fall over.

I can't picture the big Delta in the kitchen cooking, or even in a barn milking a cow. That just goes to show how truly different this pack is from my Uncle's.

"I think a man that can cook is the most attractive," I told him when I finally got my laughter under control. My cheeks hurt from smiling so much, but it's a welcoming pain. One I haven't felt before.

"Me too," Yasmin giggled. "You should bake for the Luna soon so she can let me try some. If your baking skills are as good as your skills at making liquor infused cream, they must be phenomenal."

Cherum's blush traveled all the way down his neck from Yasmin's praise, making all of us laugh even more.

...Until a tense presence makes our attention turn towards the door. Our laughter then cut out into awkward silence.

Lachlan was standing near the entryway, looking upset.

No, upset might not be the right word. He looked livid.

Val whimpered inside me at the familiar sight. This is the Lachlan we were used to seeing in the last year of our marriage in our previous life. After the first year of neglect and completely ignoring me, using all means to avoid me. All while the betrayal pains damaged my bond to him, and after Mimi was gone and I was all alone in the castle, this is the Lachlan that we saw most often. When he would appear before us, he would be wearing this same expression before yelling at me for things that I had done to offend him in the most minuscule of ways.

A familiar panic started to fill me, making my chest tighten, my mind racing for an explanation or reason for his temper.

"Is it because we are in the dining hall?" Val asked.

"He told us to eat here, though. He even sent Cherum to bring me, didn't he?"

*"Wait,"* Val said in my head, studying his face more through my eyes, *"It is not us that he is looking at this time."*

My eyebrows drew down as I started to really study his face. His nostrils are flaring angrily, but his eyes are not on me, but on someone behind me. Or is it to the side of me?

I turned, and saw Yasmin shrinking in her seat under his menacing gaze. Is he glaring at her? Why? Why would he be angry at someone as helpless as her?

I turned and watched him again, and realized that it was true, that he was in fact glaring at Yasmin, and the whole room had gone silent from the furious aura rolling off him.

He started moving his feet, his long legs making long, heavy strides in his angry movements, the muscles flexing in his arms like he is getting ready to use them.

"What the hell are you doing here, Yasmin? What the hell are you doing with MY WIFE?!" he roared the last words, making her wince back.

A hiccup left her, as well as a fearful little sob. "A-a-Alpha, I-I'm sorry. I can expl-"

"LEAVE!" he growled, slamming his fists on the table, making the drinks in front of us jump, and one of them tips over, all over the front of Yasmin and Percy.

Her white tunic shirt became see-through with the water saturating it, and Percy was quick to shrug out of his jacket, placing it over her shoulders before helping her up, completely ignoring his own wet pants.

"Alpha, you need to-" Cherum started to say something, but Lachlan was quick to snarl at him, cutting him off as he pushed his aura out even more.

It was smoldering, the weight of his anger and authority making me want to choke, but then my pendent started to pulse around my neck once again, and a different kind of magic spread through me, helping me to fight off the effects of Lachlan's aura.

"You told me you dealt with them. You and Nilo both said you told all the whores to stay out of the packhouse! WHY IS SHE HERE, SITTING AND EATING WITH MY WIFE?!"

My own fury overtook me, and before I knew it, I was on my feet, and I slapped Lachlan as hard as I could across the face, making the whole room gasp. Even the men I was just sitting with jumped to their feet in surprise, ready to defend Lachlan or myself, I don't know.

I do not care. I don't care if he takes his anger out on me for this, he will not treat a woman who has gone through enough already in this way, making her feel terrified and belittled for no reason. Yasmin deserves respect, just as much as any other member of his pack. I don't know what eating with me brought about his anger, and I don't know for sure why he didn't want her here, though I can guess....

I'm not that naive, but he shouldn't be this rash. It's cruel.

Cherum was on his feet, standing close behind me in a split second after slapping his Alpha. Gone is the blushing baker who makes fresh cream from scratch and cherishes his mother's recipes. He was my protector and I felt his protective aura washing over me from behind.

Lachlan was staring down at me, looking confused by my action. The surprise of my slap made his aura recede, and without it, Yasmin was panting, finally able to breathe comfortably again.

How dare he. How dare Lachlan try to shame her and oppress her this way. And for nothing.

"Percy, take Yasmin to my room, and ask Gemma and Mimi to help her wash up and get changed. She is not going anywhere."

Percy looked from Lachlan, who was still staring at me, too stunned to speak, to Cherum. Cherum must have given him some signal that it was okay to obey me, because Percy nodded at me before he wrapped a protective arm around Yasmin left, towing her along with him, shielding her from further humiliation.

"Lira, she's a brothel who-"

"If you use the word 'whore' again to address my friend, or any woman for that matter, or if you try to throw her out, I will be leaving with her," I snapped, cutting off that horrid word before it could leave his mouth again. He gulped nervously, no longer looking angry, but panicked. "If you just want her to leave because *you* have guilt for past relations with her, or any of those other women you invited to our reception yesterday, I think that makes you more worthy of the title *whore* than any of them."

~

***Lachlan***

"Lira," I said in a measured, warning tone, feeling a heat inside my chest and a ringing in my ears. I tried to reach out for her, ignoring the feeling building inside me, but she sneered, moving to avoid my touch.

A growl escaped me, my anger breaking through my stunned reaction.

Her calling me a whore, then avoiding me, like I was filthy or something, hurt far more than her slap. I barely felt the sting of her hand slapping against my cheek, but I felt the pain of her words shredding my pride as an Alpha.

Killian is howling at me to calm down; to apologize, but I couldn't register his words through the haze of my anger.

Cherum puts a protective hand on Lira's shoulder, pulling her back towards him like he was ready to move her further away from me if needed.

This fuels my anger more, making it scalding white hot as it raged inside me.

"*You* want to condemn *me* for being a whore, and protect the actual one?" I felt my canines and teeth sharpening, my anger drawing on Killian's form. He is fighting me, trying to pull his strength back from me, preventing me from taking any more of his menacing and imposing features.

I still couldn't stop myself. The memory of feeling her betrayal pains as she probably sold herself the same way Yasmin does each night and day is overwhelming my thoughts. That was probably why she is sticking up for the woman. She can relate to being a whore too. How dare she accuse me of being one, acting all pure and noble.

I huffed out a humorless laugh. "I suppose women like you both will always stick up for one another. It would be cruel of me to fault you for that. But you will not accuse me, *your Alpha*, of being as lowly as the both of you."

She snorted, her aura just as strong and imposing as mine. She does not back down. "You are no Alpha of mine."

I snarled, reaching for her throat, but the fear that flashed momentarily in her eyes made me slow at the last millisecond, Killian roaring and snarling in my head for me to stop. That gave Cherum the fraction of a second he needed to pull her behind him.

He snarled, planting himself between me and my wife. "Alpha, I think this is not the place," he said out loud, moving his eyes back and forth to point out the audience, then in a mind link added, "*Your rash actions are going to ruin any chance of getting the lass to stay with you, and I already warned you of what would happen if you caused me to loose my Luna. We will speak of this later.*"

His voice was low and full of warning, and I could feel his Delta aura seeping out to protect his Luna from the threat she was currently facing; me.

It's a sobering realization, like ice water being thrown over the fire of the raging anger that was just spilling out of me.

All my warriors and pack members present were watching, mouths agape in stunned disbelief. I just had Nilo reinforce the fact that Lira was my Luna, my mate, and the most important person to me, then in a fit of rage, I almost hurt her in front of all of them.

No matter what she did, or ever does to me, she does not deserve what I had just done. I just tried to lay my hands on my mate, to hurt her, though I promised never to hurt her again.

A quick glance at Lira is all the evidence I need of the damage I just did. Her small frame, that just moments ago felt as powerful as mine, is now shaking in stunned horror, looking much like she did last night as she was suffering with her night terrors.

She was gripping Cherum's sleeve from behind, her eyes closed tight like she was ready for a blow from me.

"Lira…." I pleaded in a hoarse whisper. She cringed into Cherum at the sound of my voice.

Oh, my Lira. What have I done?

~

***Cherum***

"That's enough for now, Alpha. I think the Luna needs to rest," I told the bastard.

He seemed to finally be back to normal. I haven't seen him like that in some time. The rumors about him being a cold-blooded monster didn't come from nothing. There is no turning back for him usually when he gets that worked up.

His anger was a powerful tool in war, but here at home, it was always hard for him to put that part of him away. Killian, his Lycan, is an animal. A dominant Alpha Lycan is terrifying in their own right, but Killian was the thing of nightmares. Killian manifested in war when Lachlan was barely more than a lad, which made him ruthless to any adversaries. Having two ruthless parts made Lachlan a viciously strong Alpha in the best of ways, but also sometimes the worst.

When you get on his bad side, pushing him the way Elelira just did, he would normally not hesitate to kill you, or harm you severely. He did not tolerate disrespect. Killian must be restraining his power right now to keep Lachlan from becoming the blood-thirsty monster he can be.

I'm glad at least one side of my Alpha has some sense right now.

I thought being mated to someone like Elelira would be good for him, since she is equally as strong, but in a more selfless, graceful way. Her actions this morning, extending an invitation to Yasmin when she saw the woman needed help, and then yesterday, the way she was willing to sacrifice anything to keep Niomi with her, were proof to me of how well suited she is for the role of Luna. Her selflessness and strength are that of a true Luna.

I may have questioned at first about her really being Lachlan's mate because of her hatred towards him, but if she truly wasn't the Luna I was meant to serve, my aura as a Delta would not have reacted to the danger she was facing. Danger she was in thanks to my own Alpha.

She *is* my Luna before he *is* my Alpha. That is the Delta's code. That is how the connection is between a Luna and her Delta, and now that I can feel it, the connection, she will come before everything else for me, even my mate when I find her.

Lachlan is watching Elelira, his face now back to showing regret for what he almost just did and the words he just said.

Good.

I could understand his anger, being hit and humiliated in the presence of so many members of our pack, but I can understand my Luna wanting to protect Yasmin more. Lachlan should never have reacted like that. As Yasmin's Alpha, that was out of line.

If he was to ban every woman he slept with from speaking with his wife, that would prevent a large portion of the women in our territory from ever getting to know their Luna.

An Alpha should be an Alpha before all else, and he was willing to throw out and humiliate a woman of his pack that came to the packhouse for safety and refuge for such selfish reasons.

Even if I wasn't Delta and I witnessed this scene, I would have taken the Luna's side. She was defending a woman who needed help, and Lachlan was trying to hide his past, without even stopping to assess the situation or consider why Yasmin was with Elelira to begin with.

Then, to insinuate that the woman who already hated him, his wife who he has been trying to impress and speaking of nothing but getting her to trust and accept him all morning, is a prostitute as well….

I shook my head, turning away from him to see that Elelira was far more distressed than I anticipated. She looked terrorized, her eyes closed tightly and her breathing ragged. "Ela?" I whispered her nickname, the one she said her mother gave her and she asked us to call her, but she didn't respond, her shaking wracking her whole body.

My poor Luna. I lifted her in my arms tenderly, cradling her to my chest tightly to try and curb her shaking, and she gripped onto my shirt.

She deserves better than this, and if my Alpha doesn't start showing her better soon, I may just help her to find something better myself.

# SIXTEEN

"Excuse me, Alpha," I said, hoping to the goddess that he freely moves and doesn't make this scene worse than it is.

Elelira was clinging to my shirt, her eyes closed tightly, and her small body was shaking like a leaf in my arms.

Lachlan's eyes focused on my hands gripping her, and I could see the conflict of wanting to tell me to get my hands off his wife again, but to my relief, he stepped to the side, giving me room to pass without saying a word.

Elelira's hold on me remained tight as I walked with her out of the hall. My men followed me out, sensing as much as I did that their Luna needed them.

Once outside the large, heavy wooden doors, as we began to go back to her room, I heard a fierce growl I was all too familiar with echo behind us, and the crashing of what I assume was a table he had just flipped.

"EVERYBODY OUT!" he roared, and I was sure Killian was pushing his way to the surface now.

Elelira startled and jerked, whimpering softly as she clung to me more.

"I got you, lass. No one will be hurting you on my watch, Ela," I whispered to her.

The pack members started to flow from the dining hall. I nodded to Maurice, telling him and the others in the link, "Don't let them come this way, stay behind and have everyone give her space. She can't handle more surprises right now."

*"YES, COMMANDER,"* they said in unison, then fell back to direct our fellow pack members away from their Luna.

I looked down at the lass in my arms, and saw her gripping a necklace tightly in the hand that was not holding onto me. Tears were streaming from the corners of her eyes and she had bitten through her bottom lip.

I could punch the living daylights out of the Alpha for the damage he just did; for scaring her like that.

She was so strong, facing off with him, until his hand shot out to grab her, then my aura and connection with her kicked to life, pulling her behind me right as her dominant aura collapsed into the broken woman she is now.

Lachlan insinuated that she was a whore, probably because of the rumors of her mother being one in Alpha Wayne's pack, but I don't think that is the case. She would be more numb to abuse, like Yasmin and the other brothel women are.

No, this lass was hurt by someone in her past, and from the way her uncle and his men acted in the brothels and bars last night, I could only imagine the things she had to endure.

Damn it, I wish we could have chased them out of our territory the moment the wedding was over, but our pack needs their help and protection. We need the alliance or the threat of the North will come trying to destroy our home once again.We need time to rebuild and strengthen our pack, which was the reason we tolerated the disgusting Alpha and his lack of humanity and morals. The alliance also brought us Elelira.

If he hurt her..... Goddess help him, because he will need saving from my wrath. Not to mention the wrath of Lachlan. And Killian.... Killian will drown him in his own blood.

"Ela, lass, you're safe now. We're almost to your room. Do you want to go in, or do you want to go someplace else and collect yourself before facing others?"

Her body started to relax. I could tell she was focusing on her breathing to try and get control over her panicked state.

After a few minutes, and right before we reached her door, she took another deep, steadying breath and finally looked up at me, a small smile playing on her face, but it didn't reach her eyes.

"I'm okay, Cherum. I'm sorry. I should have held myself together better. I just…." she bit down on her bottom lip again. She looked at her hand holding the necklace before looking back at me, "I'm fine now. I can walk."

"You sure, lass?" I asked her, doubting her words in her current state.

"Yes, I'm sure. I need to speak to Yasmin and make sure she is alright. I can walk now. I don't want to startle her."

Oh, my sweet Luna. You are so worthy of that title, more than anyone else.

"I'll put you down, Ela, if you would answer just one question for me."

She tilted her head to the side, "What's that?"

I hesitated, not sure if it was appropriate to ask this, but I needed to know.

"Were you hurt in your previous pack? Did men do to you something like what was done to Yasmin last night?" I let the words escape me, probably sounding like an insensitive dolt, then held my breath, hoping she didn't find offense at my asking.

She didn't want me to ask Yasmin what happened to her, so she probably won't like me asking her the same, but I need to know. I need to know how to protect her and keep her safe.

"I don't mean to make you uncomfortable, Luna. I want to protect you from everything, though, including situations that can make you react like you did back there. If someone hurt you in that way-"

"I'm still a virgin, Delta," she cuts off my words, "My ... misfortunes were many in my uncle's pack, but if you are worried about defending my virtue, it is still intact."

I'm stunned by her straightforward way of speaking.

Well, I guess Lachlan does have some restraint, considering his young, lovely wife he is so obsessed with, despite his rash actions just now, is still a virgin. The poor fool.

My cheeks became hot, and I'm sure my face was as red as my bum when my mother would spank my arse for acting out when I was a lad.

"Luna," I tried to hide my embarrassment with a cough, "Not all abuse of that nature would cause you to, uh, lose your virtue."

She smiles sadly, "I know, Delta. I know that all too well. That is why I can never attach myself to an Alpha that would condemn those who are in the most need of help. I don't want to be the kind of person who lets victims suffer and endure by themselves. I know how lonely that can be. That is why I need you to put me down, and let me get my bearings, because that woman in there needs someone. Someone who can stand up for her when she feels too weak to stand up for herself. No one should be cast out to suffer alone. Especially for things they couldn't protect themselves from or that were done against their will."

Wow....

My Luna.

I silently say a quick prayer up to the heavens, overcome by adoration and respect for the woman in my arms. She was weak and seemed helpless only a few minutes ago, but is pulling herself together to be the strength for someone else.

Oh, my goddess, I pledge in this moment to put this resilient and gloriously strong woman before all else in this life, because you know how badly we need her. We need a Luna as steadfast and empathetic as her, and I will be eternally grateful to you for giving me a Luna so worthy of serving.

I set Elelira on her feet, gently holding her arms as she got her balance.

She patted my cheek when she was steady, smiling a true smile. "Thank you, Cherum. I know I was probably unpleasant when we first met, and I apologize for that, but I am grateful that you stood by me today. You have no clue how much that means to me."

There goes my bum red cheeks again, though this time I feel the blush heating down the back of my neck.

"I will forever be happy to serve you, my Luna."

~

***Elelira***

It takes me a moment to regain my composure. Being kissed by Lachlan when Val was the one who initiated it was very different to the fear I felt when I thought Lachlan was going to strike me. When his hands went out towards me faster than my brain could register, it was like the whole world faded around me.

Vivid and horrific memories of before my death overcame me, and the feelings that accompanied them. Val screamed in my head, louder than I'd ever heard her scream before. She had succumbed to the illusion that Lachlan cared for us, but that shattered with his actions just now.

Now we are both back on the same page; wanting to bide our time until we could leave.

"*Can we find a way to leave now?*" She asked, worried about what Lachlan might do to me next time we see him.

I'm more worried about what he will do if we leave before giving him an annulment or divorce. He can not take a chosen Luna until he does, at least not without going through great lengths, and then dealing with the broken alliance treaty with my uncle.

"We would have no place to go."

"Maybe someone here can take us in? Just until you get your magic back?" She suggested.

"*Who? No one here will go against Lachlan, and we shouldn't put them in that position. I shouldn't have even faced off with him like that in front of so many in his pack.*" I don't regret sticking up for Yasmin, and never will regret standing up for a woman in such a helpless position, but slapping and degrading him in front of his warriors and staff was not wise. I probably made many enemies just then. I'm surprised that Cherum stood up for me the way he did. I can't imagine where I would be now if he hadn't.

I'm mortified that I let that many people see me that weak. I vowed to live like the dead, but the rage I felt at that moment, watching Lachlan's unjust anger towards Yasmin, who had obviously come to the packhouse for safety after what I'm sure was a hellish night, I couldn't take it. I could not be an observer to such cruelty.

I know how it feels to suffer alone. I never wish that on anyone else.

"You did the right thing," Val told me. "Don't doubt that, Ela. If you didn't stick up for her, no one else would have."

"*I know.*" That's another thing that scares me about leaving this pack.

With Cherum, I felt like I had the strength and backing I needed to protect women like Yasmin. Women that others would just cast aside and label a whore. In my short two years here, if I can help just one other woman with the new power I have as Luna in this life, it will make all the suffering I endure under Lachlan worth it.

"I still like Killian," Val whimpered.

"There is no way to have one without the other," I told her solemnly.

"*I know,*" she sighed heavily.

Cherum opened my door for me once I had myself together. Inside, Percy was sitting at my table with a book I was gifted with the wedding presents, while maids were moving about organizing clothes and belongings that were clearly not mine in the closets and in the adjoining rooms.

"What is all this?" I asked, momentarily surprised at the disorganization.

It was a little messy after I opened and unpacked everything before leaving for breakfast, but not to this extent. This is far, far more than what I was given by my brute of a husband. Because of the dark colors and the more masculine designs, I have a sick feeling that I know what is happening.

"The Alpha ordered us to move his belongings into this room, Luna," Ingrid, one of the maids, tells me. "He is giving his room to Niomi so she can be closer to you, and ordered his things to be brought over here for now."

"Oh, good goddess," Cherum huffs, exasperated. He said what I'm feeling.

Great. I can't even argue or decline the intrusion if it is for Mimi's sake. Maybe I can sneak off to my old bedroom in the cold tower at night. I truly do not want to share a room fully with Lachlan after what just happened. I don't know why he would want to share a room with an unwanted wife he thinks is a whore anyway.

I sighed, "Where is my guest I sent ahead of me?" I asked Ingrid, but it was Percy who answered.

"Changing in the bathroom, Luna. Niomi and Gemma are in there, just like you requested."

I smiled fondly at the warrior. "Thank you, Percy. And thank you for helping her back here to clean up."

"You are welcome, my Luna. Are you alright, though?"

My smile faltered, but I tried to quickly compose myself as I nodded. "Of course. Thank you."

Mimi and Gemma emerged from the bathroom a few moments later, Yasmin following behind in one of my cousin's old dresses my uncle had sent with me when he brought me here.

"You could have given her one of my new dresses. That one is quite old. But it does look far better on you than it would on me." She is the right size and height to fit in the dress, unlike me. I should give her the rest of the dresses from my cousin too.

Yasmin's face turns red, making her freckles stand out as she brushes her hands down the skirt. "I am grateful, Luna. I will wash it and bring it back later tonight."

"No. You keep it, Yasmin. You will need it, as you will be staying here to serve me."

Her eyes looked stunned as they moved back up to mine. "But…the Alpha…."

"I will deal with him, lass," Cherum said behind me, "If my Luna wants you here, here is where you belong."

Her eyes started to glisten and a sob escaped her. "I don't have to go back?" she asked in a weak voice.

I smiled sadly, then walked towards her, resting my hands on her shoulders. "We will go together to get your belongings later today," I looked to Cherum for reassurance that it was okay. When he nodded, I continued, "but after that, you will never have to go back. No one can ever make you do anything you don't want to do again."

Her tears spilled over, and she threw herself in my arms, crying on my shoulder while I rubbed her back and combed my fingers through her hair.

"Thank you. Thank you, Luna. I thought I would die there after last night, but had nowhere else to go. Thank you, so, so much."

My heart ached for her, and I could feel her relief, because it was my own. That moment of relief when I finally decided to die, when I decided to free myself from all the pain and agony; if her relief is anything like that, then it fills me with pride knowing I helped her to not face the same fate.

"Yasmin. Would you mind taking a walk with me along the beach? I have a story I wish to share with you, and once I'm done, I hope you can tell me your story too.

# SEVENTEEN

Cherum and Percy accompanied us outside, but after a little pleading, I got them to agree to watch us from the stone walkway while Yasmin and I strolled down to the water's edge by ourselves.

After ridding ourselves of our shoes, we walked barefoot in the sand. The grainy particles between my toes were warm and soft. The waves were crashing on the shore, the water soaking the bottoms of our skirts made us giggle as it tickled our feet. The fragrant ocean air soothed me and helped to keep me calm as I began to tell her my story.

As we walked along the beach, I told Yasmin about my mother, and the suffering she went through because of my uncle and his men. There are so many rumors of my mother being a whore and a loose woman, but she was forced into doing those things by my uncle, until the day of her death.

I even brushed over some of the abuse I endured, leaving out the more gruesome details that had yet to happen. I did tell her that I knew her pain. I had been in similar situations where I was forced to endure abuse, and then left all alone in my suffering, trying to manage my pain on my own.

She never should have feared seeking help. She never should have been humiliated and almost thrown out.

"I'm deeply sorry that you had to suffer such humiliation from your own Alpha, Yasmin," I told her, reaching out and gripping her hand.

She gripped my hand firmly, like she was trying to draw on my strength. She could take as much of it as she needed.

"I understand why he acted that way, Luna. I am a prostitute and have a shameful past. I am not worthy of being your maid, let alone shamelessly use your protection like this. And I'm sure he was just trying to avoid humiliating you, Luna." She bit her lip nervously, her eyes carrying a lot of guilt and sorrow.

"Yasmin," I stopped walking to look at her, "I'm under no assumptions of the relationship you had with your Alpha. I know he sought your services before, and I would never fault you for that. Anyone that would is a hypocrite. You came here this morning, looking for somewhere safe, right?"

She studied my face anxiously for a few seconds, then nodded. "I was. When I tried to speak up about….about what happened, I was told to leave. I just wanted to be treated for the wolfbane so I asked Lady Vera to call for a doctor, and Lady Vera was asking why. I was about to tell her but Leona interrupted me, dragged me to another room to threaten me and kicked me out, saying I caused problems for our guests."

Leona? Is that the name of the woman that was with Lachlan last night?

"Can you tell me what happened last night?" I asked, pulling her along with me as we walked to a piece of driftwood, then sitting down, patting the spot beside me for her to join me. "I would never tell anyone, Yasmin, but I know how much it hurts to keep things like that to yourself."

She slowly sits beside me, looking worried about speaking.

"If you don't want to tell me, you don't have to. Whatever you decide," I smiled at her reassuringly.

She bit her lip, then looked down at my hand before reaching for it. I gladly gave it to her. "I hope you don't mind, Luna. It helped me feel stronger earlier when you did this."

"I would never mind lending you my strength. We are not alone in our struggles, either one of us anymore," I told her, gripping her hand enthusiastically, swinging them back and forth.

She sighed in relief. "Thank you."

We sat in silence, just watching the ocean and its majestic rhythm as the waves danced before us. The sun shining on the water makes the ocean glitter, its bright rays reflecting back to the world, making its beauty blinding.

I miss it.

After several minutes of comfortable silence, Yasmin started to speak.

"Last night, we had a couple of high ranking clients from out of town come in. They were rough and cruel, but money is money, so they were not turned away. I don't think Lady Vera could throw them out if she wanted to. They asked for Leona, but when they told her what they wanted, someone weak and scared for their *act*, which Leona was neither, she sent me to them instead.

"Lady Vera would never allow the things that they wanted to do to one of her girls, but Leona told the men to gag me and she would never know. They….they used ropes that burned my skin around my hands and neck, and….." she looks away, wiping a tear from her eye, "It was a long night.

"I was left there for quite some time after they left, still bound. Leona came in early this morning and untied me, then took almost all the money that was left behind for a 'finder's fee'. I think she expected me to keep quiet from embarrassment, but I needed to heal. I can't work with burn marks and bruises on my body, and the wolfsbane was causing other areas not to heal as well.

"I asked Lady Vera to call a doctor, then when Lady Vera asked me why, it was as I told you before, Leona dragged me away, threatened to sell me like that every night if I said anything, then told me to leave and not come back."

How horrible. Leona is just as cruel as Lachlan. Seems the two deserve each other. Maybe I can demand Lachlan spend his nights with his *friend* rather than imposing on me.

"I'm sorry, Yasmin," I switched hands she was holding, giving her my other so I could wrap my arm around her shoulders. "Do you have a family you can go back to?"

She cringed, then shook her head. "My parents are the ones who sold me to Lady Vera when I was only 10."

"Ten!?" I asked in disbelief.

She nods, "Lady Vera didn't have me serving men for several years, but I worked in the kitchens and when I got a bit older, I cleaned the rooms after the clients were through. Many girls were sold to her like me, but she let us pay off the cost she paid for us in honest work, then gave us the choice to stay once we reached the right age. I was grateful for her kindness, so I chose to stay with her when it came time for me to choose. There wasn't anything else waiting for me. I'm a werewolf, not a Lycan, so I was less likely to get a job among humans or Lycans. We had decent regulars in the brothel too. I mean, as decent as they can be. Things weren't horrible there until Leona came."

"*Wow,*" Val whispers. Yasmin's story, being sold into prostitution by her own parents, was so heartbreaking. This morning, she must have felt so lost and alone.

"Lady Vera sounds like a good person," I told her.

She smiled fondly. "She is. She's tough. She has to be in her business, but at the core, she's a good employer. None of the other brothels would take a ten-year-old, so when she agreed, I was terrified. The first thing she did after paying my parents and sending them away was tell me to get all my tears out that night, because the world is cruel and tears would never help me, only my determination would. She didn't want to see me crying again. She fed me the first meal I had in I don't know how long, then sent me to my own room with a lock on the door so I could prevent anyone from wandering in, then put me to work in the kitchen washing dishes the next day."

"*That's a woman after my own heart,*" Val told me, making me chuckle at her inside my head.

I squeezed Yasmin's hand, smiling at her. "I'd like to meet Lady Vera one day."

"Oh, but she's human, Luna."

I looked at her in confusion, wondering why that would matter.

"Um, Lycans and humans don't, uh, meet. Not for friendly matters, anyway."

This damn pack and their issues with races. The war really damaged many relations, it seems. Not just between this pack and the fae, vampire and demon races, but with the different races within the pack.

"Such things do not matter to me," I told her.

How can they? I'm half siren, something that would get me exiled or killed if it was made known.

"I'd still like to meet her, if I can."

She bit her lip nervously. "Do you want to go back with me to get my belongings, then? I don't think the Alpha will like it," she giggled, "But I don't think that would bother you."

I laughed with her, "No. It makes me want to go even more."

~

***Lachlan***

"GAAHHHHHH!" Killian roared and snarled viciously as he threw a table across the room, shattering a glass window. That was the last table and last window in the room that was left in one piece. Not anymore....

"HOW COULD YOU!?" he yelled, his threatening tone directed at me.

"HOW COULD YOU HURT MY MATE!?"

"*Our mate,*" I told him feebly.

"No. No, you don't get to call her *your* mate. Not after what you just did. Not after you tried to....to...."

He plays the scene in our head again, of Lira's face when I struck out for her, and the horror that filled her emerald eyes and washed all the color out of her features before Cherum thankfully pulled her away from me.

I did that. I hurt her again, only this time I have no excuses. I knew she was my mate. I knew she was easily triggered. I knew she thought nothing but horrible things about me. I just proved everything she thought of me to be true. I ruined any progress I might have made this morning, and I have no excuse besides I'm a fool.

Killian stood at the center of the destroyed room, huffing as he stewed over my mistakes. If he could kill my half of us off, I know he would right now. He was thinking of throwing us over the side of one of the cliffs skirting above the town just so Lira didn't have to deal with me and the stress I caused her anymore.

Doing that would ruin our pack, though. The North would hear of my death and overtake us in a single night, so for now, he has to deal with me living.

"You hurt her," Killian tells me once again. "You made her scared of us. She will leave us sooner at this rate. Her father will come for her if he hears of what you've done."

My heart wrenches inside my chest. The thought of her leaving scares me, but the thought of being the reason for her pain hurts me more.

"Maybe we should let her go," I whispered.

"Or maybe you should stop being a jackass and apologize."

Killian dropped to the ground, right in a pile of discarded food and broken glass before giving me back control, forcing the shift. I winced when the glass tears into my ass, but welcome the pain. I deserve to bleed a little after what I just did.

I saw red when Yasmin was right across from my beautiful wife. After the scene with Leona yesterday, I thought another bar-maiden from the brothel interacting with my mate would ignite the same distrust and reservation towards me that incurred yesterday.

And it was Yasmin.

She was the one I called for the most. She was the calmest and easiest to deal with, never wanting more than to do her "job" and leave. She didn't have disillusions of anything more between us, and I appreciated that about her.

She also looked the most like Lira.

I didn't realize it then, but I do now. Her blonde hair and lighter coloring, and her meek personality were so much like Lira from before.

Meek would never be a word I would use to describe Lira now. No, she is fierce. She may be broken, but her edges are sharp, and if you try to stand up to her, you will get cut down.

She's a Luna. It's in her blood.

I just don't understand why she would stick up for Yasmin, though. They had no relationship in her past life. They didn't even cross paths.

That doesn't matter. Whatever the reason Lira was trying to protect Yasmin, it doesn't matter now. I just need to find her and beg, grovel at her feet to get her to forgive me.

"*Cherum,*" I mind link the Delta, "*Where is she?*"

"I don't think that should be any of your concern yet, Alpha. She does not wish to see you, and I'm not going to let my Luna fall into distress at your anger again."

My heart is racing hearing my Delta getting defensive for his Luna. I must have truly hurt her for him to have the will to defy me. That should only happen if his Luna's well-being comes before my order.

"*Is she okay?*" I asked meekly.

Cherum snorted, "Aye. The lass is resilient, that is for sure, but I'm still not going to let the one who triggered such a reaction from her go near her right now. I'm not telling you where she is."

"*Why?*" I almost snarled at him, getting frustrated with his attitude.

"Because she is laughing and enjoying herself right now, and I won't have you come do the same damage that you did this morning."

She's laughing. I smiled slightly, and Killian relaxed inside me when hearing that she was okay.

"I won't do anything harm to her again. I just need to see her."

"No can do, Alpha. She is with Miss Yasmin, and she doesn't want you to be around either of them."

I growled, not wanting to deal with another obstacle to get to Lira right now. "Just tell me. I….I'm trying to apologize to her. I need to apologize to my wife, damn it."

Cherum laughed dryly, "It is not your wife you should be apologizing to first, Alpha. If you do that, you will only disappoint the lass more."

"What do you mean?"

He sighed heavily, "You were wrong with the way you spoke to Yasmin this morning, Alpha. She came to the packhouse because she was forced to do things outside her job requirements last night. Gruesome things, by the looks of it. She was poisoned in the act, and went to the packhouse for somewhere safe. You, her Alpha, tried to throw her out after your wife took her under her protection."

"*She looked fine to me,*" I said, though thinking back, I'm not sure that's true. I was so focused on getting her away from Lira that I really didn't notice much about her.

"She wasn't. I think the Luna could relate to her pain, and took personal offense to your treatment of her. If you want Ela to forgive you, it is not her forgiveness I would ask for first."

"You want me to apologize to a whore?" I asked in disbelief.

"No," he growled, "I want you to apologize to the young woman, and member of your pack, that you almost threw out into the streets for coming to the packhouse for help. She didn't come here to seek Ela out. She came here bruised, burned and hurting, and Ela helped her, like a Luna should. She didn't see the hurting woman as a whore, even knowing the relationship Yasmin had with her husband. I'm disappointed that I can't say the same for her own Alpha. You used her for your pleasure, but were going to throw her out without any hesitation when she needed help."

Shame washed over me, and even Killian is feeling the weight of our Delta's judgment. Killian, just like me, wanted Yasmin away from Lira. He wasn't as ferocious about it, but he made a snap judgment too, thinking another whore had come to drive a bigger wedge between me and my wife.

"Okay," I told my Delta solemnly, "Just tell me where she is. I won't come to her, I just need to know where she is."

I could feel Cherum's hesitation in the link. I fear that he still won't tell me, but to my surprise, he does.

"We are in town, Alpha. Yasmin needed to get her belongings, as she will be moving in to be Ela's handmaiden alongside Niomi. Yasmin is going to be sharing a room with Gemma from today on."

I cursed under my breath. Lira told me that Yasmin was staying with her, but I hoped that was just a bad joke.

Wait….

"Lira went with Yasmin to get her belongings? At the brothel?"

Silence rang loudly in the link for far longer than my nerves can take. Cherum wouldn't allow for that, surely?

"She insisted, Alpha."

"You let my wife go to the damn brothel?!"

Cherum was silent again for several seconds, then said, "Alpha. No one can make that lass do anything. I did not let Ela go. She told me she was going, and I was welcome to come along."

Killian snorted in my head, knowing the words our Delta said to be true. We knew the moment she rejected us that her meek personality was just a display of her reserved power. She had more strength and resolve than I could have ever imagined.

"I brought Percy and Maurice with us, and Mel sent extra patrols out to keep the areas we travelled safe. She will be fine, Alpha," Cherum adds, probably trying to appease my anxiety.

"She better be. Let me know where all you go and when you are traveling back. If you don't keep me updated, I won't be able to hold myself back from coming to see for myself that she is okay."

Cherum sighs, "Yes, Alpha. I'll keep you informed.... for now."

I growled at the 'for now' in his reply, but kept my anger at bay as I cut off the link.

Looking around the destroyed dining hall, I groaned, knowing my anger ruined more than just my beautiful wife's day.

I dusted myself off, pulling the glass from my ass and legs after standing up, then dusted for the staff to come and assist me in clearing the mess I made. At least this mess will be much easier to deal with and restore than the mess I made of my relationship with my wife.

# EIGHTEEN

It took hours to get my mess cleaned up, and after apologizing to the kitchen staff, I ordered them to use the great hall for meal times until the new furnishings could be built for the dining hall again.

Cherum kept me updated on everything Lira was doing. She was finishing having tea and lunch with Yasmin, the last he told me, and getting ready to pay the orphanage a visit; the one she was supposed to go to today with me.

If I could go back and redo this morning, I would, but I've already been granted one redo. I need to make this right on my own.

I hurried back to my room, deciding to create a chance encounter with her at the orphanage, or at the very least, watching her from afar just to see that she was really okay.

Killian has been anxious about her because of the last image we have of her on repeat in our mind. I just need to see her to put him and myself at ease.

Walking into my bedroom, I stopped when I realized that it's no longer mine. With all the chaos from today, I had forgotten.

All my belongings were gone, and two single beds are sitting against the wall that used to have my bed against it, with a chest between them. I was turning to leave, when I jumped back, startled to have Niomi almost run right into me as she opened the door.

"Oh, my," she pressed her hand to her chest to catch her breath from the surprise. "Alpha, we have to stop running into each other like this," she almost laughed.

"I apologize, Niomi. Are you alright?" I put my hands out, as if to help her, but she waved away my concern.

"Oh, I'm fine. Just had to restart my heart, is all. Um, is there something

I can help you with, Alpha?"

I shook my head, "No, I was just checking the progress of your move. How do you like your new room, Niomi?" I smiled at her. Lira cares deeply for this old woman. With the devotion Niomi already shows to Lira, I'm starting to like her quite a lot myself.

"Oh, I barely did a thing. After helping that young woman get cleaned from the coffee spilled all over her earlier, Delta Rosewood insisted that I take it easy and gave me a few helpers that packed and moved my belongings. A good looking bunch, too," she chuckles, "Did my eyes good watching them work."

My smile faltered a little hearing about her helping Yasmin, but she didn't notice. Niomi speaks her mind, for sure. It almost makes me laugh hearing her talk about watching the warriors move her things.

"I'm glad. Well, I had best get myself cleaned up. Take care and enjoy your relaxation in your new room," I told her, going to move around her to leave.

"Um, Alpha," she stopped me. "It might not be my place, but," she pursed her lips nervously, "I just wanted to ask you to maybe be careful of how you treat Yasmin in front of Ela. Ela's mother, the poor woman, was forced into a life similar to Yasmin's and I think that is one of the reasons why Ela was trying to protect her."

I sighed heavily, "Did they tell you what happened?"

She shook her head, "No. Miss Yasmin just said she spilled coffee on herself, but as I was helping her change, I noticed scarring from wolfsbane on her arms and legs. And….and other places too, Alpha. She went through quite an ordeal. I heard Ela tell her over and over again that her profession did not give anyone the right to mutilate or harm her after they got back from their walk on the beach. Gemma heard about what happened in the dining hall when she went to launder the clothes and told me. I know it's not my place, but the Luna I serve suffers when she sees others suffering."

Guilt ate at me again. As a man, I have no feelings for Yasmin, but I should have been open to helping her as her Alpha. I've been so focused on getting Lira to trust me and fall in love with me that I'm doing a shit job of running my pack. I'm doing a shit job of earning Lira's trust and love too.

I smiled tightly at Niomi, "I'll keep that in mind. The last thing I want is to make my wife suffer." I've done that enough already.

Niomi breathed out a sigh of relief, "Thank you, Alpha." She bows as I leave my old room; her room now.

Lira's room, our room now if she still allows it, is tidy with everything put away. Her closet now houses all my clothes on one side, hers on the other, and all my other belongings are put up around the different rooms. I quickly washed myself of the grime from cleaning the dining hall, then dressed to hopefully impress, in the few light-colored clothes that I own.

Well, the shirt is white. My pants are still in my usual black. Black hides blood, which is why most of my clothes are black.

I don't want to be that same blood-thirsty, angry man with my wife. I should have new clothes bought for me too. Things I can wear specifically for Lira.

My wardrobe didn't change in the years we spent married or the time after she left me. Maybe changing my clothes is the kickstart that I need to change everything else about myself.

"You should change your piss-poor attitude first," Killian growled at me, still upset.

*"I'm trying,"* I sighed. Turning off the defensive, war-focused way I think and react isn't that easy. I felt like I've been on the defense since I was a child, and that mindset was hard to overcome.

After I was ready, I spent more time than I should have staring at the bed, thinking about the face Lira made earlier and comparing it in my mind to the face and reactions she had last night with her night terrors.

I thought that was trauma from some form of abuse, but what if it was from me? What if she was remembering the ways I used to yell at her, and all the times I was unfaithful? I was a brute. I never laid hands on her, but I did yell at her and belittle her more than a few times.

"I told you, that wasn't it," Killian sighed, "You've seen as well as I how the victims of the demons' horrific acts would react when triggered. They would suffer night terrors just like hers as well."

I growled, "I can't even think of someone doing such things to Lira. I would kill them."

"Yes, we would. Oh, their death would be long, drawn out and so, so bloody gruesome."

I grunt, happy me and my Lycan can still come together on some things.

After leaving the room, I went the long way out of the castle; the way that leads along the docks and the water. It's a habit after the long months of searching for some sign of my lost siren mate. I would walk this path endlessly at times, desperately waiting for some sign of Lira in the open water.

There never was one.

I stared off in the distance, like I once did in hopes of spotting her, but instead of a void ocean, I saw a familiar figure floating in the water near where I saw him yesterday.

Shit.

Her father.

King Brennus looked livid, but waves me over in the direction of the secluded dock that houses my ship where we met just yesterday. Just yesterday he warned me what would happen if I hurt his daughter again, and my stomach is now tied into knots as I wondered why he was back already.

He can't know what happened this morning, can he?

He dove under the water's surface, and I groaned, feeling sick as I made my way to our meeting spot.

King Brennus was impatiently floating between the dock and my ship when my boot started stomping against the creaking planks of wood alongside him.

"Hello, King Brennus," I feigned a welcome attitude. "I didn't expect to see you again so soon."

He remained silent for some time, glaring at me with his menacing green eyes. I try not to fidget nervously under his glare. This man has the power to take my whole world from me if he wants.

"Alpha," he finally said, surprising me as his eyes glowed and the water around him lifted him to be level with me. Maybe a fraction of an inch taller. "What did I warn you of just yesterday?"

I scowled, wondering what he knew. "What do you mean?" I tried to appear ignorant. With a flick of his fingers, water rushed out toward me, soaking the front of my shirt and my entire face.

Shit, not again. I just got cleaned up.

"THE NECKLACE, Alpha!" he snapped, "WHY DO YOU THINK I HAD YOU GIVE IT TO HER?!"

"The necklace?" I repeated, wiping the water from my face and pushing my wet hair off my face. Shit. I had forgotten about the necklace. "What about it?"

"IT CONNECTS ME TO HER!" he stressed, then huffed loudly as he tried to hold back his rage. "I can feel her distress and it calls on my magic to help her when she needs it. Do you know how many times it has called for me since we last spoke? 6 times! 6 times, and the last time, I felt how severe her pain was. I felt her distress so strongly, I left everything behind to check on her. Imagine my relief when I saw her on the shore, walking joyfully with another woman unharmed, but something big must have happened to her before that, or I wouldn't have felt what I felt."

I cringed back, and Killian started cursing at me in my head. "It was a misunderstanding, King Brennus."

"Oh," he scoffed, "I'm sure."

He moved out of the water, and I was surprised to see his fins turn to legs before they landed on the wooden planks. He was very naked, and more imposing than I want to deal with right now, as I'm struggling to contain my defensive tendencies.

"I have sent her a protector in my place," he stated, taking a threatening step towards me.

"A protector?" I asked, standing my ground, trying not to let him intimidate me.

"Oh, yes, and you are to welcome him with open arms, Alpha. Because if you don't, Cedric will be taking Elelira and hiding her away from you and the rest of the world until she comes of age."

"Him," I asked in a growl, making King Brennus smirk.

"Yes, *him*. One of my top siren knights. Cedric is unmatched in his skill among my guards, and it is *him* who will be giving me weekly updates on the state my daughter is in."

He leaned in close, and I couldn't help but to snarl slightly at the threatening waves radiating off him.

"Our contract has many clauses and stipulations not in your favor, Alpha. I would try not to mess up again, because not only will I feel it, I will now have eyes on you at all times."

~

***Elelira***

This was my first time ever coming to town. In my first life, my uncle had taken me through it at nighttime, and I didn't see anything. I was too scared of the unknown and the rumors I had heard of Alpha Lachlan, and too frightened of my uncle to try and peek out of the curtains of the carriage.

Now, I'm not scared of anything. I'm gaping and opening staring at all the shops and different vendors on the street. It's amazing here. Everything is so colorful and vibrant. Everyone seemed so busy, rushing about, laughing, smiling, yelling, talking. It's almost overwhelming, but I'm too excited not to try and take it all in.

"You okay there, Luna?" Percy asked me, smirking as I circled in place to watch a man carrying a huge tray of delicious smelling bread on his head. I watched as the man carried it over to a vendor stall and set the tray on a table. A plump woman came and unloaded the goods from him. She takes a smaller loaf and breaks it in half, taking a bite of the steaming fluffy goodness inside, then hands the other half to the man, who takes a bite before giving her a kiss and heading back the way he came. It's so normal and mundane, but also so lovely seeing a loving couple in their normal daily routines.

"I'm great," I smiled at Percy.

I didn't know what to expect with the rumors about the race issues in this pack, but I know I didn't expect to see such a healthy, thriving town, especially after all the years this pack has been at war.

My uncle hadn't faced a war since before my time of birth, but his pack seemed more of what you would expect of a war-ridden town than here. There was always this dark, ominous vibe in my uncle's pack. Here, everyone seems happy.

There are no homeless, though when I asked, Cherum said there were, they just have centers the less fortunate can go to, so you don't see them often.

The streets are clean. There are children running around laughing. This seems like a great place to live, even if their Alpha is a self-righteous jerk.

"I thought with all the wars that the town would look unkept and the people would seem less lively. This place is wonderful," I told them.

Yasmin giggled at me. "You know, Luna, you seemed far older than me before, but now you're acting adorable; like a true 18-year-old for once."

"Aye, lass," Cherum chuckled, "it's a welcome sight."

My cheeks grew warm in embarrassment. I must look childish right now. I can't help myself. I feel like a child as I stare in wonder at my new surroundings.

"I'm glad you like it here," Cherum continued warmly, guiding me down the streets with a protective hand on my shoulder, like he was ready at any moment to pull me out of harm's way. "Alpha works hard at trying to protect the people so they don't suffer because of the wars. The ports stayed open because of our excellent navy, so the citizens could continue life as normal. Trade never stopped. Our people never faced poverty to aid the warfront. Alpha was able to use the natural resources from our lands to trade for provisions from other territories."

"Hmm," is all I said in response. I do not wish to hear about Lachlan right now, but it's nice to know he's not a complete jerk to everyone; just when it concerns me.

"Luna?" Yasmin came up beside me, "Are you sure you do not just wish to wait for me? The other women, the ones who also listened to Leona and crashed your wedding reception yesterday, I don't want to sound like a gossiping hen, but they were speaking ill of you last night and I'm worried they may try to offend you further."

Cherum nodded, "Aye, I heard them, but to me, it sounded as if Leona was doing all the tarnishing, and others were just agreeing to go along with her."

I raised my eyebrow as I looked up at Cherum. "You personally heard her saying these things?"

"Aye," Cherum said, then after a few seconds, he realized what I was really asking him, making me smirk as he suddenly turned red all over and looked down at me worriedly. "Not, um….I mean. It wasn't like that, Luna. I was only drinking with the boys after-"

"Relax," I laughed, "I'm just teasing you." I like it when his face turns as red as his hair. He frightened me in my first life, but when he gets shy or embarrassed, all that past fear is forgotten.

Yasmin giggled, but then sighed, "Luna, I really think you should wait for me. At least out front. I can send Lady Vera to speak with you if you still wish, but I don't think it wise for you to go inside. Not with Leona there."

I grimaced, remembering my encounter with her yesterday, and the way she kept pressing her large breasts up against Lachlan right in front of me. Val growled in my head at the memory. That Leona woman really doesn't like me, it seems, and she sounds like a vindictive person. She may make things harder for Yasmin to leave if I go inside with her.

"Okay," I smiled at Yasmin, "But please have Percy or Maurice come in with you to help keep you from another bad encounter with the woman."

"I don't mind, miss," Percy grinned, "I can carry your things too."

Yasmin's eyes fluttered, then scanned the ground as we walked, a blush making her freckles stand out on her cheeks. "Thank you."

Percy's eyes softened, watching her face, and I suddenly felt like I was intruding on a moment between the two of them.

Cherum and Maurice exchanged a knowing look, and I know I'm not the only one who picked up on the vibe emanating from Yasmin and Percy.

"Good. If she likes the warrior, she won't like our mate," Val muttered.

"We don't even like our mate," I told my Lycan.

She whimpered slightly, "I liked my mate. It's your mate who is the ass."

*"He's your mate too,"* I reminded her. I like Killian too, but I can't tolerate Lachlan and his harsh attitude to be with Killian. It doesn't work like that. *"We can't have one of them without the other."*

"I know," she grumbled. "I still don't want to see her on him like the one with the flabby chest."

I snorted in my head at her reference to Leona, *"I thought you liked Yasmin?"*

"I do like her, but that doesn't mean I want her around our unmarked mate who has a taste for women of the night."

Yeah. As much as I like Yasmin, if she were to end up in Lachlan's bed again it would be hard to continue our new friendship.

"We're here," Yasmin told me, taking me out of the conversation in my head with my Lycan.

The brothel was not what I expected. It looked like a regular shop on the outside, just with blacked out windows. The front does not have a sign, but you can tell it is a bar or saloon by the music drifting out of the swinging front door.

"Ready?" Yasmin looked up at Percy, who smiled down at her and nodded. He places a hand on the small of her back and starts to lead her towards the door. She stops right outside them and turns to me.

"You still want to meet Lady Vera?" she asked me.

I shrugged, "If it's any trouble, it can wait for another time." I really just wanted to see the woman that Yasmin seemed to look up to, especially after hearing the story about how Yasmin came to be a woman of the night. She sounded impressive, but I'm not here to put anyone out. I'm sure an unexpected visit from the new, unwanted wife of the Alpha isn't desirable. "I'm sure I will meet her eventually."

"Okay," Yasmin smiled, "We will be right back.

# NINETEEN

Waiting outside, I continued to watch the people in the town going about their daily lives. Everything seems so mundane and I find it lovely. As insufferable as I found Lachlan, I couldn't help but to be impressed by the prosperity and happiness of his town and its inhabitants. This is the kind of normal I have always craved.

He may be intolerable to deal with personally, but it's nice to see he effectively runs his pack well. The people all looked happy. There may be small issues, such as I have always heard about the pack's race discrimination because of the wars, but I think any place or territory will have its issues. This place is thriving, so unlike my uncle's pack.

Maurice made a face after a few minutes, then whispers something to Cherum before slipping inside the building.

"Everything okay?" I asked.

"Oh, it's fine, Luna. The madam just asked for a favor and Percy was busy helping Yasmin, so Maurice went to help."

"Oh," I said, thinking of what favor Lady Vera would need a warrior for.

"Delta!" I heard a shrill voice, breaking me from my thoughts. "I didn't expect to see you here again so soon." I turned and saw the woman who was with Lachlan last night. Leona.

She was wearing an outfit much like the one she wore yesterday. Her chest was almost completely exposed, spilling from a corset top, and her skirts were hiked up on one side, revealing the entirety of her left leg.

Her painted red lips quirked up in the corner in a smirk as her eyes scanned my modestly clothed frame. "My, if you are here to take out the trash for the Alpha, I don't think our establishment could use a skinny little girl like this. She has absolutely no redeeming qualities to offer a man, but

I'm sure your Alpha is already aware of that."

Cherum placed a protective hand on my shoulder, growling at the woman. Her words did not offend me. Not in the least. Not after everything I have heard of her, and the things I have witnessed myself. She seems miserable, and the type of person who tries to hurt others for the sake of her own fragile ego.

I am not offended, but after hearing of her part in what happened to Yasmin, I do not wish to tolerate her presence at this time. If I felt I had actual power as a Luna, not just the support of Cherum and the Luna's guard, I might do something drastic, such as expelling her from the pack.

She may have circumstances like Yasmin's, but that doesn't excuse the actions she used to harm another woman. I can't tolerate that, even if my husband might tolerate a number of things for the woman in front of me.

"What did I tell you about the way you speak of our Luna?" Cherum growled. "I should have you-"

"It's alright, Cherum," I placed my hand on his arm, flashing him a quick but grateful smile before turning my attention back to the horrid woman. "She is of little consequence to me. Words are merely words. It is the actions of a person that I believe define their worth, and she seems of little worth to anyone, including us. If we ignore an insignificant pest, they tend to eventually go away and die off all alone. No need to squish this one just yet."

Leona's face turned bright red, no longer holding that smug expression. Instead, she looked livid, glaring at me, while Cherum was chuckling close behind me in my ear.

"You are right, Luna. I know your husband would be most upset about this incident, though. I feel like something must be done."

I grimaced thinking about Lachlan. I doubt he would stick up for his *whore* wife before sticking up for this woman, but now is not the time to voice that thought.

"Let him deal with her, then. She is not worth my time, and it's up to him to decide if she is worth his," I muttered, mostly to Cherum.

If Lachlan chose to continue his nightly meetings with this woman, that would be his choice. I want no part in it or with her. This morning was testament that I have no control over him and he has no consideration for me in this life any more than he did in my past one.

Leona made a snide expression, almost like she was sure that Lachlan would be fine with her speaking to me this way, but then Cherum scoffed before glaring at Leona.

"I know he would be more than displeased at hearing that a mere prostitute with less worth to him than the dirt on the bottom of his boots was speaking ill of his wife. He told me just this morning after hearing of the things she said last night that if it were to happen again, exile would be the punishment," he pulled me gently to stand behind him, "I think I already gave you that warning too."

Leona took a step back fearfully.

Cherum looked about ready to drag Leona out of the territory right now. I almost want to let him do it, but speaking ill of me shouldn't be the reason she is exiled. I want her to answer for the wrongs she did to Yasmin first.Lachlan will have to be the one to do that.

I rested my hand on Cherum's arm. "Why don't you save this to deal with later after speaking with your Alpha?"

"Your Alpha?" Leona huffed. "You can't even call Lanny by his name after marrying."

Val growled in my head, hearing this woman referring to our mate in familiar endearment, but I kept my face passive. It doesn't bother me…..well….It shouldn't bother me. It does irk me a bit, but I refuse to let it show.

"You, lass, are the one who should be refraining from addressing our Alpha so familiarly. You have no clue why we are here at this place right now, do you?"

She furrowed her brows, "I already made my assumptions and was threatened for doing so. I'm not stupid enough to try guessing again."

Cherum growled, "Well, your disrespect of the Luna is just one of the things I will have to discuss with Alpha later. The other is inside packing her belongings."

"What do you mean?" Leona looked at the building behind us in confusion.

"What he means is," a large, curvy woman, with strong floral-scented perfume and a bodice so overflowing, it makes Leona's look small, and mine seem like a child's, pushed past the swinging doors with Maurice, frowning at Leona. "You put one of *my* girls, and a member of this pack, in danger in the worst of ways, you conniving little tart faced cunt. You know my damn rules, good and well, and you broke them, stealing from her in the process."

"Lady Vera," Leona cringed backward, not looking afraid of the imposing human, just annoyed that she got caught. "How did you…," her eyes narrowed as Yasmin slipped out the door behind Lady Vera, and Percy was close on her heels with a large bag on his shoulder, placing his hand on her lower back as he looked down imposingly on Leona.

She must realize that she is vastly outnumbered and outranked right now. I'm the unwanted bride of her Alpha, Yasmin is a werewolf, and Lady Vera is a human, but Leona could never intimidate the Delta and two top warriors of the pack. At this realization, she shrinks back, but the hostility in her eyes never fades.

"Quite the snitch you are, Yasmin. A man gets a little rough with you, and you go blabber like it was something unexpected? That was hardly something to get worked up about."

"Three men tying up a woman with wolfsbane infused ropes and raping her for hours on end is not something to get worked up over?" Lady Vera tilted her head, "Good to know. Next time I get such a request, the job will go to you. Since Yasmin was given a position serving the new Luna at the castle, she will not need such work any longer."

At Lady Vera's words, Leona's eyes widened, and flashed in anger while quickly looking at me.

"You hired a woman to serve you who continuously served your *husband* in the past? If I had known such a position was open, I would have gladly-"

"I created the position for a poor woman who was tricked by one of her colleagues into being brutally assulted all night," I growled. "There would never be such a position for you."

"And Yasmin will be serving no one but the Luna from this day forth," Percy snarled, "because she has already agreed to become my chosen mate."

To say I was surprised would be an understatement, but not as surprised at Leona. She almost appeared to be steaming from the ears, staring at Yasmin with so much jealousy and hatred.

She tried to ruin the girl last night, but instead it led to Yasmin's way out of such a harsh life, and now she has a wonderful man wanting to claim her as his chosen mate. It makes me curious what happened to his fated mate, since chosen mates are usually only taken in the case of a fated mate's death, but that is his business. If he or Yasmin wish to tell me one day, they can. If not, that is fine too. I am just happy for both of them.

"You would take a whore werewolf as a chosen mate?" Leona snapped, making Percy growl menacingly, stepping forward as if he wished to dismember Leona himself.

"No," Yasmin pulled on his sleeve, "I just want to leave in peace. She isn't worth it."

Cherum snorted, "The Luna said much the same."

Lady Vera threw her head back with a "Ha!" then smiled sweetly at the miserable woman. "Seems we are all in agreement then. Leona, go ahead and pack your things, for you will be leaving here at once. I will not have someone I can not trust in my establishment.

Leona scoffed, "You're throwing me out?! I'm your top earner. Everyone asks for me."

"Now, that's not true. Everyone requests Yasmin's service every night, and you try to permanently harm her to steal her favor with her clients. What madame would I be if I let you stay and remain a danger to the other women who also work here? No," she shook her head, "Maurice here has been kind enough to call for more guards, and you are to leave at once, or be forced out. Your choice."

Leona growled, "You will regret this," she then turned her hate-filled eyes towards me, "All of you."

~

Leona left with little incident, just lots of sour looks, and the guards merely stood at the doors to ensure her departure. Yasmin and I decided to eat a light lunch across the street and have tea with Cherum watching over us while Percy and Maurice stood watch outside.

Our breakfast was ruined, thanks to my ever inconsiderate and rude husband, and Cherum insisted that I had to eat. I wasn't very hungry after our run-in with Leona, but I am enjoying my time with Yasmin. She was bubbly and bright, making me feel at ease. Even Val is loving her more and more now that she knows she is no longer a threat to our bond with our mate. Not that it matters if she were. Lachlan himself was the biggest threat to our bond. No one else.

Yasmin was currently staring out the window with a lovestruck expression at Percy, and it makes my heart so happy to see her happy. Who would have thought when the incidents occurred this morning that we would reach this sort of outcome just hours later?

"So," I grinned at my new friend, "congratulations to you and Percy. I'm surprised, but so happy for you both."

Yasmin blushed, "I was surprised too. I mean, he, uh, did come to see me often after his mate died in the war, but I never knew he harbored those feelings for me. It had been a while since I last saw him, too. I thought that maybe he had forgotten about me, or he was like many of the others who like to pretend those transactions never happened."

I tilted my head, intrigued by how they got to the point of agreeing to be chosen mates. I don't want to discriminate, but it is quite surprising that Percy would take a woman of the night he used to visit as a chosen mate. "It must be difficult to separate personal feelings and remaining professional in that line of work."

Yasmin snorted, "There isn't really a professional way to handle being a whore, Luna. I just tried to keep my head down and when it was over, it was over. I never let feelings into it," she sighed, then looked out the window at Percy again, "Until one night, a grief-stricken warrior came in after losing his mate. It was hard not to have feelings when all he wanted was for someone to sit and listen to everything he would miss about her. The first time I took him upstairs," she smiles warmly, "we didn't do anything other than talk. The next time, I held him in my arms while he cried. It took him quite a few visits before we ever got to the, um, usual services. He was always kind and gentle. Unlike any man I ever had."

*Any man she ever had* momentarily made me think of Lachlan, wondering if he was rough or gentle with her, but that fostered feelings of jealousy I didn't want to feel, so I quickly put those thoughts away before Val got worked up. I felt her getting grouchy at my wayward thoughts, and I don't want to have reasons to have negative feelings towards Yasmin. It's not her fault my *husband* is a manwhore.

This isn't a time to be upset. I'm happy for her and her new love with Percy. Percy is a good man, and from the way he protected her this morning, I know he will be tender and loving with her, respecting her as a woman and not measuring her worth by her past profession.

I reached across the table and took her hand in mine. "It sounds like you both have been each other's saving grace for a while now. I truly am happy for you."

Her cheeks turned that lovely pink hue, and she smiled embarrassingly. "Thank you." She then fidgets nervously in her seat, still holding my hand in hers. "Um, Luna. About this morning, do you think maybe you should speak with the Alpha? I know he was excessively angry, but I really can understand why he didn't want me to be around you."

I tilted my head in confusion, "I thought we already talked about this? It's unforgivable the way he treated you."

She grimaced, "Maybe, but it wasn't out of malice, but probably out of concern for you. I am what I am, and he did visit the brothel on occasion. That was a known fact throughout the pack, so I don't think I am speaking out of turn to say that. Last night, though," she bit nervously on her lip, "The Beta and Gamma made sure all of the girls knew that he would not be visiting us any longer, and you were his true Luna. We were all warned to stay away from him and you. Technically, I didn't listen to that order."

"Really?" That doesn't even sound like something he would do. "Did Cherum, perhaps, orchestrate that? I can't see the Alpha saying something like that."

Yasmin shook her head. "No, because Alpha said much the same thing at your reception after you left. You should have seen how worried he was. I thought he was going to throw us all out himself then."

Hmm. Why would he have that Leona woman at his bedchamber after the reception then?

Maybe he was just trying to save face. It really doesn't look good for him to have women from a brothel entertaining him at his wedding in front of all the guests. He could have been trying to cover for himself.

"Or maybe he really is different," Val offered.

I scoffed, "Did what happened just this morning leave your mind already?"

"You know it hasn't. We share the same mind. I'm just thinking; he didn't start offending us until you slapped him and called him a whore."

"He called me a whore too!" I reminded her.

"You called him one first."

That's true, but that doesn't excuse him attacking me the way he did. I don't know how I will ever eat with the castle's inhabitants again. We embarrassed each other, but I think I have shamed myself beyond repair. How do I come back from that? I wonder if Mimi would just bring me breakfast every morning in my room?

Wait….

I'm going to share a room with Lachlan from now on. I almost groaned out loud at the thought.

"I'm sorry if I upset you, Luna. I just didn't want to be the reason you and the Alpha fought when it was just as much my fault as it could be his." Yasmin was looking at me with a worried expression.

"No," I smiled at her, giving her hand one last squeeze before letting go to take a calming drink from my herbal tea. "You didn't upset me. I was just thinking about what to do. I'm sorry to worry you."

"No," she smiled shyly, "Not at all, Luna. It's an honor to be able to worry about you."

I chuckled lightly, "You are a sweetheart, Yasmin. I look forward to a long and fruitful friendship with you. I think you might just be my first friend. Well, unless Mimi counts, but I see her more as a second mother."

Yasmin giggled, "She is very motherly." She then shifted bashfully in her seat, "And you may just be my first friend as well."

We resolved to finish our meal and tea, then head to the orphanage as was originally planned for today. As we empty the pot of tea, then get ready to stand and leave, my necklace starts to pulse around my neck, not like it did in the times I was distressed, but in an oddly familiar way that reminded me of something from my past life, a memory I couldn't quite place.

Odd. It reminds me of home. Not of my uncle's pack, but of the few times in my past life when I felt truly at home in the arms of my mother. Not just my mother, though. It makes me think of the sea. The sensation I felt the first time I felt the water between my toes as they transformed into fins.

I couldn't place where I have felt this before. It's like a memory or a feeling in a memory that is trying to break free from my mind, but I just couldn't reach it. Like when you smell a scent that brings forth a memory, but you can't pull it forward enough to see the actual memory, but remembering the feelings inhabited in the memory by smelling the scent.

It's deja vu, is what it is.

Am I forgetting something important that involves this necklace?....

"Are you okay, Luna?" Yasmin asked me, standing in front of me. That's when I realized we were standing from the table and I froze halfway up, looking odd in a crouched stance with my hand over my hidden necklace on my under chest under my dress.

Just like that, the pulsing and the sensation the necklace brought forth is gone, the memory that I feel like I almost grasped all but gone.

"I'm fine," I smiled, standing and trying not to seem embarrassed.

That's when Cherum walked to the table from where he was watching us, leaning against the wall from the best vantage point, where he insisted on watching us for our safety instead of joining us in the meal, just as Maurice and Percy had declined our invitation. I guess they take their jobs more seriously than I originally thought. This morning with their spiked coffee, I thought they would be more lenient with their duties.

"Luna? Is something wrong?" he asked, moving my hair from my shoulder to examine what I was holding on my neck.

"I'm fine," I waved away his concern. "I think I was just sitting for too long. I'm fine now. We can go."

The necklace was no longer pulsing, and I have embarrassed myself enough not to dwell on it any longer.

[illegible]

# TWENTY

The orphanage was a long walk from the part of town we were in, and Cherum tried to get me to wait for warriors to bring us horses to ride, but I was fine with the walk. I used to walk a tortuous hike up jagged rocks to do my laundry up the stream from the castle, in terrible shoes. My new shoes are quite comfortable, and I'm enjoying stretching my limbs and the conversation with Yasmin.

I'm also uncomfortable riding a horse, and do not wish to embarrass myself further today. I don't want to admit that, though. A lycan scared of being close to a horse is not something common among our kind.

When we finally got to the orphanage, I stared at it in wonder. It was a beautiful building right by the sea, with an intricate iron fence circling it, and children running around gleefully in the yard. It's made of white stones that shine in the sunlight and look majestic against the sea view. The roof is clay tiles and there are stained glass windows decorating the entire front of the building, depicting ships sailing on the sea, Lycans and werewolves, children doing various activities, like reading and holding hands around a tree. The building is like a work of art.

"This is wonderful," I smiled broadly, "It's better kept than the packhouse."

Cherum chuckled. "That's because the Alpha prioritizes the orphanages and the widow's village over the upkeep of the castle. Hidden Cove is the only pack that has a guarded neighborhood just for its war widows. The children of widows and even the older kids here that are old enough to work, apprentice under fine craftsmen and helped to construct this building. It's the Alpha's way of giving a hand up and not a hand out."

"I don't think other packs need something like that," Maurice snorted. "No one else goes to war a fraction as often as we do."

"Other packs don't have our location and resources," Percy told him. "It's either war, or give our lands over to those that covet them, and Alpha would never allow for that."

The kids running in the yard all look happy and well-kept, despite being orphaned. Every one of them has on new, clean, well-fitted clothes, looking well-fed with rosy cheeks and bright smiles.

"Wonderful," I whispered to myself, the smile on my face so big it almost hurts.

Cherum's throaty chuckling comes closer until I feel his hand on my shoulder. "Do you want to stand here all day and stare from afar, or will you go and meet them? I'm sure they would love a visit from their new Luna."

I looked back at him, suddenly nervous, "I'm not sure."

I don't feel like Lachlan's Luna, and I still plan on leaving here after my two years are up. The little hope I did have of things being different died this morning with his angry outburst. I can accept that it might be my fault as well, since Val pointed out that I hit him first and called him a whore, and then Yasmin mentioned the order given to the brothel women to stay away from me, but I still don't see us ever being close enough for me to want to commit to him for the rest of my life. We would kill each other. It would never work. I think it is only a matter of time before he turns his affections to other women, and when he starts to hurt Val again, I won't be able to forgive him. I can take his abuse, but I won't let him hurt her through the bond.

"What are you not sure about? They will be so excited to meet you. You are the mother of this pack."

"But, I don't know if the Alpha would want me to address myself as his Luna," I admitted.

Cherum's face softened and he rubbed my back sympathetically. "I know the Alpha would prefer for you to address yourself as his Luna, but if it makes you feel any better, you can just have them call you by name."

Cherum must just be trying to make me feel better by saying that. Lachlan would never think like that. A man that referred to me as a whore would never want it to be known that his unwanted whore wife is Luna, but I'm tired of arguing that point.

"Okay," I grinned, but didn't feel as excited as before. I felt uncertain and scared of what will happen tonight when I return to the castle.

Cherum must have sensed my unease, because he didn't smile back. He just continued to rub comforting circles on my back, and I actually feel the soothing effects from his touch. Strange. I know Deltas have special abilities to protect their Luna, but he shouldn't have those right now. Not without my bond solidifying with Lachlan, and that sure as all get out is not happening any time soon. I'm not *mating* with him, and we will not be marking one another.

"I'm ready," I said, stepping away from his touch, not wanting to feel less worthy of being Luna than I already do. Cherum's generosity and protectiveness when I'm thinking about leaving the pack makes me feel guilty. "I'm really fine," I lied, "I just wasn't sure what to address myself as, but that's silly. I'm just here to play with the kids." I don't have to be Luna or Lachlan's mate to do that.

"Okay, lass," Cherum sighed, "Let's go play with some kiddos."

~~

The kids were excited about meeting us; all of us. Yasmin was in heaven with two little girls on her lap, tracing the freckles on her face. Percy looked like he was in heaven himself watching her.

Maurice was reading a book to a group of kids, all enraptured by his storytelling as he used a different voice for each character and talked not just with words, but his whole body. It was almost like watching a live play with his ability to bring the story of a wolf saving three little kids building houses out of different materials from a wild boar with a taste for human flesh. It sounded kind of gorey for a children's book, but the kids were not complaining.

Cherum had a group of older boys teaming up against him, trying to tackle him to the ground. It was endearing seeing him act like a living piece of play equipment, having multiple boys hanging from each of his arms. His roars of laughter mixed with theirs, making everyone join in periodically each time the boys almost succeeded in pulling him to the ground. I think he was letting them think they had a chance of winning against the Goliath red-headed man, when they truly did not.

I had a little boy named Westley with eyes as blue as the ocean sitting beside me, telling me all about his rock and shell collection he had hidden under his bed from his visits to the beach.

"Do you think we could go look for more rocks and shells now, Miss Ela? The teachers keep saying they will take us, but then they forget. I haven't been down in two whole days."

"Oh, no!" I tried to keep from giggling, "So many shells could have washed to shore during that time."

"I know! If I don't get down there soon, the townie kids might take all the good ones."

"We can't have that now, can we?" I asked. He shook his head urgently. "Well," I looked at the three warriors, all busy with their own business with the kids. Well….all but Percy, who is busy watching Yasmin with hearts in his eyes. I don't want to disturb them. I should be fine on my own. You can see the beach from here. "Okay. Let's go," I said, smiling at Westley as I stood at my feet.

He bounced on his feet with excitement, making me laugh more. The short walk to the shoreline was filled with bubbly talk about different types of shells, where they come from, and what his favorites are.

I wish so much I still had my fins and tail. I could bring him so many wonderful treasures if I could get to the bottom of the ocean floor. I could just picture the face he would make when I brought him a giant oyster or a clam. A bit of coral would have him jumping for joy.

When we got to the dry, warm sand, I slipped off my shoes, hiked my skirts up, pinning them to my sides, and let the wind caress my skin. I can't stop myself from tilting my face up towards the wind, letting the fragrant salty ocean air blow through my hair.

I miss the ocean so, so much. I miss the freedom and magic coursing through my fins. While Westley starts to search the sand for his hidden treasures, singing to himself, I mindlessly walk to the edge of the water, smiling as the water washes up towards my feet. The grainy sand tickles between my toes, and then the water comes and washes the sand away. It's a rhythmic cycle, and I love it.

I looked up, staring out at the open water, then almost startled back in surprise.

Someone is out there, watching me from the ocean.

I squinted to be sure, not knowing if my eyes are playing tricks on me, but there is definitely someone out there. A human figure floating chest up in the water.

A siren.

My heart skipped a beat, then plummeted to the ground when the figure dove below the surface, just like yesterday.

"No!" I took a step into the water, my hand stretched out as if I could stop him. "Come back," I whispered.

It's really a siren, just like yesterday. I don't want him to go. I don't want to lose a chance at finding my real father. Not again.

"Miss Ela, what's wrong?" Westley asks, looking at me curiously from where he is squatting down in the sand.

I can't find words to answer, still scanning the ocean for some sign of the mystery siren that is again, just gone.

Why does he keep appearing then disappearing just as quickly? Why is he here at all, and why does he dive under the water every time I notice him?

"Come back," I whispered to myself, then felt a pulsing around my neck. I reached up to touch my necklace, but frantic yelling coming from behind me brought me out of the trance that the magical pulse started to put me in.

"Luna!" Cherum yelled, racing down the hill to the beach, "What the mighty hell? Why did you leave on your own?"

I didn't even turn to acknowledge him, still hoping to see the siren pop up again any second, not wanting to risk missing it for anything. The pulsing from my necklace died down, but I still feel little flares of its magic emanating from it.

"ELA!" Cherum reached me, grabbing my shoulders and turning me to face him. "What?! What's wrong?"

I craned my neck to look behind me, still longing for the mystery man to show himself again.

"ELA!" Cherum shook me slightly.

"Ela, you're scaring the Delta. That man is gone. You aren't going to find him," Val told me.

"I need to find him. He may know how to find my father, Val. I have to find him!"

I could feel her pity for me in my head, "Ela, you don't know that. It is probably just a coincidence. Sirens do come to shore occasionally. This is a port token too."

I wanted to cry. I wanted the man to come back so badly, my eyes were burning with unshed tears about to burst free. My craving for the ocean is stranger than ever, so strong, I almost want to throw myself in it, praying for the man to come back to save me. Anything to prove that he was really there and I wasn't just imagining him in my head, conjuring him up from my desire to return to the sea.

"I," my throat swelled with emotion as I try to answer Cherum. "I….I just-"

What should I tell him? That I saw a fellow siren? I can't. I can't tell him what I think I saw or why I'm acting this way. He will think I'm crazy or turn on me. This pack doesn't accept races other than humans, werewolves or Lycans. If I tell Cherum I think I saw a siren and I'm close to madness because I'm a siren too and miss the ocean, he will either have me committed, or thrown in prison. Lachlan will kill me before I can ever reject him and earn my freedom. My life will just be over, or worse. I would have to repeat this damned loop again. I may wake up on the day of my wedding to Lachlan again.

"Ela, please. I can't help you if you don't tell me what's wrong."

I bit my lips and shook my head, trying to resist the urge to throw myself into the sea.

When I still couldn't say anything, Cherum growled in frustration, then turned to Westley. "Did you see what happened?"

Westley shook his head, "No, Delta. Miss Ela was looking at the ocean, then just yelled 'NO' out of nowhere. I don't know," he shrugs his little shoulders.

Maurice and Percy were running from the orphanage now, Yasmin close on their heels, as well as one of the teachers from the orphanage.

The teacher runs over to Westley, helps him up and dusts off his clothes before picking him up and taking him back up the hill, muttering apologies and scolding the little boy for not asking to go to the beach. I should tell her that I was the one that brought him down here, but I'm still frozen from Cherum's questioning.

"Luna, what's wrong? Yasmin ends up running past Percy and Maurice to stand beside Cherum, pushing him out of the way to grab hold of my face and turn it towards her, "Luna?"

"I'm fine," I managed to choke out. "I just…I…I thought I saw something, but it's gone now."

"What did you think you saw?" Cherum asked, looking past me to scan the ocean, "Was it pirates? A shark?"

I shook my head, "It was nothing."

"No," Yasmin shook her head, "You wouldn't react like this to nothing. You saw something that put you in shock, Luna. What happened?"

"It was me," a smooth, velvety voice carried in the sea breeze.

We all turned to see a gorgeous man emerging from the water, with long, platinum hair, a chiseled face and body, and eyes that looked so much like the sea that I longed to dive into them and never emerge.

"Stop," Val growled at me, "He is not our mate. You will not be diving into anything of his, and he will not dive into anything of yours."

"That's not what I meant," I murmured, "He is like the living embodiment of the sea, Val. Look at him! He's….he's like us; like what we were meant to be."

"Just don't get any weird ideas," she huffed, "Your mate sucks, but I will not tolerate anyone but Killian."

I wanted to roll my eyes at her, but I was too happy to see another siren in front of me.

Cherum tried to grab me and pull me behind his body, but I pushed him away, almost falling into the water in my efforts to get to the man.

I could still see scales on his forearms and legs, and his gills were slowly fading in his transformation. It's really him. The siren.

"You," I gasped, stumbling towards him. He hurried forward, reaching out to catch me. He was very much naked, but that wasn't important to me at the moment. My focus is on other things. He's a siren, like me, and he's here. He came to me. "You're him; the siren," I whispered desperately, staring up into his deep blue eyes.

He smiled down at me, a crooked, endearing smile.

"Yes, princess. What might your name be?"

I blinked a few times, mesmerized by his beauty. He's not ruggedly handsome like Lachlan. He's got a graceful beauty about his features, and I almost reached out to touch his glowing skin, only Val growling at me is holding me back from doing so.

"Elelira," I whispered, "Elelira Meline Lambert," I gave him my full name, feeling compelled to do so for some strange reason.

The pendant around my neck pulses again, stronger than before, and I look down to see it glowing. His eyes follow mine, then a radiant smile erupts on his face.

"I found you," he stated, pressing his fingers to the glowing pendant under the neckline of my dress, and the glow died down.

"Unhand her," Cherum growled, pulling me from his grasp, "I don't know who you are, but you will lose a hand if you continue to freely touch our Luna as you like."

"Your Luna?" the man raised an eyebrow. "I think it is you who should refrain from handling my princess in such a rough manner if you do not wish to lose *your* hand, along with that rodent hanging from your chin."

"Rodent?" Cherum scoffed, pulling on his beard. He seemed more worried about the threat of losing his beard than his hand. He narrowed his eyes at the man, then growled.

"Princess?" Yasmin echoed, ignoring Cherum and hanging on to that one word.

I furrowed my eyebrows, confused by his statement. "Why are you calling me your princess?" I asked.

He smiles warmly, "Because that's what you are."

He bows gracefully, completely unfazed by being naked while doing so. I tried to avert my eyes and I heard Yasmin mutter an "Oh my," behind me, followed by a deep growl from Percy.

The man straightened up, his perfect and white teeth glistening in the sunlight, "My name is Cedric, Princess, and I am here to serve and protect you."

# TWENTY-ONE

***Lachlan***

After King Brennus left, in a manner that was way angrier than when he came, if that is even possible, I was left in a state of dread and confusion.

That necklace. I forgot about the damn thing after giving it to her last night. The more I think about it, the more I can't help but recall Lira the night she rejected me. I was overwhelmed by her ethereal beauty in her thin silk slip of a dress, and then by her rejection. The sight of her when she said those words, rejecting me with so much fortitude, like she couldn't wait to leave me after the years of being trapped in our rough marriage, it's an image I will never forget.

I trembled in anguish as the feelings associated with that night came forth with the image of her, all the heartache and regret like a ton of bricks compressing on my chest. Killian is lamenting in my head, that image bringing nothing but heartache and loathsome thoughts towards me from him.

I messed up so much in our first attempt at life. Immensely. I keep messing up in this second chance too, and I'm going to lose her all over again if I don't get it together.

That image of her in my head; I recall her wearing one more thing besides the thin dress she discarded before escaping to the sea.

She was wearing a necklace.

I hadn't seen it before, and didn't pay close attention to a piece of jewelry when my world was falling apart, but I can faintly remember its presence and basic shape against her slim, beautiful throat.

"Do you think it was the same necklace that her father had you give her last evening?" Killian asked me.

"Maybe, but how would she have had it back then, but her father had it in this life?"

Killian thought for several moments. "Maybe you can ask Niomi if she has a piece of jewelry that she brought from her uncle's pack that looks similar to the one from her father?"

*"What if she got it here?"* I asked, thinking someone here may have given it to her. *"We paid very little attention to her."*

"That's not true," Killian growled, "You avoided her because of how much attention you would pay her when she was around."

That's very true. She occupied most of my thoughts before, as she does now. I was ignorant before, though. I thought it was a trick by her uncle. I should have realized sooner that I was drawn to her because she was my mate, not because of a trick conjured up by her uncle. I even thought that was why she kept seeking me out when she first got here. I thought that seeing her was part of whatever spell her uncle cast on me. I didn't see any other reason for Lira to keep seeking out a husband who was acting as if he clearly wanted nothing to do with her.

I'm such an idiot. I could have been happy with her from the start. I could have showered her with affection and love. Deep down, that's what I wanted to do. I overthought her uncle's part in our marriage. She was an adult. I never even considered she could be a siren or a hybrid. I was told she was a pure Lycan.

"It's because your life demanded for you to stay cautious and guarded, always on the defense," Killian grumbles at me, reading my thoughts, "I did tell you many times, though, to be kind to her."

"I know," I sighed, "I should have listened to you."

"Start listening to me now," Killian warned me, "I want my mate."

*"I want my mate too."* More than anything, I just want to love Lira.

The silk gown she left behind when she rejected me was my treasure up until the day I came back in time to our wedding day. I would hold it every night, her lingering scent still clinging to the fabric the only thing that would calm me enough for me to get to sleep.

My sleep would always be short, nightmares of Lira fading into the distant ocean water jolting me awake every night. Then there were the betrayal pains. That lasted just a short time until I felt her death, but there was no sleeping through that.

How Lira managed during our marriage, I will never know. That just proved her strength. It proved how much stronger she always was than me.

I never want to feel those pains again.

Anxiety starts to eat at me as that leads me back to the disturbing thought of King Brennus sending one of his warriors to watch over Lira.

What if he falls for her, and she falls for him in return? I would be helpless to stop it.

She's breathtaking and perfect in every way. It wouldn't take much for him to fall in love with her, especially if she is still resolved to reject me. Cherum and the Luna's guard, all her maids, Niomi, and even a brothel woman I used to visit all love her already. She was that magnificent. He would be a fool not to fall to her feet in worship just like I wish to do.

"Don't be an ass anymore and give her a reason to fall into another man's arms," Killian growled at me. "Better yet, just give me control from now on. I can do the feet worshiping. I don't trust you."

"Hey, I still have a pack to run. Lira may like you, but the rest of the pack is terrified of you."

*"Are not,"* Killian huffed.

"Are too, you giant ape. The only time the pack sees you is in battle or when you get pissed and take control away from me like you did earlier."

"Fine," he snarled, "But I'm taking control if I sense you about to be an ass to our mate again. You almost hurt her. That was all you, not me."

I recoiled at the reminder. Damn it, Lira might fall into the siren warrior's arms the moment she meets him just to get away from me. I couldn't do anything if she did.

I was hurrying to change, the need to go see Lira was growing stronger with my anxiety. I don't know how I'm going to approach her, still unsure of how to tell her and *Yasmin* sorry, but I'll figure that out when I get to her. I want to get to her before this siren warrior does.

"*Uh, Alpha?"* Cherum's voice traveled through my head in the mind link. "*I got a situation here and don't know how to proceed."*

*"What situation? Is Lira alright?"* I asked anxiously. I threw on my boots and started to storm down the hall towards the front doors of the packhouse.

"Oh, she's a fine mess right now. She is alright, as far as I can tell. Crying happy tears, I believe."

*"She's crying?"* I doubled my pace to get outside of the castle. "*What happened? Where are you?"* I demanded.

"The orphanage, Alpha. We're by the beach now."

Shit. Did she try to escape to the sea again? I just had that image playing in my head, so my panic skyrocketed. She shouldn't be able to shift to her siren form for two more years, though, right?

What if she figured out how? What if her father decided to take her away from me anyway?

"She's with you? She didn't try to leave, did she? Did she go into the ocean?"

I start rambling off questions to my Delta.

"Whoa there, Alpha. She's fine. She's a little excited, but she's alright. She isn't my issue. It's the man she is blubbering over that is leaving me clueless about what to do."

Killian snarled ferociously in my head at hearing about Lira blubbering and getting excited about another man.

"*What do you mean,*" I asked in a dangerously calm tone. I asked, but I already knew. It's what was driving my anxiety over the edge just before Cherum mind linked me, I'm sure.

"Well, Alpha, it seems that the Luna has some connection to a siren? One appeared out of the sea and started calling her princess, saying he's here to protect her. I tried to take her away from him, sensing he had gone mad to accuse Ela of being a mermaid, but the lass wouldn't let me. She demanded I leave them be."

I growled, knowing that I was too late. Shit. He had already found her; this siren man named Cedric, who King Brennus claimed was a very skilled warrior.

He found my mate, and my mate is blubbering and crying happy tears all over him.

"Bring him here," I told Cherum, working hard to control my anger. "He is not to be harmed. Head back now and bring him with you."

"Do you know him?" Cherum asked.

I sighed, "Kind of. It's complicated. Just come home. I want my wife back at this castle within the hour."

"Yeah. Sure thing, Alpha. There is just one problem."

"*What?*" I snapped, clenching my teeth.

"Um, he's stark naked. The orphanage has no clothing that fits the man either. Traveling through the town with the Luna and a naked siren man might now be the best idea."

Killian was pushing to the surface, angered that our mate is crying tears of joy over a naked man right now. A top siren warrior man sent by her father who I can not kill or displease without risking losing my mate again.

"Find him some damn clothes and bring me my wife!"

"Geez. Okay, Mr. Grumpy Drawers. Best get that temper under control before she gets there. I won't let there be a repeat of this morning."

I just growled, cutting the link as I paced in front of the castle. No. No repeats, but I need my wife back with me before I go mad over her myself.

~

***Elelira***

Cherum and Maurice tried to coax me away from the man while Percy retrieved Yasmin, holding her away and shielding her view of the naked Cedric with his body.

I refused to let him go, though. I finally found another siren. I don't want to risk losing him, especially without finding out who exactly he was and why he kept calling me princess.

"Luna, I must insist you let him go and come with me," Cherum tried to pull my arm to get me away, while Maurice went to grip my other arm.

Cedric, with lightning speed, slams his fist down on Cherum's wrist, forcing him to let go of me, then his arms snake around my waist, and he twists our bodies around, turning with me so I'm out of their reach, which just angers my guards further.

Cherum growled, and Maurice reached for the blade strapped to his waist.

"I believe my princess does not want to go with you," Cedric purred in a composed, elegant voice, full of certain authority. "I can't say I blame her. Witnessing just a bit of your barbaric behavior towards her, it seems I came just in time."

Cherum took a threatening step forward, a fierce snarl filling the space between us. The hair on his exposed skin was thickening as his claws extended, and I could see the challenge on his face. He's about to force Cedric to step away from me. I can't let that happen.

"Cherum, stop," I pleaded with him, "Please. He's….he's not here to hurt me. Right?" I looked at the unfamiliar man for reassurance. I don't know what else to say or how else to argue my point that I want to stay to talk with him. This was the first time that I have met the man and I'm unsure of the reasons why he is here. He may be here to hurt me, but that is a risk I am willing to take to get some answers about where my paternal bloodline comes from. He is a siren. He must have some clue or be able to give me some hint as to who my real father might be.

"I would never hurt you, princess. I would obliterate any who tried." Cedric's voice rang with conviction, and I knew somehow that he was telling me the truth. I looked at Cherum, my eyes wide and begging.

Cherum sighed, "Lass, you…..you know what he is, right? You know he's a siren. He could be using his abilities to entice you to go with him. I can't risk that."

"He can't use those abilities on me," I confessed, "I know what he is, and I know that I am safe from that magic. Please, Cherum, just trust me."

Please, please, please don't make me confess more than that. Please don't make me admit that I am a hybrid; a siren too.

"You might be able to trust him. I don't think he would do anything or treat you differently," Val told me.

"He may not, but I can't have him and the others here keep that secret from their Alpha. It's not them I don't trust. It's him."

*"Hmm,"* Val groaned, unable to argue with me. She retreated back to watching everything through my eyes, worried just as much as I am about letting Cedric go.

Cherum was scowling while staring at the man who was trying to block me from my Delta's view with his naked body. I can see Cherum's mind is racing, trying to decide what to do.

"How do you know his magic won't work on you?" Cherum then asked, "How am *I* to know that? How do I know that this man isn't here to kidnap the new Luna? He could have been sent here by the tribes of the north or the covens hidden in the hills bordering our lands? How-"

"Her necklace," Cedric cut him off, "It holds protective magic. That's what called me to her. Let me ask you this, *Delta,*" he said the title mockingly, "Was the princess in danger early this morning? Was there something that happened to her that put her in a frantic, panicked state? Anything that tried to harm her in any way?"

Cherum's scowl deepened. "I was with her. She will never be in danger with me around."

Cedric laughed dryly, "If that were true, I wouldn't be here." He shook his head, then turned to pull me beside him. His hand went to the back of my neck, startling me for a moment, and making Cherum and the other two guards growl, but then he found the necklace chain and pulled it, starting from the back, and working his way to the front, freeing it from my dress so it rested on the outside of it, in full view. "This necklace is like a beacon, infused with magic that calls to our kind when she is in trouble. It called for help this morning, loud and clear. Hence my being here. If you did not want a siren warrior sent to protect the princess, you should have done a better job protecting her," he stopped and shook his head, "One day. It took your kind just one day to prove your incapability to keep her safe."

Cherum growled deep in his chest, "So you would have me believe that *you*, pretty boy, were sent because she is wearing some siren charm that called for you after the Alpha's little outburst this morning?" he scoffed, shaking his head.

"The Alpha?" Cedric looked taken back for a moment, then fiery outrage flashes on his face. "The Alpha? As in, her *husband* was the one to endanger my princess this morning?"

Cherum and Maurice exchanged a quick, worried glance as the menacing aura emanated from the siren next to me. His indignation was rolling off of him in waves.

I don't understand why he is getting this upset over an event that had nothing to do with him, just like I don't understand why he keeps calling me princess. Maybe because I was technically an Alpha descendant from my uncle's pack, though I was never treated like one? Maybe this necklace is like a magic item that calls for help when it feels its owner is distressed, and Cedric is the outcome of that? Whatever the reason, all I know is I need to diffuse this situation. Now.

"It was a misunderstanding," I said, trying to calm Cedric's discontent, "He did not harm me, but I hit him out of anger. Of course, his temper flared for a moment, but it was all just a misunderstanding."

Cedric blinked a few times, then turned his stare down at me, looking less menacing as he does, his eyes softening into a pained expression. "What would cause you to hit the man that is your husband and the Alpha Lycan of this pack, though? It must have been something serious."

I bit my lip, staring up into his luminescent, deep blue eyes. What do I tell him that won't make his temper flare again?

"That was my fault," Yasmin called out from Percy's arms. "I was asked not to approach the Luna, but I did anyway and the Alpha was just trying to discipline me for disobeying. The Luna slapped him to stop him, sir. It all started with my mistake."

Oh, Yasmin. I want to correct her, tell her that it wasn't her mistake at all coming to the packhouse to seek help and a safe haven. I hope she truly doesn't believe that, because no matter what Lachlan, Cherum, or anyone else may have told her, she shouldn't have been told to stay away from me. Not when her safety was on the line. If he is ashamed of his past, it's not her mistake.

"And why were you told to stay away from her?" Cedric asked.

"That is not any of your business," I snapped before Yasmin said anything more. "I didn't agree with the order so I reacted badly. That's all you need to know."

Cedric studied my face for a few seconds longer, probably trying to tell if I'm being honest or if he should leave the topic about Yasmin alone. I'm glad he is studying my face and not the others, because they look slightly uncomfortable at me taking the blame for my idiot husband's misdeeds. I'm used to holding back my true feelings. I have no worries about him seeing my inner thoughts on my face.

"If you say so, my princess. Nevertheless, I'm here now, and it is my duty to keep you safe from this day forward."

I furrowed my brows. "Why? Why is it *your* job and why do you keep calling me princess?"

He smirked, "Consider it a nickname for now. As to why," he leans forward to whisper in my ear, much to the irritation of Cherum, "your father sent me in his stead, Elelira. He said to tell you that he is waiting. Waiting for the day you can join him in the sea."

# TWENTY-TWO

"You know my father?" I said in a stunned whisper. I can feel my throat clogging with pent-up emotions. All I've ever wanted was to find my father, and this man is telling me that my father not only knows about me, but he is waiting for me.

"See," Val's voice rang excitedly in my head, "This isn't the same life! Your father never knew you in your first life. This life is different."

I felt like Val's excitement was more about the possibility of Lachlan being different than about my father knowing me, but I chose to ignore that for now. I don't want to argue with her again. Not when I'm standing before a connection with my father.

Cedric smiled at my stunned expression, then nodded. I threw my arms around his neck, my tears spilling free, and after a few seconds, I felt his arms hugging me back, rubbing my back soothingly as I cried.

I can feel that familiar magic from the sea from Cedric's touch, but that relief is short-lived.

"Luna!" Cherum yelled, and then I felt his familiar protective hand on my shoulder.

"Cherum, please," I turned to stare at him, only I couldn't see well with my tear blurred vision. "Please, just stop. Let me talk to him in peace. Please."

Cherum looked between us uneasily, and then groaned. "Luna, you hanging on another man, a naked man at that, is not something I can condone."

Gosh, he's right. I let my arms drop and tried to dry my tears on the sleeve of my dress. I was so excited about finding another siren, and then about having a connection with my father, that I didn't think about how this scene could affect the pack and affect Lachlan. I don't want Cherum or my other guards to get in trouble with their Alpha because of me.

Cedric stood unwavering beside me. "Why don't you speak with your Alpha? He should have been aware that I was coming to help Elelira today."

What?

I exchanged a shocked look with Cherum, then stared back up at the siren man, wondering what other revelations he might hold.

"One sec," Cherum grumbled. It seemed he'd decided to do as Cedric suggested. "Don't you move, you flounder. If you hurt her or try to take her, so help me, I'll filet your arse and fry you over a spit."

Cedric smirked, "Noted."

"*Do you think they make spears strong enough to hold a man the size of this man?*" Val asked in my head, almost making me giggle. I resist the urge to ogle Cedric, though Val wants me to get another good look at him as she decides how big of a *spear* he's carrying himself. "*For reference later,*" she tells me, "*It would be nice to know that our mate is more manly than this man.*"

"*I hope we never find out,*" I growled at her. I don't want to see Cedric's weaponry, and I sure as it gets don't want to ever see Lachlan's. Not after what happened this morning.

"Aww, come on. I know you're curious too," Val snickered.

"*Not even a little bit,*" I groaned, but I felt my neck and cheeks burning as the thought of my mate's naked body and what it could possibly look like flinted through my mind involuntarily. Darn it, Val. I didn't know she could be such a pervert.

"You okay there, princess?" Cedric asked, staring down at me with a crooked smirk.

I nodded, averting my gaze anywhere but at him. Him being naked didn't bother me before, but with Val spewing nonsense in my mind, I'm not able to ignore it as easily.

"Are you, um, going to the castle to stay with us?" I asked to try and focus on something else, and also because I'm genuinely curious. I don't know if he plans to stay for just a few days, or if he is going to return to the sea after seeing that I'm alright. I don't want him to go. Especially now that I know he was sent here by my father.

"From this day on, I will not be leaving your side, princess. I will be with you until the day you gain your magic and your fins."

"Oh," I said, trying not to let my happiness show. I rest my hand on the necklace hanging from my neck, my fingers tracing its delicate pattern. He said this was what called him here. It called for help or something such as that. Does that mean that my father was the one who gave it to Lachlan to give it to me yesterday?

"This necklace," I looked up at Cedric, thoughts of him being naked all but forgotten now that my thoughts were focused on my father. "Was this a gift from him?" I asked.

Cedric reached for the pendant and lifts it slightly so it can rest against his palm. "It was. For reasons I can not yet speak of, he can not be with you, or let the world know you are his daughter, but he wanted to leave you with something for you to call for him, or use his magic if there was ever a need." He goes silent for a moment, then shakes his head, "He didn't expect for there to be a need this quickly. If he could take you to the sea with him now, I know he would, but without your magic and your fins, it just isn't possible."

My father wants me? He wants to take me away?

My heart was beating excitedly for a minute, then dwindled back to its normal beat, then dropped when another thought popped into my head. "If my father knew about me, why didn't he come to save me sooner? Why didn't he come back for my mother?"

A sad expression crossed his features, "He only learned of you recently, Elelira. He wasn't even aware of your mother's death until, uh, maybe a few weeks ago? Maybe months? The timeline is iffy, but it hasn't been long. He has been searching for a way to get you to him, but it will take you gaining your magic for him to finally bring you home to where you belong. This wedding and his access to you through your new husband was the only way for him to build a bridge to connect you in some way to him."

So, he didn't know about me? This is so different from my first life and I'm having a hard time wrapping my head around all the changes. My dad wanted me with him after finding out about me. My anxieties about having the same fate as before while trying to find information on my father lifts with this news. I won't meet the same cruel death if I have no reason to ever return to my uncle's pack.

"See," Val said mockingly in my mind, "I told you this life was different. I don't agree with him taking you away just yet, though."

I want to growl at her, but hold myself back. "Don't start with that. Lachlan is still the same demeaning jerk he was before. You and I both know that though Killian may be alright, Lachlan, the one in control, is still not someone we can be with."

"He might be sorry for what happened this morning. You know the rumors about his anger," Val tried to reason with me.

"Yes, but his anger was not just at me. He was horrible to Yasmin as well when she didn't deserve that. I can not trust a man like that and do not want to keep him as my mate."

*"I don't want to lose my mate, Ela! You are punishing me and Killian while you remain set on rejecting Lachlan,"* Val cried. I could feel her worry and the pain she felt at the thought of losing the mate that she just met for the first time yesterday. A mate that seemed to want her as much as she had always longed for him.

"He knew, Val. He knew at least since yesterday who my father was and that the necklace was a gift from him. He kept that from me. How can I trust a man like that? He held information from me pertaining to something I had desired more than anything for as long as I can remember, and he didn't tell me that my father contacted him. He didn't tell me that my father sent the necklace as a gift. Thinking back on it, it was almost like he was trying to hide who the necklace came from. You want me to commit my life to someone who doesn't have the decency to tell me that my father was looking for me? That my father was with him at some point, because where else would he have gotten the necklace?"

"You don't know that," Val tried to argue, though I could feel that she was trying to convince herself as well. "You don't know that Lachlan was aware that the man who sent you the necklace was your father."

I remained silent for a few seconds while I tried to work things out in my head. "If Cherum comes back and tells us that Lachlan knew of Cedric's arrival, that proves I'm right. That proves he had communication with my father."

I could feel her worry in my head, because she knows I'm right. I find myself hoping just as much as she is that I'm wrong. I'm still holding on to a fraction of hope that Cherum will come back over and tell us that Lachlan didn't know anything about Cedric being here, and that he was unaware of there being a siren in his land.

That hope died as Cherum walked back over to us waiting for him on the beach and we saw all the hostility gone from his expression.

"What did your Alpha say?" Cedric asked with a confidence that made me gulp nervously while waiting for Cherum's answer.

"Aye, he said he knows of you and to bring you along. We just have to find you some clothes first. The orphanage does not have any that could fit a fellow of your, uh, size, so I have a guard riding this way with some now."

"Is my nudity offensive, Delta?" Cedric smirked.

"Yes," Percy was the one to answer with a growl.

I couldn't even find the humor in their conversation about nudity and offensiveness now, my mind reeling and my heart sinking, as well as Vals, knowing our *mate* has broken our trust impossibly more than before.

~

***Lachlan***

*"Where are they?"* Killian growled in my head. He's restless, fearful of what this siren man might be telling our mate. Fearful of what she may be telling him. He was fearful that the naked siren she was clinging to and crying on, as Cherum told us, might be able to accomplish in the single hour I gave them to get home what I may never accomplish in the next two years. Not with the rate we are going.

I share his fears. If this man tries to steal my wife and my mate, I will be helpless to stop it.

"They still have 10 minutes to get here," I told him, "10 minutes, then we can panic."

Killian scoffed, "Don't try to claim you are not panicking now. We share a mind, idiot. I know you are just as frantic as I am."

Yes, but if I let that show when Lira gets here, I could upset her even more than I already have, and I'm trying to win back her affections, not drive them away even harder.

"Alpha! The Luna and her guard are approaching the gates!" my warrior called down to me from the vantage point above.

"*Finally!*" Killian huffed dramatically, urging me to go and meet them at the gate.

I cannot deny him that, because I wish for it too. I wish to see her, even just seconds sooner, and this time, I have to keep myself in control of my anger. I have to keep the appearance of someone she can learn to trust, because after this morning, one more wrong move and it is game over for me. Her father had already sent her his own guard to watch over her. It would take just one mistake for that man to take away the only woman I could ever love.

I'm pacing nervously, resisting the urge to jump up and down on the other side of the gate in the hope of seeing them sooner. She's so close to me once again, and I have this desirous energy flowing through me. I want to pull her into my arms the moment my eyes fall upon her, beg for her forgiveness, granting her every whim or desire until I gain it.

When she does come into view, it takes all that is in me to not repeat my sins from this morning.

A tall man, with broad shoulders and long silvery hair that is far too pretty to be on a man's head, is walking alongside my wife, his arm protectively around her shoulder. He is wearing a cape, no shirt underneath. Thankfully, he is wearing pants, but his bare chest grazing against Lira's shoulder as they walk is not a pleasant sight. He is smiling down at her, saying something, then laughing at whatever response she must have given him.

She doesn't recoil from his touch. She isn't panicking like she did with mine. She isn't looking up at him with guarded features, barely containing her disdain like she does with me. No. She is smiling a beautiful, heart-wrenching smile that lights up her whole face and makes her eyes shine more brilliantly than ever before.

Killian begins to whimper in my head, and my heart feels like it is breaking all over again. The pain I felt when she rejected me might be the only thing that could ever come close to the pain I am feeling right now, watching the love of my life, the woman I desire more than anything, my mate and the only future I will accept, smiling under the arm of another man. She was accepting him. Accepting his touch, his presence, his conversation, and I've been praying for the last several hours that she would just accept my apology.

"Alpha!" Cherum saw me, jogging ahead of the group to meet with me first.

Lira and the man, Cedric, turn to look at me after hearing my Delta call out my name, and the cheerful look that Lira just had fades to the more familiar look of disdain. No smiles and laughter for me. Not a warm greeting. Just a cold look that makes me recoil and makes my lycan whimper like a beaten dog.

"Hey, Alpha. I know you said to bring him, but I have half a mind to throw him back in the sea where he belongs," Cherum looked back disapprovingly at the man being far too familiar with my wife, "I fear that man, that *siren* man, is getting a little too chummy with the lass, and she seems enraptured with her. I don't trust the sirens, Alpha."

A low growl vibrates my chest. "There is *nothing* wrong with being a siren," I snapped. Even in my anxious state and dislike of this new man, I feel defensive of my wife. She is a siren as well as a Lycan, and I will not allow discrimination like that around her.

"But, Alpha, they can manipulate a person. They can make you feel lust or desire, even if you don't wish to feel those things."

They can, but they can not use such power against their own kind, which Lira is. A siren can not manipulate another siren, which makes the scene of my wife being friendly with this man so much harder to take.

"She is safe from such magic, Cherum. You need not worry about that," I mumbled glumly. "He has to stay unharmed. I do not like it any more than you do, but he is vital to my wife staying here and remaining our Luna. I will lose my wife if you try to drive him out, and I can not lose her, do you understand?" I can not lose my mate. Never again.

"No, Alpha, I don't understand, but I will follow your orders nonetheless," he sighed, "Just don't tear the castle apart when you lose her to a bloody fish."

A threatening but quiet growl left me, and Cherum shook his head in disapproval, but didn't say another word.

"Alpha," Percy and Maurice greeted me with a respectful bow of their heads as the group finally reached the gates. I nod back, making note of the way Yasmin is hiding behind Percy's back, and Percy seems to be angling himself to shield her from me. That doesn't hold my attention for long, though.

I focused my eyes on Lira's beautiful emerald ones, lost in their depths as my mind reels for a way to connect with her. I'm trying to think of something to say, anything, to break this tension. I thought she might be scared of me now, but she looks ready to face off with me again, the defiance in her face making her glow more radiantly as her strength shines through.

I was working hard to ignore the man with his arm still draped over her shoulder, knowing my anger and the anger of my lycan may boil over at the smallest thing, and that is not something I need right now. That is not something Lira needs from me. Though I am working hard to ignore him, he chooses not to do the same.

"Alpha," he grinned, holding his free hand out to shake mine.

Lira turned her face away, and I wanted to reach out and force her to hold my gaze longer. I want to rip her out from under this man's arm and bury my face in her sunshine hair, enveloping her in my scent and begging her to never let any other man but me touch her ever again.

I can't do that, though. After this morning, I'm lucky she hasn't yet kicked me in the groin and kissed this man in front of me, just out of spite.

Keeping the distaste off my face is impossible at this point, but I take the man's hand, more firmly than I probably should, and keep his stare, his eyes seeming to mock me and the state I am in with my mate.

"To say it is good to finally meet you may be a bit of a stretch," he said in a velvety but sarcastic voice, "but I am glad that you are cooperating. Thank you for that."

I gritted my teeth, trying not to let the profanities coursing through my head leak out. "Having no choice makes this greeting a little bit more tense than welcoming, but I do hope you enjoy your *long* stay at Hidden Cove Pack." He will not be taking my mate away from me. I will make sure of that, so he had better be ready to stay here the full two years, at the end of which he will be thrown back to the sea, just as Cherum suggested.

"Oh, I plan on enjoying my stay very much," he grinned, then looked down at my wife, who was steadily ignoring me.

Killian snarled at him in my head, and I almost think she heard it, because her neck quickly turned and she glanced worriedly in my direction. I don't know what she sees, but her expression softens for half a moment before she turns her face away again.

My wife. My mate. Please, don't let me suffer like this for too long, because I don't know how much my heart could take.

# TWENTY-THREE

I somehow managed to swallow down the growl building in my chest when Cedric stared down at my wife like she is the very reason for his existence. I wanted to rip that smile off his face, Killian wants me to rip his head off, but I know that isn't the way to get into Lira's good graces.

"While my Delta takes *my wife* to rest in *our* room, why don't you and I take a moment to discuss the arrangements that need to be made for you to stay here for the long term. I can have my Gamma make room for you with the warriors."

Cedric turned that aggravating smirk back towards me, tilting his head to the side. "Princess?" he whispered down to her, "Would you mind terribly if I left your side for a moment to speak with your *husband*."

My lip curled menacingly at the way he says *husband*, like it is an insult to the term. I somehow am able to keep my composure, even watching him whispering intimately in my wife's ear.

Somehow, I don't think he is doing it for any reason other than to antagonize me. I don't believe this man has those kinds of feelings towards my wife, because his actions are clearly a display for me, not an endearment to gain her favor.

No. Lira was not the type to be wooed with suave moves and a pretty face. If that were the case, I would have already gained back the favor of my wife. No. I think the only way to Lira's heart is through actions. Selfless and honorable actions. Cherum has a better chance at stealing my wife from me than some man who is displaying such disrespect as a guest to an Alpha in his territory.

Lira may accept his protection and friendship, but I don't think she will be impressed with this rebellious display.

"By all means," Lira said in a tense response. "Better you than me. I would love to hear more about my *father,"* her eyes flashed angrily towards me for the briefest of seconds before looking away again, "when you are done."

"Of course, my princess," Cedric grinned, then waved his hand to guide her to follow Cherum and the other guards, along with Yasmin, as they began making their way into the castle past the gates.

I watched as Lira walked away, never looking back at either of us. I don't know whether to feel sad for myself, or happy that her affection for the siren ran as deep as her interest in her father.

Shit....

I turned to Cedric after that statement and its implications hit me all at once.

"You told her about her father?!"

He smirked, resting his hands on his hips, making his cape billow out behind him. His exposed chest gleams in the sunlight, almost with a glittering glow.

I may have been upset with Cherum for speaking ill of sirens, but siren men really are the worst. They can use their beauty and charms to manipulate a woman, even without using their magic. Their seductive qualities are a temptation to all weak-willed individuals who look upon them. Being bred from mermaids and the ancient fae kind who are known for their beauty with their succubus or incubus blood, and masters at manipulation and seduction, my pack does not trust them easily. Not with our wars with the demon and dark fae kind of the North. Other packs will form treaties with the siren kings and queens for protection on the seas, but we do not. We have not, at least, until it was needed to bring my mate back.

I know after dealing with King Brennus while trying to bring Lira back from the dead that sirens are not to be feared and can be trusted. Our prejudices are just from fear from our wars, and rumors passed down for generations. That was something our pack will have to overcome after Lira's hybrid abilities come to her on her 20th birthday. I still don't like this guy, though.

"Why wouldn't I?" Cedric challenged me, "I can't tell her everything, but I think the princess deserves to know that her father is watching out for her as best he can under the circumstances. It will help her to not feel abandoned and alone, since those are the only feelings her *husband* seems to bring forth in her."

Killian snarled at the man through me, and I can feel his urge to shift. I'm the one holding him back this time.

*"Lira,"* I reminded him, *"Think of Lira."*

With that reminder, Killian settled down some, but still wants to rip him to shreds. Any Alpha would with another man being that friendly with their mate. We should be commended for keeping our temper this much in check.

"Maybe I wouldn't if I could reveal to my wife that *I* know her father too, and that…." my throat swelled painfully when I tried to mention that I was the one to help bring her back. This damn contract and all its stipulations. I guess mentioning that incident to even one of King Brennus's men is breaking the blood oath.

"That what?" Cedric's smile stretched further on his infuriating face. "That *you*, her abusive and boorish husband, could possibly have helped her to come back from the dead? How do you think that would go over with her? Learning that her rejected mate only fought for her life after her death."

"I DIDN'T JUST FUCKING FIGHT FOR HER THEN!" I roared, letting my anger flare and reaching out to grab him by the throat of his robe. He didn't even flinch, or seem surprised by my outburst. "I fought against her for two years. Two fucking years, only because I wanted her so badly, and because I thought she was a trap sent by Wayne Lambert to keep me from finding my true mate. I wanted her. There was never a day that went by that I didn't. I had to put my pack first, so I did despicable things, not knowing the truth. Now that I do know the fucking truth, I can not even reveal it to her." I shook my head, growling deep in my throat, "I fought so hard, it almost killed me to bring her back. I will be damned if I let your presence ruin this fight for me. I will never stop fighting for her, you greasy scaled fish. Never. If you think you can stop me with your taunting and arrogant attitude, you do not know Lira very well and you sure as hell do not know me." I shove him away from me, a twinge of satisfaction coming to me when he stumbles back with an upset expression. "I am in the fight of my life for my wife and my mate, my pack, my people, and most of all, my heart and very life depend on it. I won't lose her because of you. King Brennus's contract be damned, if he is going to try and take the only woman in the world that could ever be my Luna; if he plans on going back on his word to give me a fighting chance, I will move heaven and hell to keep her here, even if it means going against the king myself."

Cedric stared stoically, watching me for several seconds, then an irritating smirk slowly spread on his face. "Well, that is more like it. For a moment, I was questioning why my King would give an undeserving war-hungry mutt like you a chance at redemption with his daughter. I was all for pushing you to screw up again so I could remove her from here as soon as possible, but I see it now. I see why he decided to give you the chance, however undeserving it might be."

I was panting as I calmed my racing heart from my heated outburst. My eyebrows drew down in confusion.

"Okay, *Alpha*. I am merely here to serve and protect. Your *Luna* is safe from my charming advances. I fear the King would condemn me or send me to hell himself if I were to ever be anything but his daughter's protector. He knows the importance of a mate bond," Cedric looked out towards the sea sadly, "He knows it all too well, and the repercussions of a rejection to one's soul. He did not wish that for his daughter. No matter how unworthy you may be. As long as you do not threaten the safety or well-being of my princess, I can assure you that my motives towards her are pure. I am what is similar to your Delta. The King's descendants are each assigned a personal guard, and I am hers. She will never be a love interest for me," he then smirked, "No matter how charming she may find me."

I scoffed, "Lira can not be won over by charm, fishboy." I shook my head and looked towards the castle, past the gates. "If charm and a pretty face were all I needed to win her heart, I would have it already."

At that, Cedric is the one who scoffed, "Pretty face? You look like your face froze while taking a painful shit. Anger is not a pretty feature."

Killian snarled furiously, making Cedric laugh. "No offense. Well, maybe some offense. I'm still not your biggest supporter of winning my princess's affections. Now," he claps his hands together, "I believe we have some long-term arrangements that need to be made?"

*"Make his long-term arrangements to be in the moldy fish pond behind the horse stable near where they store the manure,"* Killian suggested, making me laugh darkly back at him in my head. I piss in that pond daily. That would be very satisfying indeed.

It would not win me any points with my wife, though.

"Follow me," I muttered, pushing past him and walking around the outskirts of the castle to the training grounds where Meldec would hopefully be. I'm ready to pass this headache off to him and find my wife to start making amends.

"Mel!" I yelled out, walking around the armory and offices for my ranked warriors. "Gamma Meldec!" I roared, getting fed up with looking for him.

I want to get rid of Cedric so I can get back to my wife. His very presence is grating on my limited nerves.

"Do even your commanders hide from you, Alpha?" Cedric mused, "My princess and her handmaiden must not be the only ones."

"Fish pond," Killian repeated, "Better yet, just give him a damn trough. The horses will share."

"I could just put him six feet under," I told my Lycan.

"Oh, I like that idea even better."

Killian and I were lost in my head for a moment, snickering about all the degrading places we could shove our merman guest, when Meldec finally appeared walking out of the warrior's lodging.

"There you are. Where the hell were you?" I growled.

He looked up in surprise, eyeing Cedric for a moment, freezing in his tracts before shaking his head and looking back at me.

"Alpha. I was just sorting out a dispute in the dorms," Mel said gruffly, "Um, Alpha, who's this?"

I sighed heavily, glad to finally be able to rid myself of the fish-smelling pest. "This….gentleman, is a siren warrior who will be staying with us for the next *two years*," I made sure to accentuate the 'two years' bit, "He will be part of the Luna guard, assigned to protect *my wife*. He will be needing a room. Cedric," I turned to address the nuisance, but then scowled when I saw his expression. "Cedric?"

He shook his head, like he's shaking out a distracting thought, the dazed expression he just had morphing back into his annoying, arrogant one. "Yes? Yes, I'm Cedric," he stepped ahead of me, reaching out his hand to shake Mel's, seeming much more friendly than he was with me. He almost seemed excited about meeting my Gamma. "It's great to meet you. Meldec, was it?" he asked, "The pack's Gamma?"

Mel looked nervously at me before taking Cedric's outstretched hand. "Yeah. Hi. Um, Alpha, where do you want me to put Cedric here?"

"Horse trough. No, the steamer room under the castle," Killian suggested eagerly.

"I don't think I would like the scent of steamed fish wafting up to me while I bathe," I snorted.

"Just any open room you can find that is available," I told Mel before I accidentally said one of the suggestions Killian is feeding me. "Get him set up and….maybe some clothes," I grimaced at Cedric's glimmering bare chest. "Help him get anything he needs. I have something to take care of."

"You got it, Alpha," Mel sighed, looking exhausted. With Nilo running around the territory on horseback, pronouncing Lira my one true Luna with news of the festival to be held in her honor, and with Cherum now fulfilling his duties as Delta, taking care of my wife's safety and well-being, most of the stress of organizing the grunt work of running the pack has fallen on him.

"When Nilo gets back, why don't you take some time off, Mel? You look like you could use some time relaxing with your family."

He grinned. "You clearly have never experienced living with 3 sisters. There won't be much relaxing. But, yes. Thank you, Alpha. I will gladly take you up on that offer."

I patted his back, ignoring Cedric's observant gaze, then started walking back toward the main part of the castle to find my wife. The headache has been passed on to someone else, and I'm hoping there are no other obstacles to get in my way.

"Be kind this time. Don't let your damn anger get control of you if she is still upset," Killian warns me.

"It was you wanting to take over to rip apart that siren's face," I scoffed at him.

"I just wanted to make the pretty boy a little less pretty. He was getting too familiar with my mate."

*"Our mate,"* I corrected him.

"No, my mate until she starts accepting you. I don't have to win her over. You do. If it was just me, I feel like I would have already won her back."

"You're a real negative Nancy. You know that?" I growled at him.

"I'm a realist. And you're really an ass."

Lord, if I could, I'd fight my own Lycan for his smart mouth sometimes.

*"You'd lose,"* he mocked me, and I can picture his wolfy smirk.

When I got inside, I ignored the many greetings and empty pleasantries from the members loitering and traveling about while heading straight for Lira's room. When I'm in the hallway, almost there, Percy and Yasmin step out into the hall, and I'm caught off guard for a moment by the way they are looking at each other.

This is different.

"Percy," I muttered deeply to get his attention.

Hearing me, he straightens up, since he was leaning into Yasmin, his forehead pressed to hers. "Alpha," he said in breathless surprise. He pushed a nervous looking Yasmin behind him, slowly, as if he was hoping I wouldn't notice he was doing it. "I was just about to head back to my quarters," he said as way of an explanation. Explanation for what, I do not know. If he wants to take Yasmin back with him, that's his business, not mine. I'm surprised Lira is okay with it after the incident that happened this morning, but it's not my concern what two grown adults do, as long as it doesn't negatively affect my wife.

"That's great," I murmured, trying to keep the boredom at his trivial information out of my tone. "Yasmin, can I speak with you for a moment?"

"Um…," she looked up at Percy nervously, then back at me, "Of course, Alpha."

"Good. If you would follow me, then-"

"Alpha," Percy took a step forward, "I mean no disrespect, but Yasmin has agreed to become my chosen mate, and I don't know if I'm comfortable with a man that was once, uh, involved with her in any way spending time alone with her."

My mouth feels like it has dropped to the floor, and even Killian is stunned inside my head. "What?" I asked, thinking I may not have heard him right.

"Yasmin is to be my chosen mate, Alpha," Percy said a little more firmly, "We were going to get her situated in my quarters. That was where we were about to head. If you need to speak with her about anything, it will have to be in my presence. I'm sorry, Alpha."

After a few seconds, when my shock fades away, a slow smile spreads on my face. This is good. This is different from our first life, but I think Percy taking Yasmin as a mate can only be a positive for everyone.

Percy's mate was killed in the last war, and he grew bitter in my first life, suffering the effects of losing his mate at such a young age. I wonder why he didn't take Yasmin back then as a chosen?

"Congratulations, both of you. Of course, you wouldn't want your mate alone with another man. That is only natural. I was just hoping to apologize for this morning." I turned my gaze on Yasmin. "I was unaware of what had happened to you. After the reception, and then after one of your former colleagues tried to cause problems for me and my wife last night, and not to mention after the warning the Delta put out to all the girls afterward, I assumed your intentions were harmful to my wife and reacted horribly.

"Cherum told me some of what happened to you, and I am deeply sorry you experienced something so painful and cruel. I should have gotten all the facts about the circumstances of you coming here, especially before lashing out, and I'm sorry for that. Was the one responsible for the trauma you faced dealt with?" I asked her, but I looked to Percy for an answer.

He stared down at Yasmin, wrapping a protective arm around her shoulders, then looking back at me. "They were visitors, Alpha. They were just passing through, and were out of the territory before they could be handled."

I groaned, thinking of who it might have been.

"We had visitors for the wedding, but only Wayne Lambert and his men went to the brothel in our last life," Killian reminded me.

"They didn't seriously harm anyone before, though. They were loud and obscene, but didn't cause any major problems."

"We were also there at the brothel, though," Killian said to me, "And if memory serves me right, we were with Yasmin that night."

That's true. Damn, to think doing the right thing by my wife in this life would cause this other woman such grave harm. It makes me feel truly guilty for my actions this morning. Before, I blamed myself more for the way I reacted to Lira. Now, hearing how one decision on my part, even if it was a step towards bettering myself for my mate, could cause someone else's future to change this dramatically, is a humbling fact to discover.

"I truly am sorry, Yasmin. I don't think I could ever find the words to truly express how sorry I am for what you had to endure," I told her.

She smiled slightly, then looks up at Percy and shows a real genuine smile that lights up her whole face. I used to choose her before all the others just because of her easy smile and kind demeanor. She was sweet and unselfish for a prostitute, and most of all, I thought at the time that she looked most like Lira. Nowhere near as beautiful, just the blonde colored hair and light complexion, but I thought her demeanor was much the same.

I don't think that anymore. Yasmin looks weak and mild, like she needs someone to lean to and depend on. That is nothing like my wife, who needs no one to survive in this harsh world. My wife is a fighter, as this morning proves. She was made to be a Luna, which I'm sure is why she was so quick to stand up to me this morning.

She wasn't going to let me, her mate and her Alpha, traumatize someone who had already been through so much. She was made for the role she now bears as my wife, my mate. After apologizing to Yasmin, I can truly say I am proud of my wife's fierce protectiveness and her strength.

I had better figure out how to win her love, because I'm not the only one who needs her. This entire pack, my whole territory needs her. They need a strong and resilient Luna who will fight for them, no matter the odds or who she is up against. I pray she will soon allow me to stand beside her and support her in that fight.

I looked to Percy, "We have trained doctors that can help overcome traumatic experiences. After you get her settled, why don't you take her to have appointments made to see someone? If she is your mate, she receives the same benefits and perks as you, so don't be hesitant to get her the help she needs."

He gave me a perplexed look for a moment, then smiled crookedly. "Thanks, Alpha. We'll do that."

Yasmin was staring up at him, wide-eyed and looking very much infatuated with her new mate. I'm happy for them as they walk away, down the hall to the warrior barracks I just left.

"Mel, if you're still getting things situated in the dorms, can you look into family housing for Percy? He took a chosen mate."

"Yeah, Alpha. I'll see what I can do."

# TWENTY-FOUR

***Elelira***

"Thanks, Alpha. We'll do that," I heard Percy say.

I couldn't believe the conversation I just heard between Lachlan and Yasmin. When I heard Percy say 'Alpha' as the bedroom door began to close, I hurried over to step in and defend Yasmin once again if I needed to. I never expected to hear Lachlan apologize to Yasmin and be so generous and congratulatory about Percy taking her as a chosen mate.

"See. He's different in this life, and he had his reasons," Val told me once again.

I'm still not convinced. I'm sure he is different in this life. That can not be argued. I'm not sure if he is someone I can trust.

"Apologizing to her was a huge sign of humility, Elelira. He's an Alpha, and he clearly had his reasons for acting the way he did towards her. He didn't have to apologize, and he sure didn't have to go out of his way to do it. I half expected him to only apologize to you, and if he did apologize to her, I thought he would do it in front of you so you could witness it."

"I did witness it," I reminded her.

"He doesn't know you did. He sounded genuinely sorry. I bet your stubborn butt isn't the least bit sorry for hitting him," she growls.

"Whose side are you on?" I grumbled.

"Mine," she huffed, "Yours too, if you quit being so stubborn. You don't have to accept the man yet, but you could maybe stop trying to provoke him. Stop expecting the worst out of him. If that's all you are waiting for, that's all you are going to see."

"Did you forget that he knew of my father and chose not to tell me?" I reminded her.

"Ask him about it!" she exclaimed, "Don't assume he didn't tell you because he didn't want to. Ask him about it before you start going on another tirade about him being the worst. He didn't sleep with anyone else last night, he has tried to be more than kind to you up until the moment you slapped him. He has just proven his character out there in the hall while speaking with that woman. He didn't even lose his head when you allowed that siren man to put his hands all over you."

"I hardly think his placing an arm around my shoulder can be described as putting his hands all over me," I said defensively.

"He was naked and you were hanging on the man in a very inappropriate way, Ela," Val scolded me, "You didn't discourage his behavior in front of our mate either. We have already established that this Lachlan is different, and you are doing to him what the other Lachlan did to you in our first life. You are the one hurting him this time, Elelira, and I think it's about time that you quit using our previous life as an excuse to shun our mate like the old Lachlan did to us."

She's right. It's obvious that this is not the same timeline as before. This is not the same Lachlan as before. I am treating him poorly and punishing him for things he hasn't even done.

Just then, Lachlan stepped in front of the cracked door and noticed me peeking out. He looked surprised for a moment, then a guilty expression spread on his handsome face.

I stood frozen, feeling awkward having been caught eavesdropping. After a few seconds of awkward silence, Lachlan asked, "Lira, uh, can I, um, come in?"

I bit my lip nervously, then nodded, moving aside to open the door further for him to come in. He smiles, breathing out a sigh of relief that I didn't say no, I'm guessing, then comes into the room.

"Where are Cherum and Niomi?" He asked.

My body's inclination when he asks me a question is to go numb and wait for him to be done talking to me or berating me. For our whole previous marriage, that's what I had to do to survive. To not go mad with my pain and sorrow. What Val told me, though, is still echoing in my head. This is not the same Lachlan as before. This Lachlan keeps trying to connect with me, and I'm just building my walls higher and higher each and every time.

Maybe I really do need to give him a chance?

"The Gamma went to the kitchens to retrieve some tea and snacks. He insisted it was time for me to eat again, though I assured him I was not hungry."

For some reason, this made Lachlan smile, and my apprehension towards him leaves me a bit more as his smile transforms his face, making it look impossibly more handsome while also appearing much less threatening.

"Mimi is still getting her room settled," I bit my lip, hesitating for a moment before I said this next thing. "Thank you. For granting her that bedroom. I'm glad she will be so close to me now."

"Of course," he grinned, scratching the back of his neck like he was nervous. "I checked in on her earlier. She seemed to be happy with the arrangement too."

"You checked in on her?" I asked in disbelief.

He shrugged. "She is assigned to help the most important person in my life. I think she deserves some perks for being up to the task."

"See," Val squealed excitedly, "he isn't the same thoughtless and cruel Lachlan."

She's right. The previous Lachlan didn't care about me, and sure as can be didn't care for Mimi. This Lachlan really isn't the same man I held so much disdain for in my previous life. I suddenly feel guilty that I am harboring hatred for an innocent man.

My cheeks felt hot from hearing him call me the most important person in his life, and my eyes drift to the ground, not knowing how to react or what to say back. I have never had someone show me favoritism or praise me before.

"You could just tell him 'thank you'," Val rolled her eyes at me.

"Thank you," I told him, still staring at the ground.

"You're welcome," he said to me softly, and we just stood in that awkward silence again, neither of us knowing what else to say. I started to gnaw on my lip harder, feeling anxiety at the prolonged silence and not knowing how to proceed. What are we to do now?

"Lira," he whispered, and I saw his feet take a step closer to me.

I looked up at him through my lashes only to see a pained expression on his face and his hands flexing at his side, like he was restraining himself from touching me.

"About this morning, I was wrong in the way I reacted. I should have found out what was going on before I behaved so appallingly. Not to mention, before I said such harsh things and acted so violently towards you. I have a bit of a temper, I always have, but that is no excuse for my actions this morning. I am truly sorry for scaring you the way I did."

I bit my lip even harder, unsure of what to say. Slowly, Lachlan raises his hand, making it very clear to me what his intentions are, before he cups my face, and uses his thumb to free my lip from my teeth. His thumb grazes over my bottom lip a few times, and then my chin, before he slowly lowers his hand back to his side. My skin is buzzing from the bond, and Valerina is mewling in my head, wanting more.

I don't know if I can handle any more with all these confusing feelings and thoughts swirling in my head. No matter if this is a different Lachlan, I still needed time to get over what felt like happened only yesterday.

I can apologize, though. He wasn't the only one who reacted badly this morning.

"I'm sorry as well. I should never have hit you or insulted you in front of your pack in such a public way."

His chest heaved, breathing deeply in excitement or relief, I do not know. Maybe both. A stunning smile lifts his whole face, making his usual scowl all but disappear.

"You never have to apologize to me, Lira. Never. I deserved far worse for my behavior."

A small, nervous smile lifts the corners of my mouth, but then the question of my father and Lachlan's knowledge of him comes to me again.

"Alpha?" I meekly murmured.

"Lachlan, Lira. I am your husband. Please just call me Lachlan. You never have to be formal with me."

I bit my lip again, unsure if I am comfortable calling him by name out loud. Leona addressed him so familiarly, but it was ingrained in me in my last life that I was never to be familiar or take those liberties with him. It may take me some time to get over those habits.

"Okay," I whispered, not ready to call him by name out loud while I was feeling so vulnerable. "Would you like to have tea with me? I have a question I want to ask you."

He grinned brightly. "Nothing would make me happier, Lira. Thank you."

"Ela, I brought the, uh...," Cherum stopped mid-speech as he walked past the door to the parlor in my bed chambers to find Lachlan and I sitting at the cozy table at the center of the room. "Alpha? I didn't expect to see you here," he stated, looking worriedly at me, as if he was gauging if I was okay with this situation I put myself in. Not that he knows that I was the one who invited Lachlan to stay. He probably assumed that I was being forced into this arrangement.

"I invited him for tea, Cherum," I smiled reassuringly at him, "Thank you for bringing it." Cherum sighed deeply, looking much relieved, then smiled as he continued walking towards the table and set the tea tray down in front of me. There are two cups turned upside down on the tray, along with a covered teapot and a plate piled high with cookies and pastries. I know he had every intention of joining me, but with Lachlan here, he sets the extra tea cup in front of Lachlan instead.

"Good to see you here, Alpha. I was just about to call one of the other guards to come be with the Luna while I went to take care of some business. You've saved me the trouble." Looking over at Lachlan, I could tell by the tension in his neck that he was nervous. What he has to be nervous about, I have no idea. I'm nervous. I'm about to ask the man about my father. I don't want to fight with Val and I really don't want to hurt her, but I'm still thinking the worst about Lachlan and the reasons he has to keep my father from me. I'm trying not to, but I just can't think of any logical reason why he wouldn't tell me my father was the one to give me the necklace.

"Thanks, Cherum," Lachlan mumbled, taking one of the small plates from his hands before Cherum could set it down in front of him like he did for me. "I think we got it from here."

"Sure you do, Alpha. Well," he looked to me for confirmation to make sure I really am okay being left alone with my husband. I nodded once again and smiled. "Guess I'll go take care of that, um, thing I had to do. You both have a good talk now. Call for me if you need me, lass."

"I will. Thank you," I waved at him, then looked at my lap, playing with my fingers nervously. What now? How do I bring up the issue of my father?

"Whatever you do or say, keep an open mind, Ela. Please," Val begged me.

"*For you,*" I told her. I will keep my composure and try not to let my pessimism show, but only for her.

"*Killian too,*" she growled, being defensive of her mate, which made me smile.

*"Okay, Val. For Killian too."* Val's desperation for her mate has grown substantially over the last 24 hours. I really need to figure out how to work through my issues because of my past life for her sake. I don't know if I can keep them apart now.

"Lira?" Lachan's deep voice caused me to look up at him. He is leaning over the table, reaching to take the cloth cover off the pot of tea and then picks it up by the handle. It's an odd sight seeing this very brusqued, burly man holding a delicate china teapot. "Do you want some?"

Gosh, I should have been the one to serve. I was the one that invited him. Thankfully, he doesn't look at all offended. He just looked at me expectantly while waiting for my answer.

"Yes, thank you," I nodded, hurrying to turn my cup over.

He smiled while clumsily filling my cup, leaving no room for milk or sugar. I am sure he has never done this for anyone else before. After he finishes pouring his own, he sets the pot back on the tray and lifts a couple of sugar cubes with the tongs, offering them to me.

I shook my head, fighting a smile, knowing how embarrassed he would be if he did put the sugar cubes in my cup. It would overflow and make a mess on the table.

He goes to put them in his own cup, and that's exactly what happens, making him jump back in alarm. His chair falls to the ground and he grumbles, "Shit," while trying to avoid the tea that is now dripping down the table's edge.

I couldn't stop myself. My laughter began to bubble out of me, but I quickly tried to cover my mouth to stop it. Lachlan's awkwardly annoyed face looked at me for a few seconds before his own deep, throaty laughter began to spill out.

"Sorry," he groaned, still smiling while rubbing the back of his neck in embarrassment, "I guess I overfilled my cup."

I pressed my lips together while I regained enough of my composure to reply. This is definitely not the same Lachlan I remember. He's flustered and it makes him look quite adorable.

"I'm sorry to you," I managed to say, "I invited you. I should have been the one to serve."

He picked up one of the folded tea towels on the side of the tray and began to mop up his mess on the floor while I dabbed at the table with my towel, cleaning up the small puddle. I lifted his tea cup slowly and carefully to prevent more from spilling out, and then sipped enough so he was no longer in danger of spilling before setting it back down, a lot further from the edge than before.

When I looked back up, he was watching me with fascination, and the look on his face made my face heat in embarrassment.

Gosh, I just drank from his glass without thinking. He probably won't want it now.

"I'm sorry. I can trade you cups," I offered.

"Oh, no," he was quick to take the cup and lift it from the table. "I want this one now, more than ever."

If my blush wasn't showing before, it definitely was now. I quickly looked down to try to hide it, nervously playing with my fingers again, but peeked up a few seconds later to see him drinking from the cup in the same spot where my lips just touched. He doesn't even appear to be drinking it. It's like he is just savoring the feeling of the glass against his lips.

"Just the way I like it," he murmured, setting the cup back down and then righting his chair so he can take his seat.

"*Tell me that* that *wasn't adorable,*" Val gushed, swooning in my head over our mate.

"Stop. I can't stop blushing as it is."

"That was like he was kissing you indirectly. So cute!"

"*Val, stop,*" I told her, biting my lips to stop me from grinning.

"Sorry," he husked, and when I looked up, his face was bright red too, "That was probably weird. Shit, I can't get anything right," he groaned.

"No," I whispered, "It wasn't, um, weird. Well, maybe a little, but it was, um, cute," I managed to say, "My Lycan was just telling me that she thought that was cute."

"Yeah, act like I was the only one," Val teased me.

"I couldn't help myself," Lachlan murmured in a deep voice, "I could still see the imprint of your lips on the edge."

"Oh my gosh! I don't care what he did this morning, that just made up for it. Absolutely heart-poundingly, adorable."

My lycan was getting a bit too excited about Lachlan just drinking out of a cup after me. You would think he had just ripped his shirt off and spilled tea down the front of his bare chest with the way she was gushing over him. Her excitement must be bleeding into me, because even I was having a hard time not finding Lachlan's behavior quite charming.

It has to be the influence of the mate bond….

"Mmh," I hummed awkwardly, not able to think of any way to respond to his comment about my lip print. Well, Val was feeding me a few things to say, but I would never let any of her suggestions leave the privacy of our mind.

"Sorry," he groaned deeply, "I'm probably making you feel more uncomfortable, aren't I?"

"No," I smiled shyly, "I was just caught off guard."

He groaned again, "Lord, I'm such a creep." I shrugged, letting a giggle slip out.

"A cute creep," I muttered under my breath, then covered my mouth quickly, realizing I said that thought out loud.

When I looked up, Lachlan was staring at me wide-eyed and with an expression that was full of surprise. His gaped mouth slowly started to quirk up into a truly radiant smile.

"Cute?" he repeated, "You think I'm cute?"

I pressed my lips together to keep my inner thoughts inside, feeling my cheeks light up as his smile stretches further on his handsome face.

"I think you're cute too. Beautiful, actually," he told me, "The most beautiful woman I have ever seen."

"You mean for a whore?" I let slip out, then regretted it instantly. Val was growling and snarling at me for ruining the mood as Lachlan's face fell. "I'm sorry. I shouldn't have said that. I said things I shouldn't have this morning as well."

He scratched the back of his neck again, looking uncomfortable. "You didn't say anything that was not true, Lira. I was the one out of line. I'm sorry that I said that. I really didn't mean it. At that moment I just….I don't know. I got defensive easily and it slipped out before I could stop myself. Killian was trying to make me stop, but I lost my head." He looked deep into my eyes, making my heart beat rapidly in my chest. "I'm sorry Lira. I really, truly am."

I smiled slightly, feeling guilty for making him apologize again.

"I told you, it was my fault too. I should not have hit you like that." I gulped, taking a deep breath before I continued, "I do want to ask one thing."

"What is it?" he sat forward, eyebrows drawn down in concern.

"This necklace," I lifted it from under the neck of my dress and held it up for him to see, "Where did it come from?"

# TWENTY-FIVE

***Lachlan***

I knew this was coming, but my stomach still drops to the floor when Lira asks me that question.

"The necklace?" I repeated her question, anxiety eating at me. How do I tell her with the damn blood oath in place? I feel my throat closing up just thinking about telling her about her father. "Didn't, uh, Cedric tell you?"

She pressed her lips together, staring at me pensively for a moment. "He did. He told me that my father was the one that told you to give it to me. Is that true?"

Thank goodness she asked a yes or no question. Open-ended questions seem to be where I get hung up on the oath. "Yes," I murmured, pleading with her with my eyes not to be mad at me. We were just caught in the first decent moment where we were both laughing so carefree, almost like the events of this morning hadn't happened.

"Why didn't you tell me?" she whispered, looking disheartened.

This is going to be the hard part. How do I tell her without telling her that I couldn't tell her? "Quit talking in riddles and just try to get her to answer her own questions," Killian tells me, "Ask questions back or be just vague enough to where she asks the questions more directly. She knows about her father. If you need to, just tell her to ask the fish since he won't be held to the same oath as you." Killian was coming to the forefront of my mind, ready to take over for me if I got overwhelmed or started to panic.

"I couldn't," I simply told her. It's the truth, and also isn't forbidden by the blood oath.

"You couldn't," she furrowed her golden eyebrows, making an adorable little 'v' between her eyes. "Did he tell you not to?"

I rubbed my hands over my thighs nervously, then nodded before looking up at her through my lashes. Screw Cedric. If he could have just explained everything to her, then I wouldn't be in this predicament. He probably wanted her to be more mad at me, though, so he didn't tell her everything on purpose. Stupid fish. Her father sure didn't seem to mind the thought of taking her from me early either. Cedric could have helped explain a bit if he really thought mate bonds were important.

"Why would he do that?" she asked, "Why couldn't you tell me? Did he want to hide himself from me?"

"I truly don't know," I muttered softly, tensing with every word in fear the oath would stop me from speaking. "I….I just did what I was told."

She looked down at her hands again, that bottom lip she has a habit of chewing on and abusing being gnawed on once again by her top teeth. "Did my father not want me to know about him? Did he….did he not want to see me?"

"No, Lira," I quickly went to her, kneeling on the ground before her and taking her hands in mine. Killian warned me a half a second too late not to scare her again by touching her or approaching her too fast, but luckily she didn't pull away frightened. She looked so somber and mournful about her father that it hurts me to see her like that. I went to her without even thinking. "I don't think it was that. I think Cedric can answer those questions better than I can, but I truly don't believe that that is the case. Why give you something that was meant to protect you if he didn't care?"

She smiled sadly, "Cedric said something similar. I just….I just don't understand why you wouldn't tell me that the necklace came from him. If he wants to protect me, then why not take me with him?"

My throat swelled and my heart raced, but it was not from the blood oath. It's from fear at hearing that she still wants to leave me and escape with her father. Killian is mewling like a kicked puppy in my head, his pain just as evident as mine.

"I don't want you to leave me, Lira. I don't want him to take you," I told her honestly.

She looked startled for a moment. "Is that why you didn't tell me about my father?"

"What? No. I really just couldn't. I'm not…I'm not allowed to." I almost breathed a sigh of relief that I could actually say that statement.

She gave me a dubious look. "You're not allowed to? How can he ban you from telling me? Did he use magic or something to prevent you from saying something? Because I don't see how someone could *not allow* you to do anything, Alpha."

I stared up at her brilliant emerald eyes, lost in the fire in them for a moment. Even her anger is beautiful.

"That's exactly it, Lira."

She startled slightly, looking down at me wide-eyed. "He used magic on you?" she asked, and I nodded. "So, it's not that you didn't tell me, but you couldn't?"

Again, I just nodded, praying that she would believe me. I hope that my little progress with her doesn't backslide again. I don't know if my heart could take much more.

"Okay," she whispered, gripping my hands back.

"Okay?" I repeated. "You believe me?"

The left corner of her mouth turned up a bit, and she nodded. "My Lycan told me that if I tried to blame you for something that isn't your fault again she was going to sing old-time ballads off key on repeat in my head for the next two years."

I laughed breathlessly, feeling relieved that her Lycan is at least sticking up for me. I felt like I was fighting against everyone in my damn castle to get closer to Lira. It's great to know that the one who is closest to her and constantly with her is arguing my case.

"*She's my mate. She said it for my sake, dumb butt. Of course she's going to fight for me. I'm not a dumbass like you,*" Killian said, but I know he is teasing me. He's boasting with pride to hear about Val telling Lira not to blame me."

"Thank you, Val," I grinned, rubbing my thumbs on the back of Lira's hands. Her eyes twinkle and I know it's Val watching. A deep purr came from Lira's chest, making her blush. My smile was so big that it felt like it was about to break my face.

Lira giggled, and the sound made me want to sing. Actually, it makes me want to do anything I can to hear the sound again, including spilling tea all over the front of me over and over again if that is what it takes.

She looked down at our hands and shivered slightly.

The mate bond. Hell, I couldn't wait to experience the sparks and tingles that came with the mate bond too. I kept running my thumbs on the back of her hands and watched her body shift and her face contort each and every time. The bond is getting to her. Now that her walls aren't as high up and she isn't fighting me, the mate bond is working its magic on her.

I might have a chance to win her over after all.

"Earn it," Killian growled at me, "You don't win her. Earn the right to receive her love. I won't tolerate you manipulating the mate bond she feels to weasel your way in. You earn her. Do it the right way, Lachlan."

"I know, jerk. I'm just saying, it's nice to know the mate bond can affect her. I'll still be working my ass off to be a man worthy of her love."

I have to. She still has thoughts of going back to the sea with her father. I can't let that happen. I can't lose her. If she chooses her father over me, I would be powerless to stop it.

"Thank you for having tea with me," she whispered softly, "I feel better about things after talking to you."

A smile erupted on my face, "I'm glad. I want you to always feel like you can talk to me."

She smiled shyly, her eyelashes fluttering nervously, making her emerald eyes sparkle like jewels. "I'll try," she murmured, "You are my husband, after all."

I wish she had said mate. If she had said mate, I could have agreed and then the biggest secret, well, one of the biggest secrets I'm being forced to keep from her, would be out in the open and maybe our mate bond could grow even more. Maybe all this fighting against myself could end because the blood oath wouldn't have as strong of a hold on me.

But she said husband, and all I can do is agree to that term for now.

"Well, *wife,*" I grinned at the term, while wishing I could say mate, "What do you say to a walk around the castle grounds before dinner?"

She smiled beautifully at that, "Sounds lovely."

~

***Elelira***

"*Thank you,*" Val whispered to me in my head.

She was happy that I gave Lachlan a chance to explain himself a little, and I didn't start accusing him of the worst-case scenario right off the bat. I wanted to, but the connection between Killian and Val in the bond is undeniable. That's the only explanation for why I was feeling the way I was towards Lachlan. Why I was getting flustered with all of his actions and why I couldn't bring myself to fully hold on to my negativity and wariness towards him.

Maybe if our Lycans had met in our first life our marriage could have been like this. Maybe that's what is different in this life compared to the other.

This life, I wasn't an annoyingly eager blushing bride with high expectations staring down the aisle at our wedding when we first met. I was the complete opposite. I know I was cold and indifferent, and I will not apologize for that. I think I had the right to be after what I had been through in what felt like just hours before waking up here. I would have to be insane to be eager to repeat the past all over again. I was leery and distant, wishing for nothing but to escape.

Maybe that is why he didn't write me off right then, thinking I was nothing more than my uncle's pawn. Because I wasn't eager for this. Then, with the reception, my indifference and disappearance may have intrigued him enough to find out why I had left, and then last night, our Lycans meeting for the first time. Maybe, just maybe, his Lycan felt a bit of the fated mate bond that connects us.

If Killian is longing for Val like Val is longing for him, then I can not separate the two of them. Not yet, anyway. Not unless Lachlan gives me a reason to.

"*He won't,*" Val tried to reassure me, and I wanted to believe her, but my first life was still fresh in my mind. "*He's different. You saw him.*"

"I saw him, alright. He is a perpetual playboy, remember. That was suave and made my heart flutter, as I'm sure it did many other women in the past."

Val snorted, "I'm sure he didn't have to work that hard to flatter the women he was PAYING to have relations with him. The money was all the flattery they needed."

"That's why that woman of the night was calling him by a nickname and not Alpha," I reminded her, "Because it was simply money and acts they were exchanging."

"Quit being a sourpuss. My goodness. We are getting a second chance, and maybe we are meant to use it to be happy with our mate this time," Val nagged me.

"*Maybe,*" I muttered, but still don't want to cling to the hope flaring in my chest.

Lachlan showed me around the castle, and instead of showing me the regular grounds, he surprised me by showing me a plot that overlooked the sea that he said he was planning on building a family suite for us on;

somewhere new to begin our marriage and life together the right way.

At the term 'family', Val became giddy like a schoolgirl inside me. My face and neck heated at the thought of what 'family' was insinuating, but I still refused to hope for that kind of future for us. I can't even imagine him and I being intimate with one another. I know I said I was willing to keep Mimi with me, but now that I know Lachlan won't force me, I don't know if I could force myself.

When we came to the cliff's edge, I looked out towards the sea. Longing and hope then crept into my heart, and I let it. Hope that my father was out there and he was watching over me, caring for me from afar. My fingers linger over the necklace from him. He sent this to protect me. He must care for me. Cedric said as much, didn't he?

And where is Cedric? I hope Lachlan's Gamma is being nice to him.

Lachlan's face became panicked, watching me staring vacantly at the sea, as I was no longer listening to his plans for the addition to the castle. He broke my thoughts, urging me back towards the regular castle grounds. He tried to cover his frenzied state by talking endlessly about Beta Nilo, telling me about a mission he was currently on, carrying the news of our marriage throughout the territory. I thought that was something that had already been done, and I couldn't focus much on the specifics of his conversation.

I tried to listen intently, but the close proximity we were walking in made the mate bond buzz with need inside me. It wasn't like this yesterday. I almost wish I could go back to being cold and indifferent, putting my walls back up, no matter how much it might annoy Val, because when I was clinging to the numbness that brought, the mate bond was easier to ignore.

My skin was itching with the need to touch him, but I won't give in. I can't. The thought of touching him in the way the bond is urging me to, the intimacy that would involve, makes goosebumps break across my skin. My heart pounded in my ears, making fully comprehending anything Lachlan is saying almost impossible.

I almost wilted with relief when I saw Cherum in the great hall where dinner was to be served until the dining hall could be repaired. Lachlan didn't miss the way I hurried to Cherum, gripping one of his arms with both hands like it was a lifeline. I had to hurry and tell him that I was just exhausted from walking around so much today, which was followed by Lachlan asking forgiveness repeatedly for not noticing.

Cherum's warm hand placed on my back was like a balm that soothed my anxieties away. It did little to calm the mate bond, though. For that, I truly believe that touching Lachlan may be the only way to sate the bond's need for him. Maybe not fully sate it with his still unclaimed and being so close to me for so long, but it would calm the itch that was nagging at me.

As dinner began to be served, I sat beside Lachlan, hoping he couldn't hear my heart racing when he pushed my chair in for me. The bond was fully awake and urged me to just reach out for him. Val was not helping the matter, begging for much the same.

When he took the chair beside me, I reached out and gripped his sleeve, unable to deny the bond or my Lycan any longer. He looked surprised for a moment, but smiled brilliantly before taking my hand, kissing my palm, then placing our interlocked fingers in his lap.

The bond instantly calmed with that, though my Lycan was anything but calm. She was leaping for joy inside my head. The sparks and electric waves traveling through my hand from his touch made her buzz with excitement.

Lachlan's tender action, and I'm sure my blushing features, didn't go unnoticed by those at our table or anyone in the room, for that matter. Cherum, who had just moments ago worried about the reasons for my relief at seeing him when we first came to the great hall, looked relieved that Lachlan really wasn't the cause of my minor distress. He was the cause, but not for the reasons he was most likely thinking. The people around us looked relieved as well, probably having felt anxious to see us together after the scene we caused this morning.

Lachlan looked happier than I had ever seen him before. He kept smiling over at me, rubbing his thumb on the back of my hand, using his other hand to rub my arm, scooting his chair closer to me so he would have better reach.

That was how Cedric and Meldec found us when they finally joined us to eat.

Cedric frowned at the way Lachlan was holding my hand and massaging my arm. Gamma Meldec looked confused, but I don't think it was because of us. He was frowning and furrowing his brows every time he looked at Cedric, which was often. I guess the Gamma is wary of fae races, just like most people in this pack. That's too bad. It doesn't make me want to let them know I'm half siren too, any more than before.

The meal was pleasant enough. Cherum informed me that Yasmin would need some time to adjust, seeing as Percy wanted to make her his chosen mate right away. I thought Lachlan might be displeased to hear one of his old flings was now permanently closed for business. He seemed happy for them though, and that just had Val reiterating that she really didn't believe that this was the same Lachlan from before.

Too much had changed in this life from my first one, and I so wanted to believe her. The evidence for her statement was irrefutable, but I still have a hard time accepting it. I don't know why.

# TWENTY-SIX

Lachlan and his men, including Cherum, had to hold some meeting on Nilo's return to the castle, so Cedric eagerly volunteered to go for an after-dinner walk with me. Maurice and Thomas followed at a distance to keep me safe.

Lachlan tried to refuse Cedric on my behalf, thinking I was still tired, but I reassured him that I was fine, feeling better after eating. I wanted to talk with Cedric alone. I had so many questions about my father.

"You and the Alpha seemed to be on much friendlier terms," Cedric told me, sounding almost amused as we walked alongside one another along the docks.

I huffed out a laugh in the back of my throat, not sure how to respond. I'm not sure if we are on friendlier terms or if the bond and my lycan are just that much of an influence on me now.

I'm scared. I'm scared because I clung to hope for so long in my first life that things could be better if I could just get a moment alone with Lachlan to tell him we were mates. I think keeping my heart open and holding onto hope is what hurt my bond more in my first life. Building that wall around myself helped to numb the bond and helped everything Lachlan did to not hurt me as sharply. Now that the bond was open, and Val was insisting that I keep my heart and mind open too, I'm scared that I will just hurt more later.

"Are you not?" Cedric asked, flinging one of his arms around my shoulder, pulling me to his side. Val growled, but I think it's more of a friendly gesture from Cedric. It felt almost brotherly and made me feel a bit less worried that I could go back to suffering alone.

"I'm not sure," I told him honestly. "We've been married for not even two days. I feel like I don't even know him."

It's true enough. This Lachlan is nothing like the Lachlan I know from before. Tea today and then how he acted at dinner proved it.

Cedric scoffed, "I think you know him well enough."

"Why do you say that?" I asked, tilting my face up to study him.

"Oh, just because," he grinned crookedly, "What more is there to know? He's your typical primitive Alpha dog."

"Hey," I frowned at Cedric when Val growled at the insult in my head. "I'm a half primitive dog too."

"You are far from primitive or a dog, princess," he chuckled.

"None of the people here are. You shouldn't talk that way when you are a guest in this castle."

He offers me a guilty smile. "You are right. Forgive my rudeness, my princess."

"I'll forgive you if you tell me more about my father," I covertly changed the topic to the subject I wanted to talk about.

He chuckled, not a fool at my intentions. He sighed, looked back to make sure we were out of earshot of my guards, then looked out to the sea. "Your father is a strong and powerful siren. That is why he can't come to retrieve or reveal himself to you yet. Many enemies would use you to hurt him. Some in quite horrendous ways. I know he left you to your *husband* because he believed the Alpha, along with your ignorance of your father, was the safest option to keep you hidden from his enemies until you gained your fins."

"Just like what our mate said," Val said smugly in our mind.

I internally rolled my eyes at her and continued asking my questions. "When did he learn about me? How did he know I was his daughter?" If he'd never met me, I don't see how he could have confirmed who I was, and I'm questioning how he even learned of my existence."

"Hmm. I know it was not long ago. I'm not sure of all the details. Your father is a private person. I merely do what I'm told, only getting the information he offers me. I do know he would have come from you sooner had he known about you. He would probably have taken your mother from your previous pack, along with you, if he learned of your existence when she was alive."

"Why do you think that?" I looked up at him confused. Did he care for my mother? I know she was forced to entertain visiting delegates and dignitaries from visiting kingdoms at times, she was forced to do worse often too, but none were ever mentioned specifically. She didn't even tell me about my siren lineage until Val came to me when I was going through puberty. I think she was trying to shield me from any knowledge of my true father. Whenever the topic came up, she would just urge me to keep my siren identity hidden. She said once I turned 20, I could escape to the sea and finally be free of the cruelty on land, something she sadly wished she could do too.

"Because I just know." That's all he said, as if it was as simple an answer as that.

"Thanks for elaborating," I snorted.

"You're very welcome," he grinned cheekily, making me laugh.

He turned and stared at the sea again, letting out a heavy sigh. I watched his features for a few minutes, and I recognized the same longing on his face that crosses mine whenever I get lost in the majesty of the open water with its dancing waves and glittering surface.

"Do you miss it?" I whispered, breaking him from his trance.

He turned his head slowly, offering me a sad smile. "Nothing compares to the feeling of freedom you get in the briny deep, where even gravity can't restrict you. A siren out of water is like a bird without wings. You can survive, but you will always long for it, the ability to soar."

I grinned at him, then we both stared at the sea. He turns us to face it, and I inhale the briny air, imagining it was the salty water entering my gills. The wind blowing my hair back from my face, I can almost pretend it is the currents rushing past as I soar through the water with the dolphins and fish.

I miss it, and really do long to soar once again.

"What do you do when you miss it?" I asked in a hushed whisper.

He chuckled lightly, pulling me closer to his side and gently kissing the top of my head. "I guess we will find out. I've never been out of the water for an extended period of time before. I will have to learn to adjust, it seems. I will have to placate myself with brief swims in the bay."

I smiled sadly, knowing that wouldn't compare to the deep waters in the center of the ocean. "Why don't we go for a dip tomorrow? I wouldn't mind a swim."

"Will your husband approve of you entering the water?"

"Ha. Like he has any authority to tell me I can't."

Cedric chuckled at my defiant attitude. "I doubt that man would tell you no anyway. He would likely drop all his work to adhere to your wishes and take a swim with you."

My face heated at the idea of swimming with Lachlan. I didn't feel any embarrassment at the thought of swimming with Cedric, but swimming with Lachlan, both of us in minimal clothing, where modesty is not attainable without risk of drowning, makes the nagging bond flare in my chest again.

"Because you find him attractive. As you should. He's your mate," Val huffed.

"You would have to be blind to not find Lachlan attractive. That's not it. Cedric's attractive too. It's just the bond making me feel this way, and you being an insistent pest."

"Insistent pest or not, you know deep down why you feel shy with our mate and not the smooth-talking fish," Val rolled her eyes at me, annoyed with my denial.

"What is this?" Cedric smiled crookedly down at me, his perfect teeth glistening in the moonlight. "Do we have a blushing bride, shy about swimming with her husband?"

"No," I lied, pushing him away and scowling at him.

"We do," he grinned, teasing me, "Is my princess too shy to ask her husband to take a dip in the water with her? If you want some alone time with him for more intimate moments, I could wander off into the deeper parts of the bay."

"Intimate moments will not occur, so that will not be necessary." I cringed, just imagining the panic attack that could cause. Holding hands may be fine, but the things Cedric is insinuating are not possible for me. That's another reason I don't want to get my hopes up with Lachlan. If he gets tired of waiting for me to be ready for that kind of relationship, he may again turn his affections elsewhere.

Cedric stared at me for a few moments, all the teasing gone from his face. "Are you afraid of being intimate with your husband, Princess?"

Even using the endearment of *princess*, I could feel the seriousness of his question. I felt like he was asking me something more than just inquiring about the intimacy in my marriage.

"I'm afraid that is too personal of a question, Cedric. One you need not worry about."

His stare continued, then he sighed heavily before looking around at the guard and then the sea. After a while, he turned back around to face me.

"If anyone were to ever hurt you, I would deal with them, princess. I can promise you that. Even if it's the rabid Alpha that you married, I would put him down if he ever hurt you or forced you to do something you were not ready for."

"I appreciate that, but I promise you that Lachlan has never hurt me. Not in the ways you are insinuating. He has never laid a hand on me. That is why I said intimacy is not to be expected."

He stared right into my eyes, not holding back and being straightforward with his next question. "Has he hurt you in other ways, Elelira?"

I pressed my lips together, not knowing how to answer. "Not yet," was all I said. That's all I could say. He had hurt me, but again, it wasn't this Lachlan. It was the one from my first life. "And I can only hope he won't," I whispered, more for me than him.

*"He won't,"* Val told me, but I can feel her uncertainty. She is certain of her mate, but I can feel in her tone now that she is still unsure of mine, no matter how much she tries to say otherwise.

"He won't," Cedric said out loud, repeating the words my Lycan just said while coming forward and taking hold of my shoulders. "No one can hurt you with me by your side."

A small, unsure smile appeared on my face. "I believe I can handle myself." I did in the past. I know how to overcome any misfortune that may befall me in this life. Nothing could be worse than what I suffered at the end of my last one.

"I believe you can too, but you are not alone, princess. Use the tools you are being given when you need them."

"Are you calling yourself my tool?" I smirked at him, trying to lighten the mood.

He smiled at my teasing, "I will be whatever you need."

~

***Lachlan***

"Did you reach all the villages in the territory?" I asked my Beta, who was kicking back in a chair in the armory, drinking a beer by the fire and scarfing down leftover stew.

He just got back and I wanted a debrief as soon as possible so I could get back to Lira. The afternoon with her has been so great and I just want to retire for the evening, not having to worry about work again until tomorrow.

*"I want to brush her hair,"* Killian had been pestering me. He wants to have some kind of contact with our mate too. He was jealous of me holding hands with her all through dinner.

*"Let's get this done, then we can ask."* I don't think Lira will mind as long as Killian agrees to not kissing her again.

"Yes, Alpha. Jeez. I did exactly as you asked, and now the whole territory is so excited about this festival that we have yet to finish planning."

"Did you even start planning it?" Meldec asked. "I thought you just had the idea. I didn't know it was a sure thing."

"Of course it's a sure thing," Cherum pushed his shoulder. "She's our Luna. It needs to be celebrated that our Alpha has finally found her."

"Yes, it does," I grinned, "I just want to shout it from the bell tower."

"Look at you, all smitten," Cherum chuckled, "Funny how much your attitudes changed after a mere tea party. I think I should get a raise for my excellent tea-making skills."

I laughed, unable to hide my happiness. "I'm feeling generous enough to almost grant that request."

They all chuckled. "I thought your marriage was doomed after this morning. I'm glad you overcame the incident so quickly," Meldec says.

"What incident?" Nilo asked.

"I'll tell you later," Cherum sighed. "He's finally in a decent mood. Let's not ruin that now."

No. Let's not. Shame still fills me each time the image of her frightened face flashes in my head.

That reminds me….

"Hey, Mel. Can you do some research for me? I want to find out how my wife was living in her Uncle's pack."

He made a face. "I can try. I think we have a ship setting sail for the West tomorrow. I can get a couple of our agents on board. Why? Do they need to find anything specific?"

Cherum is the one that answers before I can. "The lass must have endured some hardships in her short life. You don't have panic attacks like that from a one-off incident. She, uh, also mentioned encountering many misfortunes while living there."

"What kind of misfortunes?" Killian was pushing to the front of my mind with me, listening intently while fury built inside us, thinking the worst may have happened to our mate.

"She says she still has her virginity. I don't think assault of that nature was part of her misfortunes, Alpha, so tell Killian to calm his tits. We don't need two occurrences today, especially right before you head back to be with her."

Hell, he was right. I close my eyes and take deep breaths, trying to reign in my growing anger. After several breaths, I felt Killian settle enough to safely continue the conversation. I had to remind him repeatedly that Lira was with us now. Nothing would hurt her again.

"What misfortunes?" I asked Cherum again.

"Well," he eyed me warily, "I think she suffered something similar to Yasmin, but without the final, uh, act, if you know what I mean. Women can be assaulted without penetration. She wouldn't tell me the details, but she related too well to what Yasmin encountered last night to not have gone through something similar. I suspect the men who hurt Yasmin were the men from Wayne's pack too."

I growled deeply, wishing I had my people escort the Alpha and his men out of my land after the wedding.

"Yasmin from the brothel? What happened to Yasmin? Why was she with the Luna?" Nilo asked.

"You missed a lot being gone all day," Meldec told him.

"I know! Someone needs to tell me what happened. I was thinking of visiting the brothel after leaving here. I guess I can ask Yasmin there if you guys won't tell me."

Cherum chuckled, "You won't be seeing Yasmin there any longer. She has a mate."

"What?!" Nilo's eyes went wide. "Who?"

"Percy," Cherum grinned. "He took her as his chosen."

"What the hell? Anything else happen I should know about? Did you two get mates too?" Nilo asked Meldec and Cherum. Cherum chuckled, and Meldec shifted in his chair like he was uncomfortable. He didn't like the attention on himself.

"We have got a merman living with us now," Cherum told him, and Meldec lifted his face, looking at Nilo to get his reaction. I'm curious too to see what Nilo will think about a siren living in our presence without knowing that his new Luna is one.

"A siren? Why?" Nilo scrunched his face in displeasure. Meldec looked just as disappointed as I felt at his reaction.

"The Luna, it seems, has a siren Lord protecting her. Her necklace was a wedding gift that called him here from the distress she felt this morning. I don't fully understand it myself, but the Alpha was aware, so I figured it was just some weird wedding gift the sirens sent to try to form a treaty or start good relations with us or something."

"They wish to have good relations, I believe," I told him. It's true enough, and the contract won't allow for me to tell him more.

"Hmm," Nilo rubbed his chin, "Do you wish to have good relations with them, Alpha? I didn't think you would allow a siren on our land this easily. You don't trust them."

I frowned, guilt weighing on me again. No, I didn't trust any race I couldn't command in our first life, but that was before I saw my own wickedness in the way I treated Lira, my mate. The way I drove her away, losing her love and trust to my own heinous actions. I was far more monstrous than any siren I know of. If I'm to condemn an entire race, I would first have to condemn myself.

I, a noble Alpha Lycan, abused my power and hurt the person I should have been cherishing because of my own pride. I have no room to judge Cedric, or the sirens at all after everything I did.

"I don't distrust them. I don't know them, Nilo. Neither do you. Or any of us, for that matter. I do know it is wrong to judge an entire race who we have never had dealings with, so I ask that you all keep an open mind. Treat the siren man with respect. He will be staying with us for quite some time, and serving my wife. If she deems someone worthy, I will always hold her opinion over all others."

Meldec settled back in his chair with a small smile playing on his lips, and Cherum slapped my shoulder, grinning approvingly.

"Wow, Alpha. Married life suits you. You are already acting a bit more tame and it's only been a day." Nilo is staring at me like he's amazed.

I grinned. "She's an amazing woman. I would be a fool not to change to be the kind of man she deserves."

"I agree," Cherum said, "and it's getting late. I think this groom should go find his bride and walk her back to her room to retire for the night. Maybe enjoy another cup of tea together."

My smile was so broad it nearly hurt my face, my facial muscles are not used to being used this much. "I think you're right." I stood on my feet. "Don't forget to send some men, Mel. I want to know."

"I will assign the task right away. Enjoy your evening, Alpha."

"Oh, I plan to."

"*Hair time,*" Killian was leaping inside my head eagerly.

I chuckled back to him. "*Let's go ask.*"

I know she wasn't ready for anything more than hand holding, but I'll take anything I can get. Pampering her by brushing her hair before bed sounds amazing to me too.

# TWENTY-SEVEN

Cedric and I were walking back along the docks when Lachlan came out to meet us. After what Cedric and I talked about, it was hard to keep the heat out of my cheeks watching him walk towards us. He was very much an attractive man, with his strong physique and dark features set on a handsome tanned face, and now that I was trying to stay open to the bond for Val's sake, it's harder to bury down the natural reactions my body has to him.

"Lira," he said my name with such affection that I lost the battle of trying to keep a blush off my face, "I was just coming to find you."

"She's been here with me," Cedric smirks, wrapping an arm around my shoulders, making Val growl slightly in protest. "We were just enjoying a lovely stroll along the water's edge if you would like to join us."

Lachlan could barely hide his disapproval, because of both Cedric's suggestion and of his arm around my shoulder. The pestering bond was making it impossible to feel at ease in this situation. I didn't want to displease Lachlan or make him uncomfortable, and between him and Val nagging in my head, I ended up shrugging Cedric's arm off my shoulders and taking a tiny step forward.

"We were done with our stroll," I looked at Cedric accusingly out of the corner of my eye, knowing he was trying to rile up Lachlan again, just like earlier today. "Cedric was just walking me back to my room."

"I can do that," Lachlan steped forward and held his hand out towards me expectantly. I bit my lip and stare at it for a moment, but the nagging bond created this undeniable urge inside of me to go to him; to feel the tingles against my skin that states the burning need that the bond creates inside of me.

I closed the gap between us and took his hand, feeling shy all of a sudden when he threaded his fingers between mine and smiled brightly down at me. He truly is a handsome man, and when he smiles that way he is smiling at me right now, I can't fight off the budding hope inside me that this truly will be okay.

"I guess that's my sign to leave you two newlyweds for the evening. I will see you in the morning, princess. Have a wonderful night with your *husband.* If you need me," he gave me a serious, pointed stare, referring to our conversation earlier, "Call for me, your strongest and most handsome tool."

I grinned, feeling grateful, not because I was worried about the night with Lachlan. I truly feel Lachan will not try to harm me after this morning and my reaction to him last night. I'm grateful because I finally felt supported, and no longer alone. I have Cedric and others now willing to fight my battles with me.

"Thank you Cedric. Goodnight."

"Goodnight, my princess."

Lachlan stared after Cedric as he walked off towards the warrior's barracks and the training area. I guess that would be where Lachlan set up a room for the duration of his stay.

"Did you two have a nice talk?" Lachlan asked me once Cedric was out of sight, running his thumb over my knuckles. Tingles ran up my arms, making me shiver. Lachlan mistaked my shivering for being cold and quickly let go of my hand to wrap an arm around my shoulders, pulling me towards him, making the tingles intensify.

"Yes," I looked up at him through my lashes, my voice sounding soft and airy. "It was very informative. He told me a little about my father."

He nodded, like he expected that. "Did you get your questions answered?"

I curled my lips to the side of my face, not sure if I did or not. "For the most part. I'm still wondering who my father is, but he told me it was not safe for it to be known I was his daughter yet, so I'll have to wait."

He pursed his lips. "Did he tell you till when you would have to wait or what you were waiting for?"

Anxiety at telling Lachlan the truth about me made me shiver for a different reason. I can't tell him that I have to wait until I am 20 again, because that is the day my magic will be unleashed and I will gain my siren abilities. We are finally comfortable around one another. I didn't want to ruin that.

"He just said it was not yet safe," I lied, and Val groaned at my dishonesty. Lying isn't sitting right with either of us, but it's better than going back to facing his hatred and wrath every day for something that we can't change. I can't change my genes. Just like in my first life, I couldn't change that my uncle forced me into this marriage. I still don't trust Lachlan not to be that man from before, and Val, even if she doesn't like lying, feels the same.

"Hmm," is his only response, but he gripped my shoulder a little tighter, as if he is scared I may run away from his hold.

When we get back to our room, Lachlan calls for Mimi to help me dress down for bed, and he retreats to get tea and snacks for the evening.

Mimi gushed over me, like she always used to. There is a slight change in her in this life too. She would fawn over me while helping to care for me in my last life, but she would also have this underlying solemnness in all her deeds and words, like she was feeling sadness on my behalf. Now, she was bursting with energy, her aged smile bright on her wrinkled face, making her eyes crinkle enduringly in their corners. She seems so full of life, talking endlessly about how adorable she thinks me and my husband are together. She even mentions how he came to check on her progress with her move again, and how much it meant to her.

By the time I am in a new nightdress, a gift from Lachlan for my birthday, and cleaned for bed, my head is filled with all Mimi's positivity about my new husband.

I'm sitting in front of the window overlooking the ocean when Lachlan came walking back in with a tray of fruits, little desserts and herbal tea.

He smiled at my appearance, complimenting my new nightdress as he set the tray in front of me. I thanked him softly, then noticed there was only one tea cup on the tray.

"I thought it would help you to sleep. I don't usually drink tea, but wanted to get it for you."

He then leaves me for a few brief minutes as I ponder over his kindness, wondering if everything is really as simple as Val has been suggesting and this really is a new Lachlan on an entirely different timeline. Maybe we really are getting a chance for happiness with him. Maybe everything will really be alright this time.

When he came back out of the ensuite, he had a nervous expression on his face and a hairbrush in his hands.

"Um, Lira. Killian has been hounding me all evening to ask you this. If it makes you uncomfortable, you can say no."

I pulled my eyebrows down questioningly. "What?" What would Killian want to do with my hairbrush?

"Can we, uh….brush your hair?"

My mouth droped, not expecting that request. It's….I don't know.

"*It's adorable!*" Val screamed in my head. "*You better say yes.*"

It is adorable. Mimi had already brushed my hair, but there was no harm in doing it again.

"Yes, Lachlan," I smiled, "you are both more than welcome to."

I started to move my chair back, but he told me to sit still, lifting me and the chair easily and moved me to where my back is facing the room. I tried to casually continue drinking my tea, but I felt a weird buzzing in my body as he gently pulled the brush through the strands of my hair, his hand always following after the brush, like he was testing my hair to see if it's soft enough.

When Val began purring in my chest, I gave up my attempt at acting casual. He seemed elated hearing the sound, and the action made me feel adored. Truly adored and cherished for the first time in my life.

This was so much different from when my mother or when Mimi brushed my hair. This felt more intimate. It felt like he was treasuring me in a way that I could never have expected to feel these kinds of emotions.

When he was finally done, satisfied with his work, he set the brush on the table, then moved my chair and me back to where I originally was.

"You have beautiful hair. I've been wanting to touch it since I first saw it," he told me.

"Thank you," I looked down at my hands to hide my blush from his compliment.

"You're welcome." He grinned, then looked at the tray with the snacks and tea. "You didn't eat anything. Can I convince you to have some of the cookies, or at least a grape or two before we go to bed?"

I eyed the food warily. I was already still too full from dinner. My body wasn't used to eating so much, and I feel like everyone has been constantly trying to feed me all day.

"I really couldn't eat any more. I'm not used to eating so heartily. You should help yourself if you want to, though. Don't let it go to waste."

He made an unidentifiable face, then picked up a grape and popped it in his mouth.

"Mmmh. It's really sweet. You should try one."

He pressed one to my lips, and I ended up eating it, feeling shy as he personally fed me. He fed each of us a few more grapes, and even somehow got me to eat a few bites of a cookie before I had to stop him and tell him that I couldn't eat any more. He looked quite smug with himself, and I realized he played me to get me to eat more food.

Maybe he wanted me heavier? Maybe I'm too skinny for him? Leona was heavier in the hips and chest than me. A lot heavier. Like she said, I don't have a desirable body for men. Maybe Lachlan likes a curvier woman, and was trying to help me meet his expectations.

That thought made my overfull stomach turn with unease. I was just feeling cherished and a little more certain about this new life, but now I have doubts once again.

"Are you alright, my wife?" Lachlan asked.

I hurried to fake a smile. "I'm fine. Just full and tired."

He stared at me for a moment, trying to read my face. He then stood with a sigh, holding his hands out for me to take.

"Bed time it is, then. Unless your stomach is too full to sleep, then we could maybe take a brief walk through the halls?"

"No, I'm ready for bed," I grinned quickly to hide my unease, taking his hands. He led me over to the bed and pulled the covers back, kneeling and helping to remove my slippers like yesterday. He arranges the blankets around me before going around, blowing out the candles and lamps around the room before coming to lay beside me.

We lay in silence for a few minutes after Lachlan blew out the last lamp on his nightstand.

"Lira?" Lachlan's deep, masculine voice filled the dark space, making the hair stand up on the back of my neck.

"Yes?"

"Can I hold you? I will do nothing else. I just want to fall asleep with you in my arms."

I bit my lip, anxiety making my chest feel like it is swelling. "Just holding me? Like, hugging me?" I clarified, knowing holding me could have different meanings.

"Just hugging you from behind. I want nothing more than to go to sleep with you in my arms every night, and wake up the same way. I really won't do anything else."

I felt nervous, but Val was screaming for me to say yes, not having enough of her mate, I guess. The bond was making my skin itch from his request, wanting nothing more than to fill it.

"Okay," I whispered meekly.

I felt the bed shift beneath me as Lachlan moved closer to me. His strong arms wrapped around me, one arm sliding under my shoulders and the other resting on my waist. My breath hitched for a second, but then evened out as his touch satisfied the bond.

"Goodnight, Elelira," Lachlan whispered hoarsely in my ear, his voice raw and gravelly.

"Goodnight, Lachlan," I husked back, then let the bond soothe me to sleep.

~

"Here, princess!" Cedric called to me cheekily, swimming in loops around me in the water. I tried to keep up with him, but I kept getting frustrated and gave up. Without my fins, I just didn't have the strength or stamina.

I envy him for his freedom in the open sea and his being able to dive deep below the water's surface to a depth where I can no longer see him. The water is majestic from below. The sun's rays glittering the surface above fade to clear, cool currents teaming with life.

"Will you quit trying to scare me, Cedric? I know there is nothing down there that can hurt me."

"And how would you know that?" He asked, lifting an eyebrow.

Oh no. I kept slipping up. "I just know. If there was, you wouldn't be letting me swim out here, would you?"

His expression slipped back into his easy smile. "No, I wouldn't. You are right."

I kept almost slipping up and letting it be revealed that I have lived this life already. Well, not this life. This life was far different from my first. The past week has proved that.

It's been a week, and not only have I not felt betrayal pains, I have been living quite comfortably as the wife of the pack's Alpha. I'm being treated as the true Luna, not just by Cherum and the Luna's guard, but by everyone. Even Lachlan.

Lachlan has been.....exceptional. He has been diligently working every day as Alpha, as he was before, but he has also gone out of his way each and every day to make sure to spend time with me. He is so attentive that I find it almost smothering at times. The confusing way the bond makes me feel has been making it hard to keep my mind about me. I find myself giving into his small signs of affection and staring admiringly at him when he talks.

I don't want to be. I don't want to find the man that neglected and emotionally abused me in my first life attractive in any way, but the bond wants something different. Just as it did in my first life. It took almost a year of betrayal pains and then enduring Mimi's death by myself for the bond to lessen to where I could numb myself to the effects being in close proximity to my mate brought me. Then, when he did start to show me his face, after I resolved myself to endure until I could leave, his constant cruelty made both me and Val bury any budding affection that seeing him stirred in the bond.

This Lachlan was nothing like that. This Lachlan is the complete opposite of the cruel man I first married. He makes fighting the bond impossible. If I could see any of the other cruel Lachlan in this one, it would make resisting the bond easier. Besides what happened at breakfast the first morning here, he has been nothing but kind.

Val wasn't helping either. I don't want to hurt her. I've always tried to protect her above all else, but to keep her from feeling pain right now, I have to keep myself vulnerable to the bond. She wants her mate and to feel her connection to him. Lachlan and Killian are one entity, so each time she grows closer to Killian, I find myself being pulled closer to Lachlan.

It's confusing and suffocating at times, my mind and my feelings not matching my heart.

Cedric must have noticed my conflicting attitude at breakfast because once Lachlan left with Beta Nilo to begin planning some event the pack is hosting soon, Cedric offered to take me swimming, saying that I looked like a fish out of water.

Percy and Yasmin came with us. They were supposed to be watching and serving me, but had drifted off to an intimate bubble of their own behind one of the boats in the dock. Being newly mated, they aren't able to really keep their hands off one another. They had the first few days of their new relationship off from all duties, for obvious reasons, but it seems that wasn't enough for them. They still can't seem to get their fill of one another. Maurice is watching from the docks, so hopefully Percy won't get in trouble later for leaving me unattended. Cherum was reluctant to leave me with Cedric to join the meeting with the other ranked commanders and told Percy and Maurice to stay vigilant while protecting me. Percy is remaining vigilant alright, or at least attentive towards his mate, but I don't think Cherum cares much about that.

I'm fine with just Cedric anyway. Val was worried about him being too affectionate to me, but the only times he is affectionate in a concerning way is when Lachlan is around. I think he just wants to mess with Lachlan.

"Are you tired yet, princess?" Cedric asked, floating beside me.

"No," I leaned back, letting my hair fan out in the water, soaking in the sun's rays on my exposed skin as I floated on my back. "I could do this all day."

Cedric chuckled, bumping my legs with his beautiful tail. "You're a natural in the water, even if you haven't gotten your siren magic yet."

"The ocean is my favorite," I told him, keeping my eyes closed and feeling the orange heat on my eyelids.

"Did you do a lot of swimming in your former pack?"

My smile faltered as I cringed inwardly. No, I didn't. No woman would dare try to swim alone without a mate or someone to protect them. I was only out of the ocean for a short time before my uncle's men found me. Even if I wasn't his niece, I doubt they would just have left me unscathed. I thought I would be fine with my magic, but my uncle was ready for me.

"Not often," I told Cedric.

"How did you get to be such a great swimmer?"

"I'm just a natural, I guess," I said, trying to sound nonchalant.

He chuckled, "It is in your genes, I guess."

"Seems so," I sighed, going back to a vertical position in the water.

I looked to shore and saw Percy and Yasmin are now making out on the sand, no longer trying to hide it. I'm happy for them, but I wish they would do that in their room. It makes me feel uncomfortable as it makes me think about the first night I was back here. Lachlan and I never got heated like they are getting, but we did kiss twice. Something I know Val is craving to do again. I'm not ready, though. Even if it is her and Killian doing it, I don't know if I can sit back and just accept it. I will likely panic again.

I do let Lachlan brush my hair for me every night, something that feels intimate enough as it is. He also holds me as I fall asleep, which I've actually come to welcome. I sleep better every night when he does it. The bond is soothed enough by his touch to not pulse annoyingly inside me begging for a connection with my mate. I haven't accepted him, but I will accept using him to get a good night's sleep.

"Look," Cedric pointed off towards the castle.

I looked in that direction to see Lachlan and his men walking towards the docks. I nervously glanced at the couple still making out on the sand, wishing I had the ability to mind link them to tell them they were about to get caught. I can't until I mate with Lachlan and have him mark me. That will not be happening any time soon.

"Can you warn them?" Cedric asked, nodding to the couple.

"I wish I could. Let's swim back and try to beat Cherum to them," I wiggled my eyebrows at him. "I'll race you."

"Should I give you a head start?" He huffed. I splash him, then dove underwater, pushing my human body to swim as fast and as hard as I could. When he flew past me, I grabbed hold of his tail, hitching a ride until my lungs began to burn with the need for oxygen. I didn't let go as I lifted to the surface, making his muscles in his tail flex as he fought for control to break free. He turned and broke the surface with me, both of us laughing and sputtering water.

"That's cheating," he groaned, splashing me with his free hand when I grip his upper arm to prevent him from swimming off without me.

"No it's not," I laughed," You told me to do this."

"To cheat?!"

"No. To use you as my tool," I grinned.

He threw his head back and laughed, "You're using me to beat me?"

"It's called being resourceful," I smirked before diving back under.

The same thing happened again; he tries to swim past me but I grab on to his tail. We wrestled underwater for a minute, then got above the surface when I needed to breathe. I was hanging on his back, laughing uncontrollably as he tried to throw me off.

We ended up back at the shore eventually, our mission to warn the lovebirds all but forgotten. Cedric's fins were shifted to limbs, even with me hanging on his back, demanding he admit that I won. My wet clothes were bunched high on my thighs, my legs wrapped around his torso. He reached back to poke at my side and tickled me, trying to get me to let go. He was bellowing laughter and empty threats to get me off.

It wasn't until a very angry growl startled me that I finally let him go and slid off his back. I turned to see Lachlan, Nilo, Cherum and Meldec watching us. Cherum and Nilo were pressing their lips together to keep from laughing, Gamma Meldec was glaring at Cedric and me disapprovingly, and Lachlan's face….it reminded me of his face towards the end of our first marriage when he was always so angry with me.

"You're hanging on the back of a naked man. Of course he is angry," Val growled at me.

I jerked my head to look at Cedric, just now realizing that he was naked, and my face, I'm sure, is bright red now from embarrassment.

Cedric, showing no shame, placed his hands on his hips, grinning widely. "Did you men want to join us for a swim? The water is quite lovely, Right princess?"

Meldec surprised me, being the one to growl at that question. "*Princess*? Are you that familiar with the Luna to being calling her in such affectionate ways with no clothes on?"

Why is he so offended? Cedric always called me that. He just shifted back too. It's not like we were swimming together while he was naked.

"Get dressed, Cedric," I patted his arm, then looked up at him. His face no longer looks easy-going. He looked hurt by what the Gamma said, which I don't understand. He usually wouldn't care about such statements. "Cedric?"

He forced a smile and looked down at me. "Yes, my princess," he briefly kissed my temple, "Since your knight and the jesters are here, I think I'll head back to my room for a bit to rest. Thank you for accompanying me on my swim."

I smiled weakly, sensing the discord between my friend and Meldec. I'm a little offended by the Gamma's words too, but they really seem to be bothering Cedric.

After he was out of earshot, not bothering to put his clothes back on that he scooped out of the sand, just walking back naked, I turned to glare at the men, particularly Meldec.

"Did you need to be that rude? He just shifted back. He wasn't intentionally naked."

Meldec frowned at me, but looked guilty now. He opened his mouth, then shut it, then turned to follow Cedric back to the bunk houses and dorms.

"Hey! Don't be mean to him!" I started to follow after him, but Cherum wrapped an arm around my waist, stopping me.

"I don't think he is following the man to be mean to him, Ela. I think there is more going on there than it seems."

"What do you mean?" I looked up at him confused.

He shook his head. "Nothing to worry about right now, lass."

I pressed my lips together, not believing him.

# TWENTY-EIGHT

***Lachlan***

I watched Lira's face change from anger to worry. I caught on to Meldec and Cedric a few days ago. I recognized the look that would pass over Mel's face whenever Cedric was nearby. His eyes would be trained on the siren man, his emotions clear on his features.

If Cedric was laughing or seemed happy, Mel would be smiling at him too. When Cedric was being too affectionate with Lira, like just now, my Gamma would start going off in angry tirades that resulted in the men under him doing some form of physical exertion they would hate. Yesterday, when we walked in the great hall and Cedric was feeding Lira pieces of an apple that he was cutting up with a pearl-handled dagger, Mel lost his shit and had our warriors combing the training yard to find some imaginary pen he said he dropped when we went back to training. I didn't like it either, but I was just happy that someone was getting my wife to eat. She's getting to a healthier weight now, and Cedric's nonchalant way of feeding her is helping with that.

While we were in our meeting discussing the arrangements for the festival that is to be held at the end of the month in my wife's honor, Cherum let slip that Lira went for a swim with Cedric in the sea.

My panic took a leap, imagining the evening that Lira rejected and left me again, but Mel got up and started pacing the room in an aggressive manner. He couldn't focus, and I too really wanted to see Lira and make sure she was still there and not swimming off into the sea. I cut the meeting short and we all went to the docks to find my wife and her siren bodyguard.

Lira and Cedric were diving under water together, then they would pop up after some time, wrestle and splash around playfully, then disappear beneath the water's surface again. Watching Lira be playful with another man hurt, but even Killian said we had no room to get angry. She endured far worse from us. He was annoyed, but I think knowing that Cedric isn't as much of a threat as we originally thought he would be has helped to keep his angry side at bay.

Plus, she was staying open to Killian entirely. Killian was even able to feel flickers of the bond at times. When he comes forward each night to brush her hair, she will talk and laugh with him, not holding back her affections like she does with me. She likes my Lycan. I just got to get her to like me and trust me.

"Lira, my wife," I called to her, not liking her being in Cherum's hold but knowing I couldn't come right out and tell her that. I also do not like her dripping wet in nothing more than a short slip with undergarments showing underneath. I should have a proper swimsuit fashioned for her. One that fully covers her beautiful body in a darker, non-transparent material.

"*I like the transparent material,*" Killian purred in my head, pushing forward to check out or mate.

"I do too, but I don't want anyone else to see her like this."

"True. She isn't marked. Other males will want her if they see her like this."

I want to groan at his reminder. I want to hurry and mark my wife, seeing the affection that others show her constantly, since she is such an easy woman to love, but I know we are nowhere near that stage in our relationship yet. She may allow me to hold her from behind while she sleeps, but if I try anything more she begins to panic, and panic is the last response I want my touch to bring out from my wife.

Lira looked back at me with her big green eyes questioningly. I was lost in her beauty and speaking with Killian, that I forgot I had called her.

"I'm going to head back to our room for a rest. Would you like to join me?" I held my hand out to her hopefully. She eyes my hand, then looks back at Cedric and Mel one last time with a sigh before stepping forward to join hands with me. I can not keep my smile off my face at how regular an occurrence this is now. She doesn't deny me this privilege of holding her hand. I will be ecstatic about any affection that she allows of me.

I could hear Cherum behind us yelling at Percy for his inappropriate behavior with his new mate on the beach when he was supposed to be watching Lira, but ignored it. Cherum had his warrior handled. Lira must hear too because she turned to look at them with an amused grin. When she catches me watching her, she bites her lip and looks forward once again.

"Are you cold?" I asked her, seeing her shiver as we began to walk back towards the main castle.

Her cheeks turned an alluring pink, but she shook her head. "No. I'm actually quite warm."

My eyes trailed down to the stiff peaks on her chest proving she is chilly, but I quickly pulled my mind out of the gutter and looked the other way. Killian is smacking his lips at the lusty thoughts of seeing her alluring wet body brings us, but I'm working hard to not show how it's making me feel.

"You looked like you were having fun with Cedric," I told Lira to distract myself from thinking of helping her out of those wet clothes and what lies hidden underneath them.

"We were racing," she smiled, like it is already a fond memory to her. That sent a pang through my heart, but I'm also happy for her being happy. It's a conflicting feeling, the emotions running inside of me; jealousy and happiness for my mate. "I won."

"It looked like he touched land first if that is what you were racing for," I chuckled, earning myself a glare from her. The glare is adorable, making me laugh further. "I would like to swim with you some time. You looked so free in the water."

She bit her full bottom lip, making my hand flex at my side with the desire to pull her lip from her teeth and tracing the indentations out of it with my thumb.

"I feel free in the water. It's my favorite place to be."

With that one statement, my mood plummeted and anxiety gripped me. Killian whimpered as well, wishing her favorite place to be would be with us.

"Hmm," was all I managed as a response. I'm wracking my brain trying to come up with something, anything to say to make her consider only having a life on land with me,

"The gardens," Killian told me, "Take her to your mother's gardens."

My mother's gardens were beautiful. She loved to escape into her labyrinth of rose bushes and hanging flowers when she was feeling overwhelmed. The maze of fragrant flowers soothed her. Maybe they can do the same for my wife. Maybe I can give her another option besides the sea for when she wants to escape for a little while.

"Lira, have I ever shown you the gardens?"

She tilted her face up to mine. "No. I don't think I've even seen any gardens here."

"They are hidden in the forest past the stables a bit. My mother had them designed to be a refuge for herself when she was training with the warriors and needed a break." It weighed on my mother being a top warrior during the war while also being the pack's Luna. More was expected of her than any Lunas before her and she needed an escape.

Lira's radiant smile made my heart skip a beat, my breath hitching in my throat from her beauty. "I would love to see your mother's garden, Alpha. It sounds lovely, but didn't you say you needed to rest?"

I smirked, "That was an excuse to spend some time with you."

"*Smooth,*" Killian is smirking with me in my head, just as happy with Lira's bashful response as me.

"Okay," Lira whispered. "I'll go see it with you, if you would like."

"I would like nothing more." I lifted her hand to my lips and placed a tender kiss on the back of it. Her face turns that beautiful pink again, making me grin, pleased with her reaction to me.

Baby steps. It took me 2 years to destroy our bond. I don't care if it takes me two years to restore it. I just want my mate to know I love her and desire nothing more than to give her the world by the end of these two years. I can take baby steps, as long as we get to the goal in the end.

~

***Elelira***

Val is sighing constantly in my head. Lachlan is gripping my hand in his large, warm one, the sparks shooting up my arm and making my bond buzz and tingle with rejuvenation. It's like this every time our skin makes contact. No matter how apprehensive I want to remain, the bond reacting to him won't let me when we are together. Not when he is treating me like this; like I am cherished. When he is kind and gentle with me, I can't react with hostility or coldness like I tried to before.

I half expected him to get mad at me for swimming in the ocean with Cedric. I expected him to get angry and yell at Percy. My expectations from the past had me thinking the worst of him without realizing it, but he proved all those preconceived notions to be wrong. He was the same doting husband he had been all week. Now, he is even about to take me to a garden special to his mother. I never even knew of this garden before. If it's in the warrior's area and by the training grounds, that would explain why. I wasn't allowed to go there before.

*"He wants us,"* Val exhaled, simpering in my head. *"He likes us."*

"It's more than that," I told her, "Do you....do you think he knows? Do you think he feels the mate bond?"

That's the only explanation I can think of for his behavior all week. If he felt it, he would have said something, right? Killian would have. He wouldn't have been able to hold back from claiming his mate as a Lycan Alpha.

Val was deep in thought, contemplating what I suggested. *"I don't know. It would explain a lot."*

"What do you mean?" I asked.

"Well....Killian can reach me sometimes, even when we are both not in control. It's flickering, never long enough to communicate, but I can feel him reaching out for me. He also wouldn't want me at all if he didn't know I was his mate."

That's true. Could Killian be the biggest difference in this life versus the other?

I'm in the bathroom now, being changed into a new dress and having the salt water quickly cleaned from my hair. Lachlan seemed reluctant to part from me, but seemed equally excited for me to get ready so he could take me to the garden he said once belonged to and was treasured by his mother.

"Lira? Are you ready?" Lachlan asked from outside the ensuite doors.

"She's just about ready for you, Alpha," Mimi yelled out to him, running the brush through my damp hair a few more times. Lachlan called for her and Gemma to help me change as soon as we got back.

Lachlan groaned softly, making both Gemma and Mimi chuckle.

"He is so smitten with you," Mimi grinned at me in the mirror, making me blush. "The man hates it when you are out of his sight."

"It's enduring," Gemma said, placing shoes beside the bench for me to slip my feet into. They're the sandals I like, not a pair of the expensive heels or boots Lachlan gave me as a birthday present when I first got here. I like being able to slip my feet out of their restraints to feel the sand between my toes when I can. Gemma and Mimi are learning my preferences and rarely try to put me in the exquisite stuff anymore.

"I was worried after that first breakfast, not understanding how anyone could react that way to their mate, but I see that must have been a fluke because of the circumstances. He really does cherish his Luna like he should, doesn't he?" Gemma elbowed Mimi gently, making Mimi nod with a warm smile.

"Mate?" I picked up on the term since Val and I were just discussing it. "He called me his mate?"

"Oh, I know he prefers the term 'wife'," Gemma added. "The night after your marriage, though, he had Beta Nilo running around the castle declaring he had found his mate and it was his new wife. We were all surprised and ecstatic, really. He has been so lonely and untrusting since his parents' deaths. He always longed for his mate. When the, uh, incident happened at breakfast, the whole castle started to worry that he would lose his Luna and mate to his temper before you had a chance to know the real Lachlan Stiles, the Alpha who always put the well-being of the pack before anything else. We were all so happy to see you flirting at dinner that same night. We all want our Alpha's happiness, and I'm glad he found that in you. As far as mates go, I think you are both perfectly suited to one another."

Mate. He had Beta Nilo tell everyone that I was his mate? How could he know that I am his mate? How could he have felt that? My magic is still sealed.

"The necklace?" Val suggested.

I lift my hand, tracing my fingers over the intricate metal. The magic fused inside it tingles against the pads of my fingers.

"You think the magic in this could have triggered him to know that I was his mate?"

*"He did ask to share your bed and send those girls away after you put it on."* Val sounded as apprehensive as I feel, but there is no way for us to know for sure without asking. Maybe that's why Killian can hold back too. He doesn't fully feel the bond but feels just enough of it to react to me and want me.

*"Should I ask him?"* I asked Val. I am still a siren and this is still the same pack that has been in wars with the northern clans for the past decade, making them wary of other races. Lachlan did accept Cedric staying here in the pack and on the castle grounds, though. If I picked up on what he and the others were hinting at, Cedric might even be mates with Meldec. The Gamma didn't accept him or mark him yet, but he obviously didn't reject

him or have him thrown out of the pack. Should I expect the same? Will I be safe to stay here even if I tell Lachlan about my siren blood and ask him if he can feel the bond at all?

"I think you should ask him," Val told me. "Nothing hurts from asking."

"He could reject us," I whispered. "He could throw us in the dungeon."

"He would have done that to Cedric already. I doubt he would reject us. Killian wouldn't let him."

She's right. As much as I don't trust Lachlan fully, I do trust Killian. I trust Killian's relationship with Val, and even his relationship with me. I can tell Lachlan cares for me, but I can see the reasons behind it, making me constantly confused. Killian, though, is always bluntly honest with his feelings and emotions. He wants Valerina and he wants me. If nothing else, I can trust in that. Killian would not allow for Lachlan to reject me or hurt me.

"I'll ask. I want to know. I need to know. I can't keep battling these confusing feelings and emotions all the time."

I could feel Val grinning inside my head. "I think that is a very good idea. You're getting on my nerves trying to resist him all the time."

"What do you expect me to do? He is still the man that hurt us so greatly in our first life."

"He's not, Ela. This Lachlan is different. He cares for us. I want you to ask so you can see that for yourself. We got this redo so we can finally be happy. I know it."

Do I want to be happy with the one who hurt me so greatly before? Do I want to have a redo if it means this time I don't leave for the sea? All I ever wanted in my first life was the opportunity to tell Lachlan who I am to him and have him accept me. That was, until it was too late and our bond was already destroyed, making it so the only thing I wanted was to be free from him.

My father's knowledge of me and sending Cedric to protect me, Lachlan's changed behavior, and my acceptance into the pack as their Luna; maybe this life is a redo of my life so I can have a chance of happiness.

"*I'll ask.*" I simply told Val, not understanding myself and my true feelings about the matter yet to promise anything more.

All I can do is ask Lachlan, then go from there. My final decisions will be based on what he says. I can't disregard my first life completely, because the idea of going through all that and suffering for nothing would be much too depressing. I'm not ready to let go of the past completely yet. I can start making an effort for Val's sake at least, and depending on what Lachlan has to say, it may actually help me to find my happiness too.

"Are you ready now?" Lachlan called grumpily through the door, causing my handmaids to laugh, and me to smile at the notion that being away from him is what is causing him to be grumpy instead of the other way around.

Mimi nodded to me, happy with my appearance. Gemma pinched my cheeks to add color like she usually does, then helped to steady me as I slipped on my sandals.

"I'm as ready as I can be," I murmured, mostly to myself.

Mimi opened the door to my husband and mate, making my heart flutter involuntarily at his eager and handsome face staring back at me adoringly.

# TWENTY-NINE

***Lachlan***

My nerves were getting the best of me as I led Lira through the castle and out to the warrior's part of the castle. I can sense something is bothering her, her face lost in thought as she stares vacantly down at the ground. Val is flashing in her eyes a lot too.

"My mate likes me. Don't worry too much," Killian tried to tell me.

"You're mate may like you, but mine still wants to go back to the sea," I reminded him. "She could be talking about leaving me right now."

Killian huffed, "Don't be an ass and she won't."

*"I've been on my best behavior,"* I growled at him. I didn't even snap when the naked merman was swimming with her and she was all over him. I could tell they were just playing, but it didn't stop the jealousy from raging inside of me. I kept it in, not wanting to anger my wife. I'm glad I did too. She seemed mad enough with Meldec.

"You're right," Killian sighed, "But it hasn't been that long. A week isn't enough time to recover from the past. She has to learn to trust you again. Just keep it up. Hopefully, tonight will help."

*"I hope so."* I want with Lira what Killian has managed to build with Valerina in just a week. They were smitten with one another already. It's helped to keep Lira open to me, but I can still sense that she is reluctant to grow closer to me. She doesn't trust me.

We passed many warriors and pack members on our way out, everyone smiling and offering their greetings to both of us. Lira is always exceptionally kind, showing grace and poise in every interaction with my members. She is a fabulous Luna, and the impact she has had on the pack in just the past week has been amazing. People are always excited about seeing her, and they trust me more now. She had helped to tame Killian, who was always volatile and prone to outbursts. I don't snap as easily at anyone either. I had very few happy days, or days I would describe as good in our first life. I was always irritated and felt on edge, ready for the next attack or the next war to break out. I was holding my breath and waiting for Wayne to double cross me using his niece, or waiting for my lands to be raided again, my people needing a fierce leader and not a weak-willed chump who couldn't resist his tempting new wife who I thought was my enemy and not my mate.

Everything is different this time. I'm not fighting my attraction to her. I want her. There has never been a question about that. Now, I know not to fight my feelings for her. I know not to resist the urge to go to her when it comes to me throughout the day. If I want to see her, I don't get angry at everyone around me and start to lash out, then release my tension with pointless sex at the end of the day. I found her. I will drop everything to seek her out when the need arises, and I find so much more satisfaction with just watching her eat apple slices being offered to her by another man than I ever found in anything else. No amount of meaningless sex, brawling, wine or spirits could ever compare to the pleasure I get from seeing her growing healthier by the day. I find myself grinning like a fool when I'm watching her laugh and joke with Niomi, teasing Cherum, or simply enjoying a cup of tea. Her mere presence makes my life have meaning. That is being reflected back in my pack, and the castle feels like a much happier place simply because of her existence.

I was a fool before. Such an utter fool. If I hadn't been fighting myself, everyone could have had a better life, and this redo would never have been needed. I deserve to struggle right now, scraping my head on the ground to earn her trust and forgiveness. Forgiveness I can't even yet apologize to receive. Not because of the contract with her father.

One day. One day she will know, and then I can spend the rest of my life showing her how truly sorry I am. It's baby steps for now.

Lira's small hand kept flexing in mine. Not like she was trying to pull away, but like she's fighting some internal battle with herself.

"The sparks," Killian reminded me, "She can feel them even if we can't. She is resisting the effects."

I don't want that. I know Killian said not to manipulate her with the bond, but I can't help myself. I lifted her hand and kissed the back of it, making her gasp and stare up at me in surprise with her big emerald eyes.

My goddess, she is beautiful. Inside and out.

She blushed, and I wanted so badly to run my finger across the pink-hued skin on her cheeks. Her face filled in some over the past week, making her look healthier, and her skin glows with sunshine and vibrancy now. Her hair seems to have more light blonde streaks than before too.

"You're so beautiful," I couldn't help but to tell her.

She bit her lip, then looked away shyly. "We are already married, Alpha. You don't have to flatter me."

I resist the urge to groan, not liking that she just thinks that I'm trying to flatter her. "Lira, you really are the most beautiful woman I have ever seen. I'm not just trying to flatter you."

She grinned, but it didn't reach her eyes. It's more like a scoff, air exhaling from her nose in a puff. "I know you prefer more voluptuous women, Alpha. I have seen your tastes. That is why you have been insisting I be fed more, isn't it?"

"What?" I stopped us just as we walked past the armory and warrior barracks. "The only woman I prefer is you. Your eating habits have nothing to do with my taste." She is my taste in women. Anyone else I was with after we married the first time was nothing more than her replacement. None of them ever compared to her.

"I know I'm very skinny," she whispered, running her free hand down the front of her dress. "Thank you, though, for trying to placate me."

"I am not just telling you that you are beautiful as empty words, Lira. Look at me." I gently turned her to face me, resting my hand on the side of her face. She doesn't flinch away from me, which makes me ecstatic, besides the fact that she doesn't believe me when I tell her she is beautiful.

"You, Lira, my wife, are the most gorgeous woman in the entire land. Maybe in the world. I doubt I could ever lay eyes on anyone more pleasing to look at than you. It's not just your appearance, though. I find everything about you to be beautiful. The way you drink tea, the way you smile when you look at the sea, the face you make before you say something teasing to your Delta, and even the way you glower at someone when they make you angry. As long as it's not me, I find joy in everything about you. You also have the most beautiful heart. You knew the relationship I had with Yasmin, and you still helped her when no one else stepped up to. You are kind to everyone in this pack. I've even stuck off to watch you entertain the children in the orphanage. Your heart is just as beautiful as everything else about you. I'm not trying to flatter you. I truly mean it."

Her emerald eyes were staring up at me, Val shining through them, watching me with scrutiny, weighing my words, probably to detect any falsehood in what I am saying. There was none. I meant every word.

"Why?" she asked softly, leaning into my touch, probably without realizing it. She would blush if she realized she was seeking out more contact with my skin. I've noticed the bond causes her to do that at times and she usually doesn't pick up on it right away. She does it a lot in her sleep. Holding her to help to keep her nightmares at bay is how we fall asleep, but I often wake up with her body wrapped around mine. She doesn't even realize it. She just seeks me out in her sleep, and she hasn't had nightmares again since that first night.

"Why what?"

She pressed her lips together, her eyes searching mine. "Why are you so sure I am the most beautiful person to you? Do you….do you, um," she hesitates, pressing her lips together again.

"Do I what?" I asked in a husky whisper.

"Do you…..do you feel it?" Her voice was shaky, like she was scared to fully form the sentence. Feel what? What is she asking me?

"The bond," Killian told me. "She is asking if you can feel that she is our mate."

My throat swells, the contract pressing forward preventing me from outright saying it. I want to. I want to scream it. I want to tell the whole world that she was fated to me and only me. Her uncle and everyone else be damned. I want her to know that I'm treasuring my bond with her, even though I can't fully feel it yet.

"I can, though," Killian reminded me. "It's not often, and takes a lot of strain, but I feel flickers of it. I know my bond is there with Val, even if you can't feel yours with Elelira."

That's right. I may not feel it, but I can tell her that Killian has.

I tested the words in my head, imagined saying them and didn't feel my throat swell like before. I guess it's safe.

Lira was still staring up at me, waiting for my reply. She truly is the most beautiful woman alive. Even without the bond telling me that, I know without a doubt that she is.

"Killian does," I whispered, tracing her soft cheek with my thumb, marveling at the glittering in her eyes at my confession.

"He feels the bond?" she gasped, her voice sounding slightly broken with relief. "Really?"

I nodded, nervous and relieved that I'm finally able to tell her in some way that I know we are mates.

"So," she bit her lip, hesitating again, "You….you know that we are…..mates?"

"Yes," I smiled weakly, hoping she wasn't upset by the news. I shouldn't know, but I don't want to lie to her.

"Why didn't you tell me?" she said, looking a little lost; maybe stunned.

"I…," my throat started to swell and my chest pounds as I attempted to tell her that I couldn't. I couldn't tell her that I knew we were mates. I would then have to tell her how I knew, and that is forbidden. "I….I don't know."

"You don't know?" she lifts one of her brows. "You didn't know we were mates? Then, why? Why have you been treating me so kindly?"

"Because I love you," I told her honestly. "I love everything about you. I don't need the mate bond to know that."

~

***Elelira***

"You love me?" I whispered hoarsely, not believing what I was hearing. "How? You barely know me, Alpha."

He pressed his lips together, his face stressed and anxious. "I wish you would call me by name," he softly says, his thumb still tracing my cheek, making sparks dance on my face.

I huffed, not dramatically, but just a soft expulsion of air at his hypocritical request. I have asked him not to call me Lira plenty of times and he never listened.

Surprisingly, the nickname doesn't bother me as much as it did before. It actually makes my heart race a little when I hear him say it, especially when I don't realize he is near. Before, the nickname brought me dread. Now, it makes tingles erupt inside me.

Funny how much can change in such a short time when you leave the bond open. It chases away the resentment and dread completely, overriding everything with longing for him. My mate.

He knows. He knows we are mates. He said he didn't feel it, but Val was right. Killian can feel it. Not completely, not like us where it is all consuming, but he feels flickers of it, just as my Lycan said he could.

Maybe I really don't need to worry about him forsaking or betraying me in this life. I am not ready to fully accept him, but maybe I will be eventually. Maybe it's okay for me to finally let my guard down fully. It's strenuous to constantly be fighting the conflicting feelings the bond brings me. He truly doesn't seem like the man that hurt me before. The way he is staring down at me and the tender way he is touching me, I don't see any resemblance to the man from my previous life that caused me so much pain.

Maybe he really does love me, and maybe I can learn to love him. Eventually.

"Please," Val murmured in my head. "I want my mate. I love you, Ela, but we need him. We need our mate. Nothing else can fill that void inside us. The constant loneliness you try to ignore, he is the only answer. I need Killian, and you need him. Don't accept him until you are sure, but please, stay open to him for me. For me, and for yourself."

"But the past….Am I supposed to just act like it never happened?"

"No. Never. But I think you went through all that to become stronger; to better help your pack as their Luna. Look at Yasmin." She brings forth the image of Yasmin and Percy on the beach earlier today, focusing on the happy expression Yasmin has, her beaming smile as she stares at her mate. "If not for you and your understanding of what she went through, she wouldn't have that now. Never forget what you went through, but use it to make you stronger, not to carry around as an excuse for your hesitation and fear."

I bit my lip, unsure of how to respond to Lachlan or my Lycan. Do I use my trauma as an excuse? I think I do, but I think I earned that right. The right to maintain my victim's mentality, holding on to the insecurities that resulted from it inside of me.

She is right, though. Without what I had been through, I wouldn't have recognized the bruising on Yasmin for what it was. I wouldn't have had the understanding to see what she went through through her eyes, and I probably wouldn't have stuck up for her. I'm glad I did all that. I'm glad I was able to help her. I made a friend, my first one ever, and she gained happiness.

Maybe I can achieve my happiness one day too.

"Lachlan," I whispered his name, my face heating when he broke out in a broad grin, his eyes dancing with happiness that I called him so familiarly, not in a condescending manner, but with tenderness mixed with nervous hesitancy. "You barely know me. How do you know you love me? It can't be that easy. You don't feel the bond like I do."

He laughed softly. "Do you want me to give you my list again? If you give me some time, I can write up a list that stretches from here to the other end of the bay. You are a very lovable person, Lira. Everyone that meets you loves you."

I bit my lip. "You met my father. You know why I can feel the bond and you can't. Does that not bother you?"

"That you are…. not fully Lycan?" he asked, after struggling to swallow, making my anxiety rise, fearful of his answer. He knew. He already knew all this time, he just didn't say anything. Just like he didn't mention knowing I was his mate. I'm curious why he didn't say anything, but also worried he didn't say anything because he was disappointed. Meldec seemed to be struggling with Cedric. Maybe Lachlan felt the same.

"That doesn't matter to me," Lachlan finally said, holding my face between both of his hands. "You are still my Lira. My wife, and," he swallowed, looking nervous, "my mate." Once the words leave his lips, he pants, like he was relieved to finally say it. I'm relieved as well. Tears are filling my eyes, threatening to spill.

"You don't care that I'm half siren? It doesn't bother you to have a mate and Luna who isn't fully like you?"

He smiled gently, "No, Lira. You could be anything and it wouldn't change the way I feel about you. I would love you regardless," he told me, resting his head against mine, making my heart rate quicken.

That familiar panic creeps up, making my chest feel like it's tightening, but then the bond overwhelms the panic, calming it, making it ease into a gentle pulsing under my ribs. It's not gone, but it's manageable, and the more contact I have with Lachlan, the more it soothes my anxieties, making me just focus on my bond with him.

This Lachlan won't hurt me. He never touched me in my previous life. He definitely won't hurt me now. He isn't the one who ravaged my broken body. He is nothing like those monsters. I don't need to worry now. Not when he is telling me in so many ways how much he loves me. I told myself these things over and over again, and it helped to overcome the panic completely, leaving me breathless.

My tears spilled from the corner of my eyes. My relief was so great, for so many reasons. What should I do? How do I respond to his declaration? I can't say I love him too, because I'm not sure yet if I do. I'm just sure that I don't want to continue fighting him. I don't want to continue straining myself, denying myself something I once longed for more than anything.

Val was purring in my head, happy with the progress I have just made, and happy that it will help her to grow closer to her mate too.

"Thank you," I whispered in a soft, broken voice. "I was scared. I thought you would reject us, and Val couldn't take that. She didn't want to be separated from Killian."

"She never has to be," he promised, wiping the tears from my cheeks. "I never want to lose you, Lira. Killian feels the same way for Val. You are ours. Thank you for giving us the opportunity to love you."

I smile weakly. We stay like that, just being in each other's presence, breathing the same air, feeling the same wind wrapping around us, making my hair tangle around our bodies, whipping around his neck. If he minds, he doesn't say. He looks content, just like me. The sparks are traveling all over my body, serenity consuming my previous apprehension.

"My Lira," he husked, and before I realized I was doing it, I leaned my face up to his, accepting the pressing of his lips against mine.

Before, on the night of our wedding, all I felt was panic. Now, I feel anything but. The satisfaction I feel from his kiss makes me whimper in alleviation. I've never willingly kissed anyone, and the joy it brings me to be kissing my mate, knowing he accepts me, even as a siren and even without feeling the bond, is so amazing.

He wants me. My mate wants me. Hopefully, soon I can fully accept him and we can finally be mates. Hopefully, soon, the present will completely overwrite the past and I can finally be happy, never having to suffer alone again.

# THIRTY

Eventually, we did make it to the garden we originally set out for. Lachlan had this expression like he had just won the greatest prize, all from one kiss.

I can't say that I felt much different. It was a great moment for me as well. I finally felt free from the ghost of Lachlan from my past. It was a small act, but felt enormous to me. Now, I do not flinch or hesitate when Lachlan grasps my hand, kisses the back of it, or when he places his arm on my shoulder, hugging me to his side. This feels....right. Like this was how we were meant to be.

The garden that used to belong to Lachlan's mother was beautiful. It was a maze of foliage, blooming roses, and flower-covered vines over wooden archways. The center of the maze had an elaborate fountain with, of all things, a mermaid at its center. She was gorgeously intricate with her carved scales and the delicate way her tail and fins folded to the sides, like water currents were pressing down on them. Water was spewing from her uplifted hands, cascading down her marble body into the pool below.

"She's beautiful," I whispered, reaching out and bending over the pool to touch the delicate carving in her tail fin.

"She's alright," Lachlan shrugged, "You are by far the most beautiful thing here."

My face felt as if it was going to burst into flames as he stared at me, his expression matching his words. "Your overpraise is going to go to my head," I mutter.

"Good," he smirked, "I don't want you to have any doubts about how attractive you are again."

"In that case, maybe you should tell me more," I giggled, making his smile stretch impossibly wider.

"Lord, I love that sound," he hummed, pulling me to his side and resting his nose on the top of my head. He inhales deeply, then lets out a satisfied sigh. "I always want to be the reason for your laughter."

Goodness, he is saying so many embarrassing things tonight. "I laugh plenty," I told him.

"Not with me. I get so jealous watching you laugh and act playfully with everyone else. I can't even tell you how frustrating it gets seeing you be so carefree with the fish boy when I can barely get you to hold a conversation with me."

"Fish boy?" I lifted a brow skeptically. "I'm half *fish* too."

"I think you're more like a dolphin," he laughed deeply. "They're more intelligent."

"Cedric is very smart," I defended my friend.

"Devious maybe," he smirked. "The man likes to try and rile me up."

I press my lips together to keep my laughter in. Cedric does like to pick fights with Lachlan when he can.

We sat on a bench near the fountain and sat as the sun began to set, painting the sky in an array of bright colors. Lachlan has one of my hands in his, playing with my fingers, his touch lingering on my wedding band often. The setting of the sun brings the cold night air, making me shiver slightly. When he notices, he wraps an arm around my shoulders, snuggling me into his side in a very natural way, like he has done it a million times before. We fit together perfectly.

"Do you want to head back inside?" he asked, kissing the top of my head. "Neither of us brought a jacket."

"It was warm earlier," I sighed, another gust of wind hitting us and making me shiver, the cold water from the fountain spraying us slightly.

"It gets cold here at night. I'll have to start remembering to bring a jacket when I know we will be out late."

"You say that like this will be a common occurrence," I looked up, smirking at him.

"It will be," he grinned, "I want to make this our evening ritual. Walking together in this private garden, telling each other about our days. I can't think of a better way to spend my evenings."

"Oh my," Val purred, "If he keeps sweet talking you like this, I can think of any number of ways that you two could spend the evenings that would be much more fun than looking at plants and recycled water." Val plays a few very naughty images in my head, making me blush furiously.

"No way. I can tolerate this, but that," I resisted shaking my head, "No thank you. I'm nowhere near ready for that."

"I know," she sighed, "He is yummy to look at, though."

That he is. His strong jaw and handsome features would make any woman eager to throw herself in his bed. That fact has been proven plenty already. More times than I wish to think about. My only experience has left me traumatized by the act. I'm not ready for that yet. Maybe one day….

Lachlan groaned slightly, causing me to look up at him. His eyes are slightly glazed. He must be mind linking with someone.

"What is it?" I asked.

"Cherum," he sighed. "He's hunting for you. He says to take you back or he will come find you."

"Why?" I giggled at Lachlan's annoyed expression.

"He says it's almost dinner time and you can't miss a meal. I would usually agree with him, but I'm enjoying our time alone together right now. I'm not ready to share you with others yet."

"Then he can wait," I told him, "Let him find us."

Lachlan chuckles deep in his chest, making my heart beat wildly. Even his voice is attractive. "Want to make a wager on how long it will take him?"

My brows pulled together questioningly. "A wager?"

"A bet. Like, I bet it takes him 30 minutes to make his way here."

"Oh," I grinned, "I don't think it will take him that long. He seems to always know where I am."

"So how long are you thinking?"

"Hmm," I thought deeply for a moment. "10 minutes? Maybe not even that long."

"You're on," he smiled crookedly. "So, what's my prize when I win?"

"You won't win," I muttered. Cherum will be here before we know it. I wouldn't be surprised to see him pop out from behind a hedge any second.

"I might," he insisted.

I shook my head with a grin. "You won't. But on the one in a million chance you do, what do you want?"

"Hmm," he tilted his head to the side, looking up at the sky as he acted as if he was deep in thought. "How about another kiss?"

"A kiss?" I giggled. "Was one not enough?"

"One will never be enough," he smiled sweetly, making me flush.

"Okay," I murmured quietly. "What do I get if I win?"

"What do you want?" he asked, running his thumb on the back of my hand, making sparks dance on my skin. It's very distracting.

I try to think of something, looking around us for inspiration. My eyes land on the mermaid, and an idea comes to me.

"I want you to go swimming with me," I told him.

"Swimming?" He looked surprised. "I would do that with you anyway if you asked."

My blush returned as I looked down at our hands. "I would kiss you again too if you asked."

Lachlan went still for a minute, then his hand released mine, reaching up to cup the side of my face, turning my head to look up at him. "Can I kiss you right now?"

I got lost in the tenderness and longing in his adoring eyes, staring down at me with so much sincerity it made my heart race. Slowly, I nodded, wanting nothing more than to feel his lips against mine again and the relief it brought me.

His breath catches in his throat, his eyebrows pulling together and lifting with alleviation. Slowly, he lowered his face to mine, and just before our lips touched, as my eyes began to flutter close, Cherum's voice echoed in the space around us.

"Damn it, Alpha! I told you the lass needs to eat. She's finally getting meat on her bones and I'm not going to let your obsession with keeping her to yourself keep her from-"

His voice cuts off, as he rounds the last turn into the center of the garden, a surprise fluster replacing the exasperated look on his face.

"Oh," Cherum muttered. "Um, found you." Cherum was shifting awkwardly on his feet, knowing he had interrupted a moment between his Alpha and Luna. He didn't leave, though. He was probably putting my well-being and the need to eat dinner above making his Alpha happy.

Lachlan growled, resting his forehead on mine. "I'm going to kill him," he huffed angrily.

I laughed softly at his expression. "No you won't," I teased him, "And I won."

His eyebrows pulled together, and he looked searchingly in my eyes for a few seconds before his eyes dropped down to stare at my lips. That longing expression returns to his face, and he sighs deeply.

"Not yet, you don't," he rumbled, surprising me as he quickly stood, lifting me over his shoulder and running in the opposite direction Cherum came from.

"Hey!" I yelled out, "That's cheating! He has already found us," I stammered, lifting my head to see Cherum watching us with a confused look. Right before we reached the first hedge, Cherum started to take off after us, as I reached out for his help. "Cherum, help!"

"It's not cheating," Lachlan laughed. "He hasn't caught you yet."

"That wasn't in the rules!" I laughed loudly, feeling like a sack of flour tossed over his shoulder at being like this.

"It is now," Lachlan laughed with me, "I don't like losing."

"Me neither!" I squealed. "Put me down! I won! Cherum, save me!"

"I'm trying, lass!" Cherum panted out, pushing himself harder.

"Nope. You win if he catches me," Lachlan continued to race through the maze, Cherum tight on his heels, yelling for his 'damned Alpha' to stop.

"I totally won, you cheater," I tickled Lachlan's sides, but it did nothing to stop him.

He laughed freely. "Fine, but I still want my kiss."

"Fine!" I squirmed, reaching my hands out for Cherum to reach for. Cherum doesn't seem to understand what's going on, but he could tell I want him to get to me. He was trying his hardest to comply, a fierce determined look on his face.

"Damn it, you gritty bastard. Give me my Luna." Cherum was so close, just a few more inches and he could touch my fingers. Right when I thought he was finally going to get to us, Lachlan made a sharp right, turning off into a hidden path, making me scream at the sudden action. Cherum went barreling into a rose bush, one that looks like it is full of thorns.

"That wasn't nice," I scolded my husband, spanking his thigh. I watched and saw Cherum pulling himself up from the ground, growling as he pulled a thorny branch out of his shirt and another from his beard.

"He called me a gritty bastard," he huffed, "He deserved it."

I sighed, deciding fighting him is futile. I rested my chin in my hand, my elbow propped on his back and made me jerk with every hurried step. I will wait for him to finish his little game. I won. I know I did, but if winning is that important to him, I'll just go along with it.

Lachlan ran all the way through the training grounds, earning us many questioning looks. Cherum must have given up the chase. He is no longer following us and I lost sight of him back in the garden after he crashed into the bush. He really doesn't have a chance of catching us at this point anyway. Lachlan's stubborn determination is nothing to take lightly.

"Our mate is too strong," Val gushed.

"More like he is too stubborn. Like a mule. I darned pack mule with the way he's carrying me." I huffed, making her laugh with amusement.

Lachlan ran all the way to our room, only slowing down to open the door. When we got inside, he tossed me on the bed, making me grunt in annoyance at the jarring action, then threw both of his hands in the air triumphantly.

"I win!" He grinned, looking like an adorable child with a small accomplishment.

"Sure you did," I chuckled at him, shaking my head.

He bends over me, his panting breath mixing with mine. "I want my prize now."

"I hope you feel honorable, cheating the way you did," I teased him.

"Dishonor feels just fine right now," he smirked before pressing his lips to mine. He moaned in appreciation, making my heart hammer loudly in my chest. Val was doing back-flips, loving the way the bond is erupting inside of us.

When his lips started to move sensually, urging my bottom lip between his, I felt like I was melting. My hands pressed against his chest, began to grip his shirt, bringing his body closer to mine. He anchored himself on his forearms, not touching me, but I can feel the heat of his large frame above me. The bond was coursing through my veins, begging for more, but my mind still isn't ready for that yet. I barely feel ready for this, but it feels too good to stop.

When his tongue caressed against the seal of my lips, I gasped from the tingling sensation that it causes, and his tongue gently caresses against mine. He tasted surprisingly sweet and minty, making me whimper for more. I didn't know what had come over me, but I wanted more. I want the sensation of the bond to overtake me, making me forget everything else but the man treating me so tenderly, like I had never felt before.

We kissed for what feels like an eternity, and at the same time, no time at all. When he gently pulled away, resting his forehead on mine, I missed the contact instantly.

"I truly love you, my Lira," he whispered hoarsely.

I felt it. I could feel his love in every one of his actions today, in each and every word. I couldn't say I reciprocated his feelings, but I felt like I could. Not today, but some day. Someday soon.

We stayed like that, just breathing in each other's expelled breaths for some time before he pulled away from me, gripping my hands and pulling me up to a sitting position on the bed.

"I really should take you to dinner now," he sighed. "I'm sure I'll be getting an ear full from Cherum too. The *gritty bastard* probably got an ass full of thorns."

"Poor Cherum," I giggled, "You should doctor it for him to help it get better."

He snorted. "I'm going nowhere near his ass or red curly pubic hair. He will have to find someone else to nurse him back to feeling better."

"I guess I should offer my services," I sighed, standing at my feet, "I am the reason he was chasing you so enthusiastically."

Lachlan, or maybe even Killian, growled at my suggestions, making me giggle again.

"You will be going nowhere near his ass either. I'll get Nilo to help him."

"Is that part of the Beta duties?" I grinned.

"It is now, if it keeps my wife from trying to do such a task."

"Maybe Nilo needs to be pitied more than Cherum then."

"I think the only man you should put that much thought and feelings towards should be me, your husband," Lachlan grumbled.

"My dishonorable cheating husband?" I smirked as we walked down the hall towards the great hall for dinner. We are nearly an hour late now, but I'm sure they will still have something for us. Cherum likely saved food for me. I doubt he would have done the same for Lachlan though. I'll take pity on him and share my food if that happens.

"I wasn't cheating. I was being strategic."

"Strategically dishonorable?" I lifted a brow.

"Strategically cunning," he grinned, wrapping an arm around my shoulders. "I got my kiss."

My face grew hot at the reminder. "I think it's only fair that I also get my prize as well."

"Of course," he kissed the top of my head. "I'll put the pitiable Nilo in charge tomorrow and we can take the entire day to do whatever you wish."

I clapped my hands excitedly. "Can we go to the orphanage and swim with the kids too?" Little Westley told me he didn't know how to swim and I have been longing to teach him. The orphan boy thinks very highly of his Alpha and would be ecstatic if I brought Lachlan with me.

"If that is what you wish," Lachlan looked warmly down at me.

# THIRTY-ONE

***Leona***

My stomach churned as I stepped off the ship, my feet finally hitting dry land. For some reason, the Gamma sent warriors and scouts on this ship too. I was already on board when they boarded at the last minute before the ship cast off. I've had to stay hidden away like a rat in the bottom quarters of the ship ever since.

I wouldn't have even known the men were scouts if two of them hadn't been frequent customers at the brothel. They sought the mousier women, not able to handle what I had to offer, though I offered frequently. Being Lycan, not human or werewolf like the other girls, I guess I was too intimidating to the weaker customers. The Alpha was the only customer that I actually felt any joy from being with anyway.

Who wouldn't, with his dominant, aggressive bedroom manners? He didn't get as rough with the other girls as he did with me. That's how I know I meant something to him. He treated me special, being wild and rough with my body on the nights we shared. Yes, he may have been cold and distant, but I expect any Alpha to be the same.

That skinny bitch he married and Yasmin, the drab whore, who couldn't even handle multiple men at once without whining and moaning about it, ruined everything for me.

Lanny would have eventually gotten bored and came to find me again. There is no way a dismal, practically flat-chested girl could keep his attention for long. She was a true bitch, too boring and dreary for Lanny.

I checked to make sure the coast is clear, Gamma Meldec's men nowhere in sight. When I was told to leave the brothel by Lady Vera, then denied access to the packhouse, the guards claiming Lanny forbade it, I had little option on where to go next. The ship setting sail for the pack that the bitch came from seemed like a good enough idea for now. I gained that Alpha's favor when I offered Yasmin for their particular requests. He kept calling his niece a whore and bitch, rarely addressing her by name the entire evening. Maybe he will help me get back on my feet.

Looking around, I could tell this pack was very different from the one I had just left. There were very few women out and about, and the ones that were out were dressed so conservatively that I looked very out of place. I self-consciously started to pull up the bosom of my blouse, but it was cut in such a way that it wouldn't cover much more. I had to resolve myself to pull my shawl up over my shoulders. I still caught many men staring at me with a look that sent shivers down my spine, but I tried not to show how uncomfortable it is making me.

I started to walk to the town's center, hoping the packhouse was easy to find, and I could get there without running into the Hidden Cove Pack warriors.

Staying below deck, doing filthy favors for the lowest workers so they would bring me food and take care of my basic needs was trying and humiliating, to say the least. I don't want my sacrifice to be in vain by being caught once I'm finally off the confines of the ship.

"Uh, ma'am," a young boy who looked to be homeless, filthy with dirt and grime, pulled on my skirt as I walked by.

I sneered, tearing my skirt out of his grimy hands. "What? Don't touch me."

He looked down sorrowfully, his face cast over with shame. "I'm sorry ma'am. I just thought I should warn you not to go that way." He pointed down the alleyway I was about to head down. I noticed no one else was walking on the same path. It is completely vacant.

"Why?" I lifted a brow in question, looking doubtful at his warning. It's vacant, but the way seems normal enough.

"You don't look like you're from around here. That way is a trap by the guards. With the way you are dressed, ma'am, and since you are all alone, the guards will probably take you and do the things that make the women scream for long periods of time." he hung his head lower. "They did that to my mom. She didn't live long after. I sit here and warn people now not to go down that street. You're pretty, ma'am. They would definitely take you."

My sour mood towards him lifted considerably hearing about what he went through. Not enough for me to want to help him in any way. No one ever helped me. I'm grateful for his warning, though.

"I'm trying to get to the packhouse," I told him, trying to maintain my cold demeanor. It's like armor to me, and I'm not letting it drop for anyone, even a child. "Could you tell me the safest way to get there?"

"The packhouse?" He looked up at me, horrified. "Why do you want to go there?"

My brows pulled together. "That is my business. Why does it matter?"

"No one goes to the packhouse unless they have to. The Alpha…" he gulped nervously. "He isn't nice. He didn't care when mom died."

I swallowed the lump that formed in my throat. After what they did to Yasmin, I didn't think Alpha Wayne and his men would be kind. I never held that illusion for a second, but I didn't think even a child in his own pack would be terrified of him. Lanny had a mean streak, but only when you angered him. He would never unjustly hurt a member of his pack, and from what I hear, the orphans all love him.

Alpha Wayne can't be that bad. It's an Alpha's duty to take care of his pack, but also his duty to punish members when needed. I'm sure this boy's mother committed a major offense to earn her Alpha's unfavor and mistreatment. That has to be it.

I turned my nose up, not trusting the boy's words any longer. He probably isn't even an orphan. He's probably trying to trick me into going in a different direction so whoever he is working with can rob me. There doesn't appear to be anything that seems off on the path before me. He is just trying to deceive me, I'm sure.

"Thank you for your warning, child, but I think I should be on my way."

When I took another step towards the alleyway, he hurriedly gripped my skirt again, a panicked expression on his face.

"Ma'am! You can't-"

*WHACK*

I backhanded him, sending him flying about a foot off the curb where he was sitting. He whimpered, tears filling his surprised eyes. Guilt almost settled in my chest, but it was quickly replaced with disgust by seeing a dark spot spread on the rear of his pants, the stench of urine filling the air.

"Don't. Touch me," I snapped coldly, then turned my back on his sobbing, crumpled form. He will not earn my sympathy by causing me to fall for his scams. I will speak with Alpha Wayne about the filth he keeps on his streets too.

I walked for about 5 minutes, the boy's sobbing no longing reaching my ears, when a couple of guards dressed in similar attire to the ones who were accompanying Alpha Wayne at the brothel were wearing. The flame red stripes on the seams of the trousers and sleeve cuffs are a clear sign they were Alpha Wayne's men.

Fear gripped my chest, seeing the vulgar expressions on their faces. They were eyeing my exposed chest like starving men would be eyeing a roast of a spit.

I turned to run back the way I came, but two men were coming from that direction, looking at me much the same as the other two.

"What do we have here, Bernie?" One of the men from behind asked the men standing before me. I turn in a circle, then try to back into the side of a building. There is nowhere to run. I'm blocked from every angle; every escape.

"This one really does appear to be asking for it," another man said, stepping closer to me and running a finger over my collarbone and dragging it to my cleavage. A disgusted shiver traveled my body, realizing the boy was telling the truth washing over me.

"She doesn't have the scent of our pack," another one with rotting teeth grinned wickedly. "We can do as we wish, then toss her into the sea. No one would make a fuss."

"No," I whispered hoarsely. "I'm…I'm here for Alpha Wayne. Please…"

"The Alpha?" the fourth man pushed past the other three to look at me. To my relief, he was a familiar face. One of the men that visited the brothel that night. "Why?"

"I know you," I composed myself enough to sound somewhat confident, though my voice was still a bit shaken. "You were with your Alpha at the brothel I worked for in Hidden Cove a week ago."

Recognition replaced the skepticism on his face. "The Lycan wench that offered us your friend. I remember," he grinned slyly. "Did you bring her with you? She was….fantastic," a hungry look fills his eyes.

"No," I said in a measured tone. "She, uh, had to retire after that night." I leave out how she was taken as the chosen mate to one of the top warriors working directly under the new Luna.

"Understandable," he chuckled darkly. "That's too bad."

I smiled weakly, flinching involuntarily when he pressed himself up against me, holding his weight with his arm on the wall behind me. He ran his nose from my ear to my nape, breathing deeply. "You shouldn't visit our Alpha smelling like you haven't bathed for a week. Why don't I take you home for a *quick soak*, then I can take you up to see him. He won't be available for several hours anyway. He will be so excited to see you later."

I pasted on a smile, glad I would only be *entertaining* one of these men for the time being. The other three looked slightly disappointed.

"I would like that very much," I rested one of my hands flirtatiously on his chest, running my nails through the sprinkling of chest hair poking out above his shirt. I would rather chew my own toe off than gratify a man like this, but I see no other choice in this situation. I will just have to use my charm to subdue him.

"Maybe I can help?" The man with the rotting teeth spoke up.

"Why not?" The man before me chuckled. "It can be a team effort."

My smile faltered, and I wished again that I had listened to the boy.

~~~~

*The young boy wailed loudly, his cries not just for himself, his tears burning as they ran down his stinging, dirty cheek, still throbbing with the pain of the woman's slap. He's crying for more than just that. He is remembering the day his mother was taken, forcefully pulled away from her family. She wasn't alone. He and his father were walking back home with her after making a rare visit to the beach to collect shells. His father thought it would be safe since we were together as a family, the path cutting 15 minutes off their walk home. That shortcut cost more than 15 minutes of their lives. It cost his parents everything.*

*The guards took her, ripping her clothes from her body as they dragged her into one of the buildings to take down to the cellar. They had hurt his daddy when he tried to save her, breaking both of his legs and leaving him outside the building with his own measly knife he tried to fight them off with, forcing him to listen as they brutalized her. It was horrific for the boy. His father killed himself, hearing and feeling his mate being tortured and raped the rest of the day and all through the night. The boy went to the packhouse, begging the Alpha to save his mom, but the man at the gates just laughed and told him to leave if he didn't want the same to happen to him.*

*Ever since that day a month ago, the boy has sat in the same spot, all day and all night, warning women young and old not to go down the path.*

*Some of the shop owners around the square felt bad for the boy, offering him food periodically, but none had been brave enough to offer the boy a safe place to stay, worried the guards might soon discover what the boy had been doing and would look to punish*
~~~~

*him and those aiding him. He has been utterly alone since the death of his parents.*

*"Why are you crying, young man?" An older man, someone the boy had never seen before, knelt down beside him and asked. He had a different scent, not like the members of this pack. He also looked important, like someone with a lot of money. His clothing was nice and clean. His face, though scarred and rough, was kind.*

*"She didn't listen," the boy whimpered, pointing down the alleyway that the pretty woman had just walked down. She isn't screaming yet, but the boy knows it is just a matter of time. The houses and buildings all along that alleyway belong to the pack's single guards and warriors. No one goes that way except for them, and for good reason.*

*She wasn't nice, but no woman deserves to be treated the way those men will end up treating her.*

*"Who?" The man looked down the pathway.*

*"The woman," the boy whimpers. "The one not from here. She was going to the packhouse. I told her not to."*

*The man makes a face, then whistles loudly, causing two more men to appear from a store across the square.*

*Both of the new men are dressed similarly to the first man, but they are considerably younger. Their scents are similar and their faces are just as kind, looking down at the boy with a lot of sympathy. One of them even reaches into his pocket and fishes out a handkerchief, using it to mop up the tears and snot all of the boy's face.*

*"My name is Kent," the handkerchief man said, his voice soothing and tender. "What is yours?"*

*"Riley," the boy blubbers.*

*"Where are your parents, Riley?" the older man asked. When Riley's face contorted with mourning and sadness, his bottom lip quivering uncontrollably, the three men knew. He had no parents, and the older man instantly felt horrible for asking such an insensitive question.*

*The boy begins to cry again, flustering Kent. Kent decides the handkerchief is a lost cause, now creating mud against the boy's dirty skin instead of helping to clean him up. Instead, he opens his arms wide to Riley. Riley doesn't hesitate to throw himself in Kent's arms, longing for some form of physical contact after so long. He hasn't been held since his parents' deaths. Kent doesn't flinch away from the boy's grimy appearance or soiled clothing. He holds him tight, letting the boy feed off some of his strength.*

*"Can we bring him with us, commander?" Kent looked up at the older warrior.*

*"We sure as hell aren't leaving the lad on the streets with wet britches. We can get him cleaned back at the hotel, then have him on the ship before it takes off for Hidden Cove tomorrow. The captain will look after him."*

*The boy gripped tighter around Kent's neck, fearful of what they meant about the captain looking after him.*

*"Riley," Kent took the boy's hands, pulling him back slightly to look at his face. "Do you want to go someplace where there are other children that need friends like you to watch out for them? A place where you will get fed more than you could ever eat and teachers will play with you when you're not doing school?"*

*"Not the fabric mill?" Riley asked, worried about where the place could be. The only place in this pack for kids like him are the mills, and the children rarely live long in those conditions.*

*"No, lad," the commander shook his head. "It would be one of our orphanages. I think you would do well in the one near the sea. The kids take walks on the beach often and pick seashells. Sometimes our Alpha even joins them."*

*"Your Alpha?!" Riley asked in disbelief. "Alpha's don't care about kids."*

*Kent huffs. "They do. Yours just doesn't. He's a special kind of horrible."*

*"Speaking of which," the commander said, "It appears the brothel wench you spotted from the store window was seeking Alpha Wayne. Are you sure she was the one who caused the problems for the Luna and for Percy's new mate?"*

*Kent nodded. "Percy wanted to skin her alive. Leona was very possessive of the Alpha at the brothel, too. If she's here, I don't imagine it's for a good reason."*

*"She could just be trying to find a new Alpha to harass since ours found his mate," the third man said.*

*"Doubt it," Kent groaned, narrowing his eyes in the direction they saw her walking. "She was obsessed. The crazy kind of obsessed. She had the brothel women crash the Alpha and Luna's wedding reception. She even tried to get in his wedding bed before the Luna could."*

*The commander pursed his lips deep in thought while staring in the direction Riley said not to go. "Why is that way not safe to go?" He asked Riley.*

*Riley sniffled and looked down the path with a worried expression. "The guards live down there. They attack women walking that way. They got my mom. They killed her."*

*Kent grips the boy tightly against his chest, hiding his angered expression from him so as not to scare him. The commander and the other man looked appalled.*

*"Gerald, mind link the others and let them know that that woman is here. Tell them the situation and wait here to watch for her return. Don't go down that pathway unless you hear screams. Even then, notify us first."*

*"Sure, commander. Where are you two going?" The third man, Gerald, asked.*

*The commander tenderly smiled down at Riley. "We're going to get this boy checked into the hotel and cleaned up. Maybe Kent can introduce him to the captain after getting him new clothes and a belly full of something delicious."*

*The commander takes a paper bag Gerald is holding and offers it to Riley. Gerald is more than willing to part with his recent purchase for the boy's sake. Riley opens the bag, then smiles for the first time in weeks.*

*"Cookies!" Riley squealed gleefully.*

*"All for you, lad. Munch on those as we walk," the commander said as he lifted the boy in his arms, hiding his grimace as he got a closer view of the bruising on the boy's cheek from the brothel wench's slap. It's wrong, but the commander secretly thinks that if she were to be attacked, it might just be deserved. He never thought he would think that about a woman, but she seemed like pure evil. This pack would fit her well.*

# THIRTY-TWO

***Lachlan***

Since that night, our relationship has only gotten better. That walk to the garden, and finally being able to confess to my wife that I knew she was my mate, was the start of her truly opening up to me.

That evening, dinner was intimate. Most of the pack had eaten, leaving only the stragglers and Cherum. He grumbled a bit when first seeing us, asking Lira if she was alright, but when he noticed the change between us, he excused himself to another table, claiming he needed to talk with someone about a cream delivery or something along those lines.

I didn't question it, and Lira giggled at his excuse, distracting me once again. Her giggle and laughter is like a soothing balm to my anxious soul. It's the most reassuring sound I've ever heard. It's like my soul is crying out that if she is happy, everything else will be okay.

That night, I held her as I usually did while she fell asleep, but we talked, truly talked until her eyes fluttered close and her breathing evened out. We were never so open with one another, and after she slept, I just watched her for heaven knows how long, marveling at each and every one of her beautiful features.

Even the little sounds she makes, and her light snoring I find adorable. I never wanted to sleep, not wanting to miss a single movement of hers. Eventually, I did drift into a deep, restful sleep, which I was thankful for since we would be busy the next day. I thought up big plans for us while watching her sleep, wanting to have another perfect ending to a fulfilling day. I want more nights alone with her, growing closer to her as we learn more about one another.

The next day, just as I promised, we set out for the orphanage after breakfast, a small entourage of Cherum, Cedric and a few of her guard warriors accompanying us.

Cedric looked less enthusiastic than normal, not going out of his way to irritate me for once. I thought it was a good thing, but then Lira picked up on his mood and fawned over him for most of the journey.

I don't know what the issues are between him and Meldec, but I want them fixed. It's petty of me to admit, but I don't like watching my wife show concern for anyone else.

I ended up mind linking Meldec, telling him where we were and asking him to personally come and bring me my horse. Lira wanted to walk to the orphanage, but I had plans for our way back.

He questioned why he had to be the one to do it, but when I mentioned Cedric, he was quick to agree.

Lira and I played in the water with the children, one little boy in particular, during most of our time at the orphanage. The little tyke, Westley, was excited to see Lira. A little too excited. He ran to her, pulling on her skirts until she kneeled down, then he wrapped his arms around her neck and kissed her cheek.

It's not attractive for a man to be jealous of a child, but I was. Extremely so. I somehow buried that down from showing on the surface and knelt down beside my wife, the boy going shy at my appearance. With a kind smile and a few pats on the head, he warmed up to me, and I selfishly made it my mission to hold and hug the boy, even teaching him how to swim, so my perfect wife wouldn't have to.

It was a fun day. I didn't expect that. I didn't think I could have this much fun playing with children. I visit the orphanages when I can, and do things like read to the kids and help the older ones decide what to do with their lives. Many of the warriors and guards in the castle are from the orphanages. The boys that do not wish to fight or risk their lives usually end up working on fishing boats or ships. We started an apprenticeship program as well for those wanting to go into different trades. We have a partnership with many bakers, the blacksmith school in town, the tailor shops, and even a few of the doctors and clinics throughout the land have been open to taking in some of the older children to train to be nurses and medical students.

I try to take care of the orphans as much as I can, but I rarely just play with them like we did today. Playing with little Westley, having him so eager to soak up all the love and attention we would give him gave me a satisfaction I had never felt before. It makes me hopeful to one day feel this way with our own children.

I would likely get jealous that Lira was doting on our child more than she was me, then take our child from her to selfishly distract them. I would end up being so enraptured in the love and adoration of our most perfect child, because they would be perfect. So perfect, just like their mother. I would get so infatuated with the amazing and perfect life Lira and I created together that my jealousness would fade away. My love would only grow for both our child and the woman who birthed them.

I hope one day Lira will love me, and want the same future that I want with her. That was all I could hope for as we rode back to the packhouse upon my horse, Lira tucked between my arms, leaning back against my chest marveling at the ocean as we rode along the shore.

That night, we took a walk in my mother's garden again, only this time, I had the staff set up dinner for us there, so we could eat while watching the sun set, undisturbed by everyone else, including her overprotective Delta. Cherum is no longer my Delta and one of my commanders. He is entirely Lira's protector, the shadow and comfort of his Luna, and I wouldn't have it any other way…..except when I want to be the one who does all that for her. I'm tempted to have us eat alone in the garden every night to monopolize even more of my wife's time.

I had a thick fur blanket resting on the back of Lira's chair, so we could enjoy our meal for as long as we wanted, despite the cold. I would have been fine sitting beside her and holding her through the evening, but it would have made eating difficult. I would have gladly gone hungry to provide her with my body heat, but she might have found that uncomfortable. Her joy and comfort were my top priority, and the fur blanket sufficed.

Lira and I talked until it was near bedtime, Niomi coming to hunt my wife down to prepare her for bed. It was the most relaxing, enjoyable meal I think I have ever had. She was smiling and laughing the entire time, sharing stories of her mother, who she loved dearly. I told her about my parents as well. I know both of them would have loved her if they were alive today.

After Lira was ready for bed, I let Killian come forth and brush her hair like we do every night. He and Val playfully teased each other, and Killian even managed to sneak a few kisses of his own without Lira having another panic attack like she did the first time he and Val tried kissing. Being able to admit that we were mates and talking through a lot of our issues was a game changer for Lira. She is so open to the bond that she's letting my touch soothe her while awake, not just when she is asleep.

We continued talking as we laid beside each other in bed, her head resting on my arm while I gently and tenderly stroked my fingers through her long hair. She is the most gorgeous woman imaginable, and I want to fall asleep watching her and talking to her like that every night. Eventually, her eyes fluttered shut, but I continued to just stare at her for at least another hour before I pulled her against my chest and let the beating of her heart lull me to sleep.

It was truly a fantastic day. I can only hope that it's one of many.

~

***Elelira***

"Are you excited about this weekend?" Yasmin asked me as we sat in the finished dining hall, sipping tea after lunch. The men went back to work to get ready for some festival happening this weekend. Lachlan and Nilo have been consumed with preparations for it all week, but today Lachlan asked for my guard and Cherum to accompany him too. Cedric, Yasmin and I were left behind with a stern request from Cherum to not leave the castle under any circumstances. He's a worry wart.

"I haven't been to a festival before," I wrung my hands in my lap. "Shouldn't I be helping too if I'm the Luna now?"

"Psh, no," Cedric grinned, tracing his finger along the grain of the table. "Just relax. You shouldn't have to do anything when that ape you married is the one who came up with this idea, even if you are Luna."

It still felt weird to say it out loud. Being accepted by Luna and being treated like Lachlan's mate is such a weird concept for me.

I like it.

I'm starting to like Lachlan a little more each and every day. I feel like I can trust him. I trust his feelings for me. It's helping me to get over some of the trauma of my past with him, and I truly look forward to each day now, and what possibilities it could bring.

That also makes me nervous, though; having new possibilities.

I don't know what is going to happen. This festival wasn't something that happened in my first life. I don't even know what it's for. This is also about the time my Uncle first sent someone to check on me, seeing if I was with child yet.

The man didn't check me in a very pleasant way either. Lachlan didn't care before, not even making an appearance to welcome the guy, but I wonder how he would react now when some rough, shady warrior doctor from my uncle's pack showed up and demanded to check to see if I was pregnant by giving me an exam.

What if the man shows up during the festival and causes problems for the brothel women again? I don't think he came alone every time he showed up before. I'm sure what happened to Yasmin might happen again to a different woman if Lachlan isn't going to the brothels like he was in my first life. Maybe I should have Yasmin warn Lady Vera. Or maybe I should do it myself.

"Hey Yasmin. Do you still go to see Lady Vera or the women at the brothel at all?"

She quirked her lips to the side. "I've had a few of the girls invite me to eat with them or visit. Percy always tries to tag along, so I rarely go. He gets in trouble enough by skipping duties to be with me."

"He does," I laughed. "Ever since you got your mate mark, he can't stay away from you for long."

"I know," Yasmin blushed. "Speaking of mate marks, I see you still don't have one. Have you guys really not mated yet?"

Now it's my turn to be embarrassed. "You know we haven't," I grumbled.

She asks me almost every morning now, along with Mimi and Gemma. They thought Lachlan was just being considerate of me being so young at first, thinking he was just trying to ease me into being ready for that kind of intimacy. Now they are coming up with different theories as to why we haven't consummated our marriage and marked each other.

Gemma thought maybe one of us was mated to someone else, or that Lachlan accidentally marked one of his conquests and we were waiting for the next full moon so he could mark me and reject the other bond.

If you have already marked someone, or even found your fated mate who is still living and want to mark another without an accepted rejection, you have to wait until the next full moon to do it. The power of the moon at its fullest gives our Lycan side the ability to take a chosen mate and override fate, or claim your fated mate in the instance that you already took a chosen one before meeting your fated but want to do away with that bond to form your fated one.

Yasmin never met her fated mate, and Percy's fated mate had already died, so they didn't have to worry about waiting. That was fortunate for them. It's not an easy or pain-free process. You are literally tearing a reluctant bond apart in the process. If two fated mates meet and there is a rejection, as long as it's accepted by both of them, they can move on right away. If it's not accepted, they will have to wait until the next full moon to claim a chosen mate.

When the full moon passed and I still wasn't marked, Gemma realized both of us were really fated mates and Lachlan hadn't accidently marked another. They still can't believe that their insatiable Alpha was just being patient and not rushing to claim me and mark me.

"I can't understand you two," Yasmin shook her head. "I know it's crass and rude of me to bring this up, but every girl at the brothel knows how needy the Alpha can be. The fact that he is waiting until you are ready is fascinating to me."

Val growled in my head at the reminder that Lachlan shared a bed with our friend, and most other girls she worked with. I have accepted it for what it is. I don't like it, but he has been faithful since we came back to the day of our marriage. It's not Yasmin or any other woman's fault that our husband was a philanderer before me.

"Yes. It's so sweet the fuckboy is keeping it in his pants and respecting his wife like he should be," Cedric rolled his eyes. He probably thought Yasmin's statement would bother me and is speaking up in my defense. I'm not offended. Just a little stung by the reminder. "Why did you ask about the brothel women, Ela?" he asked, pushing my hair behind my shoulder. "Was there a reason?"

"Well," I bit my lip nervously. "I was thinking about speaking with Lady Vera soon if I could. I have something I wanted to run by her." Warn her about, really, but I don't want to alarm Cedric or Yasmin if it doesn't happen.

"Want to go see her?" Yasmin asked. "She liked you. I'm sure she wouldn't mind meeting you. We can go….oh." She makes a face. "I don't think the Alpha will let you go."

I grimaced. "I don't think so either." He is very protective of me. He always tries to be with me if I try to leave the packhouse for any reason, and when he can't, he sends my entire guard and even some extra warriors to keep me safe.

"I don't think Percy will either. He doesn't want me going back to the brothel for anything."

"I'm not supposed to leave the castle without my guard anyway. It's a Luna rule." Lachlan drilled it into me when I tried to take a swim with just Cedric once, without Cherum or any of the other guards coming with me, since they were in a training session with Lachlan.

"Do we need their permission?" Cedric smirked with that troublesome glint in his eye. That means he is thinking of something that is going to make my husband very mad. "You are both grown women. And you, *Luna*, are not marked yet. Don't you need to bare his mark before you can be fully considered Luna? That sounds like an exception to the rule."

"Still," Yasmin giggled, "She commands her own guard. I think finding a loophole isn't going to make Cherum okay with her breaking the rule."

"Rules were made to be broken," Cedric sat up straighter. "Just this once. It will be fun. We can disguise you so no one recognizes you. No one will recognize you anyway without half the pack's warriors following you around anyway. Don't you think it would be fun to sneak around, acting like a normal pack member for once?"

Yasmin lifted her brows, her mouth going wide, like she is about to disagree, but then a slow grin replaced her shock, making her eyes crinkle in the corners. "It would be fun. I do miss some of my friends."

I shifted nervously in my seat. "Lachlan won't like it."

"So?" Cedric scoffed. "He goes out by himself. Why can't you? It's not like you will be on your own anyway. I'll be with you."

I bit my lips together. "You're a bad influence," I said, trying not to smile.

"You love me being the little devil sitting on your shoulder. You know you want to go."

I do. This would be my only chance to warn Lady Vera too. Lachlan would want to know why, and so would Cherum. If I told them what I was expecting of my uncle, that he was probably sending a team to check and see if I was pregnant soon, or if I revealed how that horrible man would be checking me, both of them would explode. Cherum would slaughter my uncle's men. Lachlan may even do away with the treaty and start another war.

He can't do that yet. In several months, he will need that treaty. He will need my uncle's support and soldiers.

As Luna, if that's truly what I am now, meeting Lady Vera myself without involving my husband or Delta is the best decision for the pack. I need to keep the pack safe in the best ways I can.

"I don't want to make them angry," Val whimpered.

"I don't either, but we still should do this. For those women and for the pack."

"Okay," Val sighed, "You will have to calm him down when he finds out. Cedric might be fish food." Her voice lifts with humor at the end of that sentence.

"We can do it," I laughed softly back at her, "We can calm him down and save our friend from being fed to the ocean life."

'Let's do it," I told Cedric, suddenly not so pessimistic. I would be worried about Lachlan's anger and wrath in my first life, but now I trust him enough to know he would never hurt me. He might hurt Cedric, but we can deal with that. He will listen to me.

"Seriously?" Yasmin clapped her hands gleefully. "This will be so fun. I have the perfect wig for you."

"Wig?" I looked at her in confusion.

"Yes silly," she giggled. "We're going in disguise, remember."

# THIRTY-THREE

"Oh my goodness. You look so pretty with black hair, Luna," Yasmin gushed for the tenth time. "It makes your green eyes pop even more."

"It's itchy," I grumbled, scratching at the back of my head. "Why do you even have this sort of thing?"

Yasmin shrugged, pulling the hood of her shawl over her head as we passed a couple of guards on the road to town. "When you are in *that* line of work, wigs are sometimes needed. Men have different preferences," she blushed.

"Oh," I suddenly have the urge to wash my hair when we get back home. I don't mean to judge or think too deeply of the subject, but the thought of some random man performing those acts in such close proximity to an accessory I'm currently wearing I find mildly disturbing. I hope she washed it afterward.

"Does your mate have many preferences too? Does he get the urge to imagine you as a raven-haired beauty to get him going?" Cedric asked teasingly, making me gasp. I'm embarrassed just hearing that question.

"No," Yasmin slapped Cedric's arm. "I just didn't want to toss them. Wigs are not cheap. I spent a lot of money on getting them."

"I'm sure the money was *hard*-earned," Cedric snorted.

"You think you're funny, huh?" Yasmin glared at him, "I can shave you bald in your sleep and make your hair into a beautiful wig."

"That would really be a *hard-earned* wig," he chuckled with a wink. "Your mate might not approve of that."

"Oh, just my mate?" Yasmin smirked. "Might someone else's mate not approve as well?"

"Well, I don't think Ela's mate would care much," Cedric feigned ignorance. "I'm sure he's funded a wig or two of yours."

"Hey," I snapped, Val growling in warning through me. I don't want me or my husband's former acts to be brought into their conversation.

"Sorry," Cedric smiled apologetically at me. "Distasteful joke. I take it back."

"Quit playing stupid," Yasmin slapped his arm again, ignoring the comment about my husband. "What is going on with you and the Gamma?"

I've been eager to ask this too. My minor anger at his teasing and crude jokes is momentarily forgotten while I eagerly wait to hear his answer.

Cedric looked hesitant and the most awkward I have ever seen him. He's staring down the path like he's desperate for a distraction to pop out and draw attention away from him.

"Nothing is going on," Cedric sighed. "You are correct in assuming he's my *mate*," Cedric spit the word out like a curse. "He felt it the same as I when we first met. A then told me at length afterward when the Alpha left us alone about why he didn't trust sirens and wanted to mark me, but would not let me do the same until he felt he could trust me. I told him he could mark a rock and forget it. That's it."

"That's it?" Yasmin looked up at him in disbelief. "He follows you around like a puppy."

"More like a fly," Cedric groaned. "It's just the bond that makes him. I haven't had a pleasant conversation with him yet. Actually, I avoid responding or listening to him at all costs."

Meldec's comments on the beach weeks ago came to mind. "Do you think he still feels the same? I mean, about not trusting you?"

"I don't know nor do I care," Cedric scoffed. "I don't need his trust just like I don't need his acceptance. To make such an arrogant, bigoted statement based on rumors and ignorant opinions, then demand for my trust anyway, is reason enough to not concern myself with him in any way."

"What if he regrets what he said and how he acted?" I asked.

Cedric pursed his lips to the side of his face, then grimaced, his eyes narrowing more and more the longer he thought of his answer. "I don't think people change. He may feel sorry because of the fractured bond, but his ideas have likely not changed."

I pulled my brows down, contemplating his reply. "You don't think feeling sorry would cause the person to maybe change their perspective?"

"I don't, no. Prejudices are hard to break."

"Maybe," Yasmin said, "but I do think life-altering events can change a person. Look at the Alpha."

"What do you mean?" Cedric looked down at her with confusion, as did I.

"You both don't know this, but he was once cold and distant, never truly happy. He carried the grief of war and was untrusting and guarded. He was also wary of races outside the ones he could command. When he met the Luna, though," her voice lifted as a smile spread on her face. "He's a completely different person. His whole world seemed to change, to revolve around her. He even allowed you to stay here, Cedric. I know the Alpha of the past would have tossed you back into the sea without hesitation. Probably with a few fish hooks lodged through your limbs and lip."

"That's so rude," Cedric scoffed.

"Oh, and telling me my wigs were *hard-earned* isn't?"

Cedric smiled teasingly, wrapping his arm around her shoulder and bringing her grumpily pouting frame in for a side hug. "I was just teasing you. I appreciate a *hard* working woman."

She elbowed him in the side, making him groan and hug his abdomen. "I would appreciate you keeping your appreciation to yourself."

"No promises," Cedric laughed.

Yasmin growled, which just made Cedric laugh more. "I'm trying to have a serious talk with you and you're making jokes. Are you doing the same to the Gamma? He may be trying to apologize or talk things through with you, but if you are treating him with sarcasm and rude comments like you are me, then it's just as much your fault as it is his that you can't work through your problems to be mates."

The humor started to drain out of Cedric's expression. "I told you, it doesn't matter. I don't think he will change and I don't want to be tied to someone who won't trust me."

"So you are the one clinging to your own prejudices and opinions?" Yasmin narrowed her eyes. "You don't know what his true feelings are or the reasons behind them until you talk to him. He may have reasons for his distrust, just like you do."

"Like Lachlan," I murmured. I smiled sadly, then rested my hand on his arm. "I had a horrible misunderstanding with Lachlan my first morning here. I thought it was irreparable, the damage that incident caused, but after hearing his reasons for his reaction, and then seeing the changes in him, I know he has changed. I wouldn't be sneaking out with the two of you now if I didn't think he had truly changed. I know that even when he finds out about this, he would never hurt me. He might get angry, but he will most likely take it out on you and not me," I smirked. "Don't worry, though. I'm also sure that I can turn his focus back on me quite easily and we won't need to pull fish hooks out of your limbs later."

Yasmin giggled. "If that does happen, I know a certain Gamma for sure will seek revenge for you."

Cedric scoffed. "Sure he would."

I gripped his hand, making him look down at me. "Both Yasmin and I can see how much Meldec already cares about you. Why not just consider giving him an opportunity to explain himself? I just don't want you to have any regrets, and I know Yasmin doesn't either."

"No I don't. You are one of our most precious friends. We want you to be happy. We both have our mates. I want you to have yours too."

"And if it doesn't work out? If the Gamma and I are still incompatible?" Cedric looked unsure and vulnerable, making my heart go out to him.

"Then we will be there to kick his butt," I said firmly.

"And then cheer you up," Yasmin added.

"The *hard* way?" Cedric teased, his crooked smirk returning to his face, making both of us laugh, knowing he was only joking. His preferences in that department are not us, no matter what wigs or accessories we wear.

"Sure," I laughed.

"I know a club for *that* inclination," Yasmin giggled. "We can sneak out again and go together."

"Now we're talking," Cedric grinned, wrapping his arms around both our shoulders as we walked through the outskirts of town, headed for the brothel.

~

***Lachlan***

Killian was pacing back and forth in my mind, restless for some reason, making it hard to concentrate on this meeting. We were working out the final details of the festival this weekend, and I wanted it to be absolutely perfect. I wish he would calm down and let me focus.

"I need to see our mate in order to calm down, jerkface. Hurry this up and go find her."

*"She's fine,"* I sighed internally. *"That annoying merman is with her."* He likes to try and get a rise out of me, but he is diligent about keeping her safe. I saw a visiting merchant drunkenly run into her in the packhouse's courtyard and before I could even react, Cedric had him by his throat against the wall, forcing him to apologize. I ended up being glad he reacted instead of me, because Lira was upset with him about it for the rest of the night. She called it overkill when I thought it wasn't enough.

"Can we move this along?" Meldec surprised me, saying the same thing as my Lycan in my head. "This is getting too drawn out. We assigned the security aspects and have the routes covered. Am I needed any more?" Meldec was drumming his fingers impatiently on the table, looking anxious, which is very unlike him.

"What got in your drawers today?" Cherum said sarcastically. "This is a surprise for the Luna. Of course, we want it to be perfect."

Meldec ran his hand through his hair, then groaned. "I have this urge to go find my….to go find….I just need to look for someone, okay?"

We all know, but Meldec still has trouble admitting that Cedric is his mate. They have yet to claim each other too. I bet his Lycan gets anxious about being away from him as he's still unmated. Maybe that's why Killian is restless too.

"I'm restless because I can't feel her close by like normal," Killian growled at me. "I can usually feel her faintly when she is near, but I don't feel her at all right now. The pull is gone."

I furrowed my brows, concerned now since Lira is supposed to be where Cedric is. I couldn't feel the bond yet, but my Lycan usually could. Meldec, even if he won't admit it, can surely feel his bond with Cedric. If both Killian and Meldec are anxious, there must be a reason.

"Nilo will finish this meeting out. Mel, come with me."

"Alpha," he pushed away from the table, "I really need to-"

"That's where we are going, dumbass. To check on our mates," I told him, earning an embarrassed groan from him as we walked past all my commanders and the Luna's guard. "Everyone already knows, you idiot. I don't understand why you don't just hurry and claim him. He's annoying, but a hot commodity to the unmated females, and even the unmated males with that preference. Someone else might take him."

Meldec growled at my warning, making me smirk. "And that's how everyone knows that he's your mate, Mel. You make it that obvious."

"Okay. I get it." He mumbled, walking next to me as we began searching the castle for Lira and Cedric. Before we got far, Percy came running after us. "What are you doing?"

"Sorry, Alpha. I couldn't sit still. My Lycan and I both feel our bond's pull to Yasmin stretching further and further. I thought maybe she could be running an errand for the Luna, but I remembered that she was supposed to stay with Cedric and Ela." When I narrowed my eyes at him for addressing Lira so casually, he added, "Sorry, sorry. She was supposed to stay with Cedric and *the Luna*. Your most gratuitous and more understanding mate."

"She truly is his better half," Mel snickered.

"Only half?" Percy snorted.

"You're right. She's carrying all the good qualities in their relationship," Meldec added, making me growl in annoyance.

"Will the both of you shut up? Percy, can you reach your mate?" Lira was still unmarked, so not part of the pack mind link, and without Mel marking Cedric, we wouldn't have a way of reaching him either.

Percy closed his eyes for a moment, then groaned loudly after about a minute. "I tried, but she told me she would see me tonight and not to worry about it. She's put up a block."

I grumbled under my breath, knowing now that something truly was up. "You don't feel her in the castle?"

"No, Alpha," Percy shook his head. "Before she put the block up, it felt like she was to the north at the edge of town."

Meldec growled. "Why? I thought you told them to stay here?" He looked at me accusingly.

"Watch your tone," I warned him. "I can't command my wife or your mate, and I didn't think I needed to command Yasmin. And if Cedric and my wife are with Yasmin in town, I bet it was *your* mate's idea."

"Mine?!" Mel asked in disbelief.

"Yes, yours. He has a knack for trying to piss me off." That merman is constantly trying to get Lira to do things to get me riled up.

"You should have housed him in the pond," Killian reminded me.

"He might end up there later if my wife is harmed in any way," I muttered venomously.

"We can just barbecue him and serve him for dinner with chips and tartar sauce."

"I wouldn't put any part of that man anywhere near my mouth," I gagged in disgust.

"If he would just have let me mark him like I wanted, this wouldn't be an issue," Meldec groaned, pulling my attention out of my conversation in my head with my Lycan.

"You told him you wanted to mark him? Then why haven't you?" I asked.

"Well," Meldec looked away guiltily, "I may have made a minor mistake when we first met."

"Like what? I was there. Did you miss his bum and try to stick it in his ear after I left?"

Percy started laughing like a hyena at my question, but Meldec looked less than amused.

"No," he winced, "It may have been worse than that."

"What's worse than sticking your nub in his ear?" Percy cackled out.

"No, prick. I'll turn yours into a nub if you refer to mine in such an insulting way again." He focused a little too hard on strapping on his horse's saddle. "I, uh, may have made a fuss about not trusting sirens. I told him he couldn't mark me back because of it."

"Wow," I murmured. I feel for him. It's hard to break animosity when we have been at war with every other race for so long over our land and resources. All we have experienced from those races through the wars was selfish greed and terror. Never anything good. Though we never had dealings with sirens before, it's hard to just ignore rumors and legends when that is all we know. "Do you still feel that way, because in my experience, sirens are honest and trustworthy to a fault." I wish King Brennus would be kinder or less honest with his words sometimes. He isn't hesitant to admit he hates me.

"No, I don't." He looked to truly mean it. His expression is somber and full of regret. "I was worried about what others would think, and I still kind of am, but I don't think he is untrustworthy any longer. The Luna's trust in him, and even yours, is testament enough."

"That's an improvement, I guess, but why are you worried about what others will think?" If he's worried about that, he shouldn't make it so obvious that they are mates. It also sounds a little unfair to Cedric. I don't like the fishboy, but I wouldn't be embarrassed to be seen with him or associated with him. Maybe it's because Cedric is so much prettier than

Meldec? Maybe he feels insecure about himself?

"He's a siren, Alpha," Meldec stated, as if it's obvious.

"So?" I lift my brow, mounting my horse in a fluid motion. "Why does that matter?"

Meldec pulled his brows together, looking confused by my response. "What if he gets troubled because of being my mate? Our pack isn't friendly to outside races."

I growled at the assumption that a siren might be unsafe in my pack. My wife is part siren, after all. "That's a bigoted opinion on your behalf, Mel. He is more than capable of handling himself. If our pack has prejudices, then you should be an example by treating your mate with the respect he deserves. Be the change, not part of the problem."

I learned that lesson the hard way in my first life with Lira. I don't want my friend to make similar mistakes. He has the benefit of knowing they are mates. He should be treasuring that, not tarnishing it. He is hurting his bond.

Meldec was quiet on the first part of the trek to town. I used the quiet as a chance to mind link Cherum and let him know our suspicions about Lira and her companions escaping to town on their own. He was far angrier than me. I'm concerned for her safety, but I trust the fishman to keep her safe. Cherum threatened to filet him before cutting off the link to prepare a team to find her.

"Do you think I should offer to let him mark me first?" Meldec asked once the subject had finally left my mind. I was thinking up places to search for my wife and Killian was thinking up ways to get her to pay for worrying us, most of which involve showering her with presents and kisses while we take her away on a date in town, hoping we would find her before anyone else. I was so consumed with thoughts about my mate, I forgot about his.

"Huh?" I looked at him in confusion.

"Cedric. Do you think I should let him mark me first? Would that pacify him and get him to accept me? Assuming I can actually get him to have a conversation with me for once. He's been refusing to listen to a word I have to say."

*"I would too,"* Killian huffed, irritated that Mel broke us from our daydreams about dates with Lira.

"I think you should start with an apology and a conversation. You accused him of being untrustworthy, thereby breaking his trust in you. You might have to earn that back."

"Buy him clothes and flowers," Percy offered. "Yasmin loves it when I buy her shoes and flowers."

"He's a man, idiot," I scoffed at him.

"So? Yasmin and Luna are close with him and he likes many of the same things they do. He said just the other day his favorite flowers are hibiscus flowers that bloom in the warmer climates near the sea. He also likes sweets. Cherum accidentally brought the sugar cookies the Luna dislikes because they have far too much icing, but Cedric said they were his favorite and ate them all up."

"Really?" Meldec scratched his chin as he took mental notes. I'm busy grinning, imagining my wife's face when she bit into one of those cookies to discover it was too sweet for her. She makes the cutest faces. Even her disgusted face is adorable. "What else does he like?" Meldec asked.

Percy spent the rest of our ride to town telling Meldec everything he could about Cedric, and I was able to slip back into my daydreams about my wife.

# THIRTY-FOUR

***Elelira***

When we got to the brothel, Lady Vera was not only willing to talk to me, she invited all of us in for a drink. She grabbed a couple of pints of beer, even though it was barely after lunch, and sat the two of us down at a table in the corner while Cedric and Yasmin remained at the bar, talking with her friends.

"I barely recognized you with that wig on, Luna," Lady Vera commented. "It's one of Yasmin's, isn't it? I remember sending it out to be cleaned not long before she quit."

Oh good. At least now I know it's been cleaned after use. I was trying not to let it bug me, but it was.

"I would have smelled scents on it if it was dirty like that," Val tried to tell me, rolling her eyes.

*"It's just the fact it was on her head while someone was doing that to her. It's just a minor phobia."* With my past life, can you really blame me? Thinking of any man doing those acts grosses me out and makes my throat swell. My anxieties begin to rise and I feel like I'm about to slip into a fit. I lift my hand to my necklace and let its magic calm me, the thought about other men right now making my panic rise and my stomach churn.

"You don't get like that when we think about our mate in that way," Val teased me.

*"He's our mate. The bond won't let me feel disgusted or fear him now that our bond with him is strengthening."* I felt the opposite of all that with Lachlan. I feel giddy when he is near and I miss his touches after he leaves my side to go do his work as Alpha. When I see him coming my way, my heart races in a good way, and after his training, when he comes back to our room, most of the time shirtless and dripping in sweat, Val likes to plant dirty thoughts in

my mind, making me blush.

The mate bond, when it's not damaged and no one is fighting it, can be a very powerful thing.

"So why are you here today, Luna? What made you want to come and talk to an old sinner like me? I'm guessing by the wig that you had to sneak out, the Alpha not wanting you to come to an establishment like this."

I smiled apologetically. "He can be a bit overprotective."

"Oh, everyone knows. He sends an army out with you when you go anywhere. This visit is a surprise in many ways. I didn't think our new Luna was a rule breaker," she smirked, her eyes twinkling with mischief. "What can I do for you, Luna? I wouldn't want your troubles to go to waste."

I hurried and told her about my suspicions of my uncle sending men to check on me soon, and what that could mean for the girls here at the brothel.

"So, you are telling me, Luna, that more men from your uncle's pack will be paying a visit to the Hidden Cove Pack again soon, and might show up to my business again to torment my girls?" Lady Vera lifted her thin eyebrow as she looked at me skeptically.

"Yes ma'am. I was hoping that you could maybe warn the other establishments as well. I'm not one hundred percent certain that they will come here, but after what happened to Yasmin, I wanted to warn you just in case. " I looked over at Yasmin laughing with some of the women who work here at the bar, all of them teasing Cedric about his hair, adorning it with different clips and ribbons.

Lady Vera was watching them too, a small smile playing on her lips.

"That girl looks so much happier now. I would never say what happened to her was a blessing, but look at what it led to. She never laughed freely like that when she worked for me."

I grinned, happy to hear that. "She is very blessed with her mate."

"She is blessed with her Luna," Lady Vera chuckled, her heavy bosom bouncing with the action. "I think we all are, Luna. It takes a selfless woman to aid the woman your husband bedded, as well as looking after the others he used to pay for services."

Val growled in my head at her crude comment, getting more protective of her mate. I'm uncomfortable too, but the fact my husband was a philander in the past can not be changed. It is his current actions that I am trying to judge him on. His current actions are honorable and I have been more than impressed.

It is still uncomfortable to hear of my husband's past flings, though. I squared my shoulders and tried to just grit my teeth through hearing it.

"I think you, Luna, are far more than any of this pack deserves, especially that taciturn husband of yours, but I'm happy you remain here, nonetheless. Seeing my girl," she nodded toward Yasmin, "one that I raised from the time she was a child who couldn't even reach the toilet without a stepstool to the woman she's become today, who looks so happy and carefree, I feel honored to have you in the packhouse. You saw a broken woman crying out for help when others just saw a hooker paying for the crime of being less fortunate. That man there is not of the wolf kind. He is a siren, is he not?"

I looked at Cedric, who was now watching us curiously, having heard the term 'siren', I'm sure. I smiled tenderly towards him, catching the glint in his eye. He is in heaven having all these women to laugh and tease with. He has such a teasing nature and it can get pretty tense at the packhouse with his mate or Lachlan always around.

"He is a siren, but he is my dear friend."

"That's what I'm getting at, Luna. This pack is changing for the better with you here. The Alpha would never have welcomed a siren in the castle before you came. I hear words of praise for you all the time because of your loving heart towards the orphans. When testosterone runs high, I've heard of you putting yourself in harm's way to protect others. The former Luna would have been so amazed at your strength." Lady Vera smiled sadly, looking off in the distance, making me think she was recalling memories from the past.

"Did you know the former Luna?" I asked.

"Oh, yes. She was once a dear friend. When I inherited this place, and she met her mate, the former Alpha, we never had the chance to meet afterward. The former Alpha was not like his son. He was more conservative in his beliefs and thought I was too far beneath his mate's station to ever be granted an audience with her. She was a warrior and was strong physically, but not mentally like you. She didn't go against her husband's wishes." That glint returned to Lady Vera's eyes. "She would have been quite amused by you. You have the strength this pack needs right now. The strength to stand up against anyone who wishes to cause her pack members harm, even her own mate."

"I wouldn't-" I was about to say I would never need to stand up to my husband in that way, but she cuts me off.

"Oh, what happened at the packhouse because of Yasmin on your first morning at breakfast has been spread to all the pack. Everyone is telling of how heroic you were and how you tamed the beast."

Embarrassment creeps over my skin. I slapped him. In front of everyone. I would hardly call that heroic. I let my anger flare too. I actually ended up showing how weak I was at that time because of the panic I felt. Cherum had to carry me out of there. It's humiliating to think about now.

"I'd hardly say I tamed him," I murmured, taking a long sip of my drink. It's still foamy at the top and cool, the condensation from the glass dipping down onto my front.

"Oh, I hope you did," Lady Vera grinned widely, "Because he's here now, and he doesn't look too pleased."

I turned my head towards the door, and sure enough, there stood Lachlan with an angry expression on his face. His eyes narrowed at the glass in my hand, making Lady Vera laugh loudly. Many of the women at the bar around Yasmin and Cedric are watching intently, like they are waiting for a show. Cedric even grabbed a bowl of mixed nuts, eating them with a cheerful look on his face.

That look disappeared when Meldec and Percy walked in behind Lachlan, both of the men looking as angry as their Alpha. Percy muttered something under his breath and walked towards Yasmin, who had just welcomed him with a beaming smile and open arms. Meldec's angry expression vanished to one of anxiety when Cedric scoffed at his appearance. Those two really should try to have a real conversation soon.

Lachlan still looked angry, staring at me.

"There wouldn't happen to be a back door, would there?" I whispered loudly to Lady Vera. I know Lachlan heard me by the deep growl that escaped him.

"Oh, I doubt you will make it in time," she snickered, taking my beer from me in anticipation of the coming storm.

Lachlan took long strides toward me, his eyes never leaving mine. When he was right before me, he slid his thumbs into the waistline of his pants and leaned back on his heels.

"Excuse me, *miss,* but have you seen *my wife* around here?" he asked, confusing me.

"Huh?" I tilted my head to the side, not understanding him.

"She is about this tall," he held his hand up at his side, "Long, golden hair. She's got a sweet, timid personality and would *never* put herself in harm's way by leaving the castle without her guard or escort."

Oh, he just wants to tease me? I smirked up at him, intrigued by his game. "Nope. Haven't seen her. She sounds quite boring."

"She is far from it," he smirked, then bends down, eye level with me, making Val purr with happiness. "Nice hair."

"Thanks," I smiled. "It's Yasmin's."

"You should give it back to her," he chuckled, all traces of anger gone from his face. "I like your golden hair better."

"What about the defiant demeanor?" Lady Vera said to stir the pot, smirking to herself.

"She got that from me!" Cedric called out. "No take backs."

Lachlan sighed. "Well, that leaves me no choice then."

I furrowed my eyebrows in confusion. He sighed again, then bent to scoop me out of the chair, tossing me over his shoulder and making me squeal. "What are you doing?!"

"Dragging my defiant wife back home," he chuckled, "but not until we act a little defiant together. Let's blow off the rest of today and go on a date."

"A date?" I squealed, pinching his sides in an attempt to tickle him and get him to put me down. I don't know why I am trying. It never works. "What if I'm not done here?"

"What business do you have in a brothel, wife?" he snorted.

I pushed myself up against his back, the wig barely staying on my head as I hung upside down. "The same business you used to have here," I goaded him. "Put me down."

Killian growled inside Lachlan's chest, making Val chuckle at his possessiveness.

"If you think I'm putting you down now, you don't know me very well," Lachlan grunted. "I'm sure no one here would dare try and offer you those services."

"I volunteer!" Yasmin giggled, earning her a growl from Percy. "Oh, hush," she scoffed, pushing against his chest.

"I have a few services you might enjoy," Cedric wiggled his eyebrows at me. "I'm sure some of these ladies wouldn't mind helping to service you as well." Many of the girls giggled, nodding shyly in agreement.

I pressed my lips together, knowing he's joking but trying not to laugh, feeling Lachlan's irritation rise. Meldec was turning red, glaring at Cedric like he wanted to argue with him, but he was wisely keeping his mouth shut.

"We're leaving," Lachlan said, his tone rather grumpy now.

"Poor man," Val laughed. "You should just go along with him and try to lift his mood. I expected him to be a lot more furious."

*"I knew he would be fine,"* I grinned internally. Lachlan has been impressive with his behavior. I'm surprised he was able to just ignore Cedric's teasing like that, but I knew he wouldn't be upset with me.

He walked to the swinging doors with me still over his shoulder, and I waved bye to the girls and Lady Vera. "Thank you for meeting with me today," I called out to the madam of the house.

She smirked, her eyes twinkling as she watched us. "You as well, Luna. Thank you for the visit. I will consider what to do about what you told me today."

I smiled kindly at her, then tossed the wig to Yasmin as it fell completely off my head. She and many of the girls looked amused with the scene Lachlan was making, making my face heat. Cedric waved his fingers at me with a smirk, then turned on the bar stool to talk to the woman behind the counter, completely ignoring Meldec. The man looks lost on what to do.

"Is it a good idea to just leave them there," I asked after Lachlan had us out the doors and next to his horse.

"You should worry about yourself right now, *wife*." He smacked my bottom, making me jerk up with a yelp, then he lifted me to set me on the saddle of his horse. I'm glaring down at him, rubbing my butt. It doesn't hurt, but the principle of the matter calls for me to make a show of my displeasure with the action.

"That was rude," I muttered.

"Oh, I'm sorry," he chuckled darkly. He mounted his horse, pulling my body back against his, his breath fanning over my neck as he whispers in my ear. "Hearing others offering to *service* you has my wrist a bit twitchy."

I press my lips together, turning my head away to hide my smile.

"I hope it was worth it," he murmured in my ear.

"Why?" I whispered breathlessly, the bond and his breath stirring around me making me a bit dazed. "Are you going to punish me, Alpha, for leaving without your permission?"

"Oh, no," he chuckled, kissing the side of my neck. "I'm going to do the opposite. I'm going to be showering you with affection the rest of the day and you are going to let me. Killian won't take no for an answer after the worry you put us through, and neither will I." he presses his lips to my neck two, three times in a soft, sensual way. "Your Delta, on the other hand, is threatening to handcuff you to him every waking minute from now on. That's after he nags you to death. Look forward to that when we get home."

I cringed, knowing Lachlan isn't joking. "You can save me, can't you, *husband?*" I turned and tried batting my eyes at him, the way I see Yasmin flirt with her mate all the time.

Lachlan chuckled deeply, lifting my chin and pressing his mouth to my pouty lips. "I'll see what I can do. My protection doesn't come cheap."

I narrowed my eyes at him, lifting one eyebrow while I tilted my head. "What do you want?"

He smiled broadly. "I already told you. I'm going to be showering you with all my love and affection. You can't tell me no today."

I giggled at his cheesiness. "Why would I say no to that?"

"Why would you sneak out to go to a brothel?" he growled. "You are stubborn at strange times, Lira."

"No I'm not," I scoffed. "You are just extreme at strange times."

"Maybe," he smirked. "I'm only extreme when it comes to you, though."

My face was probably beet red from his words. Even Val was hiding her face behind her tail in embarrassment. How can he say such things so easily?

~

Lachlan took me to a little cafe in the center of town. We had tea and a large array of snacks. He wasn't as insistent on me eating a lot to gain weight any longer, but he still enjoys feeding me. It's turned into a habit of literally feeding me, like he likes to be the one to feed me bite after bite with his own hand. When we are in his mother's garden alone, I don't mind. I like the intimate moments with him. Here in this very public cafe where everyone recognizes us, I feel self-conscious and keep trying to wave off his efforts.

"You can't say no," he reminded me gruffly. I had to reluctantly endure the embarrassment of being fed like a child, bite after bite of all the treats.

"Please, Lachlan," I hissed at him when I couldn't take any more. "My belly is about to burst."

"Let me see," he said, then surprised me by actually resting his hand on my belly and squeezing my soft flesh. I'm sitting down and have a pooch, which made this horrifying for me. "It feels like there is still room in there for more."

I covered my face with my hands. "I can't believe you just squeezed my belly in public. People are going to think I'm pregnant."

A broad, brilliant grin spread on his face. "I like that idea."

"*Me too,*" Val purred, all for it.

"Don't you start too," I snapped at her. "I can't handle your perverted side with him getting me all flustered."

"You could just give in to temptation," she smirked in my head. "You know you want to. You know he wants to."

She's right. I've sensed he does, feeling his excitement at times when he is holding me in bed, and sometimes when he kisses me I can tell it is causing him discomfort. He has never pushed me, though. He has never asked for that, or done anything to suggest he wanted more than what I was already comfortable with giving him.

He has proven I can trust him. He has proven that he isn't the same Lachlan I knew in my first life. He is caring and devoted, filling me with ease when we are together and making my soul feel at peace when memories of my past life begin to be too much.

If it's with him, my mate, the man who has devoted every day to my happiness since I first opened my eyes again in this life, maybe, just maybe I could give in to more….

"So," Lachlan, probably sensing my fluster and taking it for anxiety, leaned back in his chair, giving me a little bit of space as he popped a grape in his mouth. "What business did you really have at the brothel today? What did the madam mean when she said she would consider what you told her today?"

I bit my lip, thinking of what to tell him, then a teasing thought entered my mind, making me grin.

"I asked her for a job."

He startled back, his eyes turning menacing. "You did not."

"No," I laughed, "but I did enjoy my time there. Cedric and Yasmin had fun talking with her old friends."

"Hmm," Lachlan placed another grape in his mouth, "So what did you tell her she needed to consider?"

I sighed. "You don't give up, do you?"

"Not easily, no," he grins.

"And you call me stubborn." He chuckled at my comment, his whole face lighting up, making me swoon from how handsome he is. "Fine," I sighed, shifting uncomfortably in my chair. "I'll tell you."

How do I tell him about my uncle sending men to check on me without making him angry or him thinking I'm crazy? I can't tell him this is my second life.

"Why not?" Val asked. "He knows you are a siren and accepts it."

"Yes, but if I tell him about my first life I will have to tell him how I died, and that would not be good for the alliance treaty. The pack will need that treaty to remain in place soon."

"Yeah," Val sighed, "You're right. Just tell him you have a suspicion for now. The same as you told the big boob lady at the brothel. That's all you can do."

# THIRTY-FIVE

***Lachlan***

I love flustered Lira. She turns a beautiful shade of pink and can't sit still when I tease her. My little pregnancy comment and the way her whole body, from her chest all the way to her hairline blushed had me wanting to push her a little on the topic, but I know better. She's still not ready. She's barely an adult and I still don't know what she went through in her uncle's pack.

I want her. Lord knows I want her. I am going to wait until she is ready, though, and if she never is, I will be okay with that. Anything as long as we are together.

I still like watching her get flustered over me.

The fluster she is in now is different from the embarrassed kind of flustered like earlier. She's anxious about telling me why she went to the brothel today.

I still want to know. I feel like I need to know.

"I didn't want to mention anything to you because of, um, your distrust in my uncle. I didn't want to needlessly worry you," she said in a small hesitant voice, looking up at me through her lashes.

"Well, now we are going to worry no matter what," Killian growled.

"Tell me," I urged her, reaching out and grabbing her hand in mine. She gripped my hand in both of hers, drawing on my comfort in the bond I'm sure. I can't wait until I can feel it too.

"I think my uncle may be sending someone to come check on me soon," she whispered.

"What? Why?" I furrowed my brows in confusion. Did he send word to her without me knowing? Does he not trust me to take care of….

Wait.

This sounds familiar to me now. He used to send people to check on her in our first life. I tried to avoid being a part of it, but I heard mentions of someone from her uncle's pack coming to visit her to check on her well-being and to see if she was pregnant every few months. It has been some time since our wedding. More than enough time to truly be pregnant and be aware of the condition.

I didn't want to involve myself with Alpha Wayne more than I had to in our first life, and I thought Lira was a trap sent by him. I wish I had paid better attention to what was going on around her back then. She is worried enough about this to bring it to the brothel madam's attention and there has to be a reason why. I fear the reason is an unpleasant one.

"This alliance was meant to bridge our packs through a child," Lira murmured. "My uncle is going to send someone to check my condition and to see if I am adhering to my duties." When she says the word 'check', Killian doesn't miss the shiver that runs up her body, like she fears all that word entails.

"How will they check if you are pregnant and performing your, uh, duties?" I had to ask, needing to know. I fear I already know, but I want to hear it from her. If my suspicions right now are correct, I don't know what I will do.

Lira shrugged her shoulders. "This will be their first time doing so. I'm not even completely sure he will send someone. I just wanted to warn Lady Vera so an incident like what happened to Yasmin won't happen again."

"It won't happen again," I muttered venomously, pulling her to my side and wrapping my arms around her. The thought of any man that could do that sort of damage to Yasmin being near my wife makes me and my beast murderous. I will destroy anyone who tries to upset my wife or disturb the peace in my pack. No one will be *checking* Lira in any way. "I will make sure no men from Alpha Wayne's pack can cross our borders without an escort to guide them, and no one will be going near you without me by your side."

I wish I could ban them from entering all together, but I'll need the alliance in the near future. Demon and vampire clans from the north will try to cross over, picking our people off in the outskirts and small towns of the pack. If I didn't have Alpha Wayne's support, my people would suffer greatly. We don't have the manpower to fight them off on our own.

I also want to know how this man plans on 'checking' my wife. Guilt makes my throat swell imagining the worst and knowing that, because of my neglect, Lira most likely had to suffer with the men her uncle sent on her own.

"*Ask her about it,*" Killian demanded, wanting to know the truth. He's ready to kill.

"*I can't. It's against the contract with her father to reveal we know this is a second life for her.*" I want to ask her more than anything, but my throat burns just imagining the words that form the question in my head. I'll never be able to ask. She will hopefully tell me one day when she fully trusts me.

"Thank you," Lira whispered, melting into my touch. Her whole body relaxes into mine.

"You don't have to thank me, Lira. You are my wife and my mate." It feels so good to call her that. It gives me hope that she will figure out the rest and I don't have to keep any secrets from her. It gives me hope that we will soon be completely open and honest with one another.

"I am," she turned her head to look up at me. "And you are my husband and mate."

I grinned lovingly down at her. "I am. I want to be your everything, Lira."

She bit into her bottom lip, her emerald green eyes boring into mine. "Everything?" she asked in a breathy whisper.

"Yes," I pressed my lips to hers. "Everything. You are my entire world already. I hope to one day be the same to you."

She shifted her hands to glide them up my chest, then traced my lips with the tips of her fingers. "I want you to be my everything, Lachlan. I want to….I want to try being with you in the way mates should be." Her eyes were intense, all sorts of emotions warring behind them, but I could see the fire of her resolve, making my breath hitch when I finally caught on to what she was saying.

"You mean, *fully* with me?" I murmured, not believing my ears. I have been patient and not pushed her once, not wanting to make her panic or have a fitful attack again. I know I don't deserve even this second chance with her. I sure as hell will never deserve *that* from her. I would have abstained for the rest of our lives if she wanted me to, but if she is wanting it too….

She bit her lip again, then nodded gently. "I don't know if I will be able to, but I trust you, Lachlan. I want to try. I want to trust you with this too. And," she looked down at where her hands were resting on my chest. "Val keeps planting these thoughts in my head. They used to make me uncomfortable, but now they make something else stir inside me."

"What?" Hell, my voice sounds desperate and weak even to me. I am so wrapped around my wife's adorable little fingers and she doesn't even know it. I'm hanging on to every one of her words like they are a lifeline. My need for her is so great, it's all consuming.

Her eyes were shining, and I could see that Val was right there on the surface, talking to her, probably encouraging her to say it. Say what she would normally be too timid to say.

"Desire," she whispered, her fingers flexing against my chest slightly. "I've never felt that before."

"Oh, Lira," I groaned, pressing my lips to hers, my heart beating out of my chest at her confession. She is kissing me just as hungrily as I am kissing her, everything around us, everyone witnessing our actions all but forgotten. It's just me and Lira, and our desire that is making the air thick as we breathe each other in.

She wants me. She desires me, just like I desire her.

"Can we go back home now?" I asked, not wanting to waste any time. My urgentness makes her giggle.

"What about our date?"

"I'll take you on hundreds of dates to make up for cutting this one short," I begged, pressing my lips to hers again, hoping the bond would do its magic on her.

It does. When I pull away, she is in a daze, her face sinfully sexy with her hooded lust-filled eyes and lazy smile.

"Okay," she grinned. "Let's head back home."

~

***Meldec***

"Do you ladies still want me to show you how to do a fishtail braid?" Cedric leaned over the bar, running his finger playfully down one of the girl's noses, making her giggle. What the hell is a fishtail braid? My beast is snarling inside me, getting more and more upset by the second as I watch Cedric continue flirting with the brothel girls, completely ignoring me even after all this time.

"Is that one of the *services* you were going to offer the Luna?" Another girl who was straightening a bright pink bow in his hair asked.

This is what I've had to watch the past hour or so. All the women here are fawning all over my mate and I feel powerless to stop it. The girl that was messing with the bow in his hair was now leaning on his shoulder, laughing at something he had just said that I missed completely because I was too busy watching her touch him.

That really gets my beast snarling, his growls echoing loudly in my head. "*You fucked this up. Fix it!*"

"I would if I could," I groaned internally. "He won't even listen to me."

"DO THE FLOWER THING!" he snapped. "Do something! Percy gave you an entire list of things he likes. Instead of glaring at him and insulting him, try being nice."

*"I don't insult him,"* I argued, though I know it's not completely true. I've let my jealousy get the best of me a number of times seeing him so close to the Luna and Yasmin, even joking and teasing Cherum and the rest of the men on the Luna's guard, but he won't give me the time of day. I snap at him instead of talking to him with respect, which isn't helping me.

"Try just asking him to go to the bakery with you or to that restaurant your sisters like for dinner. Better yet, take him to meet mom! She always knows how to win someone over."

My mother was a saint. She raised me and my sisters on her own after my father died in the wars. I knew the previous Luna well, and knew how strong of a warrior she was, but I still think my mom is the strongest woman there is. She has resilience and compassion like none other, and can resolve the hardest of issues with just a kind word or a gentle touch of her hand. She has calmed many fights with a simple hand on the shoulder and a stern look, and she always welcomes people with a warm smile and hug, despite their appearance, social standing or where they come from. Everyone is loved and equal in my mother's eyes.

Maybe I really should ask my mother for help. She and my youngest sisters don't live too far from here.

If I can't win him over on my own, then that's what I'll do. I'll recruit mom's help. She fixes everything when no one else can. My sisters would love Cedric for the same reasons all these girls seem to like him too. He's beautiful for a man, and very charismatic.

Cedric is now braiding one of the girls' hair, and my jealousy spikes again, seeing his fingers brushing against her exposed shoulders as he gathers all her hair in his hands.

"Relax your expression," Percy muttered, walking back to stand beside me. He's a lot more calm now, seeing that his mate is alright and just here visiting with her old friends. "You look like you want to start a fight. That's not going to get him to want to talk to you."

"I can't help it," I growled, "I hate seeing him flirting with everyone but me."

"I hate to tell you this, Gamma, but it's your own fault. I wouldn't want to talk to you either if you were always looking at me like that. Calm your tits and wipe the grimace off your face."

"I'm trying!" I snapped. I really am trying. It's just hard to focus with all these women all over him. If he prefers women, I'm already at a disadvantage. I'm not soft or small. I don't think there will ever be a time I need to be saved or rescued like he does with the Luna. I feel like I'm fighting a losing battle when I see him like this.

"Try harder. Start by smiling and saying hi," Percy, the insistent oaf, pushed me in Cedric's direction unexpectedly, almost making me fall to the ground. I stumbled a few steps, then embarrassment washes over me, knowing I just looked like a fool in front of the last person I wanted to see me as one.

"Oops," Percy murmured.

Oh, I'm going to let him have it at training tomorrow.

"Hello, Gamma," Kelly, the bartender, grinned at me. She is the only girl here I know well, since I only come here with the men to drink. I've never desired to be with a woman, and if I had, I wouldn't have been able to be with one in an establishment like this. Being raised by a widowed mother with all sisters makes it difficult not to feel for the women here and the circumstances that may have brought them to such a life. "Do you want your usual?" Kelly asks, wiping clean the inside of a mug.

"No. Thank you, Kelly. I, uh," I looked at Cedric nervously, who was now watching me from the corner of his eye, a wary expression on his face. "I was hoping to speak to Cedric."

Kelly smirked, knowing that I'm gay. I even told her last I was here with the men while they were busy in the rooms upstairs that I had found my mate. She probably suspects by my behavior and the timid look on my face as I stare at him that he is my mate.

She also knows that I royally screwed up our first meeting, giving him the worst first impression of me. She listened patiently as I voiced my problems. She keeps her customers' secrets and their conversations confidential, so I always felt comfortable with her.

"I'm a bit busy," Cedric stated, looking uninterested as he turned his focus back on braiding the woman's hair. The other girls are looking at me curiously, but both Kelly and Yasmin have these knowing expressions, their eyes expectant of a show, which just makes me more self-conscious.

"When you're not, would you like to take a walk with me?" I asked calmly, trying to focus on the goal and not my jealousy. My goal is to get him to accept me, whatever it takes now.

The Alpha was right. He has been nothing but brutally honest with everyone since coming here. I've heard tales of sirens using their abilities to deceive others. If he was going to do that, I think he would have already. He could have bewitched me into giving him my very soul and I probably would have gone along with it. He hasn't, though. He's been so honest with me that it hurts at times, him telling me repeatedly how idiotic and ignorant he thinks I am and to leave him alone.

Why didn't I keep my mouth shut on our first meeting?

"Because you're idiotic and ignorant," my beast growled in my head. "I told you to wait and talk with him before you made any assumptions or demands."

"You did, and now I have to figure out how to get him to forget about that and start over again."

Cedric was quiet for a few moments, looking like he was concentrating extra hard on the girl's hair, even though there was barely any hair left to braid. I can braid hair too. I had to help do my sister's hair plenty of times growing up. I may even be better than my mother. I would love to run my fingers through Cedric's hair, feeling his silky locks between my fingers.

"I should probably find Ela soon. She will need me if that Alpha of yours returns to work."

"He's not!" I rushed to say, probably looking rather crazed. I cough nervously as Cedric turns to look at me like I've gone mad. "I mean, he's not going back to work. He and the Luna are going to be on a date for the rest of the day."

He purses his lips together as he thinks. "You just want to take a walk?" he asked.

"Yes!" I hurried to say, my excitement getting the better of me again. "I mean, yes, or whatever else you would want to do. What I really want is to have a conversation, no matter the setting." I'll accept anything at this point, as long as we can talk and I can beg for a redo of our first meeting. I want to start over from scratch.

"Hmm," he rubbed his chin, fighting a smile. He really is an attractive man. No wonder I'm always getting jealous of others seeking his attention. "I could go for an ale right now," he said.

"If it's ale, we have- *omph*," one of the girls started to say, but Yasmin quickly covered her mouth with her hand.

"There is a great little restaurant down the way that serves the best ale in town," Kelly grinned at me, helping my case. "You both should head down there. It won't be busy this time of day, so you may have the whole place to yourselves."

Heaven bless Kelly.

"Alright," Cedric pushed himself off the bar stool, making my heart sing as I realized he'd just agreed to come with me. "Let's-"

His words were cut short as his eyes began to glow, and his whole face contorted in worry.

"We need to go," he stated when the glow in his eyes died down, walking past me and out the door. I followed closely behind, confused about what had just happened to him.

"Go where?" I asked, worried. He didn't even bother to take the bows and accessories out of his hair when he ran out.

"Ela," he muttered, "She needs me. Something must have happened. She needs me. The magic is calling me right now."

"What magic?" I asked, following him as he hurried down the busy streets, not needing help on knowing where to go. He is walking in the direction of the docks, which confuses me. The Alpha sent out a mind link that he and the Luna were at a cafe. Why would she now be at the docks and how is Cedric just knowing where to go?

"Her necklace," he said. "It calls to me when she needs me. I need to go to her."

Why would she need him when she is with the Alpha? What would she be going through that would have her call for my mate and not her own?

# THIRTY-SIX

***Elelira***

Lachlan and I started to ride back to the castle on his horse after leaving the cafe. It was a very distracted ride so far, though we haven't even made it to the outskirts of town yet. His hands as he helped me up to mount the beast sent tingles traveling all over me, and instead of the calming effect his touch has been giving me since I began accepting him, it's now making my skin itch with some unidentifiable need.

I know what I just confessed to Lachlan was basically an invitation, and it was the truth. I do have this desire that comes over me when I'm with him now…..

But there is also this hesitation inside me, like my heart is trying to tell me I'm still not ready.

"You're just nervous," Val grumbled at me. "It's our mate, and he wants us. There is no reason to not finally claim each other."

*"I feel like there might be,"* I confessed, still feeling unsure.

"Like what? Do you think he kicks kittens and taunts grannies by unraveling their yarn balls when you're not around?"

*"No,"* I huff, *"but this just feels….rushed."* I know I said it myself, and he didn't urge me in the least, but now that it might be happening, I can't help but feel like I didn't fully think this through. My Lycan urging me to finally give in to my urges didn't help me to think rationally either. Horny beast.

"You are being mighty annoying right now," Val grunted. "You know you want him, and you know we can trust him. Just give in. For once."

*"Okay,"* I whispered to her. *"I'll try."*

"Everything okay, Lira?" Lachlan nuzzled his nose against the side of my neck, his lips brushing against my skin, making many of my doubts rush away as a new wave of desire came over me. I leaned back against his chest, letting his touch ease my worries.

"Yes," I whispered, leaning my face back to look at his handsome features. I bit my lip when staring at him made butterflies flutter in my chest. "I'm just, uh, nervous," I confessed.

He smiled gently, pressing his lips to mine. "We don't have to fully mate, Lira. I'm happy just being by your side. I can wait."

Hearing him say that chased away the last of my doubts. I smiled up at him, shaking my head, ignoring Val screaming at me to not let this chance pass by. "I want to," I told him. "I want to take that leap with you."

If it's this Lachlan, the current one that loves and cherishes everything about me, who teases me instead of degrades me when I go against him, I can trust him. He is nothing like the Lachlan of my first life. He loves me, and it's time that I started letting myself love him too.

His smile is so brilliant, it makes me smile just as brightly, right before his mouth meets mine in another passionate kiss. Every time he kisses me like this, it feels as if my heart is going to beat wildly out of my chest.

His free hand, the one not holding the reins, moves across my side, then slides down to my upper leg, kneading and gripping my flesh. The wave of pleasure his touch brings me has me moaning softly into his mouth, making him smile against my lips.

"I can't wait to get you home," he whispered hoarsely, his deep voice surrounding me not helping me to calm down.

Tingles erupt deep in my belly, his face leaning in to deepen our kiss, but then he groans, pulling away from me, leaving me confused.

"Damn it," he muttered under his breath. "Why right now?"

"What?" I looked up at him in question.

"They need me at the docks," he groaned. "Why the hell can't they figure these things out themselves?"

"What things?"

"There was a fleet of ships that came in and apparently one of them had a member of our pack gravely injured."

"Oh no," I whispered, all my lustful thoughts leaving me at the news. "Of course you should go. If it's serious enough for them to call for you and not Nilo, the person must be pretty badly hurt."

"Maybe," Lachlan grumbled, still upset that our plans were put on hold. "The dock manager said the person asked for me and only me," Lachlan's eyes were glazed over, like he's still mind linking whoever reached out to him.

"Hmm. If they are well enough to speak, they must not be so injured that they need our mate," Val huffed.

"Be nice. There must be a reason."

Lachlan turned his horse around and started heading for the docks, holding me tightly as his horse raced at a gallop, weaving through the people loitering on the road.

"I called for Cherum to come pick you up at the docks. I may need to escort whoever this is back to the packhouse. The manager seems to be tied up with sorting things out and isn't offering me much information on who it is."

"I don't mind," I told him.

"*I do,*" Val mumbled, her disappointment souring the thoughts in my own mind. I wanted to spend more time with Lachlan too, but he's the Alpha. He has duties that can't always be blown off to spend time with me. We should be more understanding in times like these.

When we got to the docks, there were people all gathered around a certain ship in the middle of the yard. Guards were standing at the ready, as well as medical staff, but the broken body of the individual lying on the wooden planks was screaming, yelling for everyone to stay away, demanding my husband be the one to help her.

The voice was shrill and familiar, making Val snarl in my head.

Leona.

She was scarred and bruised, bleeding out from the scapes on her face and arms. Those scrapes look suspiciously self-inflicted, like she threw herself on the dock and scraped herself up. She was a Lycan, wasn't she? Why isn't her beast healing her.

I then see the bracelets embedded into her wrists, wrapped so tightly that her skin around them was raw and red, blood droplets seeping from around them. I know those bounds all too well. They are the reason Val couldn't help me when I needed her to heal me in my past life.

"WHAT IS GOING ON HERE?!" Lachlan's voice boomed, making everyone quiet and turning their attention to us. When Leona's eyes met mine, my blood ran cold seeing the hate in her eyes. She narrowed her eyes seeing the way Lachlan was holding me tightly against his body, her lips curling up.

"Alpha," A short, stocky man waddled over to stand beside Lachlan's horse, staring up at him with an anxious expression. "I'm sorry. I know you said you were spending time with the Luna today, but everyone here was at a loss about what to do."

Lachlan stared at Leona coldly, then looked back at the short man. "Just send her to the pack clinic and I'll send Nilo to deal with her later."

"That's not the issue, Alpha," the man looked back at the ship nervously. That's when a group of burly men in red-striped uniforms came forward, all with sinister expressions. I recognized most of them right away. Two of them were the last faces I saw before my death. Their sick smiles as their eyes meet mine makes all those memories come crashing back to me, a cold sweat running down my neck. I reached up for the necklace, rubbing it furiously with my fingers, seeking its comfort like I hadn't done since my first morning here. Even Lachlan's touch right now isn't enough to keep those memories from wreaking havoc on my mental state.

They're here. I knew my uncle would send men, but I never thought I would see all of them at once like this.

The mountainous warrior who acted as the medic who harshly examined me to see if my virginity was still intact each and every time he visited the castle pushed past the rest of the men. He stood before them before he slowly walked down to the dock, sneering and turning his nose up at Leona. He then walked towards Lachlan and me. His expression was cold and hard.

I want out of here. I want to go home. I want to go to the brothel; to the orphanage. Anywhere but right here.

"Alpha," the mountainous man nodded his head once in a half bow of respect, then came to stand behind the short man I could only guess was the dock manager. The dock manager bowed his head, moving back to give room for the horrible figure beside us. "Alpha Wayne offers you this traitor as a token of his loyalty to the alliance. She came to our pack not long ago, claiming to be fleeing from our Alpha's niece and her harsh punishment of banishment." The man looked at me, a chilling smile turning up the corners of his lips. "I knew she had to be spewing nonsense, Elelira. You were never one to kick up a fuss or cause someone unnecessary discomfort. Isn't that right?"

Lachlan looked down at me with a questioning expression. I couldn't do anything but sit there in fear, not knowing how to respond. No matter my response to this man in the past, he was cruel, leaving me bruised and hurting.

"You remember me, don't you, *Luna?*" He sneered the title like it was an insult.

"Issac," I croaked out in a broken whisper, answering automatically, my body remembering what would happen when I chose not to respond to him when he asked me a question.

His smile broadens. "I knew you would."

Lachlan growled behind me, pulling my body back against his in a possessive manner. His growl snapped me out of my trance of terror, and I quickly looked away, wishing for some form of exit from this situation. I'm not ready to face these demons of my past. The past is rushing back to me, making my soul cry for help.

"Ela!" Cedric's voice broke through the fog of panic in my mind. I turned in Lachlan's grip to see him rushing down the pathway to me.

When he rushed to the other side of Lachlan's horse, I dove out of Lachlan's arms for him, relieved that he was there. He held me tightly against his chest, cradling me to him. "Take me home," I whispered brokenly. "Please."

"Yes, my princess," he kissed the side of my head, cradling the back of my neck, his magic rushing forward, seeping into me, lulling me to a comatose state, making fatigue rush over me. "I've got you. I'll take you home."

~

Lachlan

I watched as my wife, my mate, threw herself into the arms of another man. Cedric caught her, cradling her head with his hands, whispering words into her ear until her head went slack against his chest.

"She was having another anxiety attack," Killian whimpered, "and she wanted him and not us."

I narrowed my eyes at the man still standing on the other side of my horse. He was watching Cedric and Lira with an amused smirk on his face. Did she panic because of him? Did he hurt her in some way in the past? She clearly remembered him, but if remembering him caused her to react like that, what was she remembering exactly?

"*My mate,*" Killian whimpered, feeling tiny bursts of her anxiety and fear in his growing bond with her. I want to feel it too. Even right now, with her not alright, I want to be able to feel her directly too, not just feeling my lycan's reactions to feeling their bond.

When I look back at Lira and her siren guardian, he had her asleep in his arms, holding her slack body tightly. He glared accusingly at me, distrust radiating off him in strong waves. He thinks I did something to hurt her again.

That hurts. Almost as bad as it hurts to see my wife seek his comfort and not mine.

"We'll talk at the castle," he stated coldly before turning to climb back up the hill with my mate in his arms, passing a confused Meldec on the way. Meldec looks at me with worry, then chooses to follow his mate. Good. Lira will have more protection on her way home.

She was in my arms just moments ago, on her way home with me. We were so close to becoming one. The thought of being accepted and having the chance to finally mark her and end all these stipulations on the contract with her father was so near. She trusted me to take that leap with me, but she still chose another man over me in her time of need.

It hurts.

"She was never one for the dramatics," the man, Isaac, said. "She was always a quiet and submissive little thing, hiding under her mother's skirts when her mother didn't have a man under them."

A low growl rumbled through my chest in warning. "That is my wife's mother you are speaking about. I would advise that you refrain from upsetting me any further than you already have."

"My apologies, Alpha," he bowed his head respectfully, though the intent behind his actions feels more perverse. "It was just nice to see that married life suits our Alpha's little niece. She seemed…..well accustomed to the role."

He's making fun of us and the fact my wife leapt into the arms of another man the moment she could. Killian is furious, snarling inside my head. If I could, I would put this man in his place right here and now. I might do it anyway if he pushes me any further. Treaty and alliance be damned.

"My wife is none of your concern," I replied in a level voice, trying to maintain my composure.

"That is not entirely true, Alpha. See, our Alpha Wayne sent us not only to deliver this filthy *traitor*," he sneered, looking at Leona briefly, "back to you. He wants to be informed about his niece's wellbeing and…..her current medical state as well. Being that she was always a little thing, a bit weaker than she should be, he wanted to make sure she could keep up with all her *wifely duties* so as to not dishonor our Alpha."

"Let's just bury him and the rest of the crew and claim they got lost at sea," Killian snarled in my head.

It's a tempting idea. Isaac's arrogant smirk slipped off his face the longer I stared at him, pushing my aura out intentionally, reminding him that though he may be a visiting warrior from a pack I am under an alliance with, I could still end him easily. His Alpha was a long distance from here, and my warriors are loyal to a fault. No one would say otherwise if I claimed these men never made it to my shores.

After a long, looming minute in my menacing presence, this bulking warrior is shifting on his feet, looking ready to piss his pants and go hide under his own mother's skirts.

I wonder how well he really knows my mate, and why she seemed so distressed upon seeing him. When she said his name, it was like she was seeing a ghost from her past. She looked at all of them that way. I thought there might have been a history between this man and my wife at first, but now maybe it was something more sinister….

Or maybe she remembers her from her first life.

She knew her uncle would send men to check on her. She didn't tell me how she knew exactly, but I already figured out it was because of our first lives. This man seems very familiar with my wife even now, though. That means he knew her back in her uncle's pack before coming here.

How? Did they have a history?

After seeing her throw herself at Cedric to get away from this situation, and the jealousy that caused me, I can't help but let my mind wander into the worst of scenarios. I need to ask Lira. I don't know how to, but I need to find a way to ask her what happened in her uncle's pack before I decide on what to do about these men.

I looked at the mess of Leona lying broken on the dock, staring up at me with those pathetic pleading eyes.

If she was hoping I would take pity on her after she ran away to another pack and put the blame on my wife, she was wrong. I know what she did to Yasmin, and I feel nothing but disgust for the woman.

"What would you have me do with her?" I asked the man, still cowering beside me. "If she wishes to be in your pack, I have no objections about it.

My *wife* did not outright banish her, but she harmed another woman in our pack and was reprimanded by her Luna for it. If she has strife with her Luna, then she has it with me as well, and I do not care to claim such a disloyal pack member."

"NO!" Leona yelled, pulling her body along the planks of the dock. I resisted the urge to wince seeing the cuffs around her wrist preventing her from healing. "I…I have no issues with…with the…..the *Luna*," she muttered the title like it hurt her to do so. "I want to stay here. Please, Lanny, don't send me back."

Isaac smirked again when Leona called me that dreadful nickname. I never liked hearing it. She came up with it on her own and insisted on using it. "She claimed you both were lovers," Isaac stated, making me roll my eyes.

"If we were lovers, she has hundreds of other lovers to claim too. I'm just the one with the highest title. My only love since the day of my marriage is my wife and no one will come between that."

Leona looked genuinely hurt over my statement, but I didn't care. I was too distracted by the desire to run back to the packhouse and check on my mate.

Just then, Cherum and a few others in the Luna's guard came barreling down to the docks, Cherum looking flustered as he scanned the area for his Luna.

"Cedric took her back first," I told him as he approached me.

"I felt," he looked around accusingly at all the unfamiliar faces of the visiting warriors, then glared at Leona. "I felt her need for me. Is she alright?"

I remained quiet, pressing my lips together, not able to give him a real answer. She was put to sleep by Cedric's magic. That's how not alright she was. Saying it out loud will do no good to my control and my image in front of these men.

Cherum could tell by the look on my face that he wouldn't like my answer. His nostrils flare as he looks around at the men visiting again, "Who did it? Who upset my Luna?"

"Go check on her," I told him, moving my horse to block him from actually attacking someone. "I have to deal with this mess. Please, just go be with her for now." I urged him with my eyes. Acting rashly in this situation is not in the best interest of my pack. I need to figure this all out, and until

I do, I don't want Lira to be stressed or anxious. I want her to have all the comfort from those around her who love her, even if she doesn't want that comfort from me.

# THIRTY-SEVEN

***Elelira***

"Lira?" Lachlan entered our room. He knocked first, but I couldn't bring myself to move or say anything. After waking up back at the packhouse in our bed, I didn't move at all. I just stared vacantly at the wall before me, only blinking and breathing.

I felt the bed shift beside me, Lachlan sitting next to me and gently placing his hand on my back. "Are you alright?" he asked softly.

Am I alright? No, I'm not. Not at all. Not only are those men here, many of whom were involved with…with the events before my death, but that man, Isaac, the way he stared at me….

It makes me sick to even think about it now. Even before, when he came to this pack in my first life to *examine* me, he would visit my mother often. I was always hidden or sent away, but I remember my mother's look of horror whenever she would see him strutting towards her.

I had forgotten that, since it has been so long for me since I was last living in my uncle's pack, but before I was sent to be Alpha Lachlan's bride, I was going to be Isaac's. When my mother died, he tried to claim me then, and my uncle only put a stop to it because he said he wanted me pure in hope of the alliance happening.

It's strange to me now to think about it, but my uncle seemed to know that Lachlan would need an alliance with him. He expected it.

Uncle had told Isaac if by my 18th birthday I wasn't arranged to be married already, he could have me. I avoided Isaac like the plague back then, always hiding among the servants, but Isaac had let me know on his first visit here to Hidden Cove Pack after he discovered that my virginity was still intact, that he was willing to take what should have belonged to him in the first place. Only Mimi interrupting his examination stopped him from doing so, and Mimi was with me for the next several visits after, up until she passed away from sickness herself.

Isaac's visits came less frequently after that, and then they stopped completely months before I left.

I had forgotten all those details, probably locking them away to avoid wallowing in my pain so I could focus on surviving. Seeing him today made all those memories come flooding back. Muttering his name made me remember all the times my mother would whisper his name in fear when she saw him coming, then quickly urging me to run and hide in the stables or kitchens until the next day.

I don't want to see him again. I don't want to experience the same things from my first life. I thought this life would be different. I thought everything was different. Why is this one thing the same?

"Lira?" Lachlan rubbed my back again. "What can I do? I need you to tell me what's wrong so I can fix it."

He can't fix it. This isn't something that will go away. Those men haven't done anything to me yet in this life. What can I tell him? Those men that are under the protection of the alliance you have with my uncle will rape and mutilate me in the future, and I know this because this is my second life. If I have them punished for sins they committed against me in my first life, that means, by the same reasoning, Lachlan is guilty of all the hardships he put me through back then as well.

This is all too much. It's too much to process right now. How am I going to differentiate between this life and my last? It's all too confusing, and the more I try to think about it, the deeper in despair I fall. I need to be numb. I need to not think, and not react at all. I need to try and stay in this vegetative state until my body is able to process everything going on.

Val whimpered in my head, wanting the comfort of her mate, but not wanting to upset me by asking for it. She feels that thin thread of sanity about to snap in my head, and knows if I were to let go of the numbness I'm clinging to like a lifeline, I would have a horrible breakdown.

We came so close to forgetting everything and letting ourselves be happy with our mate. Why did they have to come today of all days?

Lachlan let out a frustrated groan, the bed shifting beside me again until I can no longer feel the heat from his body being near.

"I'll send Cedric in, since he seems to be able to give you comfort when I can not."

What? He's leaving? I don't want him to, but I can't make myself move enough to ask him to stay.

Seconds later, I hear the door open and shut, and again, I'm left alone in this room with nothing but my warring emotions and strained thoughts. Why could Lachlan not just hold me and be with me? Why could he not just let me feel his touch and help to calm my anxieties? Is he….is he upset that our plans were disturbed? Is he upset with me now that I can no longer….no longer do *that* with him?

I….I can't. It will be nothing but pain. That's what it is…..

Pain.

I thought after hearing so much from Yasmin about her intimacy with Percy that it would be okay, as long as I was with my mate, but I just need his normal, comforting touch now and he's not willing to offer it. How can I do that with him later?

No…. It's just my anxieties, right? Lachlan is probably just busy and came to check on me. He has been so busy, and now with the added stress of visitors from my uncle's pack and….and that woman being back, he is probably just busy.

I keep telling myself this, trying to grasp the numbness again, but my final tether to rationality seems to finally snap. I turned my face into the pillow to scream as my tears started to fall.

~

***Lachlan***

"*Mate needs us,*" Killian whimpers in my head.

"*She didn't want us,*" I snapped at him, not needing his nagging too after dealing with all the shit we had come up with today. From chasing down my mate at a brothel to our time together being cut short by unwelcome visitors, I've about reached my limit.

"*She needs us,*" Killian snarls, annoyed with me for not doing what he wanted. "*Want and need are not the same thing.*"

I clenched my fist, my final shreds of control just seconds from snapping. Dealing with those shitty warriors from Alpha Waynes pack, arranging last minute accommodations and escorts for them, then also dealing with the disgusting woman who I can not believe I ever touched as she squawked non-stop in the infirmary, demanding for me……it's all made my control wear very, very thin. One little thing is going to make me snap, and I don't need my fragile mate on the receiving end of that when it happens.

As I walked down the hall towards my office, I saw Cedric as he was walking towards me, probably to go check on my mate. He had a tray with a teapot and two cups, as well a plate filled with finger foods that Lira liked. His face when he notices me changes to a mask of enmity.

"That useless Delta. I told him not to let anyone disturb her," Cedric growled.

I sent Cherum away from where he was guarding outside our bedroom door to eat, since it's now dinner time. I thought Lira might prefer me to stay with her. I didn't know she wouldn't even be willing to talk to me.

"Did you upset her more than you already have? I don't know what you did, but I will not have her-"

"I did nothing," I cut him off, my voice cold and menacing. "It was those men that came that set her off. I had no clue men from her uncle's pack would be there or I never would have brought her to the docks with me."

Cedric's face remained enraged. "She called for me. If you did nothing, why would she call for me and not rely on you?"

"I DON'T KNOW, DAMN IT!" I snapped, punching the wall beside us. My fist cracked the stone as my knuckles busted open and began to bleed. It hurt, but not as much as my pride. I did nothing to earn this treatment from Cedric or my wife!

I took deep, labored breaths as I tried to get control of myself again. "I did nothing to warrant your accusation," I told him through clenched teeth.

Cedric just stared at me as I worked to try to calm down. "*She is hurting,*" Killian whimpered again in my head, his thoughts letting me know that Lira is again having another attack. I want to go to her, but she would likely still prefer Cedric over me.

"I would never hurt her. I don't know what exactly happened, but she needs….she needs you." I took my fist out of the wall and took one more deep breath. "Help her," I strained myself, feeling Killian's anxiety grow as he longs to run to our mate, "since she didn't want help from me."

With that, I walked past Cedric to hide in my office. Once the door is closed and locked, I finally let myself boil over, shoving everything off my desk in one angry swoop. I picked up a paperweight, one that used to be my father's, and threw it across the room, breaking the window so the cool night air came blowing through, the wind's sea scent helping to clear some of my raw anger as I drop to my chair, wishing I knew how to help my mate.

We were so close. So, so close to finally being fully mated and bound to one another. I can't feel her like Killian can. I can't comfort her like the siren knight. I can't do anything for her, and the hopelessness in that makes me break as I begin to cry, feeling as desolate and helpless as the day she rejected me.

All I want is to love her, but right now, feeling rejected all over again and seeing how little she trusts me, I just don't know what to do.

~

That filthy dog. I watched him as he stormed down the hallway, his hackles raised for whatever reason. He says he didn't do anything to my princess, but under the circumstances, I don't know if I believe him.

The ladies of the brothel all had stories of their Alpha and his womanizing ways. Every one of them had claimed to have slept with the man at least once. I asked Meldec before sending him away if what those women claimed was true, and he confirmed it. Why Ela wanted to spend time in the place her husband used to frequent because of such vulgar circumstances is beyond me. She acted as if she wasn't bothered by it, but why wouldn't she be? I got jealous, despite myself, seeing my *mate* talking to the bartender in such a familiar way. I couldn't help but think about the possibility of the Gamma of this pack spending time in the brothels with his Alpha and Beta.

When Cherum and the guard showed up to the packhouse after I brought Ela back and told me a bit more about the situation at the dock; telling me about a woman returning claiming to be Lachlan's lover and demanding his help, what am I supposed to think other than he is the reason for my princess's distress.

He said it himself. If he had known who was waiting for him at the dock, he would not have brought his wife along. There must have been a lover's spat between him and his former mistress, and with the stress of everything else, it was too much for Elelira.

I hope I'm wrong. I don't like him, but he does treat his wife well and seems nothing like how the king described him. His stoic face, set in place like he smells an everlasting fart, is annoying as hell. The only time he didn't have that angry expression is when he looked at her.

His whole face transforms when she's in his sight. I thought that things were going well for them, but then today happened and I don't know what to think.

She is my first priority, above anything else. I'm not here to cater to his feelings, only hers. I've been too distracted with nonsense since coming here. I feel like I failed her right now.

When I go back to her room, Mimi is cradling Ela's head in her lap as Ela sobs uncontrollably. That Alpha just left her here like this?

I sat the tray down on the nearest flat surface and ran to her other side, sliding in bed beside her and pulling her to my chest. She struggled to cling to her elderly chambermaid, who had become more like her nanny. Mimi is like Ela's mother here in the pack, which I am eternally grateful for. Since the King's ex-mate passed away, I doubt Ela has had a woman to be that for her.

Ela feels my magic as I let it seep into her from my fingertips, and then turned to cling to me instead.

"Don't leave me," she wails, the pain in her voice is haunting. "Please. Don't," hiccups and shattered breathing wrack her body as she buried her face in my chest. "Not them. Not them."

"Them?" I combed my hand in the back of her head through her hair, letting my magic spread over her, trying to calm her so she could get her breathing under control. I looked up at Mimi with confusion. "Who is *them*? What *them* is she referring to?"

"She just keeps asking for the Alpha and saying 'not them' over and over again. I don't know," Mimi shook her head, a worried look on her face. "I heard her from across the hall and rushed over."

"Was the Alpha not here when this started?" Did he upset her then leave her to cry like that on her own?

"No. I didn't see him at all. I rushed over the moment I heard her too. She had an attack like this on her first day with us. The Delta told me to watch for it. She must have experienced something horrible in her last pack."

Let Mimi's words sink in. Maybe the Alpha wasn't responsible for this, though I'm still not happy he left her in the state she is in.

Them? Could it really have been the men from her previous pack that caused this reaction from her?

I held her, rocking her back and forth until she was back to sleep. I don't know what else to do for her right now. Her mind needs a break if this is from trauma and not heartache like I originally thought.

"If you are alright with her, Cedric, I'm going to go find the Alpha for her like she asked," Mimi tells me. "She kept calling his name when I first came in here."

I sighed deeply. "He's busy at the moment," I told her. He's busy sulking and being a shitty mate to leave his wife here to suffer without him. In his current state, I doubt he will be able to keep his temper at bay enough to calm her down. He might make this worse. "Can you get the Delta to come be with her?" He has the same ability as me to help calm his Luna. I might need to make a quick visit to the sea.

"Not the Alpha? I'm sure he would want to be with her if he knew of her current state."

You would think. I resisted the urge to degrade the man to this woman, and instead just say, "He is the one who sent me. I'm sure he will come when he can." When his temper is under control again.

"Okay," Mimi murmured, giving Ela one last look of sympathy and pity. "The poor girl. I wish she would just talk to us. We are all here for her. I wish she would let us know how to help her get through this."

I smiled tightly as Mimi turned to leave and get the Delta like I asked. If Ela is reliving trauma from her first life, it might not be that easy to talk about. She might not even know how to tell anyone she is in her second attempt at life. Her husband is under contract to not say anything, and I have been commanded by my king to not tell her more than needed.

I'm starting to feel like there is a need to tell her everything I know. For her sanity, if nothing else.

Her pain doesn't feel like heartache at all as I start gauging her emotions. It feels like overwhelming anxiety and fear. Fear of what, I don't know. I'm starting to get an idea, but I need her to be able to tell me about it to be sure.

My king told me very little when he sent me here. I don't think he even knew much of Ela's previous life, just what he learned from the Alpha and the people in this pack helping to fight to bring back their true Luna. He didn't want to leave his daughter here after learning how poorly the Alpha once treated her, but without her magic he couldn't bring her to the sea with him. The contract with the Alpha, and his changed behavior, gave him reason to believe she would be safe here this time around. He claimed it was not safe for the world to know too much about her and her relationship with him, and to let her rebuild a new life and a second chance with her mate if that was what she desired. If she didn't want her mate even in this life, I was told to take her to an allied Fae village hidden in the East of here until her magic came, then she would join us in her father's kingdom to live as the princess who would one day inherit his kingdom as his sole heir.

I'm supposed to keep my limited knowledge of her first life a secret, but I wonder if that is truly the right choice right now.

She is hurting. This isn't the pain of jealousy or heartbreak. This is something more…

This is the reaction of a person who has experienced horrific trauma, and I needed to talk to her about her first life to know what caused it.

I needed her father's permission to tell her everything I know in hopes she will be able to open up to me about what she went through.

KNOCK KNOCK KNOCK

"Everything okay?" Cherum pokes his head in. "I thought the Alpha was with her? Did she wake up?"

"She did," I almost growled, "She had a panic attack, it seems. Your Alpha doesn't believe he will be of any help to her."

"That idiot," Cherum groans, running a hand down his face. "Did he cause it again this time or was it something else?"

Again? A new bout of anger filled me hearing that. "She was asking for him, so I doubt it, but I still would prefer for you to be the one to stay with her until I get back."

"Aye, that's what I'm here for. She's more my responsibility than yours," Cedric came and sat on the bed on the other side of her.

"I doubt that," I snorted at him as we tried hard to untangle her hands from my shirt and move her to lay across his lap. He started combing his fingers through her long hair, his soothing powers from being her Delta coming forward to help keep her asleep. "She is my princess," I whisper, bending to place a kiss on her cheek before I get up from her bed.

"Yeah, yeah. You've been calling the lass your princess since coming here, but you have yet to tell me what your relationship with her is."

I smiled a bit. "It's similar to yours. After I get back, I hope I can tell you more."

"Where are you going?" Cherum asked.

"To pay a visit to my King."

Cherum furrowed his brows, his face contorted with confusion, making me almost laugh.

"I will return early tomorrow. Please stay with her until I return." I looked at Ela's now peaceful face deep in sleep. "She was scared of something. I don't want anyone to be alone with her but you until I get back."

# THIRTY-EIGHT

***Lachlan***

"*Mate needs us,*" Killian whimpers in my head again.

I've just been staring up at the ceiling, ignoring him and everything else as I tried to get myself under control for the last few hours.

My office is trashed. After my hopeless anguish dissipated, all I was left with was rage. I tried to keep my anger at those men and that whore under control, but feeling rejected by Lira made me blow up. It's like everything is imploding all at once.

"*Get your head out of your own butt and go to mate!*" Killian snapped at me, his temper rising as mine was finally settling down. "*She needs us.*"

"*I know,*" I growled. I didn't want to blow up like this around her.

I pushed myself out of my chair, my limbs feeling heavy as my guilt started to set in looking around my office. I destroyed another room because of my anger. I sent a mind link to the omega in charge of the cleaning staff to leave my office so I can clean it later. No one else should have to suffer because of my lack of control.

"*My mate needs me,*" Killian demanded again.

"*I'm going!*" I told him, "*I need to see her too.*" I needed to make sure she's alright. She was so unresponsive when I last saw her. My ego was wounded, thinking that she preferred Cedric to me, but now I felt convicted for thinking of only myself and how I was feeling and not her.

When I got to our room, I found Cherum in our bed, his head back against the headboard snoring loudly. Lira was lying on his lap, his hand resting on top of her head. I can tell she's not sleeping by her breathing. When I walked to the other side of the bed to see her face, I saw her eyes open as she stared at the wall.

She turned those beautiful green eyes, red-rimmed and raw, towards me, then a small, sad smile lifted the corners of her lips.

"Hi," she whispers, her voice sounding raw.

Thank all that is mighty that she was talking to me. I didn't know if I could handle her ignoring me again.

I squatted down in front of her, getting a closer view of her face. She cried. A lot. It broke my heart to see.

*"I told you she needed us,"* Killian snapped at me. He was frantic with his desire to touch her, to help her feel better with the bond that she can feel, and he can feel, but I still can't.

"Hi," I whispered back to her, then cleared my throat when my voice broke. "Hi," I told her again, slightly embarrassed.

"I'm sorry," she bit her lip nervously. "I….I'm sorry I couldn't speak before."

"Couldn't?" I lifted my brow questioningly.

She smiled solemnly. "I was trying not to break down, but then it happened anyway. I wasn't trying to ignore you."

"Oh, Lira," I rested my hand on her face, careful not to wake Cherum. "I'm sorry for leaving. I….," I hesitated, worried about telling her I had blown up and trashed my office. "I had a lot to deal with today and was worried I would disturb you more with my mood. I'm sorry I left you like I did."

I should have stayed. I should have let Killian take control and just stayed with her, letting him trap me in my mind for once while I calmed down so he could have been there for her.

"It's okay," she smiles, but it doesn't touch her eyes. She briefly placed her hand over mine, then sighed before lifting Cherum's hand off her head. She sat up to stretch, then looked at Cherum with a tired expression. "I asked him to go to bed, but he won't. He said he can't leave my side until Cedric comes back for some reason."

That's right. I looked around the room and realized that Cedric really wasn't there. I didn't think he would leave her side for anything after today.

"Where did Cedric go?"

Lira shrugs. "To the sea. Cherum said something about him being back tomorrow and not to worry about it for now. He said the Siren King wanted to see him or something like that."

He left to talk to Lira's father? Anxiety filled me. Is he going to try and take my mate from me now? He can't. My only crime right now is not being more sensitive to my wife's needs. Maybe he really was just called back for some other reason, but he mentioned the necklace calling out to him. Did the king feel it too?

"Lachlan?" Lira looked at me with concern. "Are you alright?"

"Yeah," I told her too quickly, trying to paste a smile on my face. "I'm fine. Just....thinking about everything that happened today. I'm sorry if it got to be too much for you." I remembered her reaction to seeing those men from her uncle's pack. "Can you tell me what happened? Why.....why did you have such a hard time?"

She looked away, pressing her lips together, and I can tell by the look in her eyes that she is talking to her Lycan.

She didn't want to tell me.

Did something happen with that man, Isaac, in her last pack? Does it have to do with her first life? I wanted to ask, but the contract prevented me from doing so. I can only hope she might trust me enough to tell me.

"Did...," I tested the question out in my mind to see if I could ask it, and nothing happened. My throat doesn't close up and pain doesn't radiate through me. "Did those men hurt you?"

She stayed quiet for a few seconds, still talking to Val, then turned her head to look at me again, faking a smile. "No. Not....not really."

She was scared of them, though. I wish she would just tell me why.

I remembered what that man said about her mother. "Did they hurt your mom?" I asked, going out on a limb with the only question permissible to me that I could think of at the moment.

Lira's eyes went wide. "Did....did he say anything about my mother?"

"*That answers that question,*" Killian mutters, bloodlust setting in to avenge our mate's mother.

"He made an off-hand comment," I told her, not wanting to lie. "I threatened him not to say more and he didn't after that."

"Thank you," Lira sighed. "I always hated it when they would degrade my mother for the things my uncle made her do."

I shifted uncomfortably, not wanting to ask this next question, but needing to at the same time.

"What things did your uncle make your mom do?"

She looked down at her hands, knotting them in her lap. "Lots of things. Women are not treated very well in my uncle's pack, Lachlan. My uncle also thought that my mom was a threat to his title. He would," she pressed her lips together, then looked up at me. "What happened to Yasmin was a regular occurrence for my mom."

Disgust filled me. "That man, the one from the docks, did he hurt your mother?"

She hesitated before she nodded. "I think so."

I gulped nervously. "Did....did he or anyone else ever hurt you that way?"

She stayed silent for a moment, shifting uncomfortably in her spot on the bed. She took a shuddering breath, then said, "No. Not really. Not....nothing has happened yet."

Yet?

Killian growled ferociously in my head, catching on before I fully did.

There are so many more questions I wanted to ask, but each one, even when I think about them, makes my throat swell. Is that man going to try and hurt my wife? Did he before? Is that why she reacted the way she did?

"*Kill him,*" Killian snaps. "*Kill him now.*"

"*I'm going to kill fucking all of them,*" I said in a deadly tone to my Lycan. All of them are dead.

My murderous rage is building inside me. Lira was looking down at her hands, but when she looked up again and I saw the fear and sorrow behind her eyes, that hardened my resolve.

"I'll take care of this," I muttered darkly.

"Take care of it?" Lira repeats. "You can't. The alliance...."

"Don't worry," I stood, leaning over and kissed her forehead. "Please stay with your guard." I don't want my wife taking any trips to town without me while I get this sorted out.

"Where are you going to go?" she asked, reaching for my hand. "Lachlan, you need this alliance."

"I need you, Lira," I told her. "I'm not going to let those men breathe much longer if each breath they take is offensive to the person who matters most to me.

"Lachlan, please," she urged me, "I don't want to bring harm to this pack."

She knows the same as I do that I will need her uncle's men soon to ward off the northern clan, but my mind is made up. I can't just let this go.

"Trust me, Lira," I told her, resting my head on hers. "Everything will be okay."

I placed my lips on her forehead one more time before I left the room, mind linking Nilo to meet me in the arms room so we can start planning what to do.

~

***Elelira***

"Lachlan," I tried to call for him to come back. He kept walking, not hearing me as the door closed behind him.

"Let him go," Cherum says, startling me.

"You're awake," I gasped, pressing my hand to my chest.

"Aye, lass," he stretched his arms in the air. "How was I supposed to sleep with all that racket?"

I didn't even notice that his snoring had stopped. I was too worried about what Lachlan was going to do. I didn't know what to tell Lachlan about my uncle's men, since they haven't done those things to me in this life. I'm not even sure they did anything to my mother in this life. I was just assuming that that part of this life is the same.

I don't want those men to be punished for something they didn't do, no matter how traumatic it is for me to see them. I think some part of me is still clinging to the idea that if the Lachlan in this life is different, maybe those men might be different as well. I'm too scared of the idea that if those men are the same, that might mean Lachlan is the same deep down as well.

"Can…can you go with me to stop him now, if you're up?" I asked, moving to scoot off the bed.

"No can do, lass," Cherum says, moving to wrap his arm around my waist and pulling me back to my spot in bed.

He tucked the covers tight around me as I stared up at him confused, then he sat in the chair beside the bed and sighed. "I heard most of your conversation and I'm in agreement with the Alpha. I'm sorry, Ela, but you are just going to have to do as he says and trust him for now."

"But, the alliance-"

"Will still be fine as long as our Alpha does things the smart way." Cherum playfully knocks his fist on my chin. "It's good to see you have the spirit to fight him again. In this case, though, I will be taking his side. Let him do what he needs to do."

~

***Cedric***

My muscles are screaming at me by the time I get near the underwater cove that was hiding our grand kingdom. It is cloaked and hidden away by magic in the center of the ocean, and I had to swim at top speed to make it here quickly. I didn't want to spend too long away from my princess. I'm worried about her. If I can't get permission to reveal everything to her, I'm scared she will just keep hurting herself by keeping everything in.

The underwater city was magnificent, the towers emitting their vibrant glow, lighting the city around it. The minimalism of everything makes the city's natural beauty shine through. Some parts of the kingdom are inside forcefield bubbles, keeping the space inside dry for whatever purposes the area serves, but most of the kingdom is entirely open to the ocean's sea life and natural elements. The towers making up the castle the king lives in with his royal court and noble knights, such as myself, are at the center of everything, a beacon for all sirens, so they can find their way home if they are gifted with the sight.

Sirens born outside of our kingdom have to be gifted with the sight by our king himself to find our kingdom. I always wondered why Elelira couldn't find this place in her first life, considering who her father is, but she was born with the siren magic inside her locked away while living on land. Her sight would have had to be gifted to her too.

I swam down alongside the towers until I reached the lower court. Many knights are still loitering about, eagerly waving to me as I swim past. I haven't been home in weeks, not since my princess first called for help.

It's strange that this place already doesn't feel like home to me anymore. I have this longing to go back to Hidden Cove. It must be because that is where Elelira is, but even as I think about it, Meldec's face is what comes to mind, not hers.

I dislodge that thought. If I wasn't so distracted by him, I would have been more aware that there were deep-rooted issues with my princess. I could have tried to help her sooner, long before those men from her uncle's pack arrived.

As I swam into the throne room, I found King Brennus in his chair with a worried look on his face as he stared at a map etched in stone beside him.

"Cedric?" he said my name with surprise upon seeing me. "What are you doing here? I felt the magic in the necklace flare for a moment, but didn't hear a word from you. Is my daughter alright?"

I looked at the map and saw different points marked with glowing stones. He must still be trying to find out how his daughter passed away in her first life. His goal since learning of her and her death has been to prevent it from happening again. There weren't any clues as to how she died. He could just feel it. He felt it when the magic inside her died, then confirmed it when Alpha Lachlan set sail to find her and he revealed that he was searching for what happened to his mate who he felt had passed away. If that necklace were attuned to Elelira from the start and not created to protect her mother and be her beacon to the king, we would have known of her existence sooner. All that my king could find of his daughter in her first life after her death was the necklace she wears now. He found it at the bottom of the sea at the docks outside her uncle's pack.

That necklace is his connection with his daughter, meant to keep her safe with his magic until hers comes in. If her mother had worn it in her life, my king would have felt it when she gave birth, and then would have felt every bit of her pain and come to save her, even after she rejected him. My king has been living with so much heartache for so long.

King Brennus did an extensive investigation into Elelira's death, but never found his daughter's body or revealed how she truly died. He had the Alpha bring him her uncle's body and used the uncle's and his own blood to complete the spell to bring her back.

My king is desperate not to let the same mistake happen to her again. He has been trying to piece together everywhere she was, where he felt her magic flare before she passed away, but he still can't seem to figure out how she died.

"She has been better, my king," I bowed quickly, "That's why I'm here. I would like to ask for permission to tell her everything."

He furrows his thick brows. "What do you mean?"

"Sir," I gulped nervously. "I, uh, think something horrible happened to her in her first life. Something truly traumatic that may be worse than just death. I would like your permission to speak openly with her. I want to tell her the truth in hopes of helping her, your majesty."

~

Elelira

I ended up falling asleep late into the night, waiting for Lachlan to return.

He never did. Whatever he is planning on doing, I'm worried even more since he spent the whole night away from me.

Val was more upset that her nightly flirting and hairbrushing ritual with Killian was skipped than she was about the fact that my husband may be punishing innocent men.

Cherum stayed by my side all night, falling asleep in the chair and waking up periodically when he would almost fall over.

I was up before him, sitting in my nook and staring out at the sea as Mimi walked in the room with a tray of food in her hands.

"Oh, good. You look much better today, Ela, dear." She hurried over to me and set the tray on the table, then felt my forehead with the back of her hand, as if last night I was just sick. I guess that was all she could think of to do. It's hard to know how to help people sometimes, but you still have that urge to help them in some way.

I smiled gratefully at her. "I feel much better. Thank you."

"My beautiful Luna. I'm here for you whenever you need me." She rubbed her thumb against my cheek, then pats it softly before turning to make me my tea.

She kicked Cherum's chair as she turned to leave, making him startle awake.

"What happened?!" He jumped to his feet, looking around for the threat.

I laughed softly while Mimi smacked him playfully on the back of the head. "You oversized meat bucket. Some guard you are. Your breakfast is over there with hers. Alpha's orders."

What? He had time to tell Mimi to bring us breakfast but he didn't have time to come see me?

"He might still be handling those jerks from your uncle's pack," Val tells me.

"*That doesn't make me feel any better.*" Those men have done nothing to me yet in this life, and I'm not even sure if they will.

Cherum and I ate breakfast quietly. He tried to make small talk with me several times, but I'm too lost in my own thoughts. He gave up with a heavy sigh after a while.

Meldec came after our breakfast tray was taken away and Mimi helped me to dress for the day. He was looking for Cedric, and is upset that he can't sense or find him anywhere. Cherum reassured him that he will be back soon. I asked Cherum where he went after Meldec leaves, and Cherum gave me the same answer as last night. I felt like all he is doing today is trying to keep me in the dark.

I asked him to call for Lachlan, wanting to know what is going on, but all he told me was that the Alpha is busy at the moment and will come see me when he can. My worry turned to annoyance as the morning carried on. I feel like a prisoner in this room, Cherum not letting me leave for whatever reason.

I understand Lachlan wants me to stay safe, but this is starting to disregard my feelings on the matter. We didn't discuss much of anything last night, and he just raced off to do who knows what to men that have yet to commit a crime against me.

Right before lunch time, Cedric came into my room, looking tired and the most unkempt I've seen him since his arrival here.

"There you are," I complained. "Where did you go?"

"I had to talk to your father, Ela," he tells me, collapsing on the bed beside me.

"Her father? You said you were going to see your king?" Cherum looks at him accusingly.

I stared at him in question, wanting a clear answer.

*"He does call you his princess,"* Val reminded me, almost as a joke. *"Maybe both answers are correct."*

"That can't be. Why would my mother have been with the Siren King? I thought only his officials visited my uncle's pack. I didn't think anyone had seen the Siren King in quite some time."

"Hey, maybe that's why we could never find any information about him. Maybe he was acting as an official or representative and not the king."

I thought for a few moments. "That's a fanciful thought, but I doubt I am the daughter of a Siren King. If I was, I'm sure Lachlan or Cedric would have told me about it."

Even as I say it, though, I'm not entirely sure they would. Lachlan didn't even tell me he knew my father. I had to ask him about it. Cedric tells me things when I ask, but sometimes he tells me cryptic answers like, you'll find out some day, or, when your magic comes, you will know.

"Cherum," Cedric looked up at him with an exhausted expression. "Would you give us some time alone? I need to speak to Ela about something?"

Cherum stared at him for a while, then said, "I'll be right outside. I won't be far. Alpha's orders."

"Sure, sure," Cedric waved a hand dismissively.

I stared at him, waiting for some sort of an explanation. When he doesn't start talking right away, I nudge him with my elbow and ask, "Where did you go? To see my father or your king?"

He turned and stared up at me, a nervous expression on his face.

"Both, I guess." He sat up, taking both my hands in his. "I went to ask your father, the Siren King, King Brennus, to speak freely with you. Elelira, I want to talk with you about your first life."

I stared at him in shock. My heart dropped to the pit of my stomach. "What?"

# THIRTY-NINE

***Lachlan***

"Did you do it?" I asked Nilo as the sun began to rise.

"Yes, Alpha. The warriors are stationed around the visitor dorms, ready to capture the men as they begin filtering out." He yawned, tired from the full night of preparations we had. I'm tired too, but my adrenaline is pumping, keeping me awake and on edge.

"Good," I told him, waiting by the armory to witness the first men being taken down.

When I left Lira last night, I came out and actually witnessed some of the men harassing one of my omegas to come with them to bed. I quickly interfered and sent her back home, telling them to leave my staff alone. Witnessing their antics just hardened my resolve to take these men out.

I sent a mass mind link out to everyone in my pack to protect their women and children until this threat is neutralized, making sure that Cherum knew to keep Lira in our room today. As my men capture Alpha Wayne's, we will be incapacitating them with wolfsbane and sending them to the dungeons to hold them until we can organize for the ship they came in on to be taken out to sea. I plan on killing every last one of these men if they don't give me the information I want about what they did to my wife's mother and what Alpha Wayne really wants from this marriage alliance. After that, I will sink them and their boat to the bottom of the ocean.

I will never give up my wife, but the more I think about it, the more I realize that Alpha Wayne really did have ulterior motives for agreeing to this alliance the way he did. I have been thinking more about the attacks from the north that will happen, and something isn't adding up. The threat was neutralized almost as soon as Alpha Wayne's forces came to our aid.

And that man, Isaac.....

He is going to die. No matter what he tells me or what information he offers, I could tell by Lira's response that he hurt her in some way, and I will not stand for his life to extend past today.

"Alpha, I just got a mind link from the docks. Our men that were sent to get information on the Luna's previous pack and her life there just got back. They want to meet with you."

"Not now," I said, moving to peer out the window as one of the men exited the dorms and started pissing on the side of the building. "Tell the commander that I'll meet with him later tonight or tomorrow. We need to take care of this first."

Alpha Wayne's man who is groggily peeing on the side of my building is taken down quickly and quietly with a blow to the back of the head, falling face first against the building, sliding down and covering his front with his own urine. My men inject wolfsbane in his neck then slide him away to toss him into the dungeons before another man can come out.

"The commander said he would see you tomorrow. He said they needed to take a trip to the orphanage anyway."

The orphanage? What for?

I didn't have time to ask as another man exited the building, stretching and yawning as he looked around, calling someone's name. He may have come out to look for his friend, the one my men just hauled off.

Jeremy, one of my best in battle, snuck up behind him and stabbed him in the neck with a new syringe, then covered his mouth with his hand, putting him into a headlock and dragging him away before he could yell.

My men were good. Trained in battle, they are unmatched compared to these men. If it came to an all-out brawl, we would have the advantage for sure. I'm trying to avoid that if I can. They shouldn't be able to mind link at this distance, but I want to take every precaution necessary to protect my pack and my wife from her uncle if he chooses to retaliate. If he was unaware of these events happening today, it would be weeks, maybe even months before he starts snooping around, demanding answers.

Within an hour, we had most of the men in the dungeons. Just Isaac and one other guard are left.

"Let's go," I told Nilo, moving from the arms room to make my way over to the dorms.

"You going to handle the big guy you couldn't quit glaring at yesterday?" Nilo asked.

I was tempted to slit the man's throat in his sleep. "*Save the wolfsbane and just do it,*" Killian urges me.

I might. If he puts up a fight or says anything I do not like, I just might kill him instead of taking him alive. I want to rid the world of such vermin, and avenge my wife's mother.

"Just deal with the other guy. I got him," I told my Beta.

Nilo chuckled darkly. "Don't torment him too much, Alpha. Leave him with the ability to talk."

"No promises," I muttered.

Moving into the dorms, all was quiet. Too quiet. No snoring and moving around.

"*They are up and know something is wrong,*" I mind link Nilo. He nodded at me, two warriors moving to flank us if we needed their assistance.

I wouldn't. Killian was pushing forward and ready, wanting to take control and handle this in the way he handles all threats. He wanted to expire them with his claws and teeth, spraying their blood and tearing them to shreds until their lives were no more.

We moved silently, listening closely for the men's hearts accelerating on the other side of their bedroom doors. In seconds, we both kick down the doors and have the last two men on the ground. I'm almost disappointed at how easy Isaac was to take down.

"I knew some shit was wrong," he sneered, my warrior sliding the needle into his neck, preventing his beast from taking form as fur began to sprout on his skin. "Is this because of that whore you took as your wife? Did she lie and say I tried to take her for myself? It's a lie! She was only 14 and-"

I pounded my fist into his stomach after rolling him over, then planted my other into the side of his face. He groaned, spitting out a tooth and blood.

"SHE TOLD ME NOTHING!" I snarled, Killian's fury bleeding into mine. "You just said it all yourself."

Fourteen? He tried to force himself on my wife when she was just fourteen? He was dead. He would not live past today. After I get all the information from him I can, I personally will deal with his death. I will be letting Killian free to torture and torment him in ways that will have him begging me for death.

"Take him away with the others," I told my men, feeling the burning urge to shift now. Not yet. I still need information.

"What do you want to do with them now, Alpha? Start the interrogations, or let them stew for a bit?" Nilo asked.

"Find Percy," I told him. "Have him identify any of the men that hurt his mate and we will start with them. Let him lead."

"You got it, sir," Nilo smirked, a glint in his eye.

~

It turned out that 3 of the men were there when Yasmin was raped and tortured. Percy took his time with each of them, turning them into an example for the others. He peeled the skin off one, slowly, coating his raw flesh with silver to prevent regrowth if the wolfsbane wore off.

The other two experienced far worse. He castrated one, then gagged him with his filthy, bloody member, and cut his fingers and toes off one by one. He then forced the last man to do to him what they did to Yasmin. He bled to death in the middle of the act, but Percy forced the last man to finish. When he was unable to, Percy started cutting pieces of him off, not letting him pull away from his dead friend.

It was gruesome and lasted hours, but no one thought any less of Percy for torturing them the way he did. His mate suffered greatly because of their hands. Any one of us would likely do the same for our mates.

I ordered the three men to be burned and their ashes be buried in the pig pen. They lived like pigs. I see no reason for them to spend their deaths in any other way.

Alpha Wayne's other men were more than willing to talk after that. They answered all our questions, but they didn't seem to know much. Just that Alpha Wayne had his eye on our pack for some time and wanted a way to acquire our resources. They were under the impression that the marriage was meant to bridge our packs, but Isaac's reaction to the questioning had me thinking differently.

"We will finish this tonight," I told Nilo, needing time to think and process everything that happened. My anger was getting the better of me again, hearing how Alpha Wayne expected his niece to become little more than my breeder, so he had a blood claim to the rights of my pack.

"Where are you going?" He asked.

"To think. Keep injecting them with the drug. I don't want their beasts breaking free, I will be in my office if you need me."

As I passed by the bloody Isaac, he muttered, "Does she know this side of you?"

"Who?" I asked in a level voice.

"Who else?" he spit a clot of blood from his mouth. "Elelira. Does she know what kind of monster you are?"

"I'm the monster?" I snarled, my lip curling above my canines. "Says the man who used to rape her mother?"

A maddened laugh left him. "Rape? That woman asked for it. I was promised her daughter, and she decided on her own to take her place until her daughter came of age."

Killian pushed forward, extending my claws as they sank into his neck, choking him. "The fact you don't see how monstrous that is gives me all the more reason to kill you."

"Do it," he choked, spitting in my face. "It won't stop anything."

Not yet, I told myself. He obviously knew more than the others. I need to regroup and come back when I'm sure my temper was under control enough that I wouldn't kill him before I got the answers I wanted.

That doesn't mean I can't let him suffer some more while he waits for his fate.

"This one looks a little weary from his travels," I told Nilo, releasing my claws from his neck. "I think he could use help getting over his sea legs. Prepare him a basin of our finest wolfsbane to soak his feet in for a few hours. That should help."

Nilo smirked darkly. "His hands are looking a little dry too, Alpha. Can I give them a good soak as well?"

"Why stop there?" I grinned, Killian shining in my eyes, my aura pushing forward, making it hard for the man before me to breathe with his unhealing wounds on his neck and my oppressiveness. "A full bath. Just the neck up left out. I still want his mouth working so he can speak later."

Nilo rubbed his hands together, eager to get started. "One wolfsbane bath with silver-laced bath salts coming right up."

~

I forgot that my office is a mess. Walking in, I groaned loudly, wishing I had just let the omegas clean it for me. I tried to get the worst of it picked up, but gave up when I got to my desk and everything scattered around it.

I'm too tired and feel disgusting after this morning's events. My hands were still covered in blood and grime, not really working effectively in cleaning. I left bloody smears on everything I touch. A lot of the papers that were on my desk were for Lira's festival this coming weekend and I didn't want to get them dirty if I could help it.

I fell down in my chair with an exhausted huff, then leaned back, closing my eyes, wishing for all this to be over so I could get back to my mate. If I go see Lira right now with my appearance, she might panic again. I need to get cleaned and look less monstrous before I go to see her.

"I didn't get my mate time last night," Killian whined.

"I didn't either. Stop complaining. I will give you extra time with her tonight."

"Good," Killian huffed, "I want more kisses."

I did too. I could kiss and hug her the rest of my life and I don't think I could ever get enough. I could never get enough of anything about her. We could have done more than kisses and hair brushing last night if these damned men didn't have to show up. We could be fully mated and I wouldn't be bound by the damned contract anymore. I could tell her everything, then find out how she really died so I can prevent it from happening again. Her father told me he was going to take care of that part, but I haven't heard from him in some time.

Cedric went to go see him. I hope that went well and they aren't planning on trying to take her away from me. I doubt Lira would willingly leave me at this point, but you never know what Cedric or her father will say or do to try and protect her. They both think the worst of me.

I mind linked Cherum and made sure Lira was still okay. He lets me know that Cedric was back and talking with her now while he stood guard outside of her room. Why he wasn't in the room with them, I do not know, but I'm too exhausted to ask.

Lira wouldn't let Cedric continue thinking that I was the reason for her distress. I should trust her to handle him while I worry about handling those men in my dungeon.

I can't believe that man, Isaac. He truly thought it was okay to try and claim Lira as a child? He has to be at least twice, if not three times, older than her. It's disgusting. I should let him suffer worse than the men who hurt Yasmin. I can take some pointers from Percy. I don't know if I have Percy's patience for a slow and painful death, but I can make sure it's as painful as can be.

My beautiful mate must have suffered so much in her uncle's pack. I'm glad that, for whatever reason, he arranged her marriage to me. I need to dig more into the reasons why he chose to marry her off to me, but I'm still grateful he did. There is a reason he chose to force a marriage alliance on me. I know it. Whatever the reason, I'm going to treasure Lira now that I have this second chance with her. She is my everything. My perfect and amazing Luna, wife, and mate.

I wish I hadn't been such an idiot in our first life and treated her the way she deserved. Everything would have been so much better for us if I had just gotten my head out of my ass and listened to my heart and my Lycan before.

If I had just talked to her, she might have just told me that we were mates. Our first wedding night could have been the first day of our happily ever after.

I end up dozing off while thinking about what could and should have happened on our wedding night in our first life. I should have thrown all my love I could towards her from the beginning. I can just imagine how perfect the night would have been. The taste of her skin, her soft, long hair wrapped around us as we became one. The feel of her hands on my body as my hands roamed over hers. I have never made love before, but I would love to have that with Lira. Slow and sweet, savoring everything about her.

I should have loved her from the start. We might have had children quickly, then she would be teaching our kids how to swim and not just the children at the orphanage.

Dreaming about making babies with Lira, I can almost feel the sensations of the act coming over my body. Her soft skin, her perfect body with her….

Wait.

I felt a body up against mine right now, but it was not the silky soft skin I'm familiar with. It was fattier flesh than Lira's. The chest pressed against mine is far too….

My eyes flew open in surprise when I felt lips caressing against my lips and down my neck. Then a hand glided down into my unbuttoned pants in a way that made me feel sick and not at all aroused. It made me want to puke, and I probably would have if there was anything in my stomach.

Leona.

I was so exhausted and consumed in my dream I didn't even notice anyone else was there or had entered my office. She is straddling me in my chair, her body pressed up against mine, her skirt hiked up all the way to her waist and her top completely unbuttoned, her chest on full display.

It made me sick.

I tossed her off me, making her fall back against the desk.

"What the hell are you doing?!" I sneered at her.

Her eyes went wide in surprise. "I heard you imprisoned those men to avenge me, Alpha," she batted her eyes in a flirting way, making Killian growl ferociously through my chest. It didn't discourage her. She tried to glide her hand up my thigh as she was now sitting on my desk and leaning over me. "I came to thank you."

I grabbed her by the throat and threw her back on top of my desk, choking her with one hand. I'm about to threaten her to join the men in the dungeon, but a light gasp made my words freeze in my throat. I looked up at emerald eyes staring at me from my open doorway.

"Lira," I whispered brokenly, seeing the tears filling her eyes as her hand clenched her chest. "No, this isn't-"

She bolted away before I could say this isn't what it looks like. The devastation on her face made Killian howl in pain as I tossed Leona to the ground to chase after my wife. I passed Cherum, who looked ready to bolt after Lira too.

"Get that whore out of my office and into the dungeons!" I yelled at him, not waiting for a reply, too desperate to catch my wife, my mate, before she ran or hid somewhere I couldn't find her.

She turned a corner, running outside, leaving my line of sight for a moment. I could hear nothing but Killian's snarling pain, a reflection of Lira's.

She felt it. I wasn't betraying her, but she had to have felt it as such. Why didn't I lock my office door? Why didn't I wash up and go to bed in our room? Why didn't I put that whore in the fucking dungeons to begin with?

Lira was clinging to her necklace, and when she ran towards the docks, the necklace began to glow brightly, almost blinding me as I continued to stare after her. When I hear the fabric of her dress tear, my fears intensify, knowing her Lycan is giving her all her strength to get away from me. She's shifting.

Killian howled, pushing forward, ready to shift too, but before he could, Lira took a hard right down my private dock where I first saw her watching the ocean on the day of our wedding in this life. She runs to the end of the dock, then dives in, Val more in control than Lira at this point. Her dress floated behind her to the surface as she dove under the water. I tried to dive in after her, but I was blasted with this outpouring of power. It shot up from the water, making me fall back on my ass.

I felt this power before. The day that Lira rejected me in our first life. The moment before that, when she unlocked her powers and magic as a siren, I felt this same energy.

It felt as if my soul was leaving my body. It can't be. She can't be gaining her magic already. She can't, because then that would mean….

When the power lessened, the magic faded back into the water. I crawled to the edge of the dock, hoping to catch sight of my wife in the water below. Nothing. There was nothing there.

I heard splashing off in the distance, and when I looked up, I saw her several hundred meters in front of me, too far for me to swim in my human or Lycan form.

When her fin broke the water's surface as she dove back below, I knew I lost her. I lost my siren mate, my siren Luna, and I don't know how to get her back.

This can't be happening. Not again.

# FORTY

*Earlier…..*

***Elelira***

My heart was racing while listening to Cedric. My father was the Siren King? My mind couldn't keep up with everything he was telling me. Not only who my father was, but the fact that my father was the one who gave me this second life. He brought me back from the dead and sent me back in time, but....why? Why do all this for a daughter he never met? A daughter he still chooses not to meet?

I thought this might be some alternate reality and, by some miracle, I was given a chance at happiness. I really, truly prayed it was. If this is the same life over again, then that means…..

That means this is the same Lachlan as before. He is the same.

No. He's different. He can't be the same husband I was married to in my first life.

"This doesn't make sense," I whispered, resting my head in my hands. "It can't be. If this is the same life done over again, then why is….why is Lachlan different? It can't be the same life."

Cedric grew quiet, causing me to turn to look at his anxious expression. "You and your father aren't the only ones who kept your memories of your first life. Your husband was key to your coming back, Ela. He has his memories too."

My gut twisted. Val was stunned, not knowing what to say or think. She was so sure; so, so sure that this was not the same man who hurt us in our first life. Hearing that he is not only the same man, but he still has every single memory that has been haunting us since we woke up in this life is crushing.

I feel like we were played. I feel like everyone deceived us. Why did he treat us differently, then? Is it because this time he knew we were his mate and he didn't want to lose his Luna? He didn't want to hurt his pack by rejecting me and hurting me like he did the first time?

"No," I whispered. He said he loved me. I felt like he did. He can't be that same man who destroyed our bond every day with his betrayals and rejections in my first life.

"I should let him tell you about his part, but I should warn you that he can't-"

"Why?" I asked, cutting off his words.

"Why what?" He furrowed his brow.

"Why are you telling me this now?" If he didn't tell me, I would have just gone on thinking my husband in this life was different than in my first. I would have….I would have mated with him. I would have been stuck in this without knowing the truth.

"Your father agreed that keeping this from you and letting you think this is all different is no longer in your best interest. We thought you might have just died from an accident since he couldn't find a trace of your body. Those men coming yesterday and your reaction to them made me think that maybe you suffered more than just death in your first life, Ela. I want to know how to help you. Your father is going to come and-"

"My father thought keeping everything from me was beneficial to me? Is that not just some excuse for not taking responsibility for his part in any of this? My mother…" I pressed my lips together and closed my eyes, getting choked up while remembering how much my mom suffered to keep me safe. She never told me much about my real father, just what he was and that she thought him to be a good man. Would a good man have used my mother like that, though, and then abandoned her? Why didn't he come back to save her? Why did he give me this second chance at life but keep everything from me? He never came to see me once. I still have no clue who my father truly is. Hearing that he is the siren king means nothing to me. I would have been happy with a peasant of a man as my father, as long as he knew about me and wanted me.

This did not make me feel wanted, safe, and I feel like everyone has been playing me for a fool this whole time. I have never felt more alone.

"You want to know what happened to me in my first life? The same thing happened to my mother. But you know what, he should not concern himself with me or my life, death, any of it anymore, and neither should you. Leave!" I stood on my feet and pointed to the door,

Cedric's eyes went wide, "What? No, Ela. I'm here to help you."

"You've helped enough. I've been deceived enough. Leave. I do not wish for my father's pity or yours. I lived my first life alone. I don't see why this life should be any different."

"Ela, please just-"

"OUT!" I screamed, causing Cherum to race inside the room. "GET OUT!" I yelled again.

Cedric made a pained expression, then sighed heavily. "I won't be far, my princess. Please, let me know when you are ready to talk."

Cherum held open the door for him as he solemnly walked out. Cherum's expression was a mask of shock and confusion. He was looking between us for an explanation, but I didn't offer him one, and neither did Cedric as the door closed behind him.

What explanation can I give? Does he know everything too? Does everyone? Have I just been made a fool of this whole time?

I started to pace the room, my thoughts jumbled up inside my head. I feel like a fool. I feel like everyone intentionally deceived me, trying to pacify their own guilt. My father gave me this second chance but he didn't think of coming to see me? He sent Cedric instead and told him not to tell me anything?

Why didn't Lachlan tell me?

That thought hurts the most.

*"Maybe he couldn't, like Cedric,"* Val tried to make up an excuse for him.

"He couldn't or wouldn't? Was he scared I would leave him again if I knew the truth? Think of our first morning here. He…." I closed my eyes tightly, remembering that horrible morning. "He acted as he did before. I lashed out for the first time against his anger. What if that is the only reason he changed?"

"No," Val whimpered, "Killian wouldn't deceive me like that. He loves me. He loves us."

"But does Lachlan?"

That's the question that keeps plaguing me. If he really loved me like he claimed, despite everything that happened in our first life, how could he deceive me like that? He…he was going to mate and mark me yesterday. How could he think of doing that when….when it would have been a lie. Everything he did and said, everything I started to feel towards him feels like a lie now.

"Luna," Cherum hesitantly said my name. No, not my name. The title that I have grown used to going by. The title that I was denied in my first life but Lachlan was too eager for me to go by in this one. "Are you alright? What was that about? Did he do something to upset you?"

I stopped pacing and stared at him. "Did you know too?"

"Know?" his thick brows furrowed, "Know what?"

I pursed my lips, trying to keep my tears at bay. "Cedric said that only you, your father and Lachlan had your memories," Val reminded me.

"Yes, but Cedric KNEW this was my second life. Others might know as well."

I stared at Cherum, waiting for his answer. I could tell by his confusion that he had no idea what I'm talking about. I sighed heavily, looking around the room to try and figure out what to do.

I need to talk to Lachlan. I needed answers.

"Take me to Lachlan," I told Cherum firmly, not leaving any room for argument.

"Ela, what's wrong?" He took a step towards me, reaching out to grab my arm. I move out of his reach, not wanting to be soothed and comforted right now. I don't want anything preventing me from getting my answers.

"Where is he?" I demanded, "Why has he not come back yet? Where is the Alpha?!"

"He's been busy," Cherum looked hurt by my anger. "He's indisposed. He'll come see you later tonight or tomorrow, I'm sure."

That's not going to work for me.

I pushed past him, leaving the room. When he tries to stop me, Val pushes forward and snarls at him, making him stagger back in surprise. She wants answers too.

She used the mate bond, pulling on it and using her senses to follow his scent to the part of the castle where his office is located. I have rarely been to this part of the castle. I wasn't allowed to be here in my first life and had no reasons to go this way in this one. Lachlan always comes to find me.

I could almost see Lachlan's office door from far down the hall when I felt this sick feeling in the pit of my stomach. Val grew restless, then howls of pain echo in my head when a sharp ache shots through my chest.

No….

We've felt this pain before. We felt it all too often in our first life.

I staggered to the office, using the wall for support. Cherum is following behind me. He tries to help, but Val growls ferociously through me, not letting him touch me.

I smelled her. I could smell that horrid woman the closer we got. I could tell Cherum smelled her too from the strangled sound that leaves him and the worried look on his face.

When I got to the door, it was already partially opened. I nudged it the rest of the way and that is when I saw them. Lachlan had his pants undone and that woman was lying practically naked on top of her desk, his belongings scattered all over the place.

He had a grip on her throat, his hand not far from her bare chest, his face just inches from hers. His expression sent chills down my back. I know that face well. That was the face I used to associate with Lachlan from my first life. This is all too familiar for me. His crazed look of anger and his betrayal still shocks me, making me gasp.

When his eyes met mine, I couldn't think. I didn't know how to handle this. This was it. This was the final straw. I didn't want this life again. I didn't want to suffer like this again.

Before I could do or say anything, Val pushed forward, taking control.

"*We run,*" she told me, her heart breaking into a million pieces.

That's what she did. She pushed my legs and feet to move, bolting past Cherum and down the hall as both Cherum and Lachlan yelled for me to stop. My hand drifts up to my chest, the pain radiating through me still. My hand connects with the necklace, and its magic flows through me, intensifying as Val's anger and need to protect me grows. It filters through every inch of my body. Val is in full control, starting to shift as she sprints for the docks.

The shift taking control of me feels different as the magic mixes with our transforming muscles. It feels like.... like fins are growing instead of Val's Lycan body.

~

Lachlan

I fell to my knees on the dock. My anguish is suffocating. It's choking me. My lungs can't get enough oxygen. My body was trembling. Killian's howls of pain went off endlessly in my head.

What should I do?

This was like my rejection all over again, only this time….This time it really felt hopeless. I was trying. I was trying to fix everything, every wrong I ever committed against my mate. One misunderstanding, one thing that wasn't even my fault ruined it all.

She left me.

Again.

"Alpha," Cherum fell to his knees beside me, staring out at the ocean just like me, only in shock. "She was….she's….a siren."

I didn't reply to him. He saw as well as I did. He doesn't need me to confirm it. I didn't know if I can speak without choking up anyway.

"That's what that flounder meant," Cherum mumbled.

"What?" I choked, then looked at him from the corner of my eye, then quickly turned them back to the ocean, not ready to give up hope of my wife coming back yet.

She should know it wasn't as it seemed. She knows my love for her is too deep to do that. She should know deep down I didn't betray her.

"Cedric. When he got back, he told Ela that he came from seeing her father, but he also told me that her father was the Siren King. It makes sense now."

I furrowed my brows. He told Lira that her father was the Siren King? That wasn't allowed.

"What else did he say?" I asked, turning to grab the collar of Cherum's shirt.

He looked at me with surprise. "I don't know, Alpha. They fought, I know that," he sputtered, trying not to fall back from my sudden movement. "She made him leave."

They fought? Over what?

Wait, Cedric could go after her. He can follow her where I can't.

I looked at the sea one last time, hoping to catch some movement to indicate Lira might still be out there, but there was nothing. Just the vast, open sea.

I need to find Cedric. I need to plead with him to find her and bring her back.

As if he heard my thoughts, Cedric at that moment came racing down from the castle to the docks, Meldec not far behind him.

"Where is she?" he asked in a panic. "What happened?"

I pointed out to the sea. "It seems she gained her fins somehow."

"What?" He stared wide-eyed at the ocean, then back at me. "She….she unlocked her magic?"

"So it would appear," I muttered.

"No," Cedric shook his head. "I didn't know. I didn't know it would be that great of a shock."

"What would?" I took a step forward, Killian taking focus from his despair to come forward in my mind.

"I....I told her. I told her the truth. I told her about her father bringing her back."

"What?" I stared at him in disbelief. My eyes feel as if they are bugging out of my head, my panic multiplying. "You told her *everything?* Why?" I wanted to be there when she found out so I could apologize. So I could explain my reasons for everything in our first life.

"I thought it would help her to know she could talk with us. She could tell us what happened before and....and we could help her. Those men, Alpha. I think they hurt her."

I'm sure they did. I was taking care of them all morning because I was sure they were guilty of many crimes against my wife and her mother, along with many more.

Cherum said they fought. She must not have taken the news well. "Did she say anything?"

"No," he shook his head. "She kicked me out before I could explain much further too. I merely got to tell her that she, you and her father were the only ones with those memories."

"*No,*" Killian whispered brokenly in my head. "*She....she will think we lied to her.*"

Shit. He's right.

I grabbed Cedric's collar, pulling him closer to me, surprising him and making Meldec growled. "Did you tell her your *King*," I sneered the word, "prevented me from telling her anything myself? Does she know I wasn't trying to deceive her?!"

Cedric stared at me wide-eyed. "I....I was told to leave before I could."

No, no, no. She knows I have my memories, and then she walked in on that nasty woman's attempt to seduce me.

Val had control, too. Not just Lira, but Val ran from me.

"*No,*" Killian began to sob, heartbroken because of his mate.

"FIND HER!" I screamed at Cedric, seconds away from wringing his neck. "Find my mate!" I tossed him to the ground, my rage boiling over.

Meldec snarled at me, then helped his mate back to his feet.

"Her father is coming," Cedric told me as I began to walk back to the packhouse, my mind made up to kill the woman who caused this. "King Brennus is coming. He wanted to see her himself. I…I want you to be aware."

He shrugged out of Meldec's hold then began to strip as he walked to the end of the dock to dive into the water. We stood there and watched as he shifted and began to swim out in the direction that my wife disappeared.

"Her father?" Meldec asked, still staring after his mate. "Alpha, what's going on?"

Killing the whore will have to wait. "Is that woman in the dungeons?" I asked Cherum.

He nodded solemnly. "I had two warriors take her down before following after you."

"Good," I muttered. "Call a meeting." I'm only going to explain to my men once what's going on, then I'm going to prepare to get my mate back, whatever it takes.

~

***Elelira***

We swam like never before, flowing through the water with my lithe siren body and long-missed fins. It should have been a happy moment, getting my fins back, but this was anything but.

I love the water. I missed it so much, but now that I have the magic and power I longed for to be free, freedom has never tasted so bitter.

He knew. Cedric knew. Even my father, who Cedric said brought me back to this point in my life, knew and decided deceiving me was the best option.

I don't know if I can trust someone ever again. Not after that.

At some point, Val retreated to the back of my mind to grieve and mourn, feeling heavy from her mate's deceit. I can feel all her conflicting emotions. She was heartbroken and miserable thinking her mate didn't love her enough to tell her the truth. He didn't stop his human counterpart from betraying me again. She felt sorry towards me, having urged me so many times to open myself up to the man that ultimately betrayed us again. He lied to me. Lied to her.

Everything felt hopeless now. I didn't even have the desire any longer to find my father like before. He took my death away from me, forcing this second chance to be deceived and manipulated to pacify everyone else's guilt.

What do I do now?

After swimming for so long and so hard, my tail muscles were aching. I found an island that I used to take refuge near in my first life, out in the middle of nowhere. I had never seen human life there before, but there was a small dock and a few abandoned buildings on the land. I had never ventured out onto the island before, sticking to the underwater caves to stay hidden while I rested, but Cedric might find me if I stayed in the water. I'm sure Lachlan has already forced him to come after me.

I should probably get rid of the necklace before I go on shore. It's a beacon for him to find me. It may be what gave me the magic I needed to shift, though. I touch it, and I no longer feel the magic in it. It all filtered into me, giving me the ability to gain my fins in my time of need.

I decided to keep it just in case, but I took it off when I got to shore, holding it in my hands, hoping it stopped the necklace from signaling Cedric, or worse, my father, to where I am.

The largest building was just a hut house, with a dusty bedroom inside. There were shelves with bottles of rum, coated in a thick layer of grime, and chests around the room that I chose to look through in hopes of finding clothing.

I set the necklace on the table beside the bed, then slipped on a loose-fitting shirt I found in one of the chests. It's a man's shirt. A very large man. The dark shade reminded me of something Lachlan might wear, which made my heart pang. I still choose it over the lighter colored shirts for some reason. I guess my heart wasn't ready to let go of him just yet.

Laying on the old, dusty bed, I curled into a ball as my tears started to flow from my tightly closed eyes. I loved him. I truly did. I don't know how I'm going to get over this pain residing in my heart.

# EPILOGUE

***UNKNOWN***

"Captain, do you smell that?" my first mate, Lucky, asked from beside me as we made our way up the dock.

"Aye, Luck. I do." It was the scent of a Lycan, and not a rogue one like us. Female, by the sweet smell of her. What would a female Lycan be doing on this island?

There was a tinge to the scent that was like the brininess of the sea. It reminded me of the demon ladies that sat upon the rocky sea stacks in the far North, beckoning weary sailors to their doom. It's not quite the same, but similar. Maybe it's closer to the regular siren folk that come to shore and barter their pearl harvests and purified salt for land goods.

Whatever the smell was, it was enticing, making my beast stir in my mind.

"*It's powerful,*" he purred, wanting to find its source. "*I want it.*"

I want it too. I have never smelled anything so mouth watering before.

While the men unloaded our spoils, uncovering our hidden trenches to bury the goods, I tracked the smell back to the main cabin at the center of the small island we use as one of our many hideouts.

Opening the cabin door, the scent overwhelmed me.

There, upon my bed, was the most beautiful woman I have ever laid eyes on, curled into a ball. Her face looked pained, but still exquisite. She was only wearing one of my shirts, her long, milky legs on full display.

I want her. Is this a gift from the sea gods? I want this beauty before me, more than I've wanted anything else in my life.

I brushed the hair away from her face, and she didn't even stir. Whatever she went through must have exhausted her.

I lifted her feather-light body in my arms, grabbing a blanket from the bed to wrap around her as well. Whoever left her or chased her here may be back soon, and I would rather us not be here when they returned.

"Captain?" Lucky furrowed his eyebrows at me as I exited the cabin. All the men stopped working to stare.

"Finish what you have all started," I ordered, "Quickly. We are leaving at once.

# BOOK TWO COMING SOON!

Book two, Finding My Siren Luna, will be released in September 2023.

You can find Book two, along with many other of my works on the Dreame App, or find me on Facebook.

C. Hazlewood Author

Printed in the USA
CPSIA information can be obtained
at www.ICGtesting.com
LVHW020140241024
794594LV00006B/16

9 781088 24855